MARK GREANEY

BALLISTIC

SPHERE

First published in the United States in 2011 by Berkley,
an imprint of Penguin Random House LLC
First published in Great Britain in 2011 in ebook by Sphere
This edition published in 2019 by Sphere

1 3 5 7 9 10 8 6 4 2

A CIP catalogue record for this book
is available from the British Library.

ISBN 978-0-7515-7922-2

Printed and bound in Great Britain by
Clays Ltd, Elcograf S.p.A.

Papers used by Sphere are from well-managed forests
and other responsible sources.

MIX
Paper from
responsible sources
FSC® C104740

Sphere
An imprint of
Little, Brown Book Group
Carmelite House
50 Victoria Embankment
London EC4Y 0DZ

An Hachette UK Company
www.hachette.co.uk

www.littlebrown.co.uk

*For the men and women
on both sides of the border
who work every day to end the madness*

ACKNOWLEDGEMENTS

Thanks to Karen Mayer, James Rollins, Marcie Silva, Marleni Gonzalez, Devin Greaney, Mireya Ledezma, Svetlana Ganea, James Yeager, Jay Gibson, Paul Gomez, Tactical Response, GetofftheX.com, Mystery Mike Bursaw, CovertoCoverBookstore.com, Devon Gilliland, Bob Hetherington, Patrick O'Daniel, the Andersons, the Leslies, Alex Slater at Trident, Caitlin Mulrooney-Lyski and Amanda Ng at Penguin, and Jon Cassir and Matthew Snyder at Creative Artists Agency.

Special thanks to my agent, Scott Miller at Trident Media, and my editor, Tom Colgan at Penguin.

MarkGreaneyBooks.com

Whoever fights monsters should see to it that in the process he does not become a monster.

FRIEDRICH WILHELM NIETZSCHE

In Mexico, if you have a problem and turn to the police, then you have two problems.

LORENZO MEYER, MEXICAN HISTORIAN

CHARACTERS

COURTLAND "COURT" GENTRY: The Gray Man, call sign Sierra Six, code name Violator – ex–Special Activities Division (Ground Branch) paramilitary operations officer, CIA; ex–CIA Autonomous Asset Program operative

CATHERINE KING: Senior investigative reporter for the *Washington Post*

ANDY SHOAL: Metro (cops) reporter for the *Washington Post*

DENNY CARMICHAEL: Director of National Clandestine Service, CIA

JORDAN MAYES: Assistant Director of National Clandestine Service, CIA

MATTHEW HANLEY: Director of Special Activities Division, CIA

SUZANNE BREWER: Senior Officer, Programs and Plans, CIA

ZACK HIGHTOWER: Call sign Sierra One, former CIA Special Activities Division (Ground Branch) paramilitary operations officer – Court Gentry's former team leader

CHRIS TRAVERS: Special Activities Division (Ground Branch) paramilitary operations officer, CIA

JENNER: Special Activities Division (Ground Branch) paramilitary operations officer, CIA

MAX OHLHAUSER: Former Chief Council, CIA

LELAND BABBITT: Director of Townsend Government Services

MENACHEM AURBACH: Director of Mossad – Israeli Intelligence

YANIS ALVEY: Senior officer in Mossad – Israeli Intelligence

MURQUIN AL-KAZAZ ("KAZ"): Washington, D.C., Station Chief – Saudi Arabia General Intelligence Presidency (Saudi Intelligence)

"DAKOTA": Joint Special Operations Command – Special Mission Unit team leader

BALLISTIC

PROLOGUE

The manhunter knelt at the front of the canoe, scanned the far bank as it appeared around the river's bend. Thick green rain forest morphed slowly into a rustic brown village, a settlement of hardpacked dirt and wood and corrugated rust built along the water's edge.

'This is it?' he called back to the Indian steering with the outboard motor. Only by necessity had his Portuguese improved in the past months.

'*Sim, senhor*. This is it.'

The manhunter nodded, reached for the radio tucked between his knees.

But he stayed himself. He needed to be certain.

Seven months. Seven months since the call came for him in Amsterdam. A rushed consultation with his employer, a flight across the Atlantic to Caracas, a mad dash to Lima, and then south.

Ever south. Until he and his prey came to the end of the world, and then the chase wound back to the north.

Ever north.

He'd been on the target's heels, to one degree or another, for all this time. The longest hunt of his storied career.

And it would end here. One way or another, the hunt for Courtland Gentry would end right here.

1

Outside Quito, the manhunter had come close. He'd even called in a kill team, but they'd gone wanting for a target. Foolish of him, a false start could dull their fervor the next time; he would not cry wolf again. He'd caught fresh wind of the target in northern Chile and a hint of him farther down the Pacific coast, but then he'd lost the scent in Punta Arenas.

Until Rio and a lucky break. A visiting jujitsu student from Denmark had seen an Interpol Wanted poster while in his embassy filing for a lost passport. He'd run into another white student at a dojo in the favelas. Nothing to that, but the Dane knew his art, and the white man's fighting style showed hints of other disciplines: hard, brutal, warrior tendencies that he tried to hide from those around him. The Dane recalled the Wanted poster. It was no obvious match, but he felt compelled to contact the authorities. Something about the man in the dojo had uneased him. A look, an edge, the hint of suspicion on the part of the white student, as if he knew that the Dane was sizing him up for some reason.

The manhunter got word of the sighting, arrived on a private jet mere hours later. The suspect did not show for class that day, or the next. The manhunter brought in local reinforcements for the legwork; dozens of men combed the favelas with photos and cash. Many of the crew were roughed up or threatened on the mean streets of the lawless slums, one man even relieved of his wallet and knifed in the arm. But the canvass paid off: someone talked; someone pointed a finger; someone whispered an address.

The manhunter went to have a look. He was not a shooter himself, he hadn't fired a weapon since his days in the Royal Netherlands Army, fighting the Angolans in the 1970s. But he did not want to spin up his gunmen-in-waiting on another wild-goose chase, so he left eight armed men up the street as he went on with only two. A horrid, run-down neighborhood, a shit-stained building, a piss-scented thirdfloor hall with a darkened doorway at the end of it. The manhunter's hands shook as he used another border's key and crept inside, his gunners just behind him.

A human form moved in a blur off a top bunk bed; the manhunter's life flashed before his eyes. Then a backpack heaved upon the blur's shoulder, and the blur was out a window, a full two stories down. The manhunter rushed behind him; the gunmen fired their weapons, tearing up the bed and the wall and the window frame in the blur's wake. The men reloaded as the manhunter reached the window, watched the target land and roll onto another rooftop, float across an alleyway to another building like a flying squirrel, and then leap and roll down to ground level, the explosions of small-caliber rounds chasing after him down the street as the two gunmen belatedly returned to the fight.

The target was gone. The bunk he vacated left no clues but the warmth on his tattered blanket.

That was ten weeks ago.

Last Sunday a call came from Fonte Boa, hundreds of miles north on the Amazon River. The manhunter had made lists of possible professions in which the target might find work. There were hundreds, from sheet metal worker to legionnaire. Somewhere down the list marine salvage had been noted, due to his experience in diving and his raw courage. A small operation along a remote Amazonian tributary had employed a walk-up foreign white man, a queer occurrence in the Brazilian jungle to be sure. So the manhunter had flown to Fonte Boa and shown a photo to the boatman who delivered dry goods upriver to the settlements.

And now the manhunter was here.

He fingered the radio between his knees. One call and two fat helicopters full of gunmen would descend and fan out; they'd planned their attack with satellite photos and a grease board in the watcher's hotel room in Fonte Boa. One call would turn the pristine jungle to fire and end the target the Dutch manhunter had been after for these seven long months.

But first he must make certain.

A howler monkey splashed from a tree into the water, scampered back onto the bank, and disappeared into the thick growth.

Seconds later, the launch slowed and bumped against the rubber tires tied to the dockside. The canoe's owner made to turn off the outboard.

'No,' said the manhunter. 'Leave it running. I will only be a moment.'

'Wastes gas, sir,' said the local. Some sort of Indian savage. 'I can start it again in five seconds.'

'I said leave it running.' The white man climbed ashore, started up the dirt hill towards a man idling by a shack raised on narrow stilts. The Dutchman would get some verification that this was the place, and then he would not wait around for the fireworks. He carried an ancient Webley Top-Break Revolver in a shoulder holster, but that was really just for show out here amongst the savages of the jungle. Killing was not his job. He'd use his radio, and then his job would be done. He'd head back upriver to Fonte Boa to wait at the hotel.

Mauro sat in the shade, waiting for his father to return with the morning's catch. At ten years old Mauro normally went out with his father to collect the nets, but today he'd stayed behind to help his uncle with some chores and had only just arrived at the dock when the canoe with the white man appeared. He watched the old man make his way up the hill, stop in front of the drunkard, and engage the man in conversation. The white man pulled a white paper from his breast pocket and showed it to the drunk, then handed him some cash.

Mauro stood slowly. Hesitated.

The white man nodded, headed back to the canoe, and pulled a radio up to his mouth.

Young Mauro walked towards a narrow trail that led away from the docks, away from his village. Once inside the dark protection of the jungle canopy, the boy began to run as fast as his calloused bare feet would take him.

2

Court Gentry pulled on his umbilical cable for a bit more slack then turned back to the wreckage in front of him. He reached out with a gloved hand and felt his way forward to the hulking iron wheelhouse of the sunken steamboat. Visibility in the murky river was no more than twelve inches at this time of late morning, thirty feet below the ochre surface of the warm water. Finding his place, he adjusted the angle of the flashlight on his helmet, lifted his welding torch back up, and narrowed the flame to little more than a glowing spike. Then he slowly applied the white-hot fire to the iron to begin a new cut.

A series of three strong tugs to his line pulled him off his mark.

'Dammit,' he said aloud, his voice reverberated in his brass helmet. The dive helmet's radio wasn't working so the team communicated through tugs. Three short, hard pulls meant 'surface immediately,' which meant it would take him, at a minimum, ten minutes to get back down here through the algae and oily film to find his spot again.

But he did not wait. 'Surface immediately' wasn't a message to ignore. It could be nothing, but it also could mean there was a problem with the equipment, which could be dangerous, or it could mean snakes or crocs or a school of piranha had been spotted close to his dive site, which could be downright deadly.

He broke the surface four minutes later; his gear and his weights made it impossible to tread water, so he pulled himself along his line towards the shore. When he was waist-deep, he wiped green goo off the acrylic faceplate of his helmet, but only when he unfastened the latches and lifted off the heavy headgear could he see his way forward through the thick reeds and tall grasses on the riverside. Above him stood his two coworkers, Thiago and Davi; both men were experienced salvage divers, but neither was fitted to go down today. Only one compressor was operational, so they split the time between the three of them. One man on the bottom, and two men on crocodile/ anaconda/ piranha watch.

'What is it?' Court called out to them. His Portuguese was not half as good as his Spanish, but it was functional. One jerked a thumb to the other side of a tiny lagoon that swelled off of the river like a tumor, and Court saw young Mauro standing there on the trail that led towards the dock. The boy wore a red and black Barcelona soccer jersey emblazoned with the name of a Bulgarian player who had not taken the pitch for that club since the mid-nineties, and he was barefoot. Court had never once seen the dark-skinned kid in shoes.

Gentry was surprised that he'd been called to the surface to talk to the boy – still he waved and smiled. But his smile dropped in an instant. The kid's eyes were wide, and his body was tight.

Something was wrong.

Court trudged along the marshy bank that rimmed the lagoon, his feet sucked down by mud. He climbed up to the young Brazilian, led him down the trail a few yards before asking, 'What's up?'

'You told me to come if I ever saw a white man.'

'Yes, I did.' Court's own body stiffened.

'An old man. Alone. At the dock.'

'Did he talk to anyone?'

'Yes, he asked Amado a question. Showed him a sheet of paper. Gave him some money. Then the white man talked into his radio.'

'His radio?' Gentry's eyes were off the kid, on the trail back to the dock, a kilometer distant through dense rain forest. His hands had already begun removing his old tattered wetsuit, stripping himself down to his underwear.

Thiago called out to Gentry from behind, probably telling him it wasn't time for lunch, but he ignored Thiago.

'Where is he now?'

'He left. Got back in a launch and headed upriver.'

Court nodded. Spoke in English to himself. 'The manhunter.'

'¿Quál?' What?

'Good. You did real good, Mauro. Thank you.'

'Sure, Jim.'

Seconds later Court was on his knees by his gear on the other side of the lagoon. The boy had followed him to the bank and stood above him and watched him open his large duffel bag. From it he retrieved a black sawed-off 12-gauge shotgun with a wooden pistol grip. He grabbed his wallet from the bag; it was fat with Brazilian reals, and he held it out to the boy. 'This is for you. Take some of it; give the rest to your mom.'

Mauro took it, his eyes wide with surprise and confusion. 'You are leaving?'

'Yeah, kid. Time for me to go.' Gentry's hands moved quickly as he yanked on dirty brown pants and a filthy long-sleeved cream-colored shirt.

'What about your dog?'

'He wasn't my dog; he just hung around my camp. He's a good boy. Take care of him, and he'll take care of you, okay?'

Court began lacing old tennis shoes onto his wet feet.

Mauro nodded, but in truth he did not understand any of this.

He'd never seen anyone move so fast in his life. People in his village did not leave, did not make decisions in an instant. Did not hand their wallets over to kids. Did not change their life because some dumb old man showed up in a canoe.

His uncle was right. Gringos *are* crazy.

'Where will you go?' he asked the strange American.

'I don't know. I'll figure something—'

Court stopped in midsentence. Cocked his head to the side as he lifted a small loaded backpack out of the big duffel and secured it onto his back.

Mauro heard it, too, and said, 'Helicopter.'

Court shook his head. Took the pistol-grip pump shotgun and stood up. Velcroed it tight to the right side of his backpack, grip down and within reach. A machete was already fastened similarly on the left. 'No. *Two* helicopters. Run home, kid. Get your brothers and sisters inside, and stay there. It's gonna get good and loud around here.'

And then the gringo surprised young Mauro one last time. He smiled. He smiled wide and rubbed the boy's tufted black hair, waved to his two coworkers without a word, and then sprinted off into the jungle.

Two helicopters shot low out of the sun and over the treetops, their chugging rotor wash beating the flora below as they raced in formation. They were Bell 212s, a civilian version of the Twin Huey, the venerable but capable aircraft ubiquitous amongst American forces in the Vietnam War.

In the history of manned flight, no machine was more at home streaking over a jungle canopy than the Huey.

The choppers were owned by the Colombian police but had been loaned, along with their crews, to the Autodefenses Unidas de Colombia, a semi-right-wing, semi-disbanded defense force that fought from time to time against the FARC, or Fuerzas Armadas Revolucionarias de Colombia, and the ELN, or Ejercito de Liberacion Nacional, Colombia's left-wing rebel groups. The Colombian police had thought the loan was to send this team of twenty commandos to a mountain region to combat the FARC, but in fact the AUC was working for hire over the border in the Amazon jungle.

The pilots would not report the misappropriation of resources; they were being well paid.

Each man in the unit wore green jungle fatigues and a bush hat. Each man had a big HK G3 battle rifle cradled in his arms, and each man had extra magazines for the rifles, grenades, a radio, and a machete strapped to his chest and belted to his waist.

The commander of the unit sat in the lead helicopter, screamed over the Pratt and Whitney turbo shaft engine to the nine soldiers seated with him. 'One minute! If you see him, shoot him! If you shoot him, *kill* him! They don't need him alive!' and then he amended himself. 'They don't *want* him alive!'

A chorus of '*Sí, comandante!*' roared louder than the engine. He delivered the same order into his radio to the men in the second helicopter.

A moment later the helicopters split, the comandante's craft banked hard to the left, dipped its nose toward a small winding river that snaked to the south.

Court shot through the dappled morning light flickering through the canopy above him, certain in his stride. He continued on the jungle trail, his ears tuned to the sound of the rotors behind him. Soon the single beat of the choppers changed to two as the air-craft separated. One landed behind him, probably in the swampy clearing a hundred yards from the dive site. Gentry knew the men would sink knee-deep in the muck, and this would buy him a little time to get away. The other helicopter flew on past his position, off to his left, lower than the treetops; certainly, it was skimming the river. It would be dropping off dismounts in a blocking man-euver along his path.

So much for the extra time.

Court picked up his pace even more. The smile was gone from his face, but the thirty-seven-year-old American felt confident and strong as his legs and arms pumped him onward. Adrenaline, an old friend whom he hadn't run into in a while, coursed through his body and fed power to his muscles and his mind.

He'd been here for nine weeks, nine *good* weeks, but in his adult life he'd rarely stayed in one place for so long. As he'd told the village boy, it *was* time to go.

*

11

The comandante's team fast-roped onto the riverbank; the first four down dropped onto their elbows in the muck and raised their HKs to the forest to provide cover for the second four as they slid down. The second four moved up to the dirt road, dropped down, and covered both directions. The comandante and his number-two descended last, ran up to the road, and moved out at the head of the column.

The comandante got the call that the men from the other chopper were splashing their way through a marsh; he cussed aloud in Spanish and yelled at his men to pick up the pace.

Gentry sprinted through his tiny camp. It did not take long. The camp was just a tent with a sleeping pallet, a stone-lined fire pit, a well-worn trail to a hand-dug latrine, a hammock enshrouded in mosquito netting, and a few belongings hanging from a net in a tree. He was glad to see the dog wasn't here; it was close enough to lunch time to know the little four-legged survivor had scampered down to the town's one little thatched-roof restaurant to await leftovers before making his way to the shady palms near where the fishermen returned with their daily catch. There he could rest for a while before fighting with the other dogs of the village for a chance at leftover fish bait tossed from the boats.

Court was well aware that the dog's daily agenda was more organized than his own.

He kept a Browning pistol in a locked case inside his tent, but he did not take time to retrieve it. Instead he grabbed a lighter from just inside the canvas door of his two-man tent and a small can of cooking fuel lying next to it. In seconds he'd poured the oil over the tent, his belongings in the tree, even the hammock. He lit his home on fire with neither a moment's pause nor a shred of regret, tossed the lighter on the ground, and headed off towards a small stream fifty feet away.

A man shouted off to Gentry's left. From the high-pitched exulting tenor of the voice, he could tell he'd been spotted.

They were close.

Gentry leapt into the ankle-deep stream and sprinted to the south, his footsteps exploding in the flowing water.

The comandante slid on his back down the bank and into the cold stream. He found his footing in the water and raised his weapon just as the target turned to the left, out of his sights and out of view. The men ran on past their comandante, each man wild with the chase, thrilled with the chance of a kill.

He lowered the G3 and sprinted right along with them. He knew there was a road ahead that led to the river, but he also knew that this stream did not wind directly to that road. He assumed there was a little trail that the target was making for, a trail too small to be picked up through the triple canopy of the jungle on the satellite photos. The comandante and his men only needed to get close enough to the target to see where he ducked out of the stream bed and back into the jungle, and then it would be just a matter of time before they caught him on the trail. The jungle would be too thick to hide in, the dirt road too straight for a fleeing man to duck bullets fired from the heavy 7.62 mm battle rifles that he and his men carried.

The comandante made the turn with his men, white water splashing chest high as the ten soldiers ran together. Up ahead he saw the dark-complected man with the long hair and the back-pack, both hands empty. One of his men at the front of the scrum fired a shot, blasting vines from a tree well above the target's head. Just then the man ducked left, ran out of the water and up the steep bank, and disappeared into the black hole of a small foot trail. One more rifle shot from his men chased him into the jungle.

'There he goes!' shouted the Colombian. 'Up the bank!'

3

A rifle cracked, ripping branches and brush above Gentry's head as he ran down a slight hill. The killers were close at his heels; he picked his pace up even more, and his thighs burned as the lactic acid squirted from his bloodstream into his muscle fibers.

He'd choreographed this escape, had made several dry runs, had chosen this route to maximize the effect of the natural dangers of the jungle. Natural dangers made more dangerous via certain unnatural means that he had planned.

His left hand reached back and took hold of the hilt of the machete strapped to the side of his backpack. He pulled it free of its Velcro binding, and with a single strong swing he hacked into a bush to his right. Behind the bush he picked up a smaller trail, even darker under the canopy and covered in roots and vines, and here Court went up onto his toes and pulled his knees high to keep from hooking his feet under the obstacles in his path. His pursuers had seen him leave the main trail; of this he had no doubt. They'd be on him again in seconds. He tossed the machete aside as he ran; he loved the blade and would likely need it again soon, but he had to focus all his concentration on his fast footwork and rely on muscle memory in his upper extremities to unhook the shotgun on the right side of his pack. He pulled the pistol grip and swung the weapon out in front of him, pointed it straight up as he ran, holding it with both hands, the barrel just in front of his face.

The trail went down another hill, with large thick-trunked trees on all sides. He opened his eyes wide to take in every bit of light available to him, took them off the trail for one second as he looked for just the right tree, for just the right branch, and he found it.

Another shot behind – he heard the supersonic crack as it raced past his left ear. The hunters were no more than thirty yards back; they'd be crossing the ground he now stepped on seven or eight seconds behind him.

Perfect.

Gentry ran on, passed under the tree, under the branch he'd searched for in the low light, and he fired the shotgun straight up in front of his face. He racked another round and fired once more; the weapon's recoil jolted down against his shoulder joints.

Fifty feet above him a seven-by-four-foot hive of African killer bees took the two blasts of the double aught buckshot directly at its base; the impacts blew the bottom of the hive apart and knocked the entire fat structure loose of the branch, and like a piano falling from a tree, it dropped towards the trail, slamming through branches as it came down hard.

Court was over the lip of a small rise, leaping into the air to vault a felled cypress, when the hive smashed into the ground twenty yards behind him.

The comandante was a fit man in his thirties; still, he could not keep pace with the younger men in his force. He was nearly the last in line on the trail as they ran down a hill; in the dark distance he saw the spark of flames from a shotgun. The boom of the weapon's report was absorbed into the humid air of the green jungle around him. Though nearly as wild from the chase as his men, the comandante retained the presence of mind to duck on hearing the second gunshot, and this put him at the very back of the pack on the narrow trail. He'd just picked up his feet again when he saw the huge object ahead of him falling through the few dull rays of light that made its way through the canopy.

He did not know what it was; never in a million years would he have been able to guess. Only when the tall, fat lump crashed to the earth, virtually enveloping the first two men in the column in some sort of dark cloud, did he shout out a confused and nonspecific warning to his team.

And only after the first screams, only after the first jolting burn on his forearm just above where his glove ended and his exposed skin began, only after the exploding, swarming, darkening fog surrounded his men in front of him – only after all this did he know.

Bees. Thousands – no, *tens* of thousands of enraged bees covered his screaming, writhing, frantic soldiers. In seconds guns began to fire wildly in the sky in a pathetic and futile act of desperation; well-trained soldiers ran into the thick woods along the trail and fell and kicked and swatted the air like maniacs.

The comandante was stung on the face, on the neck, again on the arm, and he stumbled and then turned to run back up the trail, back up the hill, through the outskirts of the mad swarm of livid lit cigarettes stabbing at him from all sides, the steady downpour of caustic acid rain, the viscous cloud of tiny fireballs of molten lava.

He screamed, pushed the button on the walkie-talkie, and screamed some more, and then he fell, and the stings dug deeper into his skin.

He almost made it back up to his feet, but his fleeing men – each battling panic and agony and the near-zero visibility caused by the swirling, swarming insects – knocked him back down on his chest as they retreated back in the direction of the creek.

The comandante slid a knee under his body to push himself up again, but the dark cloud enveloped him; every nerve ending in his body ignited, and he grabbed at his pistol to fight off ten thousand attackers.

Court ran on, away from the screams and the disjointed gunfire in the jungle behind him. He pictured a dozen men, but that was

16

conjecture. He'd not once looked back at his attackers. He based the number on the fact that the helicopters' distinctive sound told him they were Hueys, and everyone in Court Gentry's world knew that a Huey could carry fourteen geared up gun monkeys.

The cries of agony backed up his guesstimate. The howls of human suffering sounded like they came from about a dozen men. Which meant the other chopper would likely have the same number. Why vary the size of your fire teams?

The two helicopters circled high above; they'd dropped off their men, and they would wait for the order to come and collect them.

Gentry made it out of the thick jungle and onto the main road, turned to the south, and slowed to a jog. He had no idea where the other team was now; if they'd gotten out of the marsh, they could be on this very road, but if they were, they'd be at least a kilometer back.

He allowed himself a moment to relax as he jogged, but the moment ended abruptly as he heard a truck approaching from behind. There was only one truck in the village; it was an old flatbed owned by one of his coworkers and was used only to bring the salvaged iron up this road from the wreckage site to the dock for transport back to Fonte Boa.

Court slowed and turned, expecting to see Davi behind the wheel.

But no, one hundred yards back he saw Davi's truck, but it was full of armed men in bush hats, and as Gentry turned back to run for his life, he heard the pops of rifles.

'Fuck!' shouted Gentry as he dashed off the road, back into the thick jungle, digging his way through vines and bush and palm fronds the size of truck tires, desperate to make himself small, fast, and slippery.

As he pushed his way into the tangle of undergrowth, he worked on a new plan. His old plan had been simple. He had a canoe stowed under the little bridge just a hundred and fifty yards ahead. He'd planned on running up the road, sliding down the bank, and then making his escape via the little boat, being careful to dodge the choppers by staying under the trees that hung out over the river's edge.

But now he'd have to approach the bridge from upriver, which presented one extraordinary obstacle. Or a dozen or more obstacles, depending on how you looked at it.

Both sides of the riverbank north of the bridge were literally covered with crocodiles.

Huge fucking crocodiles.

As Court powered through the nearly impenetrable growth, he settled on his new plan – a plan that would require skill he was not sure he possessed, execution he was not sure he could pull off, and luck he was not sure he could count on.

But it was better than dancing down the road ducking rounds from a truck full of rifles.

He heard the men entering the vegetation behind him. A few fired their guns into the trees and bushes. Court knew his trail would close itself as soon as he moved through; he was not worried about the men any longer. Their eyes could not see him and their guns could not reach him.

But he *was* worried. He was worried about the damn crocodiles ahead.

The rifle fire picked up. It was as if the men were trying to tear their way through the jungle with lead. It would not work, not before Court made it clear. But that was not to say that one lucky bullet fragment couldn't crash its way through and bury itself into the back of the American's head.

Court ducked down lower, pushed through on his hands and knees, scraping them raw in the process. He ripped down spider-webs the size of fishing nets and used the barrel of his shotgun to knock a boa constrictor from a low hanging branch so he could limbo under it without fear of having the angry snake wrap around his neck.

Soon he broke out of the jungle and onto a hill above the riverbank. Forty yards to his left the wooden bridge sat invitingly in the sun. His little boat bobbed in the shade under it, a canvas tarp tight as a drum over it for protection. Below him, and for at least twenty-five of the forty yards along the water's edge, a dozen crocs ranging in size from six to sixteen feet basked in the mid-morning rays.

Gentry found a thick vine that shot out from the bank in a diagonal off to his left, ran over the riverbank, and connected to the highest, most outstretched limb of a two-hundred-foot-tall kapok tree that hung over the river like a great arm.

It might not take him all the way to the bridge, but it *would* get him to the bank right next to it. That was far enough from the crocs, and that would be just fine.

He'd tossed his machete ten minutes earlier, so he pointed the wide barrel of his shotgun just above where the vine entered the hard earth.

And then he hesitated. Panting from the exertion, stinging from the abrasions on his hands and knees and the scratches and insect stings he'd picked up along the way, he just stood there, his shotgun poised to fire. He had swung on vines many evenings with the boys in the village; he trusted their strength and their ability to get him from here to there. But in his mind's eye he saw this plan of his going very, very wrong. In fact, he could not even conjure a mental image of the next fifteen seconds going off without a hitch.

A long, angry burst from an automatic rifle thirty yards behind him in the jungle helped him focus on the task at hand. He fired the pump shotgun at the vine, it split and frayed beautifully, and he caught it with his free hand before it swung away. Hurriedly, he refastened the shotgun to his backpack one-handed and leapt into the air to take the vine at the highest point he could reach. His sore red hands gripped hard, his legs wrapped around tight, and he began swinging off the hill and over the massive reptiles below.

The vine shot him above the near bank; he passed over sleepy crocodiles warming themselves at the water's edge. Many of the crocs lay with their toothy mouths wide open, cooling their bodies with the intake of air and presenting an especially ominous image to swing over.

19

His grip was secure; he grimaced with the effort but held firm as gravity took him out over the water now, his legs jutted in front of him, his knees cinched tight against the vine, and his eyes focused on his landing area on the bank by the bridge.

The vine was supple and green and healthy; he could count on it to get him across.

But not so the high tree limb from which it hung. Termites had nested along the crook where it separated from a larger branch, weakening the joint. Without Gentry's acrobatics the limb would have held for another year, until the rainy season pushed winds across the continent and the brittle wood snapped in a storm.

But this limb did not have another year. It would fail now.

Gentry's worst-case scenario came to pass in two stages.

The first was more of a slip of the vine at the tree branch; there was a lurching and a catch. Court was well out away from the land, easily ten feet above the water and sailing fast. He kept his grip but jacked his head off of his intended destination and up towards his lifeline's connection with the tree.

He just managed to focus his wide eyes on the distant point as the tree limb cracked and broke.

Gentry's momentum, with his legs out in front of him, sent his body spinning backwards one full revolution through the air, twenty feet up. He found himself facedown as gravity took over, and he dropped towards the water emitting a primordial scream of terror.

4

Gentry let go of the vine; it was only in the way now.

He crashed through the black surface in a belly flop, well aware that the crocodiles on both sides of the bank would all be awake, alert, and pissed.

Sinking in the black with the wind knocked from his lungs, it took him longer than he wanted to get the backpack off. With it he sank into the muck; the river was only seven or eight feet deep here. After he removed the backpack, he yanked the shotgun free. Swimming while wielding a 12-gauge shotgun would be ridiculous, but leaving it down here in the mud while reptiles the size of four-man canoes roamed above would be insane.

After grabbing his weapon Gentry pushed off the bottom to shoot to the surface and lost one of his shoes in the process. He kicked the other off as his head popped out of the water. He shook his long wet hair from his eyes and turned back to the nearest bank, twenty-five yards away.

Two big crocs slid into the water before his eyes, heading in his direction. Next to where they entered the river, he noticed the bank empty. He was certain he had swung over a monstrous sixteen-footer in that spot just seconds before.

Court lay on his back in the water and kicked frantically while his head remained up and his pistol-grip weapon pointed in the direction of the bank. It was an uncoordinated half backstroke that derived no speed from its efficiency but much from its intensity.

Crocodiles do not normally eat meals that are alive. Instead they kill their prey by biting down with their clamplike jaws to take hold and then spinning it in the water in order to drown it.

But Court knew that he, as a fragile human being, would not be drowned. The bite would not kill him outright, but the spinning and the flailing and the whipping tail would shatter his neck and break his body, turn him into a lifeless rag doll, even before his lungs filled with the river's hot black water.

He had twenty yards to go to his boat; he would head straight to the bobbing canoe and avoid the bank now, as crocs were even faster on land than in the water. Panic threatened to overtake him; he knew he had not even looked at the far side of the river to see how many of the hungry fuckers over there were coming out for a quick and easy one-hundred-seventy-pound lunch of fresh meat.

Instead he focused on the white water churned up by his pounding bare feet.

There it was. The first big beast was upon him; it looked like a fat gray tree trunk through the foam until his big mouth opened, inches from the tips of Gentry's toes. With a scream of terror Court spread his legs apart and raised the shotgun.

Click.

He had not pumped another shell into the chamber after using the shotgun to sever the vine.

The reptile was on him now.

He jabbed the inside of its mouth with the muzzle of the gun.

In the two seconds since he'd stopped kicking he'd begun to sink in the water, and he felt the fore claws of the animal against his leg as they sank. The smack in the mouth caused the croc to flail back for a brief instant, and Gentry used that instant to charge a fresh shell into the chamber of his 12-gauge as he sank deeper, faceup, into the river.

He went under fully now, pushed his weapon up until he felt the neck of the reptile above him, and pulled the trigger one-handed.

Boom!

The recoil pushed him deeper, deep enough to avoid the

spinning animal's huge tail as it thrashed near the surface. Court turned and swam quickly down and away, along the bottom of the river for a moment as he neared his boat. He shot back to the surface and jacked a fresh shell into the breach as he spun back around, found a new croc on him, its mouth just beginning to open to initiate the death grip. This beast was no more than ten feet long but still quite deadly. Gentry shot the gray monster between the eyes.

The blast of double-aught buckshot was roughly akin to ten simultaneous rounds from a .32-caliber handgun. At point-blank range to the face of even a massive reptile, it was almost certainly a mortal wound. But the death throes of such a powerful creature are just as dangerous as the attack, and again Court had to kick and twist and flail at the water to get away.

He also knew the fresh blood in the water would attract hundreds of piranha in seconds; he had to get out of there immediately for way too many reasons to count. He ejected the spent shell, chambered a fresh one, and kicked frantically towards his canoe.

He heard the first snaps of gunfire as he took hold of his little boat under the bridge, but he ignored them for now. With a free hand he unhooked the ties holding down the canvas tarp from two of the cleats. He tossed the shotgun onto the tarp and pulled himself into the craft. The massive open mouth of a twelve-foot crocodile lurched from the water behind him, followed his legs up and over the little boat's edge, but the jaws snapped shut without taking hold. The animal's front leg had made it into the canoe, and his thrashing weight threatened to flip the tiny craft over with Court inside it. Court grabbed the 12-gauge and fired one-handed into the reptile's neck, flipping it back off the boat.

He tried to rack a fresh shell, but his gun was empty. The rest of his ammo was in the backpack at the bottom of the river, so he tossed the shotgun aside as he pulled the rest of the canvas cover free and let it fall into the water. Another long burst of rifle fire shot foam into the boat, but the distant soldier's gun emptied before he could hit either the canoe or the American.

Court dove flat on the bottom of the ten-foot-long canoe, pushed the outboard's propellers into the water, flipped it on, and pulled the cord.

The machine burst to life, and Gentry wasted no time turning his tiny craft upstream, away from the guns and the crocodiles and the piranha.

A minute east of the bridge he still panted and hacked river water out of his throat. He looked down and saw his wet pants ripped open at the left thigh. A long slashing wound bled from where the first crocodile had scratched him with its claws. The wound was relatively serious and could use a few stitches in the deepest part, but he knew it was a better outcome than he had a right to deserve. He shuddered thinking about the prehistoric monster on top of him in the water.

And then he let out a long sigh. Looked down at his boat, at what now amounted to the grand sum of his worldly possessions.

An old plastic flashlight, a one-liter bottle of outboard engine fuel, and a rusty speargun.

That was it.

Court wiped his long hair from his eyes, hefted the speargun with his free hand, and turned the throttle on the engine higher, steering the boat upriver towards Fonte Boa.

5

The manhunter stood alone in his hotel room, wiped sweat from his face, and opened the second-story window to let in fresh air that, while cooler than the musty room, smelled like rotten fish and donkey shit.

He fought a wave of nausea.

He turned off his radio and tossed it into his suitcase. The rest of his clothes were packed. He just had to zip up the bag, and he was out of this disgusting and humid hellhole. In ten minutes he'd be at the dock walking up the plank of the steamboat to Coari. In two days he'd arrive in a real city, even if he were only speaking in relative terms by comparing it to this backwater coffee stain on the map. Another two days and he'd be in Manaus, and there he'd run like an Olympic sprinter to the airport, catch a flight to Rio or Sao Paulo and then back home to Amsterdam.

Only then would he breathe easy again. He'd take a day or two to tend to his tulip garden, and then he would regroup. Reacquire his target.

He would find Court Gentry again. And *next* time, he told himself with finality, he'd get a team of wet boys who would not fuck up the entire operation.

He still could not believe it. Six men out of twenty killed. Including the AUC commander. Five of them by goddamned bee stings, and the other after slipping into a river full of crocodiles. Seriously? The helicopters had radioed that they were heading back over the border to Colombia with both their dead and their living.

And they were leaving him out here alone.

Bastards.

A knock at the door.

A chill ran up the manhunter's sixty-two-year-old spine. He turned away from the window and pulled the old.32-caliber revolver from its leather shoulder holster under his arm. He held it up with a quivering hand.

Slowly and quietly he took the four steps to the door, the weapon raised in front of him.

'Who's there?'

'Sir? Do you need help with your bags?'

The manhunter unlocked the bolt and flipped the latch, hiding his pistol behind the door as he opened it.

He sighed in relief. It was one of the little savages from the front desk.

'No. I can manage.'

'Yes, sir. The ferry leaves in twenty minutes.' With a nod the savage turned and headed back down the rickety staircase.

The manhunter shut the door. Locked it back tight. Holstered his ancient pistol as he turned back around to zip his suitcase shut.

On the other side of the room Courtland Gentry, his target for these many months, stood by the window. Gentry wore a short beard and hair longer than in any of the photos the manhunter kept, but it was undoubtedly him. He sported a cream-colored shirt, unbuttoned, wet, and filthy. Brown cotton pants, ripped at the thigh and blood smeared.

He held a speargun in his right hand.

The manhunter grabbed at his pistol in its shoulder holster as he cried out in shock.

The loud spring mechanism of the speargun firing snapped in the air of the hot room. The manhunter felt his body slam back against the wooden door; his arms flew out wide from his body.

Only by looking down, away from his target, did he see that

he'd been run through by a long bolt from the weapon. He was pinned to the door through the stomach. Blood wet the insides of his legs as it trickled down from the wound.

After taking the time necessary to recognize what had happened, the manhunter looked slowly back up to his target. The American tossed the empty speargun on the tiny twin bed and came closer. With a growing weakness the manhunter softly pawed again at the pistol under his arm.

The Gray Man gently moved the manhunter's hand away from the shoulder holster and pulled the revolver out. He looked it over, shrugged, and slid it into his pants at the small of his back.

'You've been on me since Chile, haven't you?' The manhunter was surprised by the gentleness of the American's voice. The Dutchman had lived and breathed Court Gentry for over half a year but realized now that he'd never heard him speak, had never even wondered what he sounded like.

Pain burned in the manhunter's gut. Weakness grew in his extremities, in his eyes. Still, he said, 'Since Quito.'

Court Gentry smiled. His face was close to the manhunter's, his tone still soft and familiar like they were father and son. 'I didn't feel you in Ecuador.' He raised his eyebrows. 'That was one hell of a chase, you and me.'

The manhunter's legs went slack, and he cried out with the pain radiating from the spike through his belly. Quickly the Gray Man grabbed him, held him up against the door, braced him to take away a measure of the agony. The American looked up into the manhunter's eyes. 'You know how it is. Men like me. We can't help what we are. It's not our fault. The man who sent you … he knew who I was. *What* I was. *He* was the one who killed you. Not me.'

The manhunter's eyes were vacant. Still, he nodded slightly.

'Give me his name, and I'll make him pay.'

After a moment, the mouth opened. A trickle of blood ran down the Dutchman's chin. He tried to speak; a small sound came out but no words.

Court leaned close to the man's face.

The Dutchman winced with pain; his eyes relit somewhat, tempered with new concentration. He *wanted* to speak.

And finally he did. So softly Gentry had to lean almost into the man's lips to hear him say it.

'Sidorenko.'

Gentry leaned away. Stood fully erect in front of the man. Nodded. Gregor Sidorenko, the Russian mafia kingpin and Court's old employer, was apparently still sore about a double-cross Gentry had engineered the previous spring.

'I'll punish him for sending you to me. You can rest now.'

Gentry pulled the spear out of the door, out of the man; the manhunter did not even feel the movement, nor did he feel himself being helped to the bed. He watched the American lay him down, lift his feet up one at a time, and pull off his boots, but he did not *feel* anything.

He wanted to rest. His eyes softened even more, and the last thing he saw before the lids shut was his target looking through his suitcase, taking his wallet and a first-aid kid and some clothes, and leaving through the front door.

The manhunter's eyes shut then, and he thought of his tulips.

He would not see them soon after all, and that was a shame.

6

Thirty-eight-year-old Major Eduardo Gamboa surfaced slowly, his black neoprene head covering, the black waterproof grease-paint on his face, the black swim mask, and the black covert breathing regulator in his mouth all helping him blend in with the three a.m. black water shifting here in Banderas Bay. Fifty meters in front of him, a one-hundred-twenty-foot luxury yacht floated, backlit by the late-night artificial illumination of the Malecon, the boardwalk running the length of Puerto Vallarta's downtown. To the north, to Gamboa's ten o'clock, the bright lights of PV's hotel district twinkled like fireflies.

The yacht was called *La Sirena*; it lay at anchor here seven miles out in the bay, wide of the shipping lanes that ran to the port or the marina but close enough to shore so that its owner and his entourage could enjoy all that Puerto Vallarta had to offer. It was long and sleek and beautiful, and crowned by a state-of-the-art black Eurocopter helicopter resting on the helipad above the upper aft deck. But Eduardo Gamboa ignored the style of the ship in front of him and focused fully on the substance. After forty minutes under water his night vision was tuned to its peak. With his naked eye he saw two guards on the upper sundeck standing near the bow. He imagined the same number on the opposite side.

Slowly another head rose from the water to Eduardo's right. Then another. Then three more men on Eduardo's left. Then two more men just behind him.

29

Eight divers in total bobbed in the water fifty meters from the *La Sirena*. And after a nod from Major Eduardo Gamboa, they each released a few ounces of air from their buoyancy-control devices, and as one they slowly lowered back below the black surface, leaving not a trace of their existence.

Gamboa and his men were from the GOPES, the Grupo de Operaciones Especiales, the Mexican Federal Police's elite special operation's group. But these eight cops were a level of elite unknown to all but a few. They'd been pulled from other police and military commando units and organized separately from the rest of the GOPES. Together they comprised a special assault-team task force run secretly by the attorney general in Mexico City.

Their mission? Extrajudicial execution of Mexico's top drug-cartel bosses.

Their target tonight? The owner of *La Sirena*, one Daniel Alonzo de la Rocha Alvarez. In a world where everyone had a nickname, de la Rocha was known simply by the initials of his last name, DLR, pronounced in Spanish as *'de, ele, ere.'*

DLR was the leader of Los Trajes Negros, the Black Suits, one of the nation's leading criminal drug and kidnapping organizations.

Four minutes later, two of Gamboa's team resurfaced at the stern of *La Sirena*. Martin and Ramses had removed their scuba gear, their masks and their fins, and they carefully climbed the sea stairs onto the lower deck. They carried suppressed Steyr TMP submachine guns and held them at the ready as they crouched at the top of the stairs. Their night vision gear helped them peer up the deck towards the galley and the bow. After a moment Ramses spoke into his headset.

'We're on board, moving into position.'

Gamboa had come along the portside hull with two more of his team. *'Entendido,'* he whispered into his radio. *Understood.*

A minute later Martin and Ramses had hoisted themselves up the helipad ladder, climbing silently in the dark. Then they lay prone on opposite sides of the Eurocopter, their weapons trained ahead on the four guards on the sundeck, some seventy feet forward on the yacht. Martin and Ramses's job was to prevent any attempt by those on board to flee in the chopper during the assault and to eliminate the deck guards when given the order by their commander. 'Team One, *listo*,' said Ramses into his headset. *Ready*.

'*Entendido*,' replied Gamboa again from the softly rolling surface of the bay. He removed his scuba gear as he spoke. 'Team Two, execute.'

'Executing,' came the call, and three men began climbing the anchor chain at the port bow, forty feet below the guards on the sundeck.

Two minutes later these men were aboard, and their suppressed weapons scanned the bridge deck. 'Team Two, *listo*.'

'Team Three, *vamos*,' said Gamboa, and he and two men rose dripping out of the water at the rear stairs, climbed to the upper deck, passed a large lifeboat covered with a tight canvas tarp, and began moving forward, proceeding cautiously. They made it to the hallway to the galley, heard noises and saw lights coming from the great room ahead, and flipped up their night vision goggles. They entered the room slowly, found two guards seated on the large white leather sofa in front of a fifty-two-inch plasma-screen television.

Gamboa took the man on the left, shot him once through the skull as he stood. The report from his suppressed weapon was drowned out by a protracted gunfight on the TV.

The officer behind Gamboa shot the guard on the right three times in the chest; both guards tumbled back to the sofa, handguns falling out of their hands and blood pools spreading out and meeting between their bodies on the white leather.

The three *federales* moved across the room quickly now. The television was running a movie that Eduardo easily recognized: *Los Trajes Negros 2*, the second in a very popular series of Mexican-made films romanticizing the life and exploits of Daniel de la Rocha, the man sleeping in the master suite just beyond.

Arrogant pendejo, Gamboa thought. It was typical of the narcissistic drug lord to have films glorifying his evil playing on his yacht. Gamboa continued across the room with his men stacked behind him and entered the hall to the master suite. They passed two other guest suites; they would clear them all after dealing with de la Rocha, but they did not expect them to be occupied. Forty-eight hours of surveillance of *La Sirena* had indicated that Daniel was on board tonight with only a few bodyguards and the crew of his yacht.

Once in place at the door to the master suite, Team Three waited. Within seconds, one deck above them, Team Two announced they were outside the crew quarters.

'All teams, execute in three. *Uno ... dos ... tres.*'

On the helipad Martin and Ramses each fired two suppressed rounds from their Steyrs into the head of each guard on the sundeck.

Team Two opened both the crew quarters and the captain's stateroom; one man trained a weapon on the captain's bed, and two more flipped on the lights of the crew's quarters and held their weapons on the eight men expected to be sleeping there.

Team Three, with Major Eduardo Gamboa in the lead, kicked in the door of the master suite. They actuated the flashlights attached under the barrels of their submachine guns but found the room already awash with light. The fifty-two-inch plasma in this room was on as well; this screen was broadcasting an interview with Daniel de la Rocha. He spoke to a reporter off camera. Gamboa ignored it and rushed to the king-sized bed. A large lump under the silk sheets was his target.

But before he made it to the bed, his weapon raised to fire, a voice to his right caught his attention.

'Welcome to *La Sirena*, Major Eduardo Gamboa.' It was de la Rocha's voice. Gamboa looked up in shock. DLR was on television looking right into Gamboa's eyes. He appeared to be in a studio, dressed in his impeccable and ubiquitous black Italian-cut suit. 'A government assassin, here, to eliminate me. *Dios mio!*'

The handsome face on the screen said it with a slight smile; his slick hair, goatee, and thin mustache gleamed black; his eyes seemingly locked on Gamboa.

Eduardo looked back at the hallway door. Both of his men stared at the television with wide eyes.

Over his earpiece the major heard Team One check in. 'All four targets eliminated.'

And then Team Two. 'Major ... most of these bunks are empty. There are only three men up here. No *capitán*.'

And then, from the television, de la Rocha continued to address the stunned federal officer. 'Major Gamboa, let me ask you something. If you work *for* the *federales*, and I *own* the *federales*, where does that leave you and your men?'

Gamboa looked to the lump in the bed, he lifted back the sheets with a gloved hand.

C4 plastic explosives, easily one hundred pounds in bricks wired together with a red detonator attached. *'¿Qué chingados?'* muttered Gamboa. *What the fuck?*

'Do you have your answer yet? Dead! It leaves you and your fucking team *muerto, pendejo!*'

Eduardo Gamboa turned away from the bomb, pushed the transmit button on his radio. 'It's a trap! Off the boat!'

Eduardo's men turned in front of him, began running down the hallway. He sprinted behind them; they had just made it into the saloon, had just passed the television playing the movie exalting the crimes of Daniel Alonzo de la Rocha Alvarez, when a flash erupted from behind them. The hot blast of fire enveloped them, and they died in the spectacular explosion of the thirty-three-million-dollar vessel.

Daniel de la Rocha bobbed in the water, one hundred yards from the wreckage of his beautiful *La Sirena*. He waited patiently while Emilio and Felipe, his two bodyguards, got the emergency life raft inflated, and then they helped him aboard. Once all three men had climbed onto the tiny dinghy, they tossed away the snorkeling gear they had been wearing since they slipped out of the wooden life raft on the upper deck and into the water of Banderas Bay. They'd managed to swim one hundred yards before the four men left behind on the sundeck were shot, and this told Daniel it was time to press the waterproof remote control that began the sequence both on his DVD player *and* on his bomb.

Now he and his men watched the flames burning on the water. He hoped it would not be long before the local harbor fire patrol came to rescue the three survivors. Daniel knew he would be a living martyr after this act of aggression by the *federales*; indeed, he had worked for months so that he could capitalize on this moment.

He would miss *La Sirena*, without question. But it was insured, his Eurocopter was insured, and a great deal of artwork that was not even on board was insured. It was time for an upgrade anyway. There was a one-hundred-sixty-foot gem that he'd seen a few months earlier in Fort Lauderdale, and he'd have his people begin working immediately on the owner to encourage him to sell it.

Sergeant Martin Orozco Fernandez and Sergeant Ramses Cienfuegos Cortillo bobbed in the black water. Both men were injured: burns to Ramses's legs that would scream in the salt water as soon as his adrenaline dissipated enough for him to feel them, and a slightly sprained left wrist for Martin that would make seven miles of swimming a special kind of hell. But they were excellent swimmers, and their wetsuits were buoyant. They would not drown.

But that did not make either of them feel much better. Because the rest of their team was dead, and it was obvious to both of them that they had been set up by their leaders, and their leaders were somewhere on the shore they swam towards. Only a few knew of tonight's attack, and Ramses and Martin knew that at least one of those few had tipped off de la Rocha.

7

As a general rule, Court liked third-world bus stations. Here he could people-watch with a minimum of return scrutiny, sit by himself in a dark corner, and soak up the experiences of others. His personal predicament, the fact that many highly dangerous people wanted him dead, necessitated a solitary existence, a distance from and a general mistrust of other human beings. For this reason the thirty-seven-year-old American by and large learned about normal everyday life and family and relationships by proxy, often in bus stations. Watching a father scold a misbehaving child, a young couple cuddle and laugh together, an old man eat his dinner alone. Court had been living this way exclusively for five years, the time that the former CIA asset had been on the run from the Central Intelligence Agency, ducking a shoot-on-sight sanction. But to one extreme or another, sitting alone and watching others live their lives had been Court's life as long as he could remember.

Nine days had passed since Brazil; he'd traveled overland ever since – bicycles and buses and shoe leather into Central America. He hadn't remained for more than six hours in a single place. He now sat at a bus station in Guatemala City, waiting on a chicken bus that would take him into the northern jungle near the border with Mexico and Belize.

He had a little money now but not much. He'd sold the man-hunter's pistol in El Salvador, and he still had some of the euros he'd pulled from the Dutchman's wallet. But he'd bought second-hand clothing in Panama and a green canvas gym bag to carry it in. That and food and bus tickets had not been much. Gentry could get by with less than virtually any other American; nevertheless, cash would become an issue before too long.

A black-and-white television hung from a metal pole in a corner of the waiting room. It broadcast a talk show from Mexico City featuring transsexuals shouting at one another over some nonsense. Court didn't pay much attention to the TV; instead his eyes were fixed on the old man and his plate of rice. It was the man who mopped the dirty floor and perfunctorily wiped the toilets here at the bus station; the American assassin had been sitting here long enough to see the man at work. Now the janitor sat at a table by the café and picked at his food, sucked the rice because he did not have enough teeth to do anything else with it. Did he have to work all night? Was there anyone to come home to in the morning?

Court found himself imagining a story for the man, and in many ways it mirrored his own.

Court did not expect to live as long as the old man, and he found perverse comfort in that because he did not want to be both lonely *and* old.

The village in the Amazon had been an eye opener for him. When Court arrived there, he'd been traveling for five months straight. A couple of weeks in Rio, a couple of weeks in Quito, a few days in two dozen other towns. All that time he thought of stopping; it never left his thoughts. He thought he wanted to find a place to stay, a job to do, people around him who, obviously, would never know his true identity but who would know him as *someone*, which was quite unlike traveling, where he was neither known nor noticed by those around him.

And the Amazon village had provided all this for him. The people were kind, and they weren't too inquisitive. The austerity had helped him focus and pushed him further away from the painkiller addiction that he'd left behind him, bit by bit, in each town he'd passed through since Caracas the previous April. He'd been clean for two months by the time he arrived in the Amazon, and the constant exercise and work and danger from nothing more nefarious than God's nature had helped his body forget about such banal trivialities as the desire for a pill's relaxation.

But there was a downside. He had come to the realization that the things which he had sought – stability, relative safety, a routine – did not satisfy him. It disgusted him to admit it, but when young Mauro came and told him about the arrival of the man-hunter, he'd felt an undeniable sense of relief wash over his body.

Action. Adrenaline. Purpose.

Court Gentry did not like it, but he could no longer deny it. After the Amazon village, after the absurd relief of an attack by choppers full of gunmen, one thing was obvious to him.

Court Gentry *was* the Gray Man, and the Gray Man lived for this shit.

Court had been sitting on a plastic chair with his head back on the greasy wall and his feet up on his canvas bag. But he sat up to move his back, to flex and then stretch the muscles high in his left shoulder where scar tissue from an arrow wound bothered him, the adhesion of the tissue needing a good daily stretch to stay pliant.

The evening news came on the little television, and Court distractedly listened to it without looking at the screen, just picking up words here and there as he leaned forward and wrapped his arms around his body to stretch the muscles under his scapulas.

The words *Puerto Vallarta* did not catch his attention, neither did *yacht* nor *explosion*.

But the Spanish word *asesinato* caused him to turn his head. He had an acute professional interest in stories about assassination.

He watched video of smoldering wreckage in the ocean, taken from a helicopter at dawn. Then a picture of a handsome Hispanic male in an impeccable black three-piece suit. The newscaster said the man's name was Daniel de la Rocha, and there was speculation that he was the target of a sanctioned murder by the Mexican Federal Police. Court couldn't understand it all, but he did pick up that de la Rocha had survived and the police who had bombed the yacht had all died.

Wow, Court thought. That was a fucked-up hit. Why blow up the yacht? Why not just shoot the son of a bitch on land?

The image on the screen changed again, displayed an official photo of a man in a police uniform sitting in front of the Mexican flag. He wore a smart hat, medals adorned his uniform coat, and his clean-shaven face was serious and stern.

Court cocked his head a fraction of an inch. Blinked twice rapidly. Otherwise, he did not move a muscle. He just watched.

The newscaster continued speaking over the cop's image, and Gentry concentrated on the words, tuned into the grammar, and did his very best to understand.

'Sources say Major Eduardo Gamboa of the Policía Federal's special operation's group led the attempt on the life of Daniel de la Rocha. As previously stated, Gamboa and all his men perished in the explosion of the yacht, along with four of DLR's bodyguards and three crewmen of *La Sirena*. Only de la Rocha and two associates survived.'

Eduardo Gamboa. 'Eduardo Gamboa.' Court whispered it softly. The image left the screen, a commercial selling mobile phone plans appeared, but Gentry still saw the face.

'Eduardo Gamboa.' He said it again softly. Then said, 'Eddie.'

Court blinked again, dropped his bearded face into his hands, and thought back to the month he spent in hell.

Laos
August 2000
Four soldiers in army green ponchos pulled the American out of the back of the truck and shoved him through the thunderstorm, up the muddy trail. He stumbled once on the pathway to the wooden shack: his manacled hands and feet forced him to move slower than his minders found reasonable, and his long,

38

rain-soaked hospital gown and bare feet hardly promoted sure footwork on the slick stones. One Laotian prodded him in the back with his old SKS rifle to encourage Gentry to pick up the pace. Once under the porch roof of the shack, Court dropped to his knees, but the guards yanked him back up and left him teetering there while the door was unlocked. He swayed with the wind of the storm as he stood and waited; finally, they moved him inside the building.

The soldiers took off their ponchos and hung them on wall pegs while an officer came out from behind his desk and unlocked a door to a stairwell that descended into darkness. Court teetered again, nearly tipped over, but strong hands on his back and shoulders guided him down the narrow stairs. At the bottom another locked door was opened, Gentry was pushed forward onto a brick floor, and his shackles were removed. The four soldiers unlocked an iron cell and shoved him inside.

He dropped in the corner of the cell, and they left him there in his wet hospital gown, the metal bars clanging shut behind him. The soldiers slammed the basement door behind him, locked it, and then retreated up the steps.

Gentry had landed on moldy sawdust; he'd caught a mouthful of it and spat it back out as he lay on his side. He opened his eyes and struggled to look around. A folded up pair of baby blue pajamas lay on the floor next to him; he could just make them out. There was a faint light emanating from a ventilation slit high on the wall above him; only a trace of dim illumination tracked down softly to where Gentry lay, but it did nothing to reveal the room around him.

He couldn't see an inch beyond his arm where it lay outstretched on the sawdust.

'Shit,' he mumbled to himself. 'Fucking perfect.'

'English?' A man's voice called hopefully from the dark in front of him, from inside the bars of the cell, maybe a dozen feet from the tip of Court's nose.

Gentry did not respond.

After a while he heard movement, the sound of a person sitting up, clothing rubbing against the stone wall.

'You speak English?' The accent was American, with perhaps a foreign background.

Court ignored the question.

The voice in the blackness continued. 'I've been here for two weeks. Spent the first couple of days checking for cameras or listening devices. Trust me, these *pendejos* aren't that sophisticated.'

Court slowly moved himself into a sitting position, leaned back against the iron bars. He nodded to the dark. Shrugged his shoulders. 'I speak English.' He was surprised by how weak and raspy his voice had become.

'You American?'

'Yep.'

'Same here.'

Court said, 'You talk funny.'

A chuckle from the disembodied voice. 'Born in Mexico. Came to the States when I was eighteen.'

'Then you're a long way from home.'

'Yeah. How bout you? What did you do to end up here?'

'Not sure where "here" is, exactly.'

'We're a couple hours northwest of Vientiane in a military camp where they dump foreign heroin smugglers. It's not an official prison; there is no judge or trial or Red Cross or anything like that. They bring the traffickers here to interrogate them, pull the names of their suppliers from them, and then when they're sure they've squeezed out everything they have to offer, they take them to a work camp and have them build roads until they drop dead. They say in three weeks the rainy season will be over and the roads will be passable, then everyone here is off to the labor camps.'

'Bummer,' Court said after another cough.

'How much dope did they catch you with?'

Court closed his eyes and leaned his head back against the cold brick wall. He shrugged. 'I wasn't running drugs.'

'Sure you weren't, homes. Just tell them it was a mis-understanding.'

'Actually I came to rescue some dipshit DEA dumbass who got himself captured by the boneheads running this place.'

An extremely long pause. Then a fresh chuckle. Then a hearty laugh that seemed utterly out of place in this black dungeon. Then the sound of movement in the dark. In the low light close to Court's face, a bearded man appeared. He looked Mexican, late twenties, and several inches shorter than Court. He wore baby blue pajamas, and the skin around both of his eyes was tainted with fading bruises, obvious even in the deep shadow. He stuck out a hand. 'Eddie Gamble. DEA, Phoenix Field Office, on special assignment to the Bangkok Field Division.'

Court shook the hand weakly. 'Hey, Gamble? How's that special assignment of yours working out?'

'How's *your* assignment working out, *ese?*'

Court smiled; the muscles in his jaw hurt. 'No better than yours, I guess.'

'So you are here to save me, huh?'

Gentry nodded.

Eddie Gamble swatted a bug from his forehead. 'Is this the part where the rest of your unit rappels down from the rafters and we all blast out of here with jet packs?'

Court looked up towards the low ceiling. 'God, I hope so.' Nothing happened. He looked back to Gamble. Shrugged. 'Guess not.'

Eddie asked, 'Who are you with?'

'Can't say.'

'I'm cleared top secret.'

'Chicks dig that, don't they?' quipped Gentry; his eyes were becoming accustomed to the low light, so he scanned the cell now, found nothing but a shit bucket and a water trough and a couple of tattered blankets as furniture.

'I mean ... I'm sure you can tell me who you're with.'

'Sorry, stud. I'm codeword-classified.' *Codeword-classified* meant only those who knew a specific code could be privy to a set of information.

'I bet chicks dig *that*.'

'They would if I could tell them, but they'd have to know the codeword.'

Gamble laughed at this, and at the situation. 'You can come rescue me, but you can't tell me who you work for?'

'The DEA is looking for you. I just happened to be in the area, sort of, so I was sent by my people to nose around.'

'And then?'

Court shrugged. 'Bad luck. I got sick. I was meeting with some contacts, and I passed out. I woke up in the hospital. I had cover for status only; my papers weren't good enough for the scrutiny of the hospital, so they called the cops. My papers weren't even close to good enough for the cops, so they called military intelligence. Military intelligence wiped their asses with my papers, basically, so here I am.'

Gamble reached out and put his hand on Gentry's forehead. 'You get stung by any mosquitoes?'

'I crossed over the Mekong about a week and a half ago. Damn bugs ate my ass up. Guess they don't get a lot of white meat around here.'

'Backache, muscle aches, stomach cramps, dizziness?'

'Fatigue, joint pain, vomiting,' Court finished his list of symptoms.

'You have malaria,' Eddie said gravely.

'Thanks, doc, but I already figured that out.'

Gamble looked at Gentry a long time before saying, 'Brother, that's a death sentence in a place like this. You need meds. Clean water. Solid food that doesn't have *cucarachas* crawling in it. You aren't gonna get that here.'

Court shrugged his shoulders. 'I'll be okay.'

Eddie stood quickly, so quickly Gentry flinched. Gamble moved to the bars and started shouting for the guards up the stairs. Court couldn't understand a word of it. The guards did not come down, and after a moment Gamble sat back down, visibly angry.

'We gotta get you to a hospital.'

'They just pulled me *out* of a hospital, remember.'

'*¡Pendejos!*'

'What does that mean?'

'It's Spanish. It's kinda like ... *assholes* or something.'

Court nodded. 'And that was Laotian you were speaking to the guards?'

'Thai. Not exactly the same, but close enough for government work.'

'Figured a DEA agent with Mexican roots would be sent to Latin America. I guess if you speak Thai, you get sent here.'

'I get sent everywhere. Before this gig I was in the Navy for six years, in the Teams. I went all over, picked up some language on the way.'

'The Teams? You were a SEAL?'

'Team Three.'

Court nodded, as respectfully as one can while resting his head on a wall. 'You've been here two weeks. You should have escaped by now, spent a week banging beach bunnies on the coast, and then made it back home with time to spare.'

Gamble bristled in the dark. Court could tell the man did not like the suggestion that he was soft. 'Sure, I could get out of here. Two guards come down to take me to the interrogation shack every morning. I *could* break their necks. I *could* grab a sidearm and make a run for the motor pool. I *could* hot-wire a ride in nothing flat. I *could* smash the front gate, make a run for the Mekong.'

'But you just stay because you like the food?'

Gamble's facial expression showed incredulity. 'Bro ... I'm *DEA*. I'm not a SEAL anymore, and I'm sure as hell not some secret squirrel, codeword, badass hombre like yourself. I can't just run around killing Laotian military.'

Court nodded slowly. He worked under quite different rules of engagement, but he wasn't going to admit that to Eddie.

43

Gamble asked, 'What about you? Can you tell me your background? I mean, you weren't *born* codeword-classified, were you?'

'I forgot everything before this job.'

'Shit, the CIA winds you singleton operators up tight, don't they?'

Court didn't bite on the comment. Didn't admit he was CIA.

Gamble gave him a moment, and then said, 'Okay. How bout a name? You got a name?'

Another shrug from the sick American against the wall. 'My cover is blown. You can make one up for me. Anything you like.'

Gamble shook his head. Shrugged. 'Okay, amigo. I think I'll call you Sally.'

Court laughed until he wheezed and coughed until he rolled into the fetal position, wracked with pain.

8

Gentry's mind left ancient history in Laos, came back to the here and now, and he looked down at the grave of Eduardo Gamboa, the freshly dug earth dry and crumbled around the tombstone.

Major Gamboa had been dead for eight days, it took three days to fish his remains from the Pacific Ocean, his funeral was the day before yesterday, and already people had defaced the white wooden cross with spray paint.

Hijo de puta! Son of a bitch.

Cabrón. Goat, a Spanish pejorative similar to *jackass.*

Pendejo. Eddie himself taught Court the meaning of the word that now adorned his grave marker.

Court's jaw muscles flexed in anger. He did not understand. Who the hell could be angry with Eddie? Apparently, there was more to the story than he had heard on the radio at the *torta* stand in Chiapas. Gentry had caught a two-minute-long follow-up report about the bombing of the yacht, and Eduardo Gamboa was again mentioned as the dead leader of the operation.

No question in his mind. Eduardo Gamboa was the man he knew as Eddie Gamble.

Court had neither seen nor heard from Eddie since Laos. He had no idea the DEA man had returned to Mexico, and this fact perplexed him greatly. Why the hell would anyone want to leave the United States to come down here and fight drug *carteleros* and

45

governmental corruption? Wasn't there enough crime and bullshit in the USA to keep Eddie happy up there?

It hardly seemed like a field trip was necessary.

When Court saw the report of Eddie's death, he'd been on his way to Tampico, on Mexico's Gulf coast. He'd heard that a lot of European cargo ships called at the seaport there, and he wanted to find a way back to the eastern hemisphere to confront and kill his former employer Gregor Sidorenko, the man who now, along with the Central Intelligence Agency, was actively seeking his destruction.

But the second news report from Puerto Vallarta changed things. It said that Major Gamboa would be buried in his home-town of San Blas, ninety minutes up the coast from where he died.

Court felt that if he were already this close, just a one-day bus journey away, he should at least go and pay his respects.

So here he was, standing on a rock-strewn hillside a mile and a half from the Pacific Ocean. The steeply graded cemetery around him was covered with cheap mausoleums made from tin sheeting and linoleum and plastic and cinderblock. Amongst these larger monuments to the dead there were less ornate tombstones, with candles, plastic statuettes, and fake flowers lying about. Fat iguanas sunned themselves on broken rock or chased one another around massive tufts of banana trees growing wild out of the tall grass. A hot afternoon breeze blew Gentry's long hair into his eyes as he looked down at the final resting place of his old friend.

Staring at the spray-painted curses he asked himself: Why were all the people around here so mad at Eddie?

Laos
2000

Eddie Gamble was right about the Ban Nam Phuong Military Detention Camp being no place for a man with malaria. Court's weakened condition deteriorated with each passing day of poor food, a cold floor of sawdust, and wholly unsanitary conditions. His mission to rescue Eddie became a joke the minute he was tossed in a cell with him, but now Eddie became the one desperately trying to rescue 'Sally.'

Once a day Gentry was pulled up the stairs, taken across the small compound and into a wooden building, dropped on the floor in front of a desk, and questioned by two Laotian military officers who spoke little English and kept one eye on the full-contact Muay Lao martial arts matches broadcast on a small television against the wall. The men drank fresh water from big plastic bottles to torment their sickened and thirsty captive. They asked him over and over how he got into the country and who he'd come to meet and dozens of other questions, without any inkling he was an intelligence operative of the United States of America. Court gave no answers, just asked for medicine and a blanket and a pillow and fresh water.

Each day the interrogators refused.

Other than a few openhanded smacks to the head, they did not beat him, but they used his illness against him, promising he would get no treatment for the malaria until he signed a confession.

And each day he would be dragged back downstairs, dumped in the sawdust, and Eddie would then be taken for his turn in front of the lazy interrogators.

After one week Gentry's physical condition had deteriorated to the point where he could barely crawl over to the metal bucket he and Gamble shared as a toilet. Eddie began caring for his 'rescuer,' helping with his bathroom duties, sluicing him with water to clean him, and even giving him half of his daily rations of potato, moldy bread, and turnip, occasionally augmented with a small tin of cold broth made with animal bones. Gamble cooled Gentry's fevers by continually dousing his scarlet forehead with a wet sock and rubbed his arms and legs when the chills came. Court protested everything that was done for him and continually encouraged the DEA agent to concentrate on finding his own way out of the camp.

Court was growing too weak to operate his body, but his

well-trained brain had not lost the ability to scheme. 'Look, Eddie. We're probably just a few miles from the Mekong River and the Thai border. If you escape from here, then you have a chance of getting home. But when they take us into the labor camps, we'll be up in the mountains, weeks from civilization, weeks from a border crossing. If you don't get out of here before we go to the camps, it's game over.'

Eddie just shook his head. 'I'm not leaving you here, and I'm not letting you go to the labor camp by yourself. You'll die.'

'I'm dead anyway, dude. You've got to concentrate on what you can do. You've *got* to get out of here.'

But Eddie was stubborn; he continued tending to his weakened cellmate and did not try to escape on his own.

With twenty-two hours a day together and literally nothing else to do, Court and Eddie spent an incredible amount of time in conversation. The dialogue was hampered by Gentry's absolute refusal to reveal one shred of information about himself, but Eddie was a talker. He talked about his life growing up in a small town on the Pacific coast of Mexico, his journey over the border into Texas as an illegal alien, his wayward couple of years in a Chicano gang in Riverside, California, and then his decision to join the military to seek American citizenship.

Eddie had joined the Navy because his father was a fisherman, but he realized quickly he himself did not want to live on a boat. He qualified for SEAL selection and excelled in the brutal training, earned the respect of the cadre and his fellow enlisted men along the way. After two and a half years of pre-deployment training and four years on Team Three, he left the military and joined the Drug Enforcement Agency. His life in Southern California had given him a hatred for drugs and drug dealers, and he worked primarily undercover in different parts of the world.

Two weeks after being brought to the Ban Nam Phuong detention facility, Court lay awake in the dark, sweat chills threatening to drive him mad, listening to Eddie drone on and on about his little sister, Lorita, and how he missed her and hated leaving her behind in the little fishing village where they grew up when he moved to the U.S. Gentry's mind drifted off Gamble's life history and turned to the problem at hand. He focused all his attention on remembering everything he saw each day when he was taken from his shack, dragged across the small camp, and dumped in the interrogation hut. It was always raining; there were trucks and jeeps sunk inches into the gravel and mud roads, maybe two dozen guards armed with Chinese-made AK-47s and SKSs.

Occasionally, he'd see other prisoners, mostly Hmong – an ethnic minority that had been getting knocked around for decades by the Pathet Lao, the Laotian Communist government. These guys likely weren't any more involved in heroin trafficking than was Gentry; they had just run afoul of the local Commies in power and were suffering for it.

While doing his best to ignore Eddie's incessant rambling – now he was talking about how, when he got out of here, he wanted to buy himself a new Ford truck to celebrate – an idea appeared in Gentry's mind. He began troubleshooting immediately, trying to poke holes in his plan. There *were* holes: some he could patch with slight tactical changes, and some he had to leave open. No plan was foolproof; he'd learned that the hard way during five years in the field.

While Gentry's mind raced, Gamble talked about his family. 'I send two-thirds of my check back to my mom and dad, been doing it since I enlisted. Still I wish I could do more for Lorita. She's nineteen now, a great kid; lookin' at me you wouldn't believe how beautiful she is. I want to get her up to the States, but she doesn't want to come. Says she wants to go to college and find a job down there.'

Eddie paused, long enough to where Court looked over at the rare silence. 'We've got to get out of here, Sally. I got too many people counting on me back home.'

'You'll get home. I promise.'

'I'm not leaving you, amigo. I told you that.'

Court changed the subject to follow his stream of conscience. 'Hey, you said you could hot-wire a car, right?'

Eddie was surprised by the change in the conversation, but he rolled up onto his arm, smiled broadly and proudly. 'Back in Riverside they called me Fast Eddie because I could boost any ride in under sixty seconds.'

Gentry nodded. 'Fast Eddie. Can you still do it?'

'Yeah. It wasn't *that* long ago. Why do you ask?'

'Just curious.' Court let it go. He went back to working on his plan.

9

'Señor?'

A woman's voice from behind startled Court, took him away from that night in the highlands of Laos, and brought him back to the warm, breezy afternoon on the Pacific coast of Mexico.

Not surprisingly, she spoke in Spanish. It was a dialect Gentry found difficult to understand. 'If you want to write something, will you please do it now so I can paint over it? I'd rather not have to come back later today. It is a long walk back to the road for someone in my condition.'

Court turned to the woman's voice. She stood behind and below him, down the hill a few feet on a dirt path that wound its way from the cobblestone road that ran down to San Blas.

She was alone, her dark hair was pulled back tight, her white cotton dress blew in the warm breeze. She carried a small white paint can and a brush in her hands and a large purse on her shoulder.

She was thirty-five or so. Very pretty.

And very pregnant.

'I'm sorry,' Court replied in Spanish. He stepped down off the hill towards the dirt path. 'I thought this man was someone I knew. I was mistaken.' He made to pass the woman with a slight nod, no eye contact, but she stepped in front of him. She held her head high and her shoulders back, boldly challenging him.

Court stopped.

51

'Who are you looking for? It's a small town. I'm sure I know most every family interred in this cemetery.' Clearly, she knew he was lying, and from the look of her confused expression, Court's accent had caught her attention.

He hesitated. He was busted, no sense in drawing out an obvious lie.

With a shrug he said, 'I knew Eddie. I was just in the area. Thought I'd come by. Sorry. I have to catch a bus. Excuse me.' He tried to move past her again, and again, she shifted into his path.

'Eddie? You are American?' She had switched to English.

'Yes.' She remained wary; she did not smile or nod. But slowly she extended a small hand, and Court took it. 'You are Eddie's wife?'

'My name is Elena. *Sí*, I was Eddie's wife.'

'My name is Joe.' He pulled the name out of the air.

He regarded the woman for a moment. 'Eddie was going to have a baby?' Court winced even as the words came out of his mouth.

'He *is* going to have a baby. A boy.'

He said nothing. Just nodded.

'You were with Eduardo in the Navy?'

'No.'

'Ah, Drug Enforcement Agency?'

'No.'

The soft features of her caramel-colored face scrunched up as she thought. 'You knew him back in California or something?'

He hesitated. He hated telling people the truth. It was not how he operated. He determined to remain vague. 'A long time ago, your husband saved my life, risked his own to do it. That's really all I can tell you.'

He felt her eyes on him for a long time. Twice he glanced to her and found her staring at his face; both times he turned his head back to the gravesite.

She smiled. Said, 'He saved many lives, I think. Here and in the United States. He was a good man.'

'I'm really sorry—'

'Are you here for the memorial?'

'The memorial?'

'Tomorrow, in Puerto Vallarta, there will be a commemoration of the eight officers who died in the bay. We are expecting a large turnout of locals who will come to honor their sacrifice. Will you be there?'

Gentry hesitated. 'I'd love to. But I have to get back on the road.'

'What a pity.' Elena looked as if she did not believe him, which to Court meant she had a pretty decent bullshit detector. 'I need to paint the cross again.' She stepped up the hill and knelt down, unsteady with the change in her center of gravity. As she opened the can of paint, she looked back over her shoulder, smiled, and extended a new invitation. 'You *must* come home with me now. Eduardo's entire family will be there, some friends, and the relatives of three of the other men killed. Everyone is at our home tonight for a dinner; in the morning we are all going together to the memorial. Eddie's mother and father will be so pleased to meet a friend of Eduardo's from the United States.'

'I wish I could, but I'd better be heading back to—'

'You have come all this way. You and Eduardo were friends. What would he think looking down on me from heaven if I did not take you home and give you a meal for your trouble?' She knelt and began working as if the matter were decided – she covered the black graffiti with the clean white paint.

Court wanted to protest more, but he could not deny he could use something good to eat. With what remained of his cash he had just enough to make his way across the country to Tampico and buy a few *tortas* or tacos from street vendors along the way. He wouldn't fight Eddie's wife on this.

He motioned at the graffiti. 'Who did that?'

'*Cabrones,*' she said, then looked up at Court with an apologetic smile. 'Just people who are fans of Daniel de la Rocha.'

'The drug lord has a *fan club*?' Court asked, somewhat taken aback.

'Oh, they say he is an honest businessman. They say that he has done much good for this area. They say my husband acted without permission. But Eduardo knew all about de la Rocha; he would not have gone after him if he were a good man.' She finished her work. A few bright splotches of white had dripped on the broken brown dirt below the tombstone. 'We will get him a nice headstone. Once the messages stop. It's not worth the trouble now.' Then she stood. She let Court take the paint can and the brush, and they began walking towards the exit of the cemetery.

Laos
2000

Flies and roaches and rats found the basement cell; the hot, sick stench of human waste saw to that. Court became weaker by the day: he'd lost twenty pounds since the hospital, and his skin was now dry and coarse from the lack of fluids and vitamins. Other than the daily journey to the interrogation shack, he had no exercise and no natural light or fresh air. At the end of the second week the interrogators told Eddie he and his fellow prisoner would be taken to the labor camps in three day's time. Eddie once again angrily demanded that his cellmate be hospitalized or at least given medicine for his malaria, but the Laotians showed no concern whatsoever for a young Western drug trafficker. Eddie flew into a rage, attacked his interrogators, and was only fought off with the butts of two big SKS rifles that were driven into the base of his skull. He was returned, unconscious, to the basement with a fat, bloody knot on the back of his head. Then Gentry was dragged up for his 'session.'

When Court was told about the impending journey north to the work camps, he stunned his interrogators.

'Okay, I'm done with this shit. I'll give you the names of my contacts in Vientiane, bank account numbers, tell you where we pick up the poppy and how we get it over the Mekong into Thailand.'

Both men's eyes turned away from the Muay Lao match on the TV and locked on the gaunt, sweat-soaked man sitting in front of them.

'Yes. You talk now!' ordered the senior man.

'No. It's better I write it all down. Easier for you to understand.'

Both men nodded. 'Yes.'

'But I want some things from you.'

'What you want?' Fresh suspicion dulled the pleased expression on the men's faces.

'My friend is hurt. I want his head bandaged. *Carefully* bandaged.'

The senior man waved a hand through the air. 'No problem.'

'I want a warm, dry blanket. I want a bottle of that water you guys are drinking.' He pointed to a plastic two-liter jug on the table. Again, the interrogators nodded. 'What else?'

'I guess some paper and something to write with would be good.'

The guards bandaged Eddie with Court lying nearby in the cell and admonishing them with his frail voice and weak gestures, ordering them to use more gauze and more tape. At first Gamble tried to push them away, insisting that the knot on his head did not need to be mummified in order to heal. But Court was adamant, and finally Eddie relented and let Court take charge of his medical care.

Court had his pad and his pen and a fresh wool blanket, and he wrote down notes throughout the afternoon and evening. During the night he opened the bottle and drank most of the clean water himself, only passing the last few swigs over to the man who'd been keeping him alive. Eddie took it and polished it off greedily, but only after Court assured him he'd had all he wanted.

When the daily ration was brought the next morning, Court surprised Eddie. 'I'm taking all your food.'

'No, I'm giving you half. Holding your sweaty ass up over the shitter burns a lot of calories, amigo.'

'Look, I need some extra strength today.' Court pulled both tin plates over in front of him as he spoke.

'What for? What's going to happen?'

'If it doesn't work out, I'd rather you didn't know. It might be better for you that way.'

Eddie looked worried. 'C'mon, Sally. You aren't in any condition to try anything. Let me talk to the guards today; if they think you are giving up some intel and I offer up some disinformation, then maybe they'll come through with that medicine you need.'

'No ... This isn't about me getting medicine. It's about getting the hell out of here.' Court began eating from both plates. Gamble looked on hungrily. Between bites of turnip and slurps of bone broth, Court said, 'Oh yeah, one more thing. I need all your bandages.'

Slowly, with no idea what the hell was going on, Eddie Gamble took the gauze and the tape from his head and handed it over.

Court spent the next half hour lying on his side under his blanket, his back to his fellow prisoner. Eddie asked over and over what was going to happen, but his cellmate would not answer.

The guards came to take Eddie to his interrogation. As they left, Court called out. 'Tell them that I need another pen. This one ran out of ink. If they bring it before I go up, then I'll have my list ready.'

Eddie looked at him a long time before relaying the message. It was obvious that he could tell something was about to go down, and he was more worried than excited.

When the door shut on Eddie and the two guards, Court used all the strength the bottle of clean water and two full meals had given him to crawl over to the cell door. He pulled out the pen he'd been given the day before, cracked it open, then removed the ink reservoir from the plastic grip. He reached through the bars, slid the ball of the pen into the lock, and felt his way through the tumblers with a shaky but practiced hand. He'd played with the lock for several days running while Eddie slept, had used lengths of straw to feel into its recesses to reveal its secrets. Using one of the broken plastic pieces as a tension wrench, he turned the cylinder. He'd accomplished this feat literally thousands of times in his training at the CIA's Autonomous Asset Development Program in Harvey Point, North Carolina, and this lock was actually much easier to defeat than most of the ones he'd been trained on.

The cell door popped open in seconds.

10

Court walked with Elena for nearly a mile through San Blas; the pregnant woman looked perfectly comfortable with the effort, though sweat covered her light brown skin. They passed roadside restaurants, the bus station; they strolled past stray dogs sleeping in the town square, chickens pecking for bugs in a garbage dump. Turning south, Elena went through an open-air vegetable market and bought a few bags of yams and mangoes. Court had questions for her; he could not help it. He learned that she was from Guadalajara, had met Eddie when he was a DEA agent working there, and they'd married shortly before he re-emigrated to Mexico to join the Policía Federal five years earlier. They'd bought a house in San Blas to be near his family, as she had no close relatives of her own.

Court and Elena left the market, turned down a dirty narrow street called Calle de Canalizo. Though unpaved, it was lined with midsized gated properties, and after a few minutes of strolling, Elena stepped through an open gate. Court followed her up a short driveway towards a two-story gray cinderblock home surrounded by bougainvillea and vine. Eddie's house. Dogs ran and played in the front garden amidst several locals; policemen and policewomen wearing yellow polo shirts and batons on their belts strolled around the driveway and the front yard.

A big, silver Ford F-350 Super Duty pickup sat in the driveway. It was decked out with tinted windows, a rack of floodlights, a big winch in front, chrome all over, and a weathered U.S. Navy sticker on the back window. Eddie's truck, Court had no doubt. He remembered Gamble talking about his love of big Ford pickups, and seeing the idle vehicle made Court sad.

Elena led him inside the plain dwelling. In the front family room a dozen people stood and sat, chatting together as loud accordion music played from a boom box on the floor. Court stood behind Elena as she greeted an older couple; she then introduced them as her husband's parents, Ernesto and Luz. They spoke no English, so Court introduced himself in Spanish as an old friend of their son from the United States.

Luz Gamboa was in her sixties, short and thick with a wide face that showed at once a friendly smile and a deep sadness in her eyes. Her husband was taller and thinner, maybe five years older, with deep, dark creases covering his face. A lifetime on a small fishing boat in the Pacific Ocean with the wind and sun had left salt-etched evidence of the years and the sea on his skin. He seemed a little suspicious of the American standing in his dead son's family room, but the two men shook hands and Ernesto welcomed 'Jose' to San Blas.

Elena handed the produce she'd bought in the market to a boy of sixteen, a nephew of Eduardo's, she said as an introduction, and the boy disappeared towards the back of the simply furnished but spacious house. Then the pregnant woman took the American around, introducing him to aunts and uncles of Eduardo, a few more nephews and a niece, two brothers, and several friends from the area.

Cesar Gamboa, one of Eddie's uncles, put a cold bottle of Pacifico beer in Court's hand and exchanged pleasantries with the American in the hallway at the back of the house, while Elena disappeared to greet more guests. As they talked, Court looked around at the pictures in the hall. The walls were adorned with Eddie and Elena's wedding photos. Court remembered that wide grin from Laos – back then he found it amazing that the guy could have smiled at a time like that. There were also several pictures of Eddie with a white-haired American man on a fishing boat. Together they held a massive marlin in one picture. Suntans, Ray-Bans, and smiles covered their faces.

Then Gentry scanned the framed pictures of a much younger Eddie with his SEAL team. The men posed with their weapons. Eddie looked impossibly young and fit, and though the rest of the men with him were a head taller than the Mexican American, Eddie Gamble looked comfortable and 'in charge.'

Elena tapped Court on his shoulder from behind. Court turned around to find himself standing in front of the old man he'd just seen in the picture with Eddie and the marlin. He was short, seventy or so, and he wore a blue U.S. Navy cap.

Fuck, thought Court. *A gringo.*

Elena spoke in English. 'Jose, I would like to present you to one of Eddie's dear friends, Capitán Chuck.'

'Chuck Cullen, United States Navy, retired,' the old man said as they shook hands. His grip was long and fierce in an obvious attempt to intimidate; his eyes were anything but trusting. He was old, but he was trim and fit, and he sure looked like he took damn good care of himself.

Elena continued speaking, perhaps sensing an initial mistrust between the two men. 'Jose was a friend of Eduardo's.'

Cullen's craggy suntanned face wrinkled in a sour smile. 'Well, any friend of Eddie's is a friend of mine,' Cullen said, but Court could tell he didn't mean it. Gentry considered his own appearance, knew he looked too much like the roadie of a heavy metal band to garner the respect of a seventyish ex–naval officer. With the overt suspicion on display now, Cullen asked, 'How exactly did *you* know Eddie?'

'I met him when he was in the DEA.'

'So, you are DEA, or did he arrest you once?' Cullen asked with a smile as if it were a joke, but Gentry sensed the old man considered the 'long hair' in front of him to be a human being worthy of suspicion. Cullen began to say something else, no doubt another chiding remark. But Elena returned and interrupted the conversation.

'I almost forgot. Come, Joe. We have more people to meet. You two can talk at dinner.'

It was a short walk down the narrow hallway to the kitchen. Here a half dozen women of various ages prepared the meal; they used every possible flat surface in the small room to slice fruits and vegetables, ice down beer, stir large pots of soups and rice, and butter bread fresh from the oven. Two were introduced as Eddie's aunts, another as a sister-in-law.

At the sink a woman with short black hair washed sweet potatoes; she wore an apron and her back was to Court and Elena, but she turned to ask Eddie's wife a question.

Court's eyes locked on hers, and he found himself unable to pry them away. She was beautiful, extraordinarily so, but not like Elena. She was smaller, with café au lait skin that was a bit darker than that of Eddie's wife. Her sparkling brown eyes were massive, half-hidden under bangs that she blew out of the way as she toweled off her hands. She was almost boyish in frame and mannerism, and her shoulders showed hints of muscularity under her simple white blouse, which had a hand-sewn floral print.

Elena said, 'This is Joe from los Estados Unidos. Joe, this is—'

Court finished the sentence. 'Eddie's little sister. Lorita,' he said it softly, reverently. He could see a lot of his old friend in her. In a flood of memories the weeks in the shit-splattered Laotian cell came back to him. Eddie had spoken of her nonstop, and his one regret about running to America had been leaving the little girl behind. He sent most of his meager enlisted-man's pay back home, supporting his parents and sister from afar, but it was painfully clear that he felt he'd abandoned the kid by leaving her behind here in San Blas.

Lorita finished wiping her hands on a rag and stepped forward; she shook Court's hand, and he felt her eyes on him. He mumbled something in Spanish about being an old friend of her brother's. His words sounded stupid to him.

61

She spoke to him in English. 'No one calls me Lorita for long time. I'm Laura. It is a pleasure to meet you.'

'*Igualmente.*' Court said *likewise* in Spanish, indicating to her she could continue in her mother tongue if she wished.

'You were with Eduardo in the Navy?' she asked, but quickly Elena stepped in.

'He can't talk about how he knows Eduardo. Some kind of secret mission, I think.' She winked at Court. There was sadness in her eyes but a conspiratorial playfulness as well.

Court nodded, and said, 'It was a while ago. He was a great guy.'

Laura nodded. 'Yes.'

He looked in her eyes and caught himself backing away. He continued in Spanish for her benefit. 'I spent ... a lot of time with Eddie. He talked about you. You were just a kid then, I guess.' He stammered for something else to say, but nothing original came. 'He talked about you.'

She smiled at first, but in seconds her round eyes narrowed to slits and her face reddened. She began to cry.

'*Lo siento,*' *I'm sorry,* she said with an embarrassed smile. She lifted her apron and wiped her dripping eyes with it, then left the room quickly.

Elena ignored the display of emotion; she had already moved and began working on the sweet potatoes in the sink.

Court stood there by himself in the center of the kitchen, now afraid to say one more fucking word.

Dammit, Gentry.

Laos
2000

For ten minutes Court leaned his back against the wall next to the door to the stairwell with the water bottle in his hand. He'd filled the empty plastic bottle with fuzz from the wool blanket and the gauze from Eddie's head, and he'd wrapped the outside with a piece of the blanket enshrouded in the white medical tape.

This exertion threatened to put him to sleep for hours. He fought it with all his might. He'd just begun to nod off when he heard someone coming down the stairs.

Gentry hurried to his feet. He sucked in musty air tainted with the stench of his own waste, filling his lungs with the oxygen he needed to give him a burst of strength for the coming moments.

The door opened. A guard came through with a pen. He stopped as he was closing the door, noticing now that the prisoner was not in the cell.

Court Gentry moved from behind the door, slammed into the man in a bear hug, knocked him to the ground with body weight.

Court made it up to his knees. Grabbed the stunned soldier's head with both hands, lifted it, and smacked it against the stone floor. Once, twice, three times.

The young man's eyes remained locked open in death. Court fell on top of him. Utterly exhausted.

Seconds later he reached back with his bare foot and pushed the door shut. He finally recovered enough to pull the Chinese-made Type 77 pistol from the Laotian's gun belt. It fired a weak 7.65 × 17 cartridge, which Gentry would have hated to bet his life on, except in the situation in which he now found himself. He struggled back across the floor, fought a wave of diarrhea that wanted to expel from his bowels as he moved, and finally made it to the door and to his water bottle. He jabbed the muzzle of the weapon into the neck of the stuffed plastic device, satisfied himself it was as secure as possible, and tried to climb back to his feet.

Nothing doing. He had neither the energy nor the balance to stand.

He'd have to fight while lying on his back.

The water bottle would serve as an adequate suppressor for the small pistol, at least for a round or two. The report of the pistol would be muffled, but it would hardly be silent, as the suppressor could do nothing for the mini sonic boom created by the bullet breaking the sound barrier.

Still, this ersatz suppressor, just like the highest-end

militarygrade silencer, was designed not to make the weapon silent but to make it not sound so much like a gunshot when the weapon fired.

Looking at the dead soldier next to him on the floor, Court amended his operational plan yet again. He'd planned on dragging the man inside the cell and covering him with the remains of the blanket to fool the guards returning with Eddie. But the American operative knew good and well that if he could not even stand on his own, he hardly possessed the strength to pull the dead weight across the floor.

Instead he lay back on the floor, five feet from the door, and waited.

He fell asleep, woke up with a start as he heard a key in the lock in the door in front of him. He would have liked for Eddie and the guards to enter the room and close the door behind them so that the muffled gunshot would not be heard above. But with the dead body lying just a few feet from the door, he knew that was not possible. So as soon as the key was turned and the latch engaged, Gentry sat up, hoping like hell there were only one or two guards with Eddie.

But there were five men coming down the narrow stairwell single file. They were all soaked from the thunderstorm above, and they were tightly packed together, no man more than two steps from the next; Eddie Gamble was the third in line. The first guard still had his hand on the door latch when he stepped in. Gentry held the pistol in his right hand and held the homemade suppressor tight to the muzzle with his left hand. Before the first soldier could react, Court pointed the water bottle at the man's face and fired a single round. The end of the bottle burst open with a loud but manageable pop, and the soldier's head snapped back. He spun backwards to the ground with his hands rising to his bloody face.

Court did not hesitate. He raised the pistol and the smoking silencer up higher and shot the man just in front of Eddie. The Laotian had not even begun to make a move for his weapon before he took a small bullet in the right eye, and he fell dead instantly.

The wool in Court's silencer burned and smoked now, the second report was twice that of the first. He raised it at Eddie Gamble, who wisely dropped down to his knees on the bottom step of the stairs. Court shot the man behind him in the throat just as the soldier's handgun rose at the surprise threat down in the basement.

This time, Court's burning water bottle shattered completely, sending a barb of sharp plastic into his left thumb. The gunshot was muffled, unquestionably, but much less so than the first two rounds. The weapon was now useless as a covert tool. Court tossed the bottle aside and pointed the pistol at the remaining sentry.

The last soldier in line did not reach for his gun; instead he turned to run back up the stairs. Eddie Gamble spun around, clambered over the thrashing Laotian with the spurting juggler vein, and grabbed the escaping man by the ankle. The soldier screamed out just as he fell, crashed face first, and then tumbled back down, dragging his wounded comrade and his prisoner along with him as he fell. The four bodies rolled down the steps and collided with Gentry at the base of the stairs, coming together on top of the first soldier to be shot, six men in a ball of twisted arms and legs. Blood from the gurgling throat wound of the dying guard coating everyone and everything with a thick, hot, crimson stream.

Court ended up on his back, the pistol fell away from his hand, and his weakness prevented him from engaging in the fight that was happening on top of him. Eddie and the fourth sentry kicked and punched and bit and clawed at each other while Gentry just lay there, his arms out wide. The battle rolled off of him, leaving the man with the throat wound, now dead from blood loss, lying across his feet. Gamble's size, strength, and training eventually gave him the advantage against the soldier. Finally, after a brutal struggle of thirty seconds, Eddie got off a clean cracking punch to the guard's face, knocking him out cold.

Eddie rolled off the Laotian gasping in exhaustion but then quickly recovered and crawled over to Gentry. Eddie's eyes were wide in shock. Amid pants and wheezes he said, 'Get up, bro! We've got to get out of here!'

Court wasn't going anywhere under his own power. He just shook his head and gave orders. 'Listen carefully. Grab a gun from one of these guards. Put on a poncho and walk out the front door like you own the place. Go to the motor pool to the left of the interrogation shack. You'll need to pick a car you can hot-wire. Go!'

'Not without you, amigo,' replied Gamble, and he pulled a gun from one of the dead guards and then heaved Court up and onto his back.

'Give it up! You can't get me out of here!'

But Gamble ignored the comment. As he fought his way slowly up the stairs, pulling himself upwards with both hands on the wooden railing, struggling with the dead weight of the weak and sick man on top of him, his knees buckled more than once. But he made it to the top of the stairs, out into the one-room shack, and found it empty. He lowered Court to the ground and then grabbed a couple of green ponchos that were hanging from pegs by the door. He dressed Gentry with one and took one for himself. Court fought his way back to his feet on his own, using the desk to help himself climb up. Both men pulled their hoods down over their faces and walked out together, Gentry leaning against his friend.

The late morning rain beat down in near horizontal sheets, obscuring the view from the guard towers and the porches of other shacks around the waterlogged compound. Court stumbled, Eddie grabbed him tighter, and they walked directly across fifty yards of pathways to the motor pool. They passed close enough to a small warehouse to see a group of four soldiers inside, looking out at them in the rain. The men did not come after them, but they did not look away, either.

At the motor pool the men found a dozen jeeps, cars, pickups, and flatbed trucks. Eddie lowered Gentry into the backseat of a small Chinese-made sedan, and then he jumped in the front and dropped down below the steering column.

Court fought to pull himself up to see out the window. He heard the sounds of the DEA man cracking the plastic steering column, cussing in Spanish as he struggled to hot-wire the vehicle with soaking wet hands, poor lighting, and the pervasive threat of imminent death.

Gentry saw them through the rain running down the rear windshield. Two soldiers approaching from the fence line, their wooden-stocked rifles hanging from their shoulders, their poncho hoods obscuring their faces like Grim Reapers. They walked directly towards Eddie and Court.

'Hey!' Court said, 'Fast Eddie? You're gonna be Dead Eddie in about fifteen seconds if you don't get this thing moving.'

'I've never boosted one of these. Shouldn't take too much longer.'

'Figure it out! We got company coming!'

'Okay! Just have to . . .' The engine started. Court looked up to see Eddie making the sign of the cross over himself, then kissing his fingertips and touching them to the dashboard of the little car. He put the transmission in gear, looked back to Gentry, and said, '*Vamanos*.'

The Chinese sedan rolled forward over gravel and rainwater. Eddie turned for the compound's main gate, doing his best to drive slowly and naturally. Court looked out the back window again. The two soldiers had unslung their rifles. They seemed confused for only a moment. Then both men raised their weapons at the departing sedan.

'Punch it!' shouted Court.

The rear windshield snapped, glass blew into the backseat, and Eddie Gamble stepped on the gas.

They barreled ahead through the rain; the cracks of rifles from overhead told them they were below the twin guard towers just inside the compound's entrance. Eddie screamed to his passenger to brace himself, and the little four-door smashed through the wood and wire gate, just as more rounds blew out the rest of the rear windshield. A tight corner to the left sent the car skidding on the paved road, but Gamble turned into the slide and righted the vehicle just as its two right-side tires reached the edge of the blacktop.

The sedan and the two American escapees left the prison behind.

11

As dusk descended on Mexico's Pacific coast, dinner was served at several picnic tables lined up in the large backyard of Eddie's house. On the back driveway an old open-decked twenty-three-foot Boston Whaler rested on blocks. Leaning against the wall near the back gate were a couple of bicycles; fishing rods hung from hooks next to the little garage. These were Eddie's things, and it felt weird for Gentry to sit here amongst them without his old friend. In Laos Eddie had a set of filthy baby blue pajamas, just like Court. Nothing else. Now that Court was in Eddie's world, he saw what Eddie enjoyed doing, he saw who Eddie loved, and Gentry could not help but feel like he was encroaching on Eddie's world.

Court counted thirty-two people at the tables, including the Gamboa family, the families of a few of the other dead GOPES officers, local friends, and several individuals he'd been introduced to who were in charge of the memorial in Puerto Vallarta. The unarmed local cops whom he'd seen earlier watching over the gathering had grown into a force of eight that wandered around the driveway, out in the street in front of the house, and even patrolled the garden around the dinner tables. He didn't know why they were there, if they thought some sort of trouble was possible, or even what they'd do about it if trouble appeared.

Court Gentry knew of no real trouble that could be quelled with a whistle and a stick.

Three brown roosters wandered the garden as well; their patrol seemed oddly similar to the unarmed cops. A small pack of mixedbreed dogs of different sizes lounged close to the diners, begging for scraps. Court related to their primal motivations. He was, more or less, doing the same thing here.

Captain Chuck Cullen sat at the head of the row of non-uniform tables, his back to the kitchen and a big charcoal grill alongside the back of the house over his right shoulder. Long black lizards scampered up and down the white stucco wall behind his head.

Court had been placed at the opposite end, facing Cullen; the old man stared him down silently for long periods of time. On Gentry's right were Elena and her in-laws, and he did his best to stay out of their conversation. Instead he dug into an excellent grilled marlin, more fresh salad and vegetables than he'd eaten at any one time in his life, and he drank beer so cold the bottles stung his fingertips.

Court imagined there had been many dinners just like this, right here, with Eddie Gamble sitting in the chair that Cullen now occupied.

Court noticed the American geezer staring intently at him again, across the length of the tables, over thirty-two big plates of food. Court did his best to ignore him. Instead Gentry found himself gazing at someone.

At Laura.

She was midway down the table on his right, sitting between her two aunts and constantly running back to the kitchen for more plates and bowls and bottles and pans filled with food and drink.

She glanced his way once, maybe twice. Surely, she'd caught him staring at her. He hoped he did not look to her like Cullen appeared to him, overtly eyeing everything he did.

This was no fiesta. The conversations were subdued and hushed; the attendees were sad and angry. Court's training in reading people was employed as he went up and down the table, trying to discern exactly what was going through each person's head.

He was good at this. He was so good at it that it was sad, divining the individual misery and fury of thirty people, most of whom had just lost someone important to them. Someone strong and fearless. Someone better than the rest.

Court looked down to his plate, scooped up a forkful of his fried plantains. He told himself he'd drink another beer and hit the road.

Laos
2000

'You hurt?' asked Eddie from the front seat.

Court checked his body for bloody holes. Finding none, he replied, 'I'm fine.'

He then pulled himself up in the seat to look out the remnants of the back window. 'They'll be close behind, but this weather will help. It will keep choppers out of the air.'

But Gamble's mind was on something else. '*Please* tell me you had sanction to kill those guards? I don't want to escape out of here just to go straight to Leavenworth.'

'I have sanction.'

'So you can just whack whoever you want, no questions asked?' He couldn't believe it.

'Stay on my good side, and you won't find out.' Gentry mumbled it as he lay back on the seat; he was so tired and weak he found himself nauseous, and even holding himself in a sitting position was too much. He'd spent 110 percent of all his energy in the escape, even with Gamble carrying him part of the way.

He was no use to anyone now.

'Seriously. Tell me we're okay.'

'We're okay. *You* haven't killed anybody.'

'I sure as shit would love to know who you work for. I mean, I've run with the CIA, and they don't look or act like you.'

'I think you need to concentrate on the road, Eddie. The Laotian Army will have roadblocks set as soon as they can.'

The DEA man sighed in frustration but did what he was told.

They'd gone no more than five minutes when the road ended at a T-intersection. Gamble turned right, making for the Mekong River.

Court had nodded off, but he awoke when the car stopped in the road and began backing up. After a few seconds they turned around.

'What is it?'

Eddie answered with a grave tone. 'Roadblock. Military. A quarter mile up. Four vehicles. Fifteen dismounts easily.'

Court looked out the window and noticed the rain had stopped. 'Okay. Find a place to dump the car. You need to go overland. It can't be too far. You can make it to the river if you go south. Find a guy with a boat, stick your gun in his face, and ask politely for a lift across to Thailand.'

It was quiet in the car for several seconds. Court said, 'You're going alone.'

Gamble clearly had been worrying about the same thing. 'Look, Sally, maybe we can—'

'No. I can't walk, and you can't carry me. I'm not going anywhere.'

Eddie looked like he was struggling mightily, but obviously, Court was right. Finally, Eddie nodded. 'I'll find a hide for you. Cover you up and mark the spot somehow. I'll go for help, come back, and get you as soon as I can.'

Court could tell Eddie did not believe Gentry would survive the night out in the elements. 'Get over the river into Thailand. Tell your people where you left me. My people will come and get me.'

Gentry tried to sound convincing, but it was a lie. No one would come for him. He knew it, and surely, Eddie must have suspected it.

*

Twenty minutes later the roof of the Chinese sedan sunk below the surface of a pond. Air bubbled out of the car with a gurgling sound, and soon the water stilled and lily pads returned to cover the breach near the bank created by the vehicle's entry into the water. Court Gentry lay nearby on his back, twenty-five feet from the water's edge and fifty feet down a steep slope from the road, his body shielded by tall grass. Eddie had covered him in banana leaves and surrounded him with a small makeshift wall of stones and branches. Just a few feet away a small foot-path ran off to the south past the pond, in the direction of the Mekong River.

Gentry was invisible from the road above, but if anyone ventured down the hill, they would likely notice the man-sized anomaly in the grass.

Eddie knelt down next to Gentry; they could barely see each other through the foliage.

'There's going to be UXO out there,' Court said weakly. Eddie knew that UXO was unexploded ordnance. 'We dropped more bombs on this country during Nam than we did on Germany in WWII. A lot of those bombs didn't explode; they're just out in the jungle, waiting for someone to come by and kick them. You do *not* want to go off the beaten path out here.'

Eddie looked down the trail. 'Good advice. I knew I brought you along for something.' Gamble's tone turned serious. 'You won't have any food, but H_2O won't be a problem. Just keep your mouth open and let the rain drip from the banana leaves.'

'Okay.'

'I'll make sure someone comes back for you, I swear.'

'Sure. Thanks for everything. Someday you'll make someone a hell of a wife.'

Eddie nodded. Hesitated. Clearly, he was torn apart about leaving his former cellmate behind. 'I'll see you in a couple of days, tops. You'll be at a hospital in Bangkok hitting on exotic nurses, and I'll stop in and bring you something. Any requests?'

Court smiled. He'd play along with this fantasy if it would help Eddie save himself. 'A root beer would kick ass.'

'You got it.' Eddie patted Court on the forehead through the leaves. 'See ya soon, homes.' He stood and began walking towards the pathway to the south.

12

Court looked down at his watch and found it was past nine o'clock. Some of the dinner guests had drifted away; others were sitting around in clumps in the back garden, on the driveway by the boat, and throughout the downstairs of the house. The local police wandered around on the outskirts of the event. Laura and Elena had brought each of the cops a big plate of dinner and a tall plastic cup of iced *horchata*, a cinnamon-vanilla flavored drink made from boiled rice and sesame seeds. The cops ate while standing, careful to keep one eye out the gate towards the street.

Court took another sip from his fourth sweating bottle of Pacifico and began wondering about where he would sleep tonight. Bus service in San Blas had surely halted for the evening, and he did not have money to blow on a hotel. He figured he'd find a bench in the little central park a few blocks to the north, then be on the first bus out in the morning back to Puerto Vallarta.

There was another option. He'd learned through others that the retired U.S. Navy man, Captain Cullen, lived down in Puerto Vallarta. Court considered asking him for a lift back to PV, but only briefly. A ninety-minute car ride with the icy geriatric was more scrutiny than the international outlaw wanted to subject himself to.

Gentry was pleased to notice that the rest of the crowd had forgotten him; he sat alone at a small picnic table near the back wall of the compound, away from the rows of lights strung over the garden and the flaming torches stuck into the ground here and there, and away from the conversations going on all around him. He eyed the back gate. It was closed but not locked; the darkness beyond called to him.

He'd make an invisible escape now; he'd come to pay his respects, and his respects had been paid. Now it was time to disappear.

Standard operating procedure for the Gray Man.

Court finished his beer. Stood slowly.

'Why is it I find myself so curious about you?'

Court turned around, found Cullen ten feet behind. He held a bottle of tequila in one hand, with thumb-sized plastic shot glasses over the bottle's spout, and a pair of shiny green limes in his other hand.

'I don't know.'

'Join me for a drink?' Cullen did not wait for an answer; he sat down at the small picnic table across from Court, put the bottle down in front of him. Cullen retrieved a pocketknife from his cargo shorts, sliced them each a wedge of one of the limes.

Court hesitated. 'I've got to be going.'

'Where you headed, ace?'

'Uhhh. Back to Puerto Vall—'

'Not tonight, you aren't, unless you want to blow a hundred bucks on a cab. Elena said you arrived by bus.'

'Well ... I'll find a hotel here.'

'I can give you a lift to PV.'

Court sat back down. Cullen poured thick clear liquid into two tiny cups, passed one to Gentry. Court sipped the tequila, bit down on his lime wedge, and changed the subject by turning the conversation away from himself. 'How did *you* know Eddie?'

Cullen leaned back and smiled. Took off his USS *Buchanan* cap and held it up. His silver hair shone in the light from the torches burning throughout the yard.

'You met him on your boat?'

The Captain shook his head. 'No, no. I never knew him in the Navy. I met him in PV, 'bout four years ago. I run on the beach every morning, used to anyway. It's more of a walk now but faster than most of the old expat farts around here. Anyway, one morning, after my run, this tough-looking Mexican hombre saunters over to me on the boardwalk. I thought he was going to go for my wallet. But he pointed to my hat. Asked me about my service. We got to talking, and he said *he* was Navy, too. Of course I'm thinking Mexican navy. When I found out he was an ex-SEAL, you could have knocked me over with a feather.

'Eddie and I became friends. We used to go fishing on my boat whenever he was down in PV. I've been up here, sitting at this very table, many nights. Eddie sat right where you are now.'

Cullen sighed a little. He was old enough to have experienced much loss in his life. Still, Court could tell how wounded the man was by the death of his younger friend. 'I spent a lot of hours getting to know that fine young man.'

'Yes, sir.'

Cullen put his cap back on and leaned forward. 'I gotta tell ya, a stranger showing up at his house, right after he's killed. How does that look to you?'

Gentry shrugged. 'I'm just a guy who came to say good-bye. If I had my way, I wouldn't even be here right now.'

Cullen nodded, sipped his tequila thoughtfully, and looked back over his shoulder to the house full of people. 'It's going to be tough for them now. Eddie is a villain to a lot of people around here. The press is portraying him as just another *sicario*.'

'*Sicario?*'

'An assassin. The general consensus is that he and his men were working for a cartel in competition with de la Rocha. After he died the *federales* and Nayarit state police came here, went through all his personal belongings, confiscated his computer and his guns. Even his pension has been held up pending an investigation. It's bullshit: he died following orders to protect the people here, but they see him as another corrupt *federale*.'

'Why do they think that? I don't understand any of what's going on here.'

'No matter, ace. You'll be gone tomorrow. No sense in learning the intricacies of the local conventional wisdom.'

Gentry knew he was being chided by the old man. Treated as if he was just some drifter passing by. It angered him. Court would die for Eddie Gamble. *If* there were still an Eddie Gamble to die for.

'Tell me.'

'Why?'

'Because I *care*. And because I suspect you have some opinions on the matter.' Court reached for the tequila bottle, poured two more shots.

Cullen nodded slowly and sliced off two more wedges of lime.

'Eddie led a team of eight men. His unit took orders directly from the attorney general in Mexico City, who'd been authorized by the president to eliminate the top cartel chiefs of Mexico.'

'Eliminate?'

Cullen nodded.

'A sanctioned hit squad?'

'Exactly.'

Court did not blink an eye. 'Go on.'

'Eddie and his men were good. They assassinated the leaders of four of the top six cartels in the Mexican interior in the past six months. Daniel de la Rocha would have been number five.'

'But the entire team was wiped out in the process.'

'I'm afraid so.'

'I don't understand why he blew up the yacht.'

Cullen shook his head. 'Me, either. There's a lot that I don't get. Of course Eddie never told me about operational details, just chitchat here and there.'

Court sipped his drink. 'What's with all the support for this de la Rocha shithead?'

Cullen waved his arm in a wide circle. 'Not just around here. Everywhere. There are movies, books, and songs about him.

He's a celebrity, a rock star. His father was a bit of a legend, too. He ran the Porfidio de la Rocha cartel in the eighties and nineties, worked directly with the Colombians to move their product to the U.S. But Daniel took no favors from his dad; instead he joined the military and then the GAFES, the Grupo Aeromóvil de Fuerzas Especiales, an elite army paratrooper assault unit. He trained in the U.S. at Fort Benning and Fort Bragg, and at the School of the Americas. He left the army when his father was killed by the government in '99. Daniel went to prison himself for a couple of years; when he came out, he surrounded himself with former military colleagues, men from his commando unit. They are a really tight group, all fixed up like a cross between businessmen and paramilitaries. They all have the same haircuts, wear the same suits, they keep themselves in shape, and they always travel together in a convoy like a military operation. The press started calling them Los Trajes Negros. The Black Suits.

'Since getting out of prison, de la Rocha has stayed officially clean; he owns a domestic airline that ferries commuters from the big towns on the coast to little towns and villages all over the Sierra Madres. He has a bunch of other businesses, too. Orchards, farms, logging mills. All completely aboveboard. He claims that's where his money comes from, and he's apparently bought off enough government employees to where no one is scrutinizing his balance sheet.'

'But you're a hundred percent sure he's dealing cocaine?'

The older man finished a sip of tequila before shaking his head. 'DLR deals with some coke, some heroin, some pot, but that's not where the bulk of his money comes from. The Black Suits run the second largest *foco* cartel in the world.'

'*Foco?*'

'Crystal meth. Most Mexican cartels don't specialize in a certain drug, rather they control a territory or a distribution route. There they will deal in anything, pot, coke, meth, kidnapping victims, even pirated DVDs. But de la Rocha has his own business model, combining both manufacturing and distribution. He supposedly has these massive crystal meth processing plants – they're called super laboratories – somewhere up in the Sierra Madres. But no one knows where they are, and even if they were found, I doubt they could be directly tied back to de la Rocha.'

'I still don't get the love for this guy around here.'

Court could tell that Cullen had warmed up to him to some degree. The older man's tone did not contain any of its earlier reticence. 'Most of the *narcos* are ghosts, but not Daniel. He takes control of his image like a movie star, doesn't fit any mold for a *cartelero*. He's only thirty-nine. He's got six kids, doesn't cheat on his wife, dresses like the Prince of Wales, and supports half the legit charities in the nation. Here in Nayarit, down in Jalisco, and over in Michoacán, the state police have been accused of protecting him. It's a safe bet that the accusations are valid.'

Court sipped his drink and looked up at the bright stars.

Cullen leaned forward. 'Don't think of Daniel de la Rocha as a drug dealer. Think of him as Robin Hood. He provides for the needy, protects the helpless; he supports more legitimate causes down here than anybody else.'

'So the locals don't care about what these drugs do?'

'Nobody but nobody in Mexico gives a damn that millions of drug addicts in the United States want a product. Nobody here feels sorry for them for fucking up their lives. They hate the murder that the *carteleros* bring down here, sure. Who wouldn't? But the average Jose on the street knows the last way to go against the *narcos* is by supporting the cops or the government in the war. The corruption down here is massive. Pervasive. Anyone with a brain knows there are only two ways to protect yourself and your family. Either stay the hell out of the way, or join the cartels. Well, guess what, ace? Joining the cartels pays a lot more than sitting on the sidelines. Plus, it's a lot safer.'

As Court had suspected, Cullen *was* an opinionated old cuss. 'Cops, judges, soldiers, mayors ... you can't trust *anyone* here.

A lot of guys start out with the best of intentions. But the *narcos* give them a choice. *Plata o plomo.*'

'Silver or lead,' Court muttered.

'A better translation would be money or bullets. The *narco* will give you one or the other, take your pick.'

Court nodded then pointed to the police standing around the back garden. 'These cops here. The guys and girls with the batons. They seem like they think Eddie was a good guy.'

Cullen waved a hand through the air, rendering them irrelevant to the conversation. '*Municipales*. San Blas cops. Yeah, they like the family. Ernesto, Eddie's dad, has lived here forever. But the cops down in Puerto Vallarta? Rotten to the core. The state police? Can't trust them. Ditto large swaths of the *federales*. Even the army stationed around these parts is crooked. I don't even know what to think of Eddie's own unit, the special operations group. It seems a bit fishy that all of de la Rocha's regional competition has been wiped out in the last few months, with one exception.'

'Who's the exception?'

'Fellow up north in the Sierra Madres named Constantino Madrigal Bustamante. They call him el Vaquero, "the Cowboy." He's an even bigger son of a bitch than de la Rocha. Some people are saying Eddie's police commando unit was secretly working for the Madrigal Cartel. Taking out all the competition.'

Court's eyebrows furrowed. 'If there was a list of shitheads to go kill, how do we know Madrigal wasn't just the last guy on the list?'

Cullen smiled ruefully. 'Mexicans don't think that way. There is a lot of conspiracy theory in play down here.'

Court had heard this before. He was no stranger to Latin American culture.

'So, Captain, who *are* the good guys?'

Cullen considered the question for a long moment, like it was an impenetrable mathematical puzzle. 'I know Eddie was a good guy. I don't believe the Madrigal conspiracy for one second. Some of the other *federales* are good, no question.'

81

'How do I know a *federale* when I see one?'

'You can tell them apart from the local cop; they wear black uniforms, body armor, and ski masks. Their cars and motorcycles and helicopters and armored cars say PF, Policía Federal.'

This was the type of intel that Gentry had picked up in the thirty or so other areas of operation in which he'd worked or traveled in his career, both as an asset of the CIA and as a private hit man. 'So ... the good guys wear the masks around here. I'll have to get my head around that.'

'Yes, but so do a lot of the bad guys.'

'Perfect.'

Court looked at four local cops hanging out on the patio, leaning against their beat-up mountain bikes. Laura was standing among them, refilling their plastic cups with milky *horchata* poured from a plastic pitcher. 'How come the cops on our side are the ones with the sticks and the bicycles, and the cops on the other side have the guns and the helicopters?'

'Maybe we picked the wrong team.'

Court drank his tequila down. 'I'm beginning to think maybe Eddie did.'

Cullen looked at him thoughtfully. 'I wish I knew who you were, *Joe*.' The old man even said the phony name in a way that demonstrated that he knew it was bullshit.

Court changed the subject again. 'Why did Eddie come back home? Did you ever talk to him about that?'

Cullen waved a hand. 'To save his country. To fight the *narcoterroristas*. To bring his skills from the USA down here where they could do the most good.'

'But?'

'But that's not why he came back.' Cullen turned back to the driveway, pointed at Eddie's little sister, Laura Gamboa. '*That's* why he came back. For her. One hundred percent. Laura's husband was killed five years ago up north. He was a lieutenant in the army. His truck was ambushed by *matamilitares*, special bands of *sicarios* who kill military men. He was beaten, his eyes were gouged out while he was still alive, and he was shot like a dog. His body was burned in a fifty-five gallon drum, and his head was stuck on a fence post within sight of the Arizona border. Laura was a mess afterwards.

'She has two other brothers, but they are both worthless losers. Drunks. One is an out-of-work auto mechanic and the other is an out-of-work appliance salesman.' Cullen pointed to the two fat men standing by the door to the kitchen, smoking and drinking. Rodrigo and Ignacio. They both looked shitfaced. Court had read their body language during dinner; he could tell neither man wanted to be here. 'When Laura's husband died, Eddie left the DEA, moved down here to San Blas, started working with the Feds.' Cullen took a long breath. 'I've got to assume little Laura blames herself for Eddie's death now. She's taken it even harder than Elena or his parents.'

'Shit.' It occurred to Court for the first time tonight that close family ties had drawbacks as well as benefits.

As if on cue, Elena stepped out of the back door and walked across the yard to the two men. In English she said, 'Joe ... I've made your bed; I can show you where it is when you and Capitán Chuck finish your drinks.'

'Thank you, but I need to get back to Puerto Vallarta.'

Elena shook her head. Court had only met the woman a few hours earlier, but already he knew her to be intensely strong willed. 'You are staying with us. Just one night. Francisco, Eddie's uncle, is driving down to Sayulita early in the morning; I'll have him run you to the bus station in Vallarta.' She took his hand and squeezed it; she seemed genuinely offended that he would consider leaving her home in the dead of night.

Court glanced at Cullen, and Cullen smiled, raised his eyebrows, and nodded.

Gentry said, 'I guess I can stay.'

Cullen switched to Spanish to speak to Elena. Court could not tell if he was just proud of his command of the language or if he was trying to keep the other American out of the conversation.

'Listen, Elena. Have you given any more thought to skipping the protest tomorrow?'

Court butted in, but in English. 'What protest?'

Elena answered. 'I told you. In Puerto Vallarta.'

'You called it a memorial.'

She shrugged. 'To me, to the other family members here, it is a memorial. We will speak out for our dead loved ones. But Capitán Chuck thinks it will turn into a rally against Los Trajes Negros.' She looked at the older American. 'He does not want me to go.'

Cullen said, 'They are expecting a big crowd. I just don't see it as a great idea for a woman seven months pregnant to be down in all that rabble. There is a lot of anger, a lot of tension after . . . ' His voice trailed off.

'After Eduardo died fighting against them. I know that, Chuck. That's why I should go.'

Court could not help but take sides. 'I agree with the captain. You are pregnant; you don't need to be in the middle of a riot. Pushing and shoving—'

'It's not a riot, and I will be on the dais, not down in the crowd. I will be fine.'

Cullen shook his head. 'I don't like it. Eddie wouldn't want you to get in the middle of that.'

'Eduardo would have gone, and you know it.'

'Yes,' Cullen said, 'Eddie would have been there with a tactical team and an assault rifle, and he would have protected the protest from all threats from the monsters who support DLR. But he would not want *you* to be there, his family to be there, his unborn son to be there. It's too dangerous.'

Elena smiled at the older man for a long time. 'You worry too much about me, Capitán Chuck.' Then she smiled. 'You have been a good friend to the family.'

Cullen sat up straighter in the chair. 'And I will be as long as I live. Eddie's death did not change that.'

Court liked the old man, even if the old man wasn't as crazy about him. Court wished there was something he could do for

Elena and the Gamboas, but he couldn't think of a thing. He said good night to Cullen as the old man headed out front to his car; Court followed Elena inside, past at least a dozen others finding little corners with blankets and pillows to bed down for the night. She took him upstairs to a small bedroom, where she'd laid out a mattress with a blanket and a pillow for him.

The walls of the room were a fresh coat of baby blue. Court imagined Eddie had painted it himself for the son that he would never get to see.

13

Laos
2000

The afternoon humidity clung to his skin like barnacles on a ship's hull. Gentry drifted in and out of consciousness for the rest of the afternoon. The fever from his malaria caused him to shake some of the banana leaves off his hide, but he managed to shield himself from the sun by pulling the foliage back over his exposed skin.

Night brought relief from the sun. It also brought out a breeze that was strong enough to blow away his protective covering but somehow not strong enough to keep away the mosquitoes. With a weary hand he scooped mud off the ground next to him, wiped it thickly across his face and neck to try and cover as much skin as possible, but it didn't really work.

The bug bites kept him awake all night, spiders scurried across his body, and he had nothing left in the tank to kill them or even flick them off. He just lay there like a fallen log as creatures made trails all over him.

The fever caused his brain to swell inside his skull, and with the swelling he lost touch with reality and began seeing visions. Several times he believed he had died; he felt no more pain or heat or hunger or weakness, only a lightness and a peace. But the visions were cruel, like a desert mirage they teased him with their tranquility, and just like in the desert, when they dissipated, they brought about renewed despair.

He saw a big Chevy pickup truck pull up next to the pond. From it stepped his father and Chase, his younger brother. They beckoned him to get up and jump in the cab; they told him they were heading into town for pancakes, and they wanted him to come along.

Court spoke back to them, and with the movement of his scratchy vocal chords, the vision dissipated, leaving him right where he'd lain for fourteen hours.

Dammit.

He wanted to die. He did not want to be alive when the sun rose the next morning.

In the bright moonlight a helicopter hovered just overhead, landed next to the pond, and from it leapt Maurice, his CIA principle trainer and long-time mentor.

'Get your lazy ass up, Violator!' the old Vietnam vet shouted, calling Court by his code name.

Court did not reply at first. He just shook his head. He thought to himself, *I'm too damn tired.*

'Charlie don't care if you're tired!'

'I can't, sir,' replied Court aloud. 'I can't.'

But when he spoke, when he brought true noise to the night, the vision disappeared. He was alone. Frail, hurting.

Dying.

But he did not die that night; he lived to see morning. The three hours of daylight before the storms came were the worst of his ordeal. He prayed for rain, and when it came, it cooled him and quenched him, but the mud all around his body caused the water to pool, and it became deeper. A few times he even felt his body move slightly, he was floating in the downpour over the saturated earth. He wondered if he would be pulled into the pond, and he was horrified at the thought of drowning in the murky water.

But mercifully, the rain lulled him to sleep.

He awoke to the sound of birds, then voices, human voices. He knew it was day, the rain had stopped, and the sun singed through the humid air and burned his skin.

He heard voices once again; this time he assumed the voices to be nothing more than the beginning of another vision. He did not feel elation or fear; he only lay there, barely alive but drifting away.

The voices were soft at first, but they became louder, as if the speakers were getting closer. Court began to realize he was not dreaming, was not imagining this, and he felt a faint sense of concern. He had no weapon, not like it mattered – he wouldn't have been able to thumb a safety catch or pull a trigger, much less identify a threat and point a weapon towards a target.

The voices were all around him now, and they were speaking Laotian. They had found him, and as far as he was concerned, they could have him. They could shoot him right here; that would surely be preferable to them dragging him up the hill and hoisting him into a vehicle only to bounce around on the shitty roads on his way back to a cell in which he would certainly die within hours.

Fuck it, he thought, his mind incredibly lucid on this one subject. He'd fight them. These little bastards weren't taking him anywhere.

Two men knelt over him, peeled off the few banana leaves that were left covering his body. He reached up to punch one, but his arm just sort of wiggled a little next to his body. There was no swing, no punch.

More men came, and he was lifted off the ground and into the air; he screamed in protest and then in pain as his left arm was yanked in a different direction from the rest of his body. He felt himself being hauled up the hill; he heard the men's guns clanking against metal on their belts as the weapons swung free; his legs were dropped once, and men fell along with them, yelled and barked at one another until he was lifted up again.

The steady *slap*, *slap* of boots in mud as they left the muddy pond behind.

Their clipped and impenetrable language felt like ice picks into his ears.

They hoisted him onto the road finally and hauled him towards a black van. Gentry was carried headfirst and faceup, but his head hung upside down and bounced with the strides of the soldiers. The back of the black van opened, and it was dark inside. The men spoke quickly and gruffly amongst themselves, as if they were arguing with one another. Their uniforms meant nothing to him, but their weapons were AKs and long SKSs, the same as the local cops and the prison guards.

They slid him into the back of the van, and the doors shut. The van lurched and sped off, bouncing on the gravel alongside the paved road. Court tried to lift his head but gave up, rolled it from side to side. It took a moment, but he soon realized none of the soldiers had gotten in with him.

He was alone.

Huh?

No, he was *not* alone. A figure moved into the back from the front passenger seat; Court's weak neck muscles had dropped his head back on the hard surface of the van, and it rolled towards the wall.

A hand went to his forehead as if taking his temperature. 'Bad news, Sally, no luck on the root beer. I brought you some Beerlao. It's the local brew. That work?'

Court smiled and even that hurt; it stung his sunburned face. But a painkilling wave of relief began in his heart and shot out across his body in all directions. A new energy forced his neck muscles to fire one more time. He turned towards Eddie. He felt tears welling in his eyes, and he fought them. His voice was faint and rough. 'Is it cold, at least?'

Eddie shook his head. His eyes were wide and relaxed. That big Eddie Gamble smile widened as he spoke. 'Hot as hell, amigo. Tastes a bit like yak piss. Sorry.'

'The soldiers. Are they from Thailand?'

'I didn't leave the country. You didn't have time for me to get out and for some other group to come back and find you, so I went to Vientiane. Called in some favors I'd earned with an insurgent force. They aren't half as badass as they think they are, but I figured they were good enough to help me scoop a guy out of the mud and toss him into a van.'

Court hoisted an arm up with all his might, and Gamble grabbed it and shook it. Court said, 'Thanks for coming back.'

Gamble grinned, pulled a large backpack from between the front seats, opened it, began pulling out bags of fluid and syringes and medicines. 'You start crying, and I'm gonna tell your buddies in the CIA. You'll never hear the end of it.' He prepped an IV and jabbed it into Gentry's arm. 'Let's get you home, amigo.'

14

At eleven o'clock in the morning Court stood in a slow-moving line to buy a bus ticket at the Central Camionera de Puerto Vallarta, the city's main bus terminal. His green canvas bag lay on the floor in front of him. Every minute or two he'd kick it forwards and take a step along with it.

He'd awoken early, folded his bedding, descended the stairs silently, stepped over guests sleeping on the floor, and then left alone through the kitchen door. He'd taken the first bus of the morning from San Blas, and he'd stared out the window at the Pacific Ocean for much of the three-hour journey. Thinking of Eddie. Eddie's family. Eddie's sister. Court tried to shake the thoughts from his head a number of times but found it hard. Long-dormant emotions tugged at him. Longing. Loneliness. Lust.

He *so* needed to get the fuck out of here.

To that end, he had a plan. He'd buy a ticket to Guadalajara, and once there, after a day or two, he'd catch a bus to Mexico City. From there he would make his way to Tampico. He imagined it taking him a week or more to cross the country at the pace he planned on traveling.

The station was busy, but the pace of the line picked up a bit. He was only four from the counter when a security scan of the room caused his shoulders to pull back and alarm bells to go off in his head.

Entering the station with the charging, purposeful gait of a military officer was Captain Chuck Cullen.

Cullen scanned the room himself; Court had no doubt the old man was looking for him, trying to pick him out of the mass of travelers. Gentry turned away out of force of habit; he knew he could duck the man and remain invisible until he left.

But there was something about Cullen's walk, his intense, seeking expression.

Court knew something was wrong.

The Gray Man came out of the shadows, hefted his backpack, stepped out of the line, and walked towards the only other American in the crowded hall.

'What's up?' he asked, warily.

Cullen did not hide his surprise. He'd been hopelessly searching for a man who had just somehow materialized in front of him. He recovered. 'Elena said you didn't wait around to say good-bye.'

Court shrugged. 'Tell her I said good-bye.'

Cullen glared at Gentry for a while. He clearly wanted to say something, but twice stopped himself from speaking. Finally, he cleared his throat. 'Young man. I don't quite have a handle on who or *what* you are, but I have the impression that you may be helpful right now. And, whoever the hell you are, I *do* believe you want to do right by Eddie's family.'

Court cocked his head slightly but nodded. Said slowly, 'Absolutely.'

The captain nodded. Continued. 'Elena and most of her family are going to the rally downtown.'

Court wasn't surprised. 'Yeah, that's what she said last night.'

'I live downtown. This morning I woke to the sound of a car with a PA system driving up my street; the announcer was telling everyone to get out to the memorial this morning and protest the government's assassins. They've been talking about it all morning on the radio. There's a boatload of ill will on the local stations towards the Policía Federal's assassination attempt, and the DJs are encouraging certain ... elements to come out and make themselves heard. Supporters of de la Rocha and his Black Suits. The authorities are saying they are expecting thousands; they'll be roping off streets. It just sounds ... off. I am going to be there just in case something happens. I'd like you to come, too. I'm not as young as I used to be.'

'You really expect trouble?'

'Organized trouble? Maybe not. But at this point in time, DLR has more fans in Puerto Vallarta than Eddie Gamboa does. Depending on the crowd, the disposition of the cops holding back traffic, the extent to which the pro–de la Rocha group fires up the audience, the number of drunks and lowlifes who stagger into the protest ... Christ, I could see this getting out of hand really easily.'

With only a moment's hesitation, Court hefted his green canvas bag off the ground and slapped the older man on the shoulder. 'Good call, Chuck. Let's go.'

They drove south in Cullen's red two-door CrossFox. Traffic was heavy, but the seventy-two-year-old American weaved through it expertly. Court recognized that he could not have driven these streets half as well as the old man.

Cullen filled Court in as they drove. 'It's Monday, so there will be a cruise ship in port. Thousands of tourists down on the Malecon, the boardwalk lining the beach. Plus locals come into downtown on Mondays. The streets would be tight, even *without* this protest going on. I know a place I can park east of the event, just up the hill from the action.'

'The site of this rally. What's it like?'

'It's called the Parque Hidalgo. Used to be a park, but the city cleared out the grass and the trees and the market, so now it's just a flat, open cement plaza sitting on top of an underground parking lot. I guess the plaza is about fifty yards square, 'bout three blocks inland from the beach. There is a big staircase running off the plaza to the left that leads up to a street on the hill above. The Talpa Church sits up there.'

93

'Does the church provide overwatch on the location?'

'Overwatch? Hell, son, I never was a ground pounder, but I get what you mean. Yeah, it might. Not sure, to tell you the truth.'

'And in front of the plaza?'

'Just a busy downtown road. Three lanes, all one way, and gridlocked this time of day. Buildings on the other side. Commercial property. My dentist's office is right in there. There's some construction going on if I remember correctly. Everything is four stories high or so.'

'I need a phone,' Court said as a plan of action began to form in his head.

'Here, take mine.' Cullen reached towards the BlackBerry on his belt.

'No, I need my own, so I can contact you after we split up.'

'Why are we splitting up? We need to stay around Elena and the family. She's seven months pregnant; somebody throws a beer bottle, and she won't be able to get out of the way. Ernesto and Luz aren't as old as me, but they aren't as fit, either. Laura can handle herself, but Eddie's brothers are worthless; his uncles and aunts are mountain people who've probably never even seen a crowd this big before. We need to protect the family.'

'We will. Look, trust me. Let's do this my way.'

Cullen looked at Court out of the corner of his eye while he drove through thickening traffic. 'Help me understand just what skills you are bringing to the table.'

Court's game face slowly hardened. 'If I were armed, I'd be bringing more skills to the table.'

The captain sighed. 'We don't want to do anything to make a bad situation worse. Somebody charging in in a blaze of glory is not going to—'

'I'm not looking for glory. If the shit doesn't hit the fan, you won't even know I'm there.'

'Good.'

'This rally ... Do you expect the press to be there?'

'Most definitely.'

94

Court reached over to Cullen, pulled the USS *Buchanan* cap from his head. He put it on his own and pulled it down low.

Cullen looked at him as he drove.

By way of explanation, Court said, 'I'm a little camera shy.'

'Do I want to know why?'

Court shook his head, looked out at the road. 'You really don't.'

Cullen turned back to the road himself; the creases in his face deepened in thought and worry.

'What have you done, son?'

'I'm just like the other good guys down here. There are enough bad guys around that I don't want them to see my face.'

Cullen nodded, but it was obvious he was still suspicious. He reached into the backseat and pulled an identical *Buchanan* cap from the floorboard and put it on his silver-maned head.

They pulled into a supermarket, and Cullen rushed inside, came back a few minutes later with a cell phone and a wired earpiece in black plastic. Court had already ripped the devices out of their packaging before Cullen had pulled the CrossFox out of the parking lot.

The memorial had begun by the time they parked the car a few blocks behind the large stone Talpa Church, on a steep hill above the plaza. They followed the rumbling noise of the crowd, and canned patriotic music played on a tinny public address system as they walked down the hill. The music stopped, and a woman began speaking to the crowd. It was not Elena Gamboa's voice, but Court thought it sounded like one of the other police wives from the dinner the previous evening. She railed against the *narco* traffickers, the lack of opportunity for the youth of Mexico, and the corruption in the local police force. Gentry could not understand more than half of it, but it seemed pretty rambling and disjointed, even if it was delivered passionately. He and Cullen passed some Puerto Vallarta Municipal Police manning a wooden barricade just as the speaker called out their department as being in the back pocket of the 'terrorist' Daniel de la Rocha. The cops glowered down the hill towards the protest with their right hands resting on their pistol grips.

'This shit could turn ugly,' Court said as they began pushing through street vendors and stragglers at the top of the long stone staircase that ran alongside the big square.

'Yep,' Cullen said tersely; he looked over the edge of the railing down towards the podium, searching for the Gamboas.

Moving down the big staircase was an exercise in both diplomacy and aggression. Court would tap one person on the shoulder and politely ask permission to pass, and then physically adjust the next person to make way for himself and the old man. The plaza below to his left was every bit as crowded, easily two thousand people crammed into a single city block to listen to the speaker. Court worried there were some in the crowd here to encourage trouble, and likely others who were just trouble-loving spectators hoping for a little excitement.

Finally, at the bottom of the steps, Court said, 'Why don't you get close to the family? Be ready to move them away and out of the action if this all breaks bad.'

'Alright. But what about you?'

Court turned slowly, 360 degrees. Then he looked back to Cullen. 'I need to stay on the perimeter. Get a feel for the action, the crowd, the streets. The vibe.'

'How is that going to accomplish anything?'

'I'm pretty good at this. You brought me here because you think I might be able to help. Let me help.'

Cullen nodded. 'Call me if you see something.'

'Let's establish coms right now and keep the line open between us.'

Cullen called Gentry, popped his earpiece in his ear, and Court put his earpiece in and answered. 'Good luck,' the Gray Man said into his mike, and the men set off in different directions.

Moving west through the mass of humanity, away from the stage, Court immediately ID'd troublemakers in the crowd. There were groups of dissenters here and there; around him he heard angry comments, arguments, even some pushing and shoving. A woman mumbled that the Policía Federal shouldn't be blowing up boats in the bay, and another woman snapped back that DLR was a son of a whore and the only pity was that he survived.

Within sixty seconds of leaving the captain's side Gentry spotted men who clearly did not belong. Heavies, stone-faced tough guys watching the others around them instead of focusing on the speaker. He passed two of these individuals within yards of each other, picked them out as undercover operatives working for the police, the government, or maybe even one of the drug cartels.

Court saw bulges on their hips, evidence the men were wearing guns secreted into the waistbands of their blue jeans. Plainclothes police agents were common at Latin American protest rallies; it was nothing Court hadn't seen before in Brazil or Guatemala or Peru or a half dozen other places. Often they weren't as dangerous as they looked, but still he knew to keep an eye out for these assholes.

Court spoke into his mouthpiece. 'Chuck, have you made it to Elena yet?'

'Just about. I'll get up on the dais with the family. One more speaker after this broad and then it's Elena's turn. When she's finished at the podium, I'm going to do my best to get everyone back up the stairs and away from this crowd.'

'Roger that.'

Court arrived at the three-lane street just below the Parque Hidalgo. There were a few cars and trucks parked along the curb, but no traffic flowed. Instead, PV cops had the street blocked to the north, and easily two hundred people stood in the middle of the road or on the sidewalk next to it, their eyes riveted to the stage.

The speaker finished, and she received polite applause from some and angry whistles from others. Gentry passed another tough-looking hombre who neither clapped nor paid attention to the speaker; instead he made eye contact with the bearded gringo pushing to the east before turning his eyes towards another part of the audience.

Court's gaze settled on a building that overlooked the park. The first two stories were finished; they housed a dental office, a travel agency, a pharmacy, and a few other offices. But high above street level the third and fourth stories were construction; iron beams, rebar, cinderblock, electric wires, scaffolding, and big, dark open windows that overlooked the entire crowd and the stage. To a man like Court Gentry, it looked promising. Here was an overwatch, a place where he could get a bird's-eye view of the event.

He began walking towards the building.

The next speaker at the podium was male, a state prosecutor. He began extolling the brief but illustrious career of Major Eduardo Gamboa, in advance of the late-officer's wife saying a few words.

Finally free of the gridlocked crowd, Gentry headed down an alley that ran west all the way to the beach. On his left an archway opened to a hallway that ran under the partially finished building. At the arch he passed the doorway to a pet store; a dozen bird cages hung from the roof off the hall alongside the shop's windows, forcing him to duck as he walked on. Moving slowly down the narrow hallway, he stepped around more chirping finches and budgies in their wooden cages, which jutted out into his path. Pigeons sauntered around at Gentry's feet as he moved slowly towards a light ahead. A stairwell at the end of the dark hall.

And then, thirty feet in front of him, a shadow from the left. Court stopped in his tracks. A man crossed the hallway in the light, from a room on the left to the stairwell up on the right.

The man was dressed from head to toe in black, and his face was covered with a black ski mask.

He was a *federale*, or dressed like one at least, but his skulking movement and mannerisms were not those of a cop here to keep the peace.

Gentry froze, willed the man not to look up the dark hallway as he passed and just continue to the stairs.

The man did *not* look, he *did* walk on, and just before disappearing from view, Court saw a squat black submachine gun in the *federale*'s left hand.

Then Court heard a vehicle pull into the alleyway behind him. He looked back and saw a black armored Policía Federal SWAT van stop directly under the archway by the pet store from where he had just come, essentially blocking him in unless he could find another open exit.

Court stood alone in the hallway for nearly half a minute, not sure what to do. Ahead of him, somewhere up the stairs, an armed man who seemed to be up to no good. Behind him, who knows how many more shady cops showing up a block away from the event.

'Cullen, you read me?'

The reception was shit in the hall. Court heard an echo of the man speaking into the public address in his phone's earpiece, but he couldn't hear Chuck.

Damn. He began heading towards the staircase.

The second-floor door was locked, and Court didn't think the man had gone through it, as Court would have heard the latch echo down the stairwell to the hallway. He whispered into his mike, again trying to raise Captain Cullen, but the reception in the stairwell was even worse than in the hallway.

He slipped off his tennis shoes so that he could move without footfalls echoing up the stairwell, and he began walking up the concrete stairs in his stocking feet.

On the third floor Court left the stairwell and entered the construction area of the building, looking for the lone *federale* with the sub gun. The unfinished floor provided open windows out to the Parque Hidalgo and the streets around. He half expected to find the masked policeman here, amidst the darkness and the building materials, but there was no one. Gentry stepped forward to check the crowd.

The plaza below was packed tight; from this vantage point he could better see the incredible congestion in the space. The speaker finished his comments and turned the lectern over to Elena Gamboa; clapping and cheering drowned out the yelling and cursing, but Court could make out the differing camps reflected in the gathering. Shoving, finger wagging, and other animated gestures expressing displeasure were sprinkled in amongst those clearly here to honor the fallen men.

Then loud car horns began honking below and to his right, drowning out the applause. First one, then two, and finally five large white SUVs pushed their way slowly through the mass of humanity. They moved in the wrong direction up the one-way street. The big trucks continued honking, and the angry waving of the SUVs' drivers out the windows encouraged the crowd to part. Finally, the big white trucks stopped, and men began filing out. So dramatic was their entrance to the event that even Elena Gamboa paused her opening comments from the riser to see what was going on.

Court wondered if this was part of the memorial, but one look to the dais dispelled that notion. The families and other speakers standing up there looked confused by the new arrivals.

Puerto Vallarta police hung around the outskirts of the crowd, but they did not move on the vehicles or the men. They just stood about like all the other spectators.

Tentatively, Elena Gamboa began speaking again, thanking the organizers of the memorial for putting the event together and thanking the audience for coming to pay tribute to the work of her husband and his fallen comrades. But Court kept his eyes on the SUVs. A man in a goatee and a black suit and tie emerged from the second truck. Court watched him take a bullhorn from a similarly dressed man and climb atop the hood of the big vehicle. Immediately, before he even spoke, both cheers and gasps of horror emitted from the crowd.

'*Damas y caballeros!* Ladies and gentlemen! Your attention, *por favor*,' the man said, his voice tiny and hollow compared to the PA system Elena's voice had passed through.

Court spoke into his headset.

'Hey, Chuck, can you hear me?'

'Loud and clear.'

'Who's this asshole?'

There was a pause. Gentry looked across the park, picked Cullen out of the people lining the back of the stage, standing on his toes to get a look at the white trucks and the man atop the hood. Soon the older American exclaimed, 'Holy hell! It's him!'

'*Him* who?'

'*That* is Daniel de la Rocha.'

15

Court couldn't believe the balls of this guy. This entire event was to commemorate the police who died trying to kill him, and he shows up, a flagrant insult to both the police and the families of those fallen men. 'What is he doing here?'

'Doing what he always does. Putting on a performance.'

Confusion mixed with concern in Gentry's brain. He thought of the plainclothes men he'd seen in the crowd. Were they *sicarios*, assassins who were part of de la Rocha's entourage? Or were they in the employ of Constantino Madrigal, his archenemy. Was there more here than the threat of drunks and fistfights and beer bottles? 'I don't like this. Get the family out of here. Now.'

'I just tried. Elena won't budge until she finishes her speech.'

'Dammit,' Court said, and he hurried back to the stairs to find the masked man here in the building with him.

De la Rocha continued speaking into the bullhorn, and Court could hear every word, and what he did not understand, he put together contextually. 'I have come before you today, to tell the people and the authorities that I am not in hiding. I have nothing to hide! The assassination attempt against me on my yacht failed, *gracias* only to my protector and savior. The assassination attempt was made by government *sicarios* working directly under the orders of el Vaquero, Señor Constantino Madrigal Bustamante, the *real narcotraficante* , the *real* criminal to threaten the region and our poor nation. Madrigal and his bought-off police gangsters want me dead because I have evidence of government corruption at the highest levels in Mexico City! In my hands I have the names of the corrupt working for Madrigal.' De la Rocha turned his attention from the general crowd and to a dumbstruck Elena Gamboa, still standing behind the microphone on the stage. 'Señora, I ask your forgiveness for saying so, but your husband's name is on this list!'

'*¡Mentiroso!' Liar!* Elena shouted into the microphone on the podium.

De la Rocha ignored her, and once again addressed the crowd at large. 'I came today, putting my own life in jeopardy, because I believe that there should be no rally in support of murderers and villains and dishonest police officers ...'

He continued speaking, the crowd seemed split down the middle in their reaction now; the arrival of Los Trajes Negros seemed to intimidate some and rally others, even as it incensed many in the crowd.

But Court Gentry tuned it all out. He was back in the stairwell now and heading up, looking for the skulking *federale*. At the top of the stairwell he began moving through another dark floor of dusty construction, again towards the windows overlooking the park.

Then he saw him, ahead in the shadows. The masked man held the submachine gun, and he knelt behind the cinderblock wall, hiding his body and looking down towards the crowd. Court could hear Elena's voice over the loudspeaker, trying to argue back against DLR while the crowd both cheered and booed her words.

The cop pulled a radio off his belt, began speaking into it softly. Court could not hear what was being said. He moved a little closer in his stocking feet, staying close to the walls.

He stepped into the dark room with the officer now, moved left along the wall towards the corner, and went prone behind a low stack of wallboard that lay on the dusty concrete.

The policeman spoke again, and once again, Gentry could not

103

make out his soft speech, but Court absolutely did *not* trust the guy. Why would he be up here, crouched down, conspiratorially whispering into his radio to someone? It didn't seem like the actions of a policeman on the job.

Slowly, the cop raised his weapon; Gentry recognized it as a Colt 635, called a Shorty, a 9 mm submachine gun. The *federale* lifted the barrel over the cinderblocks and pointed it down towards the crowd. Gentry still did not move, did not know what the hell was going on. Was the policeman there to protect those on the stage, and did he see some threat? Or was he planning on killing Elena Gamboa? The Colt was no sniper rifle, but a long burst from the gun could send thirty rounds of 9 mm bullets streaking one hundred and fifty feet to the podium, knocking everyone standing there dead to the ground.

Shit, thought Court. He did not know what to do. If this man was a good guy, he sure didn't want to kill him, but if he was a bad guy, he didn't want to sit by and watch while he blasted innocents.

He did not know, but instinct told him that the situation before him smelled bad, and his instinct had been honed and refined through years and years of danger. In a moment of semi-resolution, Gentry stood in the dark room, walked across the cement on the balls of his stocking feet towards the black-clad man. Fifteen feet, ten feet, five feet behind him. His footfalls were quiet, and what sound they did emit was drowned out by the noise from the street and the park.

Court knelt down, out of view of the open window, directly behind the crouching cop.

'Hi.'

The Mexican federal officer spun on the balls of his feet, his head whipped around only to meet a vicious left jab from the American assassin. With a pop and a crack, fist met face. The cop's dark glasses flew off, the wide eyes of the policeman quivered, and the man went limp, a one-hundred-forty-pound sack of flour dropping towards the cement. Court caught him, more or less, and laid the unconscious man down on his back. Quickly, Gentry took his weapon.

Court looked down through the spaghetti-like mass of electric wires and telephone cables strung from his high perch here, across the street to poles down at street level by the park. Below these wires, directly under his position, he saw a fresh group of black-clad figures pushing through the crowd in the street. They were Policía Federal as well, and they'd come from the alleyway with the armored truck. They were dressed exactly as the policeman lying at Gentry's knees.

Below Court and to his right, de la Rocha continued rambling on into the bullhorn. Twice more Elena Gamboa tried to speak, but both times the immaculately dressed man standing in the sun on the hood of the white SUV continued talking, forcing her to give up and just stand there at the podium. He said something about the lack of an indictment, something about the corruption of the special operations group of the federal police, something about how songs and action movies are merely entertainment and are no basis for judging a man guilty. He waved folded sheets in his hand, his 'list' of conspirators against him, and he railed against Constantino Madrigal and *los Vaqueros*, 'the Cowboys.'

Court peered down at the Feds pushing through the crowd. The crowd itself had begun pushing and shoving to get away from them. Five cops at least, maybe more; it was hard to count their numbers the way they moved into the pulsing and recoiling mass of civilians around them, everyone burning under the hot noon sun.

'Señor!' shouted Elena now towards de la Rocha. 'I speak for my dead husband! You *will* allow me to finish!'

Court spoke in his cell phone's mike. 'You've got five plus suspicious-looking fuckers working their way towards the podium in the crowd. Federal officers.'

'Shit.' Court heard Cullen relay this information to Laura, and he saw her step behind the lectern to talk to Elena. Elena

105

pushed her sister-in-law away gently as she continued addressing de la Rocha.

Court looked back to the *federales*. Civilians literally scrambled out of their way now, but the masked men moved aggressively through the citizenry, shoving with hands and arms, and then ... yes. Guns! Where their hands before had been empty, he now saw black metal. They had drawn weapons: Colt submachine guns for some and black semiautomatic pistols for others.

Every sight and sound and sixth sense Gentry had seen or heard or felt since arriving in the plaza suddenly made sense; it all formed together into a solid mass of certainty in his gut.

He understood now.

There would be no riot.

This was going to be a massacre, and he had a bird's-eye view of it all.

'Yank her ass off the stage, Chuck! It's about to go loud!'

'Okay!' the old man shouted back.

Court heard the captain yell at Elena. *'¡Vamanos!'* Let's go! Court looked above and across the two-thousand-strong crowd in time to see the white-haired American with the blue ball cap take Elena by the arm.

And then a gunshot rang out.

Court looked back to the *federales*, but immediately his head followed the source of the noise, below and to his right. His mouth opened in shock. Daniel de la Rocha dropped his bullhorn, his hands wide from his body; a second shot sent him tumbling backwards, stumbling off the hood of the huge white Chevy Suburban Half-Ton and down into the arms of his black-suited bodyguards.

Pistol smoke rose from the crowd in front of the SUV.

'I'll be damned,' Gentry muttered to himself.

He sure hadn't seen *that* coming.

16

'Somebody just whacked de la Rocha.' Court said it into his mike, but a burst of gunfire ahead to his left turned his head again. The black-clad *federales* fired into the crowd as they pushed towards the podium, shooting at the civilians in their way.

The white SUVs were honking and screeching their tires, doing their utmost to back out of the crowd.

Court had to do something; he could not just sit up here and witness mass murder.

The Gray Man rose to his feet, stood in front of the open fourth story window. He lifted a two-foot rebar hinge from a stack of fastenings next to him and took the bent iron rod in his right hand, slung the sling of the Colt Shorty over his neck with his left, and in his silent stocking feet he stepped onto the cinderblock window ledge. With only a quick glance down he leapt out over the crowd, over the screams and the honking horns and the crackle of gunfire, and dropped towards the street, four stories below.

As he fell he heard a submachine gun go cyclic off to his left, draining its magazine of bullets.

Gentry caught the rebar hook around a mass of telephone wires just three feet below the window, got his right hand under the wires, and took the bar on the other side as he fell, squeezing as tight as he could with both hands. With a violent wrenching in his shoulders, the wires caught him, and he managed to hold on.

His legs and torso shot out to the right, spinning him almost horizontally before gravity caught up with him and he began sliding down at a forty-five degree angle towards the Parque Hidalgo, the metal rebar stripping rubber from the phone lines as he slid down.

He hurtled down over the street now, above the bedlam of the packed audience desperately trying to break the gridlock and get away from the men with the guns.

At thirty feet in the air he was skidding down at top speed; he fought to maintain his grip. His cell phone and his wired earpiece flew away from his body and tumbled to the street below. The crowd in front of the cement steps between the sidewalk and the park scattered with the flying lead coming from both their north and south; a fresh crack up near the staircase to the Talpa Church sent some of them in the opposite direction from the masses and caused a virtual mosh pit of flailing and falling bodies on the sidewalk near where Court's telephone wire terminated at a metal pole.

He chose these unlucky people as his landing zone. As he shot down the wire, he let go of the rebar while his feet were still eight feet off the ground and he was halfway over the three-lane street. He flew through the air, tucked his knees in tight, saw a big man in civilian dress with a radio in one hand and a silver revolver in the other. Court slammed into his back, and he and the fat man tumbled hard, crashing down into those who'd already fallen on the sidewalk.

Court struggled back to his feet, faster than anyone else taken down by his dive-bomb attack from four stories high. He ran across the back of a young man who was facedown on the concrete, and then he leapt onto a small wall running along the sidewalk and began heading for the stairs Cullen planned to use to get the Gamboas away from the park.

More gunfire barked from ahead, and the crowd shrieked. Men, women, children all running and fighting and screaming to get away from the bloodbath. Court searched for the origin of the fire as he ran, blading his body and using his free hand as a spear to knock the shocked and stunned out of his way as he advanced on the threats ahead. He arrived at the first of the victims now: bullet-riddled dead bodies and writhing injured civilians whose misery continued as others tripped over them trying to escape the pandemonium. Court pushed his way with the crowd towards the long staircase leading up to the road and the church above; in front of him an utter logjam of panicked and shrieking humanity fought its way up the steps towards safety.

By now Chuck Cullen had moved Elena and her family off the stage; the Captain quickly ushered her, Laura, Ernesto, and Luz towards the staircase leading away from Parque Hidalgo. Moving with them, either behind, alongside, or in front, depending on the chaotic flotsam and jetsam of the crowd, were the other eight members of the Gamboa family: Eddie's two uncles, two aunts, his two older brothers, a sister-in-law, and his sixteen-year-old nephew. Along with them, family members of other PF officers killed on *La Sirena* fled the stage to the stairs. But the crowd was thick, and Cullen's hasty escape plan bogged down immediately. The steady rhythmic gunfire seemed right on top of them, but they could barely breathe, much less move away. After what seemed to him to be an eternity of shoving, Cullen finally got the Gamboa family to the wall alongside the staircase. He began pushing and fighting his way along it to make the turn to go up, but the swarm of horrified protestors moving in the opposite direction pushed back at his scheme.

Finally, he turned at the base of the stairs, and he led the way, held Elena by the hand, and alternated between looking back to make sure the rest of the family had not been left behind and scanning forward up the stairs towards more pandemonium, searching to avoid threats or discover opportunities to hasten their flight from the danger.

More gunshots from behind, from different areas of the park and the street, and from different types of weapons. Laura trailed her parents, pushed at her father who, along with his wife, was suffocating at the bottom of the stairs, packed like cordwood amongst the others.

From just above them, 'Go! Go! Move! Move!' Cullen spoke excellent Spanish, but he shouted in English, certain his meaning was obvious to all.

For much of his slow and arduous progression through the gridlocked park, Court could not see more than a few feet in front of him. He fought against the masses, punching and pushing and scratching to make his way. *'¡Muevate! ¡Muevate! ¡Muevate!'* *Move! Move! Move!* Nearing the staircase, stepping and leaping over dead and wounded along the way, he caught up to three *sicarios federales*, their backs to him. These men pushed forward, reloading their smoking submachine guns, completely unaware that an armed enemy was behind them.

The men wore big bulletproof vests, so with cruel determination the American assassin knelt to the hot pavement, thereby creating a flight path for his bullets that would not send them through his targets and then into innocents. He carefully fired a short burst into the back of each man's head below the helmet. They pitched and tumbled forward into fleeing civilians; their Colt sub guns and Beretta pistols flew from their hands and fell silent. Court held his rifle in his right hand and fired again at the men on the ground, double-tapping the forehead of each man as he pushed past them.

He came to a group of terrified civilians frozen in fear; they were obviously a family, a father nearly hysterical as he tried to shelter his wife and three children from the flying lead and thrashing and kicking bodies as he attempted to get out of the way of it all. Just as Court caught the terrified eyes of the man, the Mexican's head lurched to the side, and blood erupted from his jaw. Gentry spun his head to find one of the plainclothes agitators in the crowd re-aiming his big silver revolver, having missed Court with his first shot. Court ducked and rolled on the ground, crashed into others around him like a bowling ball, but he successfully dodged another pistol shot that no doubt struck an innocent person behind him.

The Gray Man emptied his Colt 9 mm into the fat man's gut at twelve feet, sending him into spasms before he tumbled back dead.

Court dropped the spent submachine gun, crawled forward on his hands and knees, and hefted the dead man's smoking pistol.

He rose, sprinted forward towards the stairs; his new weapon dripped blood, and he shoved and pushed and even pointed the gun at innocents so they would get the fuck out of his way. He did everything within his power to catch up to Cullen and the fleeing Gamboa family, obscured still by the hundreds pushing in both directions on the wide steps running up to the street in front of the Talpa Church. At one point he found himself climbing onto a bench, jumping high onto the backs and heads of the crowd, literally bodysurfing over a particularly tight gathering of Puerto Vallartans too terrified to move.

17

Chuck Cullen was eighty feet above and ahead of Court, just more than halfway up the stairs with the Gamboas and the other GOPES family members right behind him. The crowd ahead thinned suddenly on his right, so the retired captain decided to shift his entourage in that direction. He led Elena forward and past him so that he could take Luz by the hand to pull her through the surging riot of screaming people all around.

At the top of the stairs, another thirty feet away, three federal policemen on Suzuki motorcycles drove through the mob and dismounted; they drew pistols from their drop-leg holsters and looked down the stairs towards the gunfire. They waved the escaping memorial attendees past, encouraging them to run for their lives, and they seemed to cover them with their guns, scanning for threats down in the plaza.

More gunfire. More honking horns. More screaming and shouting. More cries of agony.

Elena Gamboa led her family up the stairs now. She slowed when she noticed the *federales*, but she saw their motorcycles, just like Eduardo's; their uniforms, just like Eduardo's; their ski masks and sunglasses, just like Eduardo's. She ascended the crowded stairs just as fast as her pregnant body would allow.

The policeman directly above her at the top of the stairs beckoned her forward with his free hand as he furiously searched the crowd for threats.

More gunshots from behind Elena as she hurried towards the safety of Eduardo's colleagues.

Chuck Cullen got Luz moving again, checked quickly to see that Laura held Ernesto around the waist and kept him pressing forward behind his wife. The aunt and uncles and nephew and brothers had pushed on ahead; they passed Cullen on the left-hand side of the staircase. The seventy-two-year-old retired American naval officer turned to see Elena advancing quickly up on the right; she'd gotten ahead of him while he helped Eddie's mother. He rushed to arrive at the top of the stairs at the same time as she so he could protect her from any danger there as well as direct her up the alley behind the church where his car was parked.

He was still a few feet behind her and to her left when he saw the policeman, at the top of the stairs and seven steps above Elena.

The two other *federales* stood to his left. They all held automatic pistols out in front of them. As one their weapons' muzzles left the threats at the bottom of the stairs and leveled instead on the families of the dead GOPES men rushing up towards them.

These men weren't protecting anyone. They were assassins.

Chuck watched in utter horror as a handgun's barrel pointed directly at Eddie Gamboa's pregnant wife.

Captain Cullen moved faster than he'd moved in forty years, hurtling himself upwards, throwing himself up the four steps, and jamming his body between the weapon and the woman.

The pistol barked, pain tore into the old man's gut, still he grabbed at the cop, pulled him tight in a bear hug.

The other masked police began firing as well, pouring lead down the stairs into the Gamboa family as they approached the top of the staircase.

Captain Cullen was shot again in the ribcage by the man in his grasp, his arms relaxed the hug, and he slid slowly down the cop's body, onto his knees at the top of the stone staircase. Slower still he slumped forward onto his chest as Elena screamed.

*

To avoid the crowd on the staircase Gentry leapt high in his stocking feet onto the wide and steep stone railing that ran up the right side of the steps; he began running upwards with his arms out for balance and the revolver he'd taken from the plainclothes gunman jutting out from his right hand. He looked away from his feet for an instant and up towards a new commotion in the thick crowd at the logjam at the top of the stairs. Before his eyes could fix on the action a pistol round cracked and Court saw Elena. In front of her was the captain, and in front of him stood a black-clad *federale*.

Court understood everything in an instant. The cop had been gunning for Eddie's wife and unborn child, and old Chuck Cullen had thrown his body over the gun.

More gunshots, rapid-fire pistols blazing, and Court saw the other two officers murdering the families of the special operation's group as they ascended towards them.

Gentry sprinted upwards on the stone railing. He raised the silver Smith and Wesson revolver and put the weapon's front site on the back of Elena Gamboa's head, shifted aim a fraction to the right, and fired a single .357 Magnum round.

The bullet left the weapon, tracked up and over the crowd on the stairs, passed two inches to the right of Elena Gamboa's ear, and struck the killer of Chuck Cullen on the left collarbone above his Kevlar vest, blasting bone and blood and muscle out of the man's shoulder and spinning him away and down to the ground as his pistol flew out of his hand and twirled in the air above him like a whirligig.

Court was still thirty feet from the top of the stairs. Gunfire continued, and the crowd behind the Gamboas turned as one and began running down now, away from this new danger above them. Some of the younger and more ambulatory on the steps jumped over the railing, falling fifteen to twenty-five feet to the concrete Parque Hidalgo below just to escape the flying lead. Some of these people crossed Gentry's line of fire, kept him from getting clean shots on the two remaining police assassins.

Court was near the top now; finally, he got a sight line on a target ahead. Both cops were kneeling behind their motorcycles, reloading their pistols. Court aimed at the first man, began pressing the trigger as he leapt off the railing and onto the steps, but again someone got in his way. In half a heartbeat he took his finger from the trigger.

It was Elena, she was falling backwards; the crowd had cleared the top portion of the steps and behind her nothing but hard concrete for ten feet awaited her.

Gentry threw himself at her, dropping the revolver to free both hands. He landed behind her and caught her; he slid his arms around her head and belly, and the two of them slid with the other bodies cascading down the stairs.

Court took the brunt of the impact as they fell; he kept Eddie's wife safe and her head and belly protected as they slid.

A long blast from an automatic rifle below him focused Gentry's efforts on stopping his slide, getting back on his feet, and pushing back upwards. He lifted Elena into his arms, cradled her, struggled with her weight as he ascended, pushed through the pain in his back and arms caused by bumping down the steps. He shifted his ascent to the left, doing his best to keep other civilians between him and the gunmen below.

To his left, men, women, and children fell; from the corner of his eye he saw both of Eddie's uncles and one aunt in a pile of dead and wounded flowing down the stairs, smearing long splatters of fresh blood across the steps as they tumbled and slid.

He kept climbing with Elena in his arms. He put his foot on the revolver he'd dropped and took a moment to kneel and pick it up; his thighs quivered with the effort of raising back up while holding Eddie's pregnant wife. Soon the sheer number of civilians, an unrelenting stampede of humanity, shoved forward from behind Court, and those with nowhere to run but straight *through* the killers pushed the hit men at the top of the staircase back, knocked them down, and by the time Gentry arrived at the sidewalk above, the cops had abandoned their cycles and had begun retreating north, reloading their depleted weapons again as they did so.

Court looked down at Chuck Cullen's body. He lay facedown and violently contorted, splayed along on the top three steps; his USS *Buchanan* cap had fallen off his head and lay beside him. Gentry put Elena down gently, looked for the loose weapon dropped by the man he'd shot in the collarbone, but he could not find it.

'Fuck!' he shouted, surrounded by the dead and the wounded and the terrified, and now more bursts of gunfire cracked at the bottom of the staircase.

18

At the road above the Parque Hidalgo, just in front of the church, Gentry held Elena Gamboa's hand, his head swiveled back and forth, searching for anyone in her dead husband's family left alive. Screaming civilians ran off in the distance, but he did not see any of Eddie's loved ones among them.

Finally, a voice called to him from the front door of la Iglesia de la Virgen de Talpa. 'Joe! *¡Estamos aquí!*' It was Diego, Eddie's sixteen-year-old nephew, beckoning the American into the church. He and Elena crossed the one-lane street and ran together inside.

The sanctuary was big and dark, and the cries and shrieks of those who'd sought shelter there echoed like church bells. There were twenty or so people inside the old building, many of them GOPES relatives, standing and shaking together near the altar. They cried and hugged and comforted one another. A priest stood above them in his white robes, his hands on his hips and his face a mask of confusion, uncertainty, and fear. Gentry took a moment just inside the doorway to check Elena out. Understandably, she suffered from shock. There was no color in her face; this he could tell even in the candlelight and the meager sunlight that filtered through the stained glass windows. But she did not seem wounded. He held her hand, began moving through the pews with her; Diego was speaking to him but too fast and frantic for him to understand.

117

'Are we safe?' Asked Elena softly. 'Is it over?'

'I seriously doubt it,' Court answered honestly, and kept moving with her towards the altar.

There was no time for a head count; Court would help whoever was here to get out of here, but there was no way in hell he was going back out front where the snapping gunfire continued. He was certain most of the Gamboas were dead, but Luz and Ernesto were standing at the altar unhurt, as was Eddie's younger sister, Laura. Court blew a quick sigh of relief when he saw her.

'They killed my parents!' Diego shouted, and this Court understood.

He did not know how to respond. What came out was cold and efficient Spanish. 'We'll worry about that later.'

When he looked back up, he saw many of the survivors at the altar knelt in prayer. The elderly frocked padre stood above them still. He did not participate.

Idiots! Court thought to himself.

'Hey!' He interrupted their prayers. 'What the hell? We've got to get the fuck out of ...' He switched to Spanish. *'¡No hay tiempo para eso!' There is no time for that!* Those kneeling turned back to him, eyes still wide with the shock of the event.

He began running up the center aisle towards them.

Laura rose from her knees and turned; Court realized she had a Beretta pistol in her right hand, likely the weapon he had not been able to find by the cop he'd shot at the top of the stairs. She raised it quickly towards him, and he stopped dead in his tracks. He lifted his arms slowly.

'Laura. It's okay. Put it on the ground. It's going to be okay.' Instead he saw her sinewy forearm flex as she pulled the trigger, Court dropped flat on the floor of the center aisle as two shots rang out, right over his head. Through the echo in the sanctuary and the ringing in his ears, he heard a body hit the floor behind him at the entrance to the church. He looked back over his shoulder and saw a *federale* fall flat on his face in the open

118

doorway forty feet behind, a Colt SMG skittering along the tiles next to him.

She'd shot the man in the head.

'Okay,' Court said as he slowly crawled back to his feet. 'Why don't you just hold onto that for now?' She nodded blankly. She was clearly in shock, as bad as Elena. But she sure as hell could shoot.

'Everybody, listen up!' Gentry said in English, then again caught himself and switched to Spanish. 'Where are your cars?'

Ernesto Gamboa, Eddie's father, spoke for the group.

'They are in the garage below the Parque Hidalgo.'

Court cussed aloud. They might as well be on the dark side of the moon. They were *not* going back down there. And there was no way he could transport everyone in Chuck's little two-door parked behind the church, even if he had the keys for it, which he did not.

He stepped up to the priest, who stood as still as Jesus on the crucifix behind him. 'We are going to have to borrow your car, Padre.'

The elderly man shook his head emphatically. 'Out of the question! The church van belongs to my parishioners, and they need their van!'

Without hesitation Court pulled the hammer back on the revolver, still held at his side. The metallic click echoed in the dark sanctuary. 'Your parishioners can have a van, or they can have a priest. It's your call.'

The priest stared at the weapon. Slowly, he reached into his robes, pulled out his keys. Handed them over.

Gentry nodded. 'Good call, Padre.'

Out of the corner of his eye Court caught a vicious look from Laura Gamboa. He assumed her Catholicism was clouding her pragmatism at the moment. But he did not have time for niceties. Ignoring her disgust, he lowered the hammer on the gun and shoved it into his waistband, and he led the civilians out the back of the church and into the van. He thought about running back for the Colt Shorty dropped by the dead cop at the door, but he did not know how long it would be before another team of assassins entered the church to finish off the survivors.

The van filled with passengers. Court climbed behind the wheel, with Elena in the front passenger seat, and they took off to the north.

19

Three miles east of downtown Puerto Vallarta five white Suburban Half-Ton SUVs idled in an orderly row on a hilly gravel road. Their five drivers stood outside the open driver-side doors, each wore a button-down shirt, loose tan tactical vest, and khaki cargo pants. Each held a black Mexican Army–issued Mendoza HM-3 submachine gun in his hand. Five more men, bodyguards in identical black Italian-cut suits, knelt or stood alongside the vehicles. They wielded AK-47s, referred to as *cuernos de chivos*, 'goat's horns,' so named because of their long, curved magazines. The men's eyes and the barrels of their AKs were pointed back down the hill towards the town.

In a clearing some twenty yards off the side of the road, Daniel de la Rocha knelt in the grass, his head bowed in supplication and a tight, intense expression on his handsome face. His left hand clutched the right hand of the man kneeling beside him, Emilio Lopez Lopez, de la Rocha's personal bodyguard and the leader of his protection detail. And his right hand squeezed the hand of the leader of the assassination and kidnapping wing of Los Trajes Negros, Javier 'the Spider' Cepeda Duarte.

Around these three kneeling men, seventeen more knelt or stood close. Everyone wore matching black three-piece Italian-cut business suits, and they all carried handguns on their hips or in shoulder holsters or, in the case of the Spider and a few others, Micro Uzi submachine guns.

The twenty men were packed so tightly together they were able to hold hands, wrap arms around shoulders, or simply press their bodies close. A tight knot of brotherhood, all with heads bowed in front of a garish roadside shrine.

Daniel de la Rocha was closest to the shrine, and he took his hand away from the Spider's clutches just long enough to lift a white rose from the grass at his knees and place it at the feet of a six-foot-tall skeleton made of plaster that sat on a throne made of plywood. The skeleton's head wore a long black wig and was covered with a sheer veil. Its torso and extremities were enshrouded in a full-length purple bridal dress that shimmered in the sun even though it was partially protected from the elements by the small tin roof erected over it. The right hand of the female skeleton held a scythe of wood and iron, and her left hand clutched a lit votive candle.

De la Rocha tucked his single white rose between dozens of varied flowers and several candles, many of which had burned down to leave nothing but colorful wax smears on the cement slab below this throne of bones. Amidst the flowers and candles were dozens of other offerings for the icon: cigarettes and cash and bottles of tequila and bullets and DVDs and apples.

The skeleton sat passively amidst all this booty, stared ahead vacantly with an icy grin.

Finished with the presentation of his flower, Daniel put his hand back in the hand of the leader of his *sicarios*; he clenched his eyes tight and said a prayer to la Santa Muerte.

The Saint of Holy Death. There were hundreds of roadside shrines just like this for la Santa Muerte positioned all over the country. The icon had been adopted by the poor and helpless, and by many in the drug trade.

Daniel spoke, his voice low and reverential. 'Glorious and powerful Death; thank you for saving me today, for stopping the bullets that raced to my heart and to my throat, for protecting me from those who would do harm to my brothers and myself.

'Death Saint, you saved me today. You are my great treasure;

never leave me at any time: you ate bread and gave me bread, and as you are the powerful owner of the dark mansion of life and the empress of darkness, I want you to grant me the favor that my enemies are at my feet, humiliated and repentant.'

He continued to pray aloud, with the rest of the Black Suits clutched close alongside him, while the ten men by the SUVs surveilled the road down the hill towards the city and glanced nervously at their watches.

Nestor Calvo, at fifty-seven the oldest man in Los Trajes Negros's inner circle by over a dozen years, was tight in the scrum of prayer by the shrine, but he himself could not help but crack open an eye and steal a glance at his Rolex. He heard the sirens down in Vallarta, the helicopters circling just to the west of their location, and he knew that there were hundreds of police and military desperate to secure the bloodbath that had just taken place. Soon enough they would branch out, look for evidence or gunmen in the hills, and they would come to this place. Calvo wanted to be long gone by then. He wished he knew exactly when 'then' would be.

It was the not knowing that got to him. As director of intelligence, his job was to know things, all things, before his boss asked him a question. Since leaving the Parque Hidalgo not fifteen minutes earlier, he'd received a few quick updates from his sources there on the scene. He'd learned that many of the GOPES families had been wiped out, according to plan. But the biggest prize of all, the immediate loved ones of Major Eduardo Gamboa, had managed to escape. Surely, there was more information available at present; his mobile phone had been vibrating nonstop since de la Rocha ordered the escaping convoy to pull over at the first shrine of la Santa Muerte that they passed as they raced away from danger. But Calvo had business to attend to, and this ridiculous pit stop for the joke of a cult that his leader and the majority of his colleagues worshipped was beyond asinine.

But there was nothing he could do but stand there and wait. His *patrón* was a believer, an idolater, and separating an idolater from his idol was never a good idea, especially when the idolater signed your paychecks and carried a gun.

Daniel de la Rocha had asked the Death Saint for a sign; he knew she did nothing for free, and she had given him a great gift today. He wanted to repay her, *needed* to repay her, and he knew the white rose was nothing. What did she want from him? How could he settle up with her? He waited quietly there on his knees for three minutes. His men around him were silent; they would give him all the time he required here at the shrine. Even old Nestor Calvo, who was probably shitting in his pants right now due to the delay, knew better than to disturb de la Rocha.

It was quiet. He heard only the birds in the trees and an occasional crackle from a radio in the SUVs behind him on the road, and of course he heard the choppers and the sirens down near the ocean. But nothing else. It was so quiet he could hear the beating of his heart, and this self-awareness finally caused him to focus on the bruising on his chest and on his throat where the bullets had struck him but had not penetrated.

Sí!

His eyes opened slowly, and they opened wide. He looked down to his chest, saw the hole in the left lapel of his jacket, and in an instant he knew he had his sign. He took off his tie quickly, opened his coat and pulled it off, slipped off his vest and, under it, his hand-tailored white shirt, which barely contained the muscles in his shoulders and arms. He began to unbutton the shirt but found his hands trembling too hard to continue, so excited was he by what he knew he would find. Giving up on this dexterous task, he instead tore open the shirt; ivory buttons fired into the air in all directions like shot from a scattergun. The men clutching him in prayer stepped back so that he could get his shirt off, baring his ripped chest and back, and the holsters and grips of the twin silver .45-caliber pistols on his hips.

Daniel Alonzo de la Rocha Alvarez looked down at his body, at the single red bruise where the first bullet had struck, just over his heart. It was centered perfectly on the belly of the large tattoo of the Santa Muerte inked into his chest – the skeleton bride reached an imploring hand forward.

The belly of the woman.

Tears formed in de la Rocha's eyes.

He had his sign. He knew what his matron wanted from him. He knew how to repay her.

'Nestor?'

Nestor Calvo, the oldest man in the group, looked away from his watch quickly and answered back. '*Sí, jefe.*'

'The major's wife, she survived, yes?'

'*Sí, jefe.*'

'She is pregnant?'

'*Sí, jefe.*'

'Spider?'

'*Sí, jefe.*'

Daniel de la Rocha stood slowly, those kneeling next to him did the same, though Emilio Lopez Lopez stayed down long enough to pick his *patrón*'s coat, vest, tie, and shirt off the ground. He tossed it all to one of the other bodyguards and shouldered up to DLR.

De la Rocha stood face to face with the shrine of the hollow-eyed skull under the sheer white veil. He kissed his fingertips and reached out, pressed them to the smiling plaster teeth. 'Spider ... Find the woman. Kill the baby. La Santa Muerte has spoken.'

'*Sí, jefe.*'

A minute later they were back in the five Suburbans and headed east; DLR rode in the middle seat of the third vehicle. His suit coat was back on, though he'd left the shirt and vest and tie off. With him in the truck along with the driver were Emilio, his bodyguard; Spider, the leader of his armed wing; and a couple of Spider's best riflemen. Also riding in the Suburban was Nestor Calvo, DLR's intelligence chief and personal advisor. Daniel felt Calvo's unease. He turned to the row of seats behind him and smiled towards his older consigliere. 'What is wrong, Nestor? You don't like my visits to the skinny girl? Still you do not see the power of la Santa Muerte?'

The gray-bearded fifty-seven-year-old shrugged. 'It wasn't the Death Virgin who stopped the bullets racing to your heart. It was the one-hundred-twenty-thousand-peso Kevlar suit you are wearing, it was the tailor in Polanco who designed it, and it was my suggestion that everyone in the inner circle of the organization wear them every day.' He shrugged, bowed sarcastically. 'Apologies to the holy virgin sitting on the side of the road back there with pigeon shit on her head.'

De la Rocha laughed aloud, a roar in the tight confines of the full SUV. Calvo was funny when he was frustrated, and Daniel knew that he frustrated the man to no end, which gave him great pleasure. The leader of Los Trajes Negros actually appreciated honesty and candor from his men, but the natural order of things had all but eliminated the personal opinions of his underlings from daily discourse. He'd killed employees and associates with whom he did not agree, many times, and although he'd found it necessary to do so, he recognized that this stifled outspokenness in his workforce.

But Nestor Calvo had been his father's best friend, and Calvo was a genius when it came to the world of the cartels. As intelligence chief of Los Trajes Negros, he served as a go-between in DLR's relationships between him and the government, the police, and the military, and Calvo, therefore, knew he was immune to violent retribution. De la Rocha loved the grumpy old goat like his father, may la Santa Muerte keep his eternal soul, and he'd listen to Nestor say anything he wanted. Even if it was blasphemous.

Daniel pointed to the bruise on his throat. 'Do you see this, Nestor? Do you see where this second bullet hit me?'

'In the knot of your necktie?'

'¡Sí!'

'In the knot of your *Kevlar* necktie?'

'Dammit, Nestor, I know the tie was bulletproof, but the bullet came one inch from hitting above the tie, striking my throat.'

Nestor shrugged. 'Therefore, your conclusion is that a resin skeleton in women's clothing somehow controlled the trajectory of the bullet? If you had not insisted on coming to the rally in the first place, standing on top of a truck with a megaphone, thereby making yourself an easy target, I imagine you would not need the magic of your bony girl. Even without this attempt on your life, the hit teams Spider arranged to attack those on the dais created a dangerous environment to which you should not have exposed yourself.'

Spider Cepeda spoke up angrily. 'My men knew where the trucks would be, and they knew to keep all fire towards the dais. The man who shot don Daniel was not one of my *sicarios*.'

De la Rocha started to enter the argument, but Nestor grabbed his vibrating mobile phone to answer a call. So Daniel turned to Emilio, the leader of his protection detail, who was seated to his right. 'The man who shot me. Did you get him?'

'I think so, *patrón*.'

'You *think* so?'

'I was on the other side of the truck, but one of my men swears he killed *el chingado cabrón*.' *The fucking asshole.*

'Your job, don't forget, is to kill *los chingados cabrones* before I get killed or hurt. If I was hurt, you would be dead now. You know that, don't you?'

Emilio said, 'La Virgen de Muerte has honored us both with a gift today.'

Daniel stared the man down for a long moment, then smiled broadly, reached out, and hugged him. 'Indeed she has, amigo.'

Now de la Rocha's mobile buzzed. He looked down at the screen and answered it. It was his wife. '*Hola, Mami*. No, no, I am fine, thanks be to God. Oh, some *pendejo* tried to shoot me but he failed. Emilio and his men took care of him. How are the kids? *Excellente. Bueno, mi amor*, give them each a kiss for me. I will be home soon.'

De la Rocha hung up the phone, took a sip of water that burned going down due to the bruising on his throat.

'¿Jefe?' It was Nestor Calvo; he was putting his phone back into his pocket.

'What is it, nonbeliever?' he asked with a smile.

Calvo did not return the smile. 'That was my contact with the local cops. There was a gringo there, at the Parque Hidalgo.'

'Yes, I saw him, the old man in the blue hat on the stage.'

'No, not him, another. A young hombre with a blue hat and a beard. He killed five of our *federales* and one of the Puerto Vallarta police working for us.'

De la Rocha just stared for a long moment. His face reddened slowly. Finally, he shouted back at him. 'Six *sicarios*? I haven't lost six men at one time in two years fighting Constantino Madrigal and the government. Who the fuck was this gringo?'

Spider hung up his own phone and addressed the question. 'I've learned that he escaped with the Gamboa family. I don't know who he is, but I *will* find out.'

Calvo called out from the rear seat. 'I'm on it, too.'

'What about the families of the police assassins?'

'At least twenty dead.'

De la Rocha shook his head, still confused by the fact a foreigner had appeared from nowhere and taken down an entire squad of Spider's *federale* hit men. It wasn't supposed to go like this. The *sicarios federales* were supposed to shoot everyone on the stage and then disappear. Now there were dead police back there who could be identified. Some may even be tied to his organization. Still, he knew there would be no major investigation. The government here was in his pocket, as was the media and many officers of the military garrison at the northern end of town. This would be a mess, but it would blow over.

Anyway, he had Nestor to take care of the political fallout; that was not de la Rocha's main concern. His role in the next day or two would center on public relations.

And appeasing la Santa Muerte by killing Major Gamboa's unborn son and laying the body on her altar.

20

Court Gentry drove the church van north, out of Jalisco State and into Nayarit State. They had dropped the surviving members of other families off along the way, at the airport and the bus station and a rental car office. Everyone just wanted to get the hell away from Puerto Vallarta.

Left in the vehicle with him now were the survivors of the Gamboa family: Eddie's wife, Elena; Eddie's sister, Laura; his brother Ignacio; his nephew Diego; and his parents, Ernesto and Luz.

The van's radio was tuned to a station that reported on nothing other than the shooting in Puerto Vallarta. The reports said first eleven, then twenty-two, and finally twenty-eight people had been killed, including prominent businessman and suspected drug lord Daniel Alonzo de la Rocha Alvarez, three Puerto Vallarta municipal police, five *federales*, a German citizen, and an American citizen. Another thirty-odd civilians and police had been wounded. The initial presumption had been that after de la Rocha had been shot by either government assassins or *sicarios* from the Madrigal Cartel, the assassins, police, and bodyguards in the crowd had all opened fire on one another, causing the largest bloodbath in the nation in nearly five months.

Laura Gamboa sat behind Court and fed him driving directions and periodic instructions. 'Make a left here.' And 'It will be dangerous in front of the army base; let's take the beach road.'

And 'There will be a roadblock at Sayulita; we can get back on the highway after that.' She seemed peculiarly well acquainted with the roads and highways and traffic patterns of Puerto Vallarta, and oddly professional and in control, as opposed to the five others in the van, who did nothing but shout and cry. Court wondered if Laura was in shock or denial, or if she had just experienced enough turmoil and danger and loss in her life to where she could, more or less, take this in stride.

Elena was on her fourth phone call now. Gentry had let it go for a while, he knew her frenzy to find out who was alive and who was dead would be all consuming. But he couldn't take this flagrant security violation any longer. 'Get off the phone,' Court demanded. Elena just ignored him, kept calling friends and hospitals and clinics in Puerto Vallarta trying to find out about Eddie's brother and aunts and uncles.

So far she hadn't learned a thing from her phone calls. Only by retelling the events amongst themselves in the church van could the family get an idea about the fate of their loved ones.

'Rodrigo was killed. I have lost another son!'

'I saw *tío* Oscar; he was shot in the stomach. I think he is dead!'

'*Tía* Esperanza was right next to me; she was screaming, but she just went quiet and fell.'

'I think the Ortega family was in front of us, but they weren't in the church. I hope that they—'

'I saw Señor Ortega lying in the street; his leg was bleeding, but he was alive.'

'Capitán Chuck is dead. Did you see?'

Court did not enter the conversation; their frantic shouted Spanish was all but indecipherable to him. And his mind was on their escape.

And then his own. He had to get them home and then get himself out of here before the cops came to question the Gamboas.

Elena dialed the number of one of the other relatives there on the podium; she did not know if the woman was alive to take the call.

'Hang it up!' shouted the American behind the wheel now. She nodded but kept listening to the ring, willing someone to answer.

Court rolled down the window next to him, reached across his body, and wrenched the phone from Elena Gamboa's hand. He threw the device out onto the highway.

'Why did you do that?'

'They can track your calls. You are a target.'

'A target?'

'Yes. Those federal cops were gunning for everyone on the stage. There was nothing random about what just happened.'

'De la Rocha was killed. Why would someone kill him and then kill the families of the GOPES men?'

'I don't know. The only thing I can think is there was more than one group in the crowd. One group trying to kill you; one other group trying to kill him.' Court shook his head. 'This place is completely fucked up.'

Elena just put her head in her hands and cried.

'We need to swap vehicles,' Court said, more to himself than to the six others in the car.

'Why?' asked Elena. 'What's wrong with this van?'

'Operational security. We left the scene in this van; we need to switch it out for something clean.'

She looked around the interior. 'It's clean enough.'

Laura spoke out from the back. 'He means something that did not come from the crime scene. Joe, where are we going to get another vehicle? We passed the last rental car office back at the airport.'

'We can get whatever car we want. I have a gun, remember?'

It was quiet in the van for several seconds, only soft sobbing from Luz Gamboa in the backseat. Finally, Laura said, 'You can't steal *another* vehicle.'

'Wanna bet?'

'It is against the law.'

Court laughed, more in surprise at the comment than anything else. 'What, are you a cop?'

'*Sí*.'

'Right.' Court shook his head, kept driving. Then he slowly looked back up at Laura in the rearview. 'You're serious?'

'*Sí*.'

Elena entered the conversation while wiping her nose with a tissue. She spoke dismissively, 'She's with the tourist police in Puerto Vallarta. Not a real cop.'

Laura snapped back at her sister-in-law. 'I *am* a real police officer. My training and responsibilities are just as—'

Elena shouted back at her sister-in-law, and the two women's argument became heated. Court recovered slowly from his shock, realized Laura's knowledge of roads and roadblocks and traffic patterns made sense now. He then took Eddie's sister's side against Elena. Like a man sprinting headlong into a minefield, he entered into a squabble between two Latin women. 'The *real* cops killed a lot of innocent people today, and I saw how Laura shoots, so I'm glad she's on our side.' He looked back into the rearview mirror at Eddie's sister. 'Why didn't you tell me you were with the police?'

She shrugged. 'You didn't ask me.'

'Oh.' Just like always, he found himself having to struggle to take his eyes from her. He forced himself to stare at the road ahead.

She continued, 'Anyway, when Eduardo died, I was suspended. Many say that he acted without permission, and I would need to be investigated and cleared before I could return to work.'

'That's bullshit.'

'I know, but that's what they said. They took my gun when they took Eddie's weapons from his house.'

'You still have that Beretta you used in the church.'

She shook her head. 'No. I gave it to the padre to hold. I cannot be caught with a weapon.'

Court sighed. Neither could he, but that didn't stop him from packing one now. He wished she was still packing. He let it go, looked back up, and he and Laura made long eye contact in the rearview. He said, 'You did good back there.'

'So did you,' she said. 'Thank you.' Court's eyes flicked back to the road ahead for just a second, then back into the rearview. Laura Gamboa continued to stare at him. She said, 'Please don't steal another car.'

For a long time the eye contact continued. Finally, Gentry looked away. 'Whatever you say, officer.'

The Gamboas prayed together: Laura led the prayer, Ernesto's voice was the loudest, Ignacio mumbled, and Luz could only sob softly along with the words. After the prayer the conversation trailed off. The six surviving Gamboas stared out the window while Court drove. He himself was worn out from the exertion and the danger, and he found himself sad about the old Navy man. Cullen was a stud, Gentry recognized. He would have enjoyed another night drinking tequila with him, hearing his stories. Hell, he would have even enjoyed the old geezer chiding him about his long hair and his vague answers.

But, Court told himself, that cranky bastard went out like a hero.

And there was something to be said for that.

They arrived back at Elena's house shortly before three p.m. Ernesto immediately turned on the television and sat down, while Luz retired to the kitchen to begin dishing out leftovers from the previous evening. Heavy-set Ignacio grabbed a beer from the fridge and went out back to smoke, Diego disappeared into the bathroom, and Elena and Laura stormed around the house arguing with each other about what they were going to do next.

Court could not understand a word the two women said.

Gentry stood in the living room with Ernesto and the TV, watched news reports from Vallarta – a reporter did a stand-up in the local morgue amid rows of bodies lined up on the floor. Bloodstained sheets and blankets covered the fresh cadavers, and only the feet stuck out; paper toe tags were attached to the left big toe of each body with red twine.

There would be cops here at Eddie's house soon enough. Court didn't know what kind of police, didn't know if they would be friends or enemies. He hoped what remained of this family had the sense to leave town for a while, maybe hook up with some friends or family in another part of the country where the Black Suits weren't so firmly entrenched.

But Court's ingrained sense of self-preservation had begun kicking into high gear on the drive up the coast, and his own predicament came into sharp focus. The Gamboas weren't out of danger by any stretch, but he had his own problems. He was in the country illegally; he'd just shot dead a shitload of people, most of whom wore badges; and any police officer he ran into would likely want to have a word with him about that.

There really wasn't much left for Court to do now, he reasoned, but disappear. He did not want to hang around to await the arrival of the authorities. Despite all the bullshit sermonizing by the Mexican government about the United States' treatment of illegals, illegals caught in Mexico were not entitled to anything much more than a jail cell.

He figured the media would show up here as well. The residents of this house had been at the memorial, the six people here with him were likely the largest surviving family of those who'd been on the stage when the battle erupted, and the reporter on the television wasn't having much luck interviewing the eyewitnesses with the toe tags.

Court began moving towards Ernesto to explain why he had to run now and to wish him and his family luck. But the image on the TV broke away from the reporter suddenly and showed the Parque Hidalgo. This was clearly footage of the incident itself: the square was full, and the camera was positioned up in the square just above the street. The videographer caught de la Rocha the moment he was shot and knocked from the hood of the truck, and then it shook and spun; people moved in front of the lens; the cameraman seemed to stumble and then to regain his balance with the jostling of those all around him.

Court sat down on the edge of the sofa and watched the replay of his day.

The crackling of gunfire and wisps of gray gun smoke above the crowd, and then ... no ... yes ... *Oh shit,* thought Court.

The camera caught it.

Court groaned as the television broadcast the image of a bearded man in a blue baseball cap, wrinkled khaki pants, and a brown shirt as he used a bent iron bar to slide down a telephone wire across the street, a short-barreled rifle hanging from his chest. He dropped and disappeared into the crowd.

There was no doubt in Court Gentry's mind that right this moment, several men and women in Langley, Virginia, coffee cups in hand, would be watching this same feed on a large monitor in a darkened room. Right about now one of them would adjust his or her glasses, lean forward a tad, and say to those around, 'Holy shit? Is that Violator?'

Court knew this was happening just like he was there in the room with them. His CIA code name would be broadcast throughout the upper echelons of the agency, and everyone who had ever worked with him would get an enhanced image of that jackass with the swinging Colt Shorty zip-lining between phone poles so they could positively identify their former employee and current wearer of a shoot-on-sight sanction.

Then the SAD would come. The Special Activities Division of the CIA wanted him dead, and now that they knew where to find him, executive jets from Virginia would be landing in PV within hours, not days.

Court said it aloud; it was the only English that had been spoken in the Gamboa house that day. 'I've got to get the fuck out of here.'

He stood again to leave; it was all he could do not to break into a sprint right there in the living room.

But the TV screen changed again, away from the Parque Hidalgo. It was an interview with Daniel de la Rocha. Court assumed it was an old interview. The handsome man with the trim haircut and laserrazored goatee wore his ubiquitous black suit and black tie; he sat in a simple Catholic church at a simple wooden pew; the reporter next to him held a microphone and spoke softly, reverentially. She was pretty, and she did her best to look serious and professional, but her body language broadcast to an expert eye like Gentry's an intense attraction for her subject.

'Tell us what happened today, Señor de la Rocha.'

'I came to the park to speak out against the corruption of the attorney general's office. Their unfair persecution of me. The memorial for the assassins who were killed acting on its behalf was an outrageous—'

Ernesto sat on the couch just to the right of where Court stood. His Spanish was native, obviously, so he understood what was going on before the American. He shouted aloud, startling Court. '¡Chingado! The monster is still alive!'

No, thought Court, *no way that asshole took two to the chest and is giving an interview three hours later.* This was a live broadcast, and the smug bastard did not seem to have so much as a scratch on him. Court had seen him plainly during the shooting, both in person and just now on the television replay. He knew the man had not been wearing body armor, not even a Kevlar vest.

'After I was shot, I thought it was over for me, I thought of my wife and my little ones, but as my associates drove me towards the hospital, I said, "Hey, guys, wait a second. I don't even think the bullets went into my body." It was some kind of a miracle, thanks be to God.' He crossed himself in the Catholic fashion and then wiped tears from his eyes. The reporter handed him a Kleenex. He took it with a nod. To Court it all appeared to be an act, as if he were hitting predetermined notes of faith, sadness, vulnerability, charm. DLR smiled at the reporter. '*Gracias.* I'm sorry. It has been an emotional day for me.'

Gentry looked around to find Luz and Elena and Laura in the room with him now. Diego came in from the hallway, and even Ignacio came in from outside after hearing his father's shout. Court saw the red anger in their faces; he wished there was something he could do for them; they were in more trouble now than he'd thought.

But shit ... he *had* to go.

By the end of de la Rocha's interview he had the reporter eating out of his hand. She asked with a concerned look on her face, 'What else would you like to tell the viewers, Señor de la Rocha?'

'Government agents working for the Madrigal Cartel have tried to kill me two times in the past two weeks because I have information linking them together. I lament the incredible loss of life today at the Parque Hidalgo, but it is only the beginning if the *policía* are allowed to kill anyone they want on behalf of the *narcoterrorista* Constantino Madrigal. It is obvious to me, and I am sure to the federal authorities in Mexico City, that Señor Madrigal ordered the massacre in Puerto Vallarta this morning in order to punish the GOPES for failing to kill me two weeks ago. This tragedy will continue as long as Constantino Madrigal remains a free man.'

While he spoke, all of the Gamboas sat in rapt attention except for Luz. The sixty-five-year-old woman disappeared down the hall towards the kitchen; she came back seconds later carrying a tray with plates of fried empanadas, beans, plantains, and salad. Leftovers from the night before. Court groaned inwardly as she tried to hand him his lunch.

Laura turned to Court. 'What do we do now?'

Gentry looked behind him, back over his shoulder, to see who the hell she was talking to. There was no one else. '*¿Cómo?*' Huh?

'What now? What is our plan?'

'What are you asking me for?'

Laura looked confused. 'I thought ... I thought you would tell us what we should do.'

'I don't have any idea what you guys need to do now. I'm not even supposed to be in Mexico. I've got to get out of here myself.'

'Go? You are going to leave us here?'

'You *live* here.'

'You think we should stay?'

137

Of course they shouldn't, Court knew. But he had neither friends nor connections in Mexico. In truth he had no real friends anywhere.

'You don't want to go with me; I guarantee you that. Find someplace safe. Contact some friends who can help you.'

Elena stepped past her sister. The pregnant woman said, 'We do not know who we can trust.'

'I don't know, either. I'm not from around here.'

'We trusted the GOPES until Eddie was killed. We trusted Capitán Chuck. And we trust you.'

Shit.

Court said, 'Surely Eddie had some friends here, in the government, the army, who can protect you.'

Elena's voice rose, a growing panic in her heart as she realized the man who had saved their lives was about to hit the road. 'His unit was wiped out. It seems likely his bosses were involved in the corruption. Who can we turn to now?'

'What about in the U.S.?'

Elena shook her head. 'Eddie worked undercover for thirteen years. Almost all of it overseas. You don't make friends working undercover. He had friends in the Navy, but I don't know them. I can not just show up, pregnant and running from killers, and ask people I do not know for help.'

Court felt completely on the spot. The entire family stared at him, and he took an unconscious step backwards, bumped into the cement block wall. Softly, he shrugged. 'I ... don't know. I think you guys should get away from here. But where you go ... what you do ... who you trust? I have no idea. I can't help you. I wish I could.'

No one spoke for a long time. Gentry looked longingly across the room at the front door. It seemed miles away.

Young Diego shook his head in disgust, turned, and disappeared up the hallway. He did not understand all of the English, but he'd picked up the fact that Joe had decided to leave.

Laura said, 'You *can* help us. You *did* help us. You took charge. The shooting and everything in Puerto Vallarta. You—'

138

Court wanted them to understand. 'The shooting and everything … that's pretty much my specialty. I don't know how to do much of anything else. My plan ran out when the bad guys disappeared. You all need to just leave town. Get away from the Black Suits. I won't be any help to you with that.'

Elena began begging him to stay.

'Leave him alone,' shouted Laura, interrupting her sister-in-law. 'He is done with us! That's fine.' She looked at him. 'Thank you for everything. We'll be just fine.' Court's interpersonal communication skills were not refined enough to discern whether or not she was being sarcastic, but he had his suspicions.

Court nodded. Shook everyone's hand, wished them luck, and left through the front door.

21

Gentry walked through the *mercado* that ran along the road north of the town square in front of the church of San Blas. He felt miserable for the Gamboas, but he had no doubt that if he didn't get the hell out of here right now, he would be found and killed by the CIA or Gregor Sidorenko's henchmen or, in what was a pretty lousy *best*-case scenario, thrown into a Mexican jail for not having papers or for murdering federal police.

He justified his leaving the imperiled family behind by telling himself that his presence around them did them more harm than good. Ernesto had a good relationship with the local cops that would deteriorate if they realized he was harboring a man on the run from both the American government and the Mexican police.

And if Russian assassins dropped into San Blas? Well, that would *really* annoy the local constabulary.

They'd be okay. Laura and Elena and Diego and Luz and Ernesto. The locals would gather around them, just as they had last night, and protect them. De la Rocha had made his point with the shooting in Vallarta; the Gamboas would be in the spotlight now, so they would be safe.

As Court had explained to Elena and Laura, he *was* helpful in a shoot-out. But, he told himself, his presence was pretty much a hindrance in most other situations. He'd been on *television* for God sakes.

And the motherfucking Gray Man did *not* go on motherfucking television!

He passed the church and neared the bus station, his arms swinging freely as he moved. His canvas bag was back in Chuck Cullen's car, so he had no belongings other than a wallet and the hidden revolver with three live rounds. He passed a barbershop and a beauty supply store, kept walking for a moment, and then slowed.

A large yellow sign on the wall of a bodega caught his eye. It looked like the other advertisements around, for a school or car insurance or a soft drink.

But it wasn't.

It was very different.

'Join the ranks of the Cowboys of the Madrigal Cartel,' it said. 'We offer benefits, life insurance, a house for your family and children. Stop living in the slums and riding the bus. A new car or truck, your choice. Members of the police, the army, or the marines will receive a special bonus for joining us.'

A phone number was written below next to photos of a smiling, happy family.

Court stopped in his tracks. Read it again, checked his comprehension. Yes, he'd understood it perfectly.

What the hell? The drug cartel is openly hiring?

This place is fucking insane.

'*Narcobanderas*, they are called. Help-wanted advertisements for the cartels. *¿Increíble, no?*' An old man sitting on a bench in front of the convenience store had noticed Court reading the ad. Presumably, he noticed Court's jaw hanging open; otherwise, he might have assumed the bearded man was interested in a job for himself.

Court looked at the man. 'Madrigal can post these ads, and the police don't take them down?'

The elderly man shrugged. 'Sometimes they do.'

Thank God. Not everyone was corrupt. 'That's good to know.'

'*Sí*, the police who support DLR sometimes take down the Madrigal ads. Or else they will write on them, put a note at the

141

bottom to say the Black Suits offer a better life insurance plan than the Cowboys.'

Court shook his head in disbelief.

The *narcos* were everywhere, even here. Like a malignant cancer, the cartels' insidious reach had taken hold in all aspects of life on Mexico's Pacific coast.

He could not kid himself. Laura and Elena and the rest did not stand a chance.

But just what could *he* do about it?

Court looked up the street towards the bus station, took a couple of steps in that direction, and stopped again.

Indecision. Complete and utter indecision.

Dammit, Gentry.

After a protracted family argument right there in the living room, Laura Gamboa Corrales took temporary control of the surviving members of her family, plus Elena Gamboa Gonzalez, her late brother's wife. Laura had announced her decision that they should leave San Blas that afternoon, that they should go to a family friend an hour or so inland in Tepic. This man was a prominent attorney, and he would help them, she was certain.

Elena had tired of arguing, had acquiesced to her sister-in-law's wishes, and then had lain down on the sofa to rest her tired back and her swollen feet. At first Ernesto and Luz fought the decision to run; San Blas was their home, after all, but when Laura promised them that if *they* did not go, *she* would not go, they reluctantly agreed.

Diego had lost his parents today. He was nominally in the custody of Ernesto and Luz, but he was mature enough to make his own decisions. He could have walked out the back door and jumped on a bicycle and pedaled away if he so desired. But he stayed with the family.

He knew that his *abuelo* Ernesto was old, and he knew that his *tío* Ignacio was a worthless bum.

Diego knew that he would have to be the man. It was not an

142

easy decision for him to make. He himself had peddled Sinaloan pot to American surfers and backpackers in PV and Sayulita, so he was actually a member of the Madrigal organization, although at the absolute bottom rung of the ladder. But that was behind him now. This wasn't about money or right and wrong; this was about family, about survival. He would do whatever it took to make his family safe.

Ignacio had gotten half drunk on beer and tequila in the past hour. He agreed to go with the family to Tepic without argument. He had no family of his own, and he had nowhere to go but back to his house, just up the coast from Puerto Vallarta.

Even with four shots of reposado tequila and a couple of beers in his system, he wasn't too drunk to realize that *that* was no option at all after today's events.

Laura was satisfied that they now had a plan, but she still would have felt a lot better if Joe had stayed to help. She was disappointed in the American stranger for leaving them. He had saved all of their lives; she had not seen what he'd done in the Parque Hidalgo, but according to the news reports, someone had killed a half dozen of the *sicarios* shooting in the crowd. Laura had only shot one, so she reasoned this mysterious American must have taken out the rest.

There was an attraction there, as well, but she quelled it now that he was gone. She had not so much looked at a man in years, not since her husband had been tortured to death by the *narcos* up north. But she *had* looked at Joe. She could not say why. She wondered if it was just that he had known Eduardo in those years when her only relationship with him had been occasional phone calls and colorful postcards of faraway cities. This made her feel close to the American, almost like they were friends from the past.

And now the mysterious American had come and gone, had appeared and disappeared in the space of less than twenty-four hours, and he had taken himself out of her life.

With everything else that had happened today, she did not really understand why she cared.

She had the family prepare to leave. The six of them would pile into Eduardo's big F-350 Super Duty. Her father began packing, her mother shuffled into the kitchen to begin getting together food and drinks, and Diego took the truck up the street to fill it with gas and to add some oil.

Elena rested on the couch, and Ignacio went out back to smoke and drink.

The phone in the living room rang for the first time since the family had returned home. Elena answered the call.

'*¿Bueno?*'

'Good afternoon, Elena. How is the family?'

'Who is this?'

'My name is Daniel.'

Elena sucked in air before speaking. She recognized the voice. 'Daniel de la Rocha?'

'At your service. We did not meet formally today. I didn't get to meet your husband formally, either. Such a pity about Eduardo.'

Elena was breathless now. 'I . . . I saw you get shot.'

He laughed. 'Señora, if your tough husband, trained to murder by the gringos, could not do me in, do you really think it would be so easy to kill me? No, there is not a scratch on me.'

'Why are you calling me? What do you want?'

'I'll tell you what I want. You won't like it, but I'll tell you. I want your baby. For the crimes of your husband, your son must pay. You give me your child, and you can have your life. I will no longer threaten you or your family.'

'My baby? You will kill my baby?'

'Yes, but it is not so bad. Listen, I will make it very easy. You can go to a doctor, and I'll talk to them and explain the situation. They will take care of you and just take from you what I want. If you do this, you can spare your own life, the lives of the rest of your family who made it out of the Parque Hidalgo this morning, and you can save the lives of everyone who tries to stop me from taking your baby. Your mysterious gringo included.'

'You want my . . . child? Are you mad?'

144

'I am far from mad. I am a reasonable businessman. And I am extending you a limited-time offer. Agree now or you will regret it.'

'You *are* insane. Leave me, my family, and my unborn son to grieve for all that you have stolen from us!'

De la Rocha's urbane tone changed, turned acidic. 'Listen, bitch! *Your* husband tried to take from *me*! *His* life did not pay me back for the trouble he caused. *His* life was not worth the shit on my shoes! You give me that baby or I will kill every—'

Elena Gamboa slammed the phone down, brought her hands to her face, and emitted a shrieking cry. Laura took her sister-in-law in her arms and hugged her tightly. Began praying aloud standing right there in the living room.

'God, protect us!'

The front door opened and together the women turned towards it. It was Joe, the American. Stunned, Laura stammered in her confusion. 'Did you ... forget something?'

He nervously shifted from foot to foot. 'I can just watch over you tonight. Tomorrow if things haven't cooled down yet, I can hide out back in Eddie's boat if the cops come.'

Immediately, Elena told him of the call from de la Rocha. Luz, Ernesto, Diego, and Laura all surrounded Elena while she spoke. Court's jaw muscles flexed when the pregnant woman relayed the drug kingpin's demand for the life of the unborn child.

'Why?' he asked. 'Why the kid?'

'I don't know. Maybe because he is Eduardo's only offspring.'

'His legacy,' Court said softly, shaking his head. 'This prick is from another fucking century.' He thought for a few seconds. 'You need to run. You need to get the hell out of here right now.'

Laura said, 'We are going to Tepic. We have a friend there; he is a prominent attorney. He can—'

'No,' Court said. 'No friends. The Black Suits can track you to any friend who lives nearby. You need someplace out of the way, someplace where you can just disappear for a day or two while we figure out who is on your side.' He hesitated. 'If you can think of someplace like this ... I'll come along, just to make sure you get there.'

Ignacio scratched his huge belly and looked at Court. 'We have cousins who have a place in Mazatlan. We can go there.'

'No. No friends, no family.'

Laura stepped in. 'I know a place.'

'Where?' asked Gentry.

'It's an old farm high in the Sierra Madres, three or four hours from here, depending on the roads. Owned by my late husband's family, but they are old now, and they moved away to the city. As far as I know, the hacienda is unoccupied.'

'*That's* where we're going,' Court announced to the family.

He was back in charge.

22

If it were just Court, he would have been long gone by now, within sixty seconds after the decision had been made to head to a farm up in the mountains. But it wasn't just him; there were six others who would be making this trip, and to a guy like the Gray Man, it felt like he had a long tail sticking out of his ass, a tail that would trail way behind him, exposed and catching on everything as he moved. He couldn't just walk out through the gate in the back garden, out into the back alleyway, and disappear in the dust. He had to wait for three women, a kid, a fat drunk, and an old man to get their shit together. He'd tried to rush them at first, but they only agreed with him that they didn't have time to waste and then continued picking things up and putting them back down as they scurried throughout the house.

While Court waited, he pulled guard duty; he had the revolver with three rounds in it. He kept it in the small of his back under his shirt as he stood out by Eddie's truck. The truck was large enough for the seven of them, barely, but it was also a powerful four-wheel drive vehicle that could go off-road if necessary. It even had massive flood lamps on the roof of the cab that might also come in handy on rough mountain roads. Diego had shown Court around the cab, how to operate the controls for the lights and the winch, how to use the key fob so that he could start the engine remotely without putting the key in the ignition.

It sure as hell was not Gentry's first choice, driving around

147

in a big brash vehicle known to the bad cops who might well be targeting this family, but he'd at least had Diego change out the front and back plates with Laura's little Honda two-door. He hoped this would be enough subterfuge to get them a few hours clear of San Blas.

As Court waited impatiently for his 'tail,' he kept his eyes on the gate at the end of the little driveway. He'd only stood there a minute or two when a middle-aged San Blas municipal policewoman appeared at the gate and peered through it at him. Court remembered her from the dinner the evening before; she'd been one of the police who'd stood around in the back garden. She'd hugged Laura several times; something he'd noticed, no doubt, because he'd been staring at Laura. Court nodded at her and gave her a quick wave. She just stared back at him. Her demeanor had changed since the previous evening, and he wondered what she knew about his involvement in the events in Puerto Vallarta.

We need to go! He said it to himself, because saying it again to the Gamboas would be a waste of time.

The policewoman stepped away after a few seconds, but then another San Blas cop stepped up to the gate. This man soon wandered off as well, but not long after, Court heard a police radio squawk in the street on the other side of the wall, and he knew the policeman, and possibly the policewoman, were still standing out there. He hoped they were here to protect the Gamboa family, although there wasn't a whole hell of a lot they could do with their stupid batons if the Black Suits showed up.

A third and a fourth cop pulled up in a battered white pickup truck. The men climbed out of the cab, and like the others, they just stood out in the street. Diego came out of the house, and Gentry helped him throw two big backpacks in the bed of Eddie's F-350.

Two more unarmed officers pedaled up on bicycles and looked through the gate. Court felt like a monkey in the zoo with all the eyes on him through the iron bars. He detected nervousness in the mannerisms of the *municipales* as they looked up the drive while speaking to their colleagues. Finally, one of them, perhaps the senior man, stepped up and stared Gentry down through the bars. Court decided to find Ernesto so he could talk to them.

He stepped back inside, walked through the entire house, was annoyed to find Laura leading everyone but Ernesto in yet another prayer in the living room, so he stormed out into the back garden. Here he found the old man just sitting in the back yard, at the table next to Eddie's Boston Whaler restoration project.

He was crying, sobbing in solitude.

Fuck, thought Court, like we have time for this.

'*Perdóname*, Ernesto.' His voice was soft but imploring. 'The *policía* are out front.'

The old man looked at Gentry. Just said, 'I lost another son and two brothers today.'

The American had no response other than, 'I am sorry.'

'My daughter.'

'Laura?'

'Will you protect her?'

'I'll do whatever I can. For all of you.'

Gamboa reached a hand out and ran it across the smooth hull of Eddie's Boston Whaler. 'Please, Jose. Please help me save the rest of my family.'

'I'll watch out for Lorita. You better go see what the cops want.'

Ernesto stood, reached out, and took the American in a tight embrace. Court held himself stiff and wooden; he couldn't imagine the pain residing in the old fisherman's heart, but there wasn't a damn thing he could do about it.

Ernesto walked through the house and then out front towards the gate; Court followed him, watched his movements from behind, and saw the unbearable loss the old man had endured manifest itself in low shoulders and a hunched neck. Eddie's dad looked physically quite robust, even at his advanced age. But mentally he was frail.

The old man unlocked the gate and opened it; the heavy-framed mustachioed officer stood in front of him.

'Sergeant Martinez. Have you heard what happened?'

'*Sí*, Señor Gamboa. I am very sorry.' The two men hugged stiffly. Court remained back by the truck; he did not want his presence, and any suspicion it may cause, to create problems.

Ernesto said, 'It is not safe for us here. Los Trajes Negros tried to kill us today. We will be leaving immediately.'

The police sergeant looked up the street a moment. He then said, 'I'm sorry, Ernesto, but I must ask that you do not leave San Blas.'

'Why not?'

'Well ... the truth is I do not know. We have received a call from the director of the Nayarit state police in Tepic; he has ordered me to ask you to stay.'

Ernesto nodded. 'I see.'

The rest of the family filed out the front door now. They carried various packs and purses and boxes, straining the limits of what Eddie's pickup could handle along with seven passengers. They loaded up the truck, and Laura and Elena soon made their way out into the street to stand with Ernesto. Shortly, they were followed by the rest of the clan. Ernesto and the sergeant continued to discuss the arrangement.

The sergeant was courteous, but he requested that the family come with him and his officers to the local station, where they would await further instructions.

Ernesto thanked him for the offer of protection, but he did not instruct his family to go along with the *municipales*.

An extremely congenial standoff began to develop there on the hot street.

Gentry stepped into the crowd, anxious to get his entourage moving. *Enough with this polite bullshit*, he thought to himself. Though friendly and hardly threatening themselves, these cops, by delaying their escape from the Black Suits, were quickly becoming a threat to Court's operation. He spoke Spanish. 'Sergeant. You

150

are asking them to stay. And they are telling you no. There is nothing left to discuss. *Adios.*' He looked to the family. 'Everyone in the truck. We are leaving.'

The police sergeant said, 'Señor, *you* are free to go. We were not told to keep you here, but the *familia* Gamboa needs to come with us to the station.' He turned back to Ernesto Gamboa. 'We will protect you all there. Come this way.' The policeman smiled at them and motioned to the pickup, as if all seven of them should climb in the bed. This vehicle was barely half the size of Eddie's big rig.

'Are they under arrest?' Court asked.

'Of course not. We would just like to watch over them for now.'

'They aren't going anywhere, except with me. Now. Get out of the way.'

'*Amigo*, if you are interfering with police business, I can arrest you.'

'You can *try.*' Court stared the heavy man down, but the machismo of the officer was something that Gentry hadn't considered. Court could stomp the out-of-shape middle-aged man into the dust without breaking a sweat, but this dude wasn't going to back away from a physical confrontation.

The two men held hard eye contact. Martinez said, 'Let me see your papers.'

Gentry did not blink. 'I'm a little light on papers.'

'Passport? Entry card?'

Court just shook his head, his steely stare fixed. '*Nada.*'

'How did you get in the country?'

'I bribed one of your colleagues down in Chiapas into letting me come over the Guatemalan border. There seem to be a lot of dirty cops in Mexico.'

The sergeant's mustache twitched with a facial tick, but the rest of his body stood as still as stone. The two men glared at each other for a long time. Court could almost see the wheels turning in this man's head: *How much trouble is this gringo going to make?*

151

Ernesto stepped forward, broke the staring contest, defused the impending encounter. '*Bueno*, Sergeant, everything is fine. We accept your offer of protection. We will come with you.'

'Don't get in that truck.' Court said it to Ernesto, but the old man and his compliant wife walked towards the police vehicle. Two local cops lowered the back gate and prepared to help the couple up into the rear. Court repeated himself to Elena as she passed him in the street. She looked nervous and confused but resigned to the fact they would not be rushing out of San Blas at the moment after all.

Laura passed him now. She spoke to Gentry softly. 'These are our friends. They have nothing to do with the *narcos*.'

'But they can't protect you. If the *sicarios* come, or if the *federales* want to take you away, they can't stop them. If the state police or the army—'

Just then a rumble up the street turned everyone's heads. Three olive drab pickup trucks turned off the road from the plaza and onto Canalizo, the Gamboas' street. Standing in the beds and leaning on the cab's roof in each vehicle were two Mexican Army soldiers with bulky green flak jackets and large black G3 rifles. Behind them in the truck beds were two more armed soldiers facing the rear, their weapons trained on the street. Counting the driver and a passenger in each cab, Court realized eighteen guns and gunners had just arrived on the scene.

'Or the army,' Court repeated, more to himself than to Laura. His three .357 Magnum bullets seemed so much worse than nothing now.

The army vehicles pulled to a stop, and the soldiers climbed out and jumped off, began speaking with the six San Blas cops, who now seemed ridiculously unprepared to protect anyone, outfitted as they were with Billy clubs and baby blue polo shirts.

23

Five minutes later nothing had been settled – in fact, the situation had turned even more precarious. Another pickup full of local cops had arrived, so now eleven. San Blas *municipales* now lined up against eighteen National Defense Army soldiers. The police sergeant and an army lieutenant argued in the middle of the street, politely at first, but now the discussion had become heated.

Behind them a scuffle broke out between the two sides. A soldier had leaned against one of the *municipales'* pickups, and a young cop had shoved him off of it. The lieutenant shouted at his men, and they raised their weapons on the police.

There was enough testosterone and machismo on the street to ignite a fight as big as what went down in Puerto Vallarta earlier in the day.

Ignacio Gamboa, Eddie's brother, had been leaning against the wall of his brother's house, taking advantage of the slight shade there. When the guns came up, the big man raised his hands in surrender. When no one else followed suit, he lowered them slowly.

Court discerned from the army lieutenant's arguing that he had been ordered by his superiors at their base in Puerto Vallarta to take the Gamboas back down to PV. And the San Blas cops made it clear that they had been told by their superiors to keep the family here until the Jalisco state police could make it up the coast to pick them up and then return the Gamboas to the

153

Puerto Vallarta police for questioning about the shoot-out at the Parque Hidalgo.

The Gamboa family did not want to go with either group. Court saw that Ernesto and his family found it suspicious that both organizations represented here in the street claimed to be doing the bidding for the same organization down in PV, but their orders were, essentially, in direct opposition to each other.

Yeah, thought Court, *this is bullshit.* At the very minimum one of the two groups here fighting for control of Eddie's family was lying. It was not hard for him to imagine that *both* groups were working for *narcos* or the corrupt elements in their organizations, either directly or unwittingly. As the standoff turned personal between the two sides, as the intractable argument turned to threats and more shoving and angrier glares between the opposing forces, Gentry felt more and more certain this power struggle playing out in the dusty afternoon street had nothing to do with jurisdictional authority – it had to do with a bounty de la Rocha had placed on the Gamboas' heads, and both groups, or at least their masters, were determined to earn it.

The Gamboas and Gentry stood in the street in front of the house. The pickup was packed up and ready to go in the drive; Court even considered briefly trying to load up the family while the argument continued and simply driving away, but when the soldiers formed into squads on either side of the road, he nixed the idea. No, they would just sit here and wait to see who would win this argument, who would win the prize of the *familia* Gamboa.

The municipal police could not possibly win in a fight, but the big, angry Sergeant Martinez was nothing if not an alpha male, and he would *not* back down.

Then the distant drone of finely tuned engines rolled in from the north and filled the air. The sound continued, grew; the machines sounded like nothing else in this little town of old cars and beater trucks with slapdash motors and dirt bikes that spewed more gray smoke than a locomotive. The riflemen standing in the pickups turned their gun barrels towards the north

154

in the direction of the approaching machines but looked to one another and their commanding officer for guidance.

Court knew that if he were an outsider, it would have been comical to watch thirty-six people, none of whom had any idea who was coming or what they would do when they got here, just stand around, trying to look resolute and tough, knowing that any new attendee to this party might just change everything.

Two motorcycles turned onto Canalizo Street from Sinaloa Street, the road in front of the Plaza Mayor. Even at one hundred yards Court recognized the uniforms, the helmets, the masks, and the dark goggles of the Policía Federal. Their bikes were white with green trim, and Gentry saw they were powerful Suzuki crotch rockets; the men rumbled quickly and confidently towards the crowd that had gathered there in the street in front of the Gamboa home.

It was obvious. Even though the two *federales* were vastly outnumbered, as far as these two dudes were concerned, *they* were in charge.

Gentry had little doubt these ninja-dressed bastards were from the same unit of men he'd shot up three and a half hours earlier in Vallarta. He wondered if these two were the very same *sicarios* who had stood on the top of the stairs gunning down the GOPES families trying to escape from the park.

He thought it a good bet that they were.

'Hooray, we're saved.' He said it sarcastically under his breath. For a moment, a brief moment, he considered slipping away, backing into the Gamboas' driveway, and then ducking out the gate of the rear garden. He could leave this all behind; he could get away.

He could run.

But he did not run.

The two men parked their vehicles in the middle of the road. They wore Colt 635 SMGs on their backs, muzzle down, and black pistols in drop-leg holsters. Their boots were black and shiny; they wore sunglasses and helmets and ski masks obscuring 100 percent of their faces. They lowered their kickstands as one, turned off their engines simultaneously, and stepped off their bikes in perfect unison. They moved into the scrum of pueblo police and regular army enlistees with a calm confidence and an undeniable air of authority.

First the federal cops walked right through the soldiers, right past the Gamboa family, and right up to the sergeant in charge of the municipal police. One of the new arrivals did the talking; he spoke softly to the heavyset cop. Martinez started to argue back, but the *federale* silenced him, placed a friendly gloved hand on the man's shoulder, and continued speaking.

Martinez tried again, puffed his chest out this time, but the smaller *federale* just shook his head, continued speaking softly but authoritatively.

After no more than sixty seconds in conversation, the *municipale* sergeant nodded, turned back to the other men and women in the polo shirts and ball caps, and ordered everyone to return to their previous duties. This matter was settled.

The Feds were taking over.

It was no surprise to Gentry that the San Blas police were the first to back down. The sergeant seemed disappointed, either because he knew how angry his bosses would be with him or because he knew he would not be receiving the bounty he'd been promised by the Black Suits, but he appeared nonetheless thankful that a higher authority had come to relieve them from the standoff that had been brewing between themselves and the soldiers.

But the departure of the poorly motivated guys and girls with the sticks did not exactly fill Court Gentry with confidence. He kept his eyes on the heavy battle rifles waving in his direction.

The pickup trucks and the bicycles and the foot patrolmen melted away quickly, and the more loquacious *federale* now turned and began talking to the army lieutenant. There was arguing and shouting on the part of the soldier, but only a calm and assertive voice on the side of the law enforcement officer. Court could barely understand a word of either end of the conversation, but he could tell the ninja was saying that the Gamboa family and the gringo were to be taken back to PV, and he and his colleague would be escorting the family and the gringo there.

End of discussion.

Court had pressed his luck by sticking around, and now he was in the same boat as the rest of them. He leaned back against the whitewashed concrete wall around the Gamboas' property, next to Laura. Ernesto and Diego had walked back into the house and gotten the bench from one of the backyard picnic tables, and this they put in the shade for Luz and Elena. The old woman and her pregnant daughter-in-law sat and fanned themselves with pieces of a newspaper they'd picked up from the gutter along the side of the road.

After a long speech by the black-clad cop, Laura, who had been standing at Court's shoulder, leaned into the American's ear. 'Did you understand that?'

He hadn't picked up a word of the men's argument in the past minute. 'No, what's going on?'

'The *federale* says he is promising to tell La Araña that this army unit deserves a reward for detaining the family until he and his associate could come and take custody.'

Court thought for a moment. 'La Araña? Who the hell is "the Spider"?'

'Javier Cepeda.'

'Okay, who is Jav—'

'He is one of DLR's top men. A Black Suit. They say he is the head of his *sicarios*. DLR's assassins.'

'Perfect.'

'We are in danger, Joe.'

He wanted to say 'no shit,' but he looked at the girl, down into her big brown eyes, and he caught himself. 'We'll be okay.'

'What are we going to do?'

'I don't know yet.'

'Then how can you say we'll be okay?'

'I have three bullets. There are two cops. We go with the cops and we'll be okay.'

157

Laura's eyes widened. 'Joe ... Please do not kill them. We can disarm them and—'

'I won't kill them unless they make me,' Gentry said, but he had every expectation that they would make him.

The *federales'* bargain with the soldiers seemed to be working. It was an interesting dynamic to a man like Court Gentry – two lightly armed cops against nearly twenty heavily armed soldiers. The cops didn't finger their weapons; they didn't bark into their radios to summon reinforcements; they didn't scream or threaten. He suspected the cops were older, more sure of themselves, intimidating to the young army lieutenant, and they pressed their authority and selfassuredness against him with polite words, like a thin glove over a metal gauntlet, to enforce their will.

Court was certain they were bad men, but he was rooting for them in this little battle.

And their browbeating worked. The lieutenant told his men to stand down, to get back in the vehicles. Within sixty seconds the three loaded army pickups disappeared towards the south, turning left off of Canalizo, behind a cloud of afternoon road dust.

The two *federales* watched them leave then turned around to face the family.

Instead they found themselves staring down the gringo's pistol at a range of five feet.

The cop who had been doing all the talking spoke slowly as his arms rose in surrender. His English was excellent. 'Get your gun out of my face, *amigo*.'

'If I was your *amigo*, I wouldn't have my gun in your face, would I? Down on the street! Both of you! Facedown, arms out.'

'You need to listen to me very carefully, señor.'

'You don't eat some dirt right now, *señor*, and I'm going to blow off your fucking head. *Comprende*?'

Both men went slowly to their kneepads and then down onto the hot, dusty street.

'You don't understand. We are not regular *federales* like the men who killed the Gamboas.'

Court's eyes furrowed. 'Oh, sweet. You guys are just regular ole hit men. That makes killing you even less complicated.'

'No. We are el Grupo de Operaciones Especiales. GOPES. We worked under Major Gamboa. We came here to protect his *familia* from the Black Suits.'

Court held his revolver steady at the men on the street in front of him. 'Bullshit. Everyone in Eddie's team was killed on the yacht.'

'No. We survived. We went into hiding to protect our families.'

Court knelt over the talker. 'So where did that blood on your pants come from?' Court had noticed a speckled splatter of red on the *federale*'s thigh.

The officer made to climb back up, but Gentry pressed the barrel of the revolver into the back of his head, made the man talk with his face in the dirt; his words blew a circle clean of dust and sand on the black pavement. 'We were coming here in my car, but we heard a broadcast on the radio channel that the Black Suits use. Two *sicarios federales* were coming here to kill Elena. We killed them fifteen kilometers south of here, and then we took their bikes.'

Court did not know what to believe, but the man's tone was extremely convincing. Even though their conversation was in a mixture of two languages, Gentry detected a tone of truthfulness. But he wanted to get an impression from the other man. He knelt next to the other masked *federale*, the one who had not yet spoken. He placed the revolver's barrel on the back of his neck. 'Do you speak English?' The man shook his head. Court switched to Spanish. '*Bueno*, so what do *you* have to say for yourself, *cabrón*?'

The man did not answer, but he looked up towards Court, turned his head slowly to do so. His right hand scooted along the hot asphalt to his face, and he pulled off his helmet, his sunglasses, and then his mask.

His right cheek and jaw were black and blue, an ugly fist-sized contusion. Court thought about the man in the building under construction across the street from the Parque Hidalgo. The masked man he'd knocked out with a punch to the jaw.

'Did I do that?'

'*Sí,*' said the officer; with the swelling his voice sounded like a tennis ball was lodged in his mouth.

'Huh ...' Court thought it over. Could the man have really been there to provide protection for the family? There was no way for him to know; he had knocked him out cold before the fighting had begun.

Court just said, 'Sorry.'

'*No hay problema.*' *No problem,* responded the man, but Gentry imagined the man's jaw *would* be a problem for him for a few days.

'What's your name?'

'Martin. Sergeant Martin Orozco Fernandez.'

Looking back to the first officer, Court asked, 'How 'bout you?'

'I am Sergeant Ramses Cienfuegos Cortillo.'

'Where did you learn to speak English so well, Ramses?'

'As a boy I lived for six years in El Paso, Texas.'

'You are American?'

'No.'

'Got it. You were an illegal alien?'

Ramses looked up at the American kneeling over him. 'I prefer the term "undocumented immigrant."'

'I bet you do.'

The Mexican smiled behind his mask. Said, 'And what about you? I saw what you did today. You are an assassin.'

'I prefer the term "undocumented executioner."'

Ramses nodded. 'You are with the American government?'

'No. I'm just an old friend of Eddie's who stumbled into the middle of all this bullshit.'

'And you stayed to help?' Ramses spoke in Spanish to Martin for a moment, then directed his attention back to the gringo with the gun. 'Do you mind if we get up?'

'Slowly.' This time Court let them both rise to their feet, but he kept the pistol on them. They brushed the grit and dust from their black uniforms. 'What were you doing at the memorial?'

Ramses explained. 'We suspected there would be trouble. We just came to watch over the families of our colleagues. Martin took overwatch; I stayed down in the crowd. I saw the gunmen standing around, known operatives for the Black Suits. Then de la Rocha himself appeared.'

'And?' asked Court. He thought he knew the answer.

'And ... I shot him. Twice.' Then he added, an unmistakable tone of confusion in his voice. 'I did not miss. I don't know how he survived. Then the massacre began.'

Court believed him. This dude's eyes, his voice, his body language, it all indicated that he was as confused about what happened as Gentry. Court slid his revolver back in his pants and told the *federales* to follow him back inside Eddie's house. Everyone else had already moved back inside the gate; the Gamboas were finished loading the F-350 now, and once again, Laura was leading her family in prayer, thanking the Lord for the end to the standoff outside.

Court asked the cops, 'So you guys are just playing dead, hanging out? Doesn't sound like much of a plan.'

'We can't go to our homes; we don't want it revealed we survived. If it were known ... our families would end up just like the others today. We are dead men – we know that – but our families are safe. And if we can help protect Major Gamboa's family, that is a death we will be honored to die. If you all are leaving now, we'll go with you on the bikes to clear the way ahead. We'll have to dump the motorcycles at some point, but for now I think we are safer using them.'

Court nodded. For a moment he considered using this as an excuse to leave again. Now Elena had friends, capable men who would protect her and her family. But no, Court recognized he was only trying to help himself with this line of thinking; these guys were probably better than any half dozen regular dirty cops or cartel assassins, but there were a shitload of dirty cops and cartel assassins running around. Court could not just wash his hands of this entire situation because the Gamboas had a couple more guns on their side.

No, he'd stay alongside them as long as they needed him, and he'd work with these men.

But, he told himself, he'd keep an eye on them. Trust was not on the table.

24

It was after nine when they reached the hacienda. They'd made it on one tank of gas; Court hadn't stopped at all, and the big 4×4 had proved invaluable on the rocky mountain roads. As Laura had promised, this hideaway of hers was secluded, wrapped in a tiny valley that sheltered it from all sides. The little convoy had rolled through the town of Tequila thirty minutes earlier, then had driven through miles and miles and miles of agave farms to get here, but the terrain around the property itself was overgrown forest and uncultivated fields. Court followed Laura's directions, leading the way in Eddie's truck as the two Suzuki bikes followed, and they turned off the one-lane road, onto a gravel track that ended at a rusted iron gate under an arch made of whitewashed stones. On both sides of the arch a white stucco wall ran off into the evening darkness. Court assumed that it encircled the property. Ramses stepped off his bike and cut off the chain lock with bolt cutters he found in the toolbox in the back of Eddie's truck; he pushed open the gate, and Gentry could hear the protesting screech of the rusty hinges even though his windows were rolled up to ward off the cool mountain air.

The cops got back on their bikes and led the way now; the three-vehicle procession followed a long, hilly driveway whose cobblestones had been pushed up out of the undulating earth. Weeds grew in fat sprigs between the loose uneven stones, and the unkempt landscaping on either side of the drive brushed against both sides of the truck as they ascended towards the main building. The property looked as if no one had lived here in years; the view illuminated by their headlights showed nothing but wild flora, fallow hills overgrown with pine and cacti and cypress and lime and orange trees, flowing vines, and tall grasses.

Laura explained that all the property, both within the walls and for miles around outside of the walls, had once been a massive hacienda, an agave plantation built back in the 1820s. The walled compound was at the center of the farm, and she pointed out several ruined stone buildings back in the woods, overgrown mostly by vines and geranium and azaleas.

Soon they arrived at the casa grande, the main house in the hacienda complex. Gentry thought it looked haunted in the dark with its broken masonry and aged whitewash and pink walls. Moneda, a green ivy that grew fast and thick, wove up the structure, wrapped around columns along the long arcaded front porch, and made its way through the ironwork on the second-floor balcony, where it integrated itself into the architecture. The truck and the two bikes parked in a round gravel driveway that had an old fountain as its centerpiece. A stone angel, probably half the size of a woman, stood above the fountain; her wings were broken, and her white eyes stared Court down through the windshield of the car. He turned off the engine and the headlights. Below the angel the fountain, even in the moonlight, looked like it was full of algae and trash.

A single light appeared suddenly in a window on the second floor. It was faint and it flickered like a candle.

'Someone is here.' Court said it looking back to Laura, and her eyes widened in surprise.

'Impossible. That cannot be. No one has lived here in three years.'

Gentry stepped out of the truck and began crunching across the gravel drive. Laura climbed out as well, chased up behind him, and grabbed him by the arm. Her fingers felt tiny yet strong. Insistent. 'We need to leave. We cannot put anyone else in danger.'

'Where are we going to go? Elena has been lying in the back of the truck for four hours on bad roads. She needs to rest. We *have* to stay here, at least for tonight.'

Laura winced in concern, but she did not continue to argue. She followed 'Joe' and the two Mexican officers up crumbling steps to a huge oak and iron door. Gentry knocked, his right hand hovering over the butt of the pistol stuck in his pants.

Laura stepped up beside him. 'It might be a caretaker or some farmer from the nearest pueblo who snuck in. Let me talk to them.'

'Go for it.'

A minute later the door opened slowly; a man stood back away from it in a dark tiled hallway, and the long double-barreled shotgun in his hand was pointed at Court Gentry's chest. Moonlight reached into the building, illuminating the old man like a gray ghost.

Gentry did not draw his pistol. He understood the man's suspicion; he just hoped like hell Eddie's sister could quickly explain the situation to this old coot's satisfaction.

Laura gasped in shock, put her small hand to her small mouth. She recovered, spoke softly, '*Buenas noches,* Señor Corrales. It's me, Laura. Guillermo's wife?'

'Guillermo?'

'Yes. Guillermo. Your son.'

This dude was ancient; this much Court could tell. Much older than Ernesto. He wore a white mustache that hung low on either side of his face. By the look of it, he'd been sleeping facedown, the bristly hair shot out in random directions.

'*Sí, Señor Corrales. ¿Cómo está Usted?*'

'Guillermo is here?' The old man asked.

Laura responded softly, 'No, señor. Guillermo is not here.'

Just then another ghostly form appeared behind the old man in the shaft of moonlight let in by the open front door. The figure moved towards the doorway from the recesses of the house.

'Lorita?' The voice of an old woman.

'Inez. How are you?'

'I am fine, little one.' The old lady shot out into the moonlight and hugged Eddie's sister tightly. 'Luis, put down the gun and let them inside.'

The old man lowered the weapon, stepped forward, and embraced Court. He spoke in Spanish. 'Guillermo, my son. I have missed you.'

It was immediately apparent, by Señor Corrales's words and actions, that Laura's father-in-law suffered from some form of dementia.

Five minutes later all eleven residents and guests sat in a massive candlelit sitting room. A stairwell led to a second-floor landing that wrapped around the dim room, but it was too dark for Gentry to see past the banisters. Inez, Laura's mother-in-law, brought a bottle of fresh but lukewarm orange juice and poured it into broken cups and plastic tumblers, laid the offering out on a long wooden coffee table. A bottle of tequila was placed next to it, there for the taking, but only sullen and silent Ignacio spiked his OJ.

This casa grande was huge, but it seemed quite literally to be falling down on top of the elderly couple. Thick cobwebs hung in the darkened corners of the sitting room, the floors were caked in dust, and the old furniture, though sturdily built from big oak and cedar logs, creaked under pressure.

The ceilings were high, the floors were stone tile, the smell of candle wax, dust, and mold was prevalent in the dim air. Voices echoed when raised above a whisper. There was a monastic feel to the interior of the big home; Gentry could not imagine living in a creepy place like this.

Thin black and green lizards streaked along the walls and ceilings, appeared and disappeared in and out of the long shadows cast by the candlelight.

Court did not want to ask, but he had the distinct impression that there was no electricity in the home other than a small gas generator that rumbled outside the kitchen. Inez had

166

a little flashlight that she used to make her way to the sconces in the blackened corners of the large room. These she lit with wooden matches, giving a little more light and a spookier glow to the scene.

Luis Corrales sat in a large wingback chair, his eyes darted around the room, watching his late-night guests. Gentry could tell his mind was clearly someplace else. It didn't take Court long to realize the old woman seemed slightly off as well. Nevertheless, as Laura carefully and honestly explained the reason for their appearance, Inez seemed lucid enough to understand the predicament her daughter-in-law had put her in.

Inez Corrales invited everyone to stay for as long as they wanted, proclaiming everyone present to be in 'God's hands,' and then she led the entourage into a dim hallway, asked the group to join hands around a *nicho*, a niche built into the wall where a Cristo, a small wooden statue of Jesus, had been placed between a circle of votive candles. She took a few minutes to light them, a red glow illuminated the miniature shrine as well as everyone's faces, and then she asked Laura to lead the group in prayer. Court didn't understand much of it, probably wouldn't have been familiar with a lot of the words even if the prayer had been in English, but everyone else seemed to know the tune. He heard varying levels of conviction in the voices around him.

After the prayer Luz went with Inez to help her find a comfortable place for Elena to lie down. The bumpy drive must have been difficult for the pregnant woman, but Court noticed appreciatively that she had not complained once. She hadn't even argued with her sister-in-law during the trip.

Gentry took Laura aside while they were unloading the backpacks from the car. Softly, he asked, 'What's wrong with them?'

'Who?'

'The old couple.'

She shrugged. 'They are a little bit loco.'

'A little bit?'

'This hacienda has been in the Corrales family for over

two hundred years. Luis has lived here his entire life; he was a Jimador, an agave farmer. But he has Alzheimer's. Inez ... well, I think she is losing her mind, too. After Guillermo died they just fell apart. He was everything to them.'

'Why did you think they wouldn't be here?'

'They moved to Guadalajara, to a home for old people. But Inez tells me they did not have money to stay, so they returned here. I never would have brought us here if I knew they were—'

'It's okay.'

'It's not okay. It's not safe for them to stay here.'

'Maybe *they* can go someplace while we're here.'

Laura shook her head. 'Look at them, Joe. Where are they going to go? We have to protect them.'

'I'm not promising that we can protect ourselves. If DLR finds out where we are, he's going to hit this place hard. His *sicarios* will kill everyone to get to Elena.'

Laura looked like she was about to cry. Instead she just gazed off into the distance, out into the forest at the front of the property. 'This is their home; if anyone needs to leave, it is us.'

'Yeah, but *we're* the ones the drug lord is trying to murder, so we'll just hang out here till we figure out where we're heading next.'

Laura's expression remained unchanged. Finally, she turned to Court. Said, 'It's all in God's hands, anyway.'

'Maybe so, but if it's all the same to you and Him, I'm going to make sure all the doors are locked.'

Shortly before ten Court walked the property inside the walls with Martin and Ramses. The three of them agreed; this big, lonely hacienda in the mountains was a great place to hide, but it would be an absolutely shitty place to defend if it came down to it. The walls around the property were ten feet high, but they were covered in vines and could be surmounted with little trouble; the massive back patio and garden could be watched over from the veranda on the second level, but there were so many wild-growing plants and trees and statues on the property, along with a four-hundred-year-old stone aqueduct and a long terra-cotta trellis, that enemies advancing on the casa grande would have plenty of both cover and concealment from most any direction.

There were many buildings inside the walls. A simple stone chapel with a tile roof, a garden shed the size of many Mexican homes, and a broken-down wooden barn and stables all made this hacienda less like a walled castle and more like a tiny walled village.

It was apparent to Court that they could not stay here long. If the Black Suits found them here, then they could be surrounded, the walls could be penetrated, and the building could be overrun.

As they walked through the dark, checking the perimeter wall to make sure the gates were locked tight and there were no gaping holes, they tripped over sharp, spindly agave plants. As they did their best to find their way, Court asked Ramses, 'How did you guys make it off DLR's yacht?'

The Mexican answered softly, his voice almost lost in the darkness. 'Our role was to cut off de la Rocha's escape via the helicopter and to kill the guards on the upper deck. The major was below with a team assaulting the bedroom. All I know is that he came over the radio and said to get off the boat, that it was a trap. We were on the helipad, we both dove off into the water, and the yacht exploded. It took us ten hours to get back to shore.'

'So you guys definitely did not bring the bomb.'

Ramses shook his head emphatically. 'No. That is a *mentira* ... a lie? Yes, we were going in to kill de la Rocha. We had no plans on leaving anyone on the boat alive. This is a difficult war; our enemies do not take prisoners, why should we? But no ... we didn't swim to *La Sirena* to put a bomb on it. If that were true, we would have attached the bomb to the hull and swam away; there would have been no need to go on board.'

Court believed him, it was the only thing that made sense. Somehow de la Rocha was tipped off about the assassination attempt. 'Who knew of the attack on *La Sirena*?'

Ramses shrugged. They'd reached a large pond that came almost to the edge of the property; they moved under weeping willow trees along its far side, putting their right hands on the estate's vine-covered wall for balance on the narrow bank. 'Only Major Gamboa and the two of us, the other five on our team, plus those higher than us, not in the GOPES but in the federal government.'

'And who would that be?'

'Only the attorney general, and the special prosecutor assigned to the project.'

'So one of those two men?'

Ramses chuckled a bit while they walked. 'I can narrow it down further. Major Gamboa felt that the attorney general was working all this time for Constantino Madrigal.'

Court stopped in the dark for a moment. 'Eddie knew his boss was ordering him to do the bidding of the Madrigal Cartel?'

Ramses shrugged, but it was clear he wanted Court to understand their position. 'Major Gamboa always said, "we will never get to the last guy, because the last guy is the one who is setting all this up." He was ... what is the word? Fatal, about this.'

'Fatalistic,' corrected Gentry.

'*Sí.* The intelligence was so good, he knew the *carteleros* were using us as a proxy force. He knew that Madrigal and his Cowboys were to be last on the list of cartels, so he assumed Madrigal was pulling our strings. But we never expected to be double-crossed on the de la Rocha hit. The only thing I can think is that, maybe, the special prosecutor was in the pocket of Daniel de la Rocha.'

'So what you are saying is, the attorney general is working for Madrigal. And the special prosecutor is working for de la Rocha.'

'And we're stuck in the middle,' confirmed Ramses.

'*Exactamente,*' muttered Martin through his swollen jaw. He'd picked up enough of the English to give his take on the matter.

'You can't trust anyone in power, can you?' Court said it aloud but to himself.

Ramses chuckled without mirth. 'You just figured this out?

Well, my friend, now I can say it. Welcome to Mexico.'

Damn, thought Court. He had worked some dicey ops in his life, had dealt with some shady motherfuckers waving the flag of freedom or justice or honor or anything else to conceal their own nefarious objectives, but he had never encountered corruption so completely ingrained into a society. If all of what Chuck Cullen and Ramses said was true, which seemed pretty damn likely considering what he had witnessed and experienced in his thirty hours in western Mexico, the Gamboas had no one they could trust.

Court thought it cynical of Eddie to knowingly work under these conditions, to take intelligence from corrupt bosses with their own agendas in order to execute his assassinations. But Court understood. Those were the rules around here.

The rules sucked, but those were the rules.

Eddie had known all along that he was in peril, that he was in too deep. Court wondered if his old friend had even expected to live long enough to meet his son. There was no way to know, but it depressed Court greatly to think about that heavy weight on the mind of his lighthearted friend.

A new resolve grew inside of Court. A resolve to ... to salvage *something* for Eddie Gamble. And for Chuck Cullen. Some tiny victory, some simple bit of retribution, some finger in the eye of those who took everything from these two good men.

25

When Court and the GOPES men returned to the casa grande, they checked the building to find the best places to position sentries to look out over the property. Old Spanish architecture, like that built in Mexico in the 1770s, borrowed much from the Moorish buildings dotting the landscape of Ottoman Spain. One common feature was the *mirador*, or 'overlook,' a balcony or atrium usually covered and usually adorned with an archway, that gave a vista of the property. This building was built in a horseshoe shape, with the concave portion facing south and surrounding the expansive patio and rectangular pool. There were three *miradores* on the second story of the casa grande, giving view to the front drive, the patio and back wall, and the overgrown fruit tree orchard that ended at the wall by the pond.

Overwatch itself would not be hard here.

The men did a quick inventory of their weapons. Between the eleven people in the home, the grand total of the arms at their disposal were the two Colt SMGs carried by the GOPES, Luis Corrales's ancient double-barreled shotgun with a box of birdshot loads, two Beretta 9 mm pistols with a couple of magazines each, and a big .357 Magnum revolver with three live rounds.

They had no night vision equipment, only a couple of shitty dimestore flashlights, and no weapons that could really reach out and touch someone at a distance.

Yeah, Gentry realized, if the bad guys came, it could get ugly. If they came hard, it would be over in minutes.

A second meeting was held in the big sitting room at ten thirty. Luis Corrales had gone back to his bedroom to sleep, but everyone else was present and accounted for. Elena lay on the couch with her swollen feet elevated on a pillow and her mother-in-law rubbing them, and the rest of the group either stood against the wall or sat on dusty chairs or tables. Court passed off Martin's pistol to Laura; the police academy and her badass, overly protective brother had taught her how to shoot, and Court recognized from her actions in Vallarta that she had no problem killing bastards who needed killing. The other pistol went to young Diego. He'd never fired a weapon, so Laura took him aside and gave him a quick primer on the location of the safety and the concept of the magazine and the sights. Ignacio had not stopped drinking tequila since the first offering two hours earlier, so Court and the two *federales* decided he'd be no help in a fight. Ernesto angrily sent his forty-five-year-old son to a bedroom on the second floor.

They talked about the security situation for a while, though the Gamboas seemed to think it highly unlikely that they would be in any danger here at the hacienda. But Court insisted they needed to do their best to be ready, and after Court questioned Inez about secure places around the property, she showed the entourage a door off the kitchen that led to a steep and narrow stairwell down to a dark subterranean hallway. The hallway ended at a long stone cellar where, back when this was a working hacienda, casks of tequila had been stored. The women moved enough bedding down there for everyone, creating a hiding place and a dormitory, but only Elena, Luz, and Inez bedded down immediately.

Court approved of the cellar as a last-ditch defensive position; he saw the benefit that it was somewhat hidden and any attacking force would be forced to send all their number up a hallway that could be turned into a fatal funnel of fire from those defending the cellar.

But he also saw there was no other way out, no possible means of escape.

Fuck it, he decided. It was the best they could do here in this humongous dark house of horrors. They did not have the luxury of choice in picking their defensive positions.

Court took Luis's shotgun and kept his stolen revolver. Before heading back to bed, the old man had wandered around for a while, calling Court Guillermo several more times. In the morning who knew what he would think of what was going on around his house? Gentry was not going to let the confused old man roam the hacienda with a twelve gauge. Court had enough potential problems on the *outside* of the hacienda.

The shotgun was old and simple, and the loads it fired would only be effective at very close range, but it was better than nothing. He'd asked Martin for his submachine gun, and the Mexican officer looked at the gringo like he was out of his fucking mind.

'I'm not giving you my gun,' he mumbled through his swollen jaw.

Court didn't blame him, and he didn't bother to ask Ramses.

There was one more security issue, and it was big, and it was one that Court saw no good way to deal with. In order for them to find a way out of this mess, to get reporters to come help or honest people in the army or somebody with some authority *somewhere* to save them, the Gamboas were going to have to use a telephone. Elena would, by necessity, be calling people who the *narcos*, either directly or through intermediaries in the corrupt police, would be monitoring. He worried someone might accidentally say something to give away their location, might tip off the bad guys that Elena was laying low somewhere and that this big dead hacienda owned by her sister in-law's in-laws just might be that somewhere.

It seemed farfetched that the connection could be made, but Court had learned in his time working both for and against drug merchants that there was enough money and murder in this industry to motivate absolutely limitless amounts of labor. Enough men tracking down enough leads would, eventually, lead the enemies of the Gamboas to Casa Corrales.

And the Gray Man knew his side could not possibly win a pitched battle, so he hoped like hell he and those he would die to protect would be long gone when the bad guys came.

But that was a problem for tomorrow. He forbade anyone to use either their cell phones or the landline in the hacienda before morning, because a nighttime attack on this dark place would be a slaughter.

Nestor Calvo spent the entire afternoon and evening on the back patio that he had converted into a makeshift office. The twenty Black Suits had been picked up by a pair of helicopters owned by de la Rocha and ferried from Puerto Vallarta to a stately mansion thirty minutes southwest of Guadalajara. Here, just like at all of the fifteenodd safe houses owned by the cartel's leadership, the building and grounds were patrolled by dozens of armed guards, all with special operations military training. An outer cordon of security, all infantry trained and their fidelity to the organization proven by years of employment, drove the highways and back roads in pickup trucks. On the roof of the casa a team of guards even kept watch with antiaircraft missiles, lest anyone – police, military, or competing cartel – try to hit the property from the skies.

Calvo smoked a Cuban cigar and sipped warm Dominican rum as he typed notes on his laptop, stayed in constant phone contact with his intelligence contacts back in PV, and kept both eyes flickering up to the large television that had been brought outside from a bedroom and wired to the satellite through a bathroom window.

The intelligence chief of Los Trajes Negros monitored international reaction to the massacre, the official government response in Mexico City, and the back channels to the military and government and police that kept him in the know.

All this was the work of ten men, but Calvo kept up, and truth be told, this is what he loved. The intrigue, the negotiations, the public media stance, and the backroom threats. This was his world, and he found it intensely satisfying.

But he had another duty today, and that irked him to no end. Young Daniel, his boss, was unequivocally more interested in finding a fetus and ending its life in order to satisfy the perceived whim of some stupid idol. De la Rocha put more stock into the gaze of a plastic figurine on his bedside table than he did in the reports of his intelligence chief, and he ordered Calvo to focus on doing the bidding of the statuette, instead of doing the business of running the second-largest cartel in the region.

To this end, for this stupid fool's errand, Calvo had made and taken over fifty phone calls in the previous three hours. And even though his heart wasn't in this task, even though he found it an idiotic, unprofessional, and reckless waste of time to divert his attention, the Black Suit's men, material, and political capital to such a trivial task as the life of one unborn child – well, Nestor Calvo was nothing if not a professional, and he did his job.

And he did it well, as evidenced by the fact that he had, in fact, determined the general location of the Gamboa family.

De la Rocha shot out the back door. It was one in the morning, but he still wore his suit and his tie; his face around his trim mustache and goatee had been shaved clean for dinner with his men, so he still looked as fresh as he had when Calvo had first seen him at eight a.m. the previous morning.

'Emilio said you wanted to talk?'

'*Sí*, Daniel.'

'Tell me you have found something!'

'I have found something.'

Daniel moved closer, sat on a leather and wicker settee next to the desk. He poured himself a shot of rum from the Waterford service next to his intelligence chief, leaned back in the sofa, and crossed his legs.

'What is it?'

'You already know that the two Policía Federal *sicarios* who survived the gringo at the Parque Hidalgo were killed in Nayarit on the way to eliminate Elena Gamboa.'

'Yes.'

'Witnesses of the attack on the road said two men in PF uniforms killed our men.'

'*Federales* killed the *federales*?'

'*Sí.*'

'Madrigal's men did this?'

'I don't think so.'

'So, if it was not los Vaqueros, what do you make of it?'

'I have a theory.'

Daniel smiled. 'Of course you do, consigliere.'

Calvo nodded. 'On *La Sirena* – Colonel Gamboa's assault force was how many men?'

'Eight.'

'And how many of their bodies were recovered.'

De la Rocha nodded thoughtfully. 'Only six.' He sipped the warm rum from the Waterford crystal glass.

'*Exactamente.* Two were never found. And then today, two *federales* appear and kill our *sicarios*. My contacts in the federal police report no desertions in the Nayarit area; all men on duty are accounted for. Of course, it is still possible that men not on duty did this, but why? The only other person in the area with any control over government forces is Constantino Madrigal, but if these men were working for los Vaqueros . . . explain to me how Madrigal benefits by killing *sicarios* on their way to kill the wife of a dead PF officer.'

De la Rocha was sold on Calvo's theory. 'Constantino does not do anything that does not benefit him.'

'I agree. I think there is a very good chance that two of Gamboa's men are still alive, they somehow survived the explosion on *La Sirena*, they killed our two *sicarios*, they rescued the Gamboas from the *municipales* and the army up in San Blas, and now they are working to protect what is left of Eduardo Gamboa's family.'

'Along with some gringo, apparently.'

'Yes.'

'Okay ... so where does this all take us?'

Calvo had a road map open on the desk, he spun it around towards his *jefe*, and as Daniel leaned forward, Nestor placed a manicured fingernail on a city in the interior of the country.

'Tequila? Explain.'

'Two Suzuki Policía Federal motorcycles, just like those owned by our *sicarios*, were seen on the road near Tequila. With them was a large Ford truck, similar to the one owned by the late Major Gamboa.'

'Do we own the municipal police in Tequila?'

'*Por supuesto que sí.*' Of course we do.

DLR stood, drained the dregs of the rum into his mouth.

'*¡Perfecto!* Get them out on the roads. Find where these people are hiding. Tell Spider to put together a local force of hit men and get them in position. We will find the Gamboas, and we will kill them all right where they hide!'

Nestor cleared his throat. Drummed his fingers on the oaken desk. 'Daniel. We have made an incredible statement today. Finding the Gamboa woman and killing her is something well within our power, but what more will it achieve? Why can't we just let it go?'

De la Rocha looked out over the patio, into the night. He sighed. 'I'll tell you why. Madrigal controls a portion of the *federales*, just like he has men in the *municipales*, the *judiciales*, the state police, and I can accept that. But the GOPES? No ... these men are too clean. If they start working for Madrigal, then I must show them—'

'There is no reason to think Major Gamboa knew he was doing the work of Constantino Madrigal.'

Daniel waved the thought away. 'Gamboa *was* smart, but he thought he was smarter than he actually was. He thought he would use the intelligence of the Madrigal group and then kill Madrigal on his own. I don't like smart men who will not play by the rules. And I want to show any other man who thinks he is so pure and clean and perfect and smart that I will start by killing him, and I will end by killing everything that he has ever loved.'

Calvo said nothing.

'You will find Elena Gamboa. Spider's men will then kill her and her baby and anyone else around.'

Calvo nodded at his boss. There would be no changing his mind. *'Sí, patrón.'*

De la Rocha turned to go into the house, but he stopped, called back to his consigliere. 'And Nestor. Do not question me again about this.'

'Sí, patrón.'

26

The hacienda did not have electricity, but it did have a telephone, and it rang at two a.m., startling everyone in the home and waking those sleeping. Laura had just come up from the cellar, and she ran into the candlelit main sitting room to answer it. She grabbed it on the sixth ring, just as Court entered the same room through the door to the back patio. He'd spent the last two hours preparing for an attack that he prayed would never come.

'*¿Bueno?*'

'Good morning, sorry to disturb you so early. May I speak with Señora Elena Gamboa?'

Laura looked up to Court, her face white. She whispered, 'De la Rocha.'

Without hesitation Court stormed through the dim, crossed the dusty tile flooring of the expansive room. Laura held the phone out for him and he pulled it to his mouth.

'Tell me you speak English, asshole!' His voice boomed against the stone walls, echoed down dark, lonely hallways, and rattled old panes of glass in the windows.

A long pause, then a low laugh. 'Ah. The *norteamericano*. The one who swings like a monkey on television. How nice to finally talk to you, man to man.'

'I don't know *what* you are, but marking an unborn child for death makes you no kind of man, you sick fuck.'

'You would not understand. There is a difference in our

180

cultures that creates a wide chasm between our belief systems. Unfortunately for you, I expect you will be in the way of my objective, so you will die along with Señora Gamboa.'

Court laughed angrily, 'You talk much better than your men fight. I've killed a half dozen of your guys already, remember?'

'Yes, I heard all about your actions. You are quite good at what you do. Do you have any idea how much money you could make working for me? Listen, obviously I have found out where you are hiding. I have men outside the hacienda walls even now. You and the family are completely surrounded.'

'And we are well armed. Tell your men to come in and get us.'

The rest of the Gamboa family had entered the room, even Ignacio stood on the stairwell, leaning against the wall, listening to one side of a conversation in a language that he did not speak.

De la Rocha laughed again. '*Cálmate*, amigo. Calm down. Just listen. We will allow you to surrender, to leave. If you want, you can take everyone except for Elena out with you. We only want her.'

'No deal.'

'Then this is the last time we will speak. You will be dead before dawn, but if this is your choice, it is okay with me.'

The line went dead. Court played with the phone for a moment to check it. Yes, the landline had been cut.

'Everyone check your cell phones,' he commanded, and for the next two minutes there was a shuffling of bodies around the living area of the hacienda as the family scrambled for their phones and tried to get a signal.

No ... the mobile tower in the area had been disabled.

Shit. Gentry realized that disabling the cell phones took some manpower and some intelligence on the part of his adversary. Court recognized that they weren't going to just get hit by a couple of fat Mexican ranch hands in straw hats. No ... de la Rocha had managed to get together a decent enough crew, even out here in the wilderness.

Martin and Ramses had been on the landing; each had come

in from his post on opposite sides of the casa grande. One had been covering the *mirador* to the north, the other to the south. Court stayed downstairs in the living room, looked slowly at each member of the Gamboa family. He did not sugarcoat their situation; he only said, 'They are coming.'

No one moved.

'Where is Luis?'

'He's in bed,' said Inez.

'Can you get him to go down in the cellar?'

She just shook her head. 'No. He won't understand. He won't go.'

Court nodded. He didn't have time to worry about Luis right now. Looking around the room at his pathetic force of nine, he just blew out a sigh. The Gray Man had always been labor, never management. He was no leader. He wished he had some profound way to rally his troops, but he didn't really know what to say. It would come down to himself, Ramses, Martin, and Laura. These other poor people – well, he just hoped they didn't accidentally shoot each other in the attack to come.

Court muttered to himself. 'We're in trouble.'

Elena stood; she'd been sitting on the sofa. 'We can stop them.'

Gentry just stared back at her. He tried to say something helpful but could not think of a thing.

Inez announced she had bread in the oven that she needed to take out. Luz followed her into the kitchen, the old women disappearing before Gentry could point out to them that there were more important concerns at the moment.

He turned back to those remaining in the room and to the *federales* looking down from the landing. 'There are four trained fighters here. Only two of us have real weapons. I just have a half-empty wheel gun and a fifty-year-old scattergun, like I'm in fucking Dodge City.' No one understood the reference. They all just looked at their American protector.

In the dim he looked at Elena and Laura, at Ernesto and Diego and Ignacio. He saw eyes of trust. Eyes of hope.

Eyes of fools.

His mind raced; he thought about the impending attack and what he could do about it.

Elena said, 'Joe, don't give up on us. We may not all be soldiers, but we can all help. Everyone can do something!'

The smell of fresh bread wafted from the kitchen.

Court sighed. 'We can't fucking *bake* our way out of this, Elena!' Elena Gamboa's face reddened in anger and frustration.

Ramses chuckled on the landing above.

'Other than pelting our enemies with chimichangas, does *anyone* have *any* ideas?'

Laura Gamboa held her pistol up. '*Sí*. I have an idea. How about we just shoot all the *pendejos* when they come?'

Court shrugged. 'Well ... yeah, that's the plan, I guess.' He stiffened. 'Everyone to your positions. You know what to do.'

Court stormed past the family towards the first set of sconces and blew out the candles there.

He passed the family again in the living room as he headed to the back door. *'Buena suerte,'* he mumbled. *Good luck.* With his hand on the latch he stopped, turned back, and looked at them one last time. They stood like stone statues there in the dark, staring back at him. Luz and Inez stepped out from the kitchen with a tray of rolls.

'Come on, goddammit!' he shouted, utter frustration at their predicament getting the best of him. 'Elena, Luz, and Inez to the basement! Ernesto to the cellar hallway to guard the women; Diego and Ignacio to the kitchen to guard the basement access; Laura on the upstairs landing to overlook this room! Blow out all the candles on the way. Move! It's not that fucking complicated! And stay away from the damn windows!'

Everyone moved off in different directions and, more or less, Court was somewhat relieved to see, in the directions of their duties.

'Fuck,' he said to himself.

He looked up at the landing; Martin had gone back to his post, but Ramses looked down at him. In the darkness the Mexican officer said, 'Good luck, amigo.'

'We're going to need it,' Court replied.

And then he stepped out the back door into darkness.

There were sixteen in the first wave. They were not elite *sicarios*, but they were nevertheless cold, ruthless men, trained in the use of their weapons and well 'encouraged' by their leadership to fulfill the wishes of the head of their cartel.

In the nomenclature of the Mexican cartels, these men were referred to as *soldados*, 'soldiers,' or more dismissively as *estacas*, in this sense meaning 'fence posts.' They weren't the top-of-the-line, but they could stand there with a gun in their hand and do their job.

Their ages ranged from seventeen to sixty-one; there were two sets of fathers and sons, and two more sets of brothers. All of them had served in the army, and one of them had been an officer, and that made him the leader of this ad hoc group of killers.

These men weren't the best that the Black Suits had to call on, but they *were* the closest to the hacienda, and for that reason they would have to do. They all lived up here in the hills and mountains; most had worked together on other assignments at one time or another for Los Trajes Negros.

Three of them were *judiciales*, state police from Jalisco, and six more were *municipales* from nearby Tequila. State and local squad cars sat parked alongside the dirt track on the other side of the hacienda's back wall, alongside two pickup trucks and three old sedans.

Spider had contacted the leader of his enforcers in this region just after eleven p.m., and it had taken all of three hours to get the muscle into the area. They'd pulled down two cell towers with a chain and a truck, and then waited for a radio call ordering them to cut the landline.

Most of them carried police issue shotguns or M1 carbines, a sixtyyear-old American rifle that is still seen all over Mexico, mostly in use by security guards at banks, department stores, and the like. Though venerable compared to any current frontline rifle, it fired a potent .30-caliber bullet from a fifteen-round magazine, and it got the job done.

Just as Gentry and the two GOPES had suspected from their inspection of the terrain, the attacking force came over the back wall, dropped down into the dark.

They moved through the overgrown grasses in pairs, kept their eyes on the dark building in the distance, still fifty yards beyond the patio and the pool. They ducked down behind the few lime and orange trees growing wild in the back, and then they ran in short, labored zigzags to the statues, and ducked down behind these as well.

They were close now; all sixteen had made it to the edge of the back patio. Seventy-five feet from the colonnade, where the rear doors to the main room sat invitingly. The teams of men began a disorganized leapfrog advancing maneuver, some nearly colliding with one another, others ducking down behind planters alongside the pool.

Fifty feet now, the former army officer, the man who was nominally in charge of this array of shooters, stood and waved all forces forward. He had not anticipated making it this far without resistance and had not planned for everyone to hit the same entry point, but the patio doors were closest, and once inside the house, his men could separate and begin the killing.

The man could already count the money that Spider would give him.

'¡Ataque!' he shouted.

Then, without warning, there was the rumble of a big engine to the right of his position on the patio, on the other side of the rectangular pool. A huge pickup truck had somehow been pulled up against the outer wall of the colonnade and covered with vines, far away from the front driveway and totally hidden from view. The sixteen men stood like the statues around them for stunned, precious seconds as the high-beam lamps and spotlight rack of the big F-350 flipped on and the entire rear patio flooded with blinding white light.

The leader spun towards the origin of the light, shielded his eyes from its glare, and raised his rifle one-handed to fire at its source.

But ten feet from the tips of his boots, in the filthy black pool, a noise and a movement caught his eye.

The Gray Man had spent nearly three minutes under the water, had spent the previous ten with only his head and shotgun above the thick, greasy surface of rotten leaves. When he heard the faint whistle from Martin that the attackers were coming, he submerged, breathing through a bamboo reed with his eyes shut tight, just waiting for the noise from the truck to tell him it was time to act. Ramses started the vehicle with the remote key fob when the *sicarios* were close enough to engage.

When Court surfaced, he was careful to do so facing away from the massive flood lamps. He immediately saw targets before him like fish in a barrel, and he showed no mercy. He rose from the water, spitting the hollow length of bamboo from his mouth as he did so, leveled the long side-by-side shotgun at the first man he saw, and he fired a barrel of bird shot into the man's ample gut.

Boom!

Above him, to his right, he heard the short belching of a 9 mm submachine gun, Ramses firing from the *mirador* on the second floor. Another pistol cracked from ground level, coming from the patio door of the house. Court did not know who that was; he had assigned no one to that position.

Boom!

He fired his remaining chamber, sending over one hundred tiny beads of steel shot into the lower torso of a man in a green police uniform who spun away from him on the patio.

Splashes of water stitched close to him, and he ducked back under the lily pads to reload his shotgun while submerged. He kept the shells in his front pockets. He exchanged two fresh ones after dumping the two spent rounds, and he kicked himself into the shallower end of the pool as he did so, so he could come back out of the water at a place other than where he'd gone under.

He shot up again from the black water into the cool night air, found two targets who had just passed his location as they ran towards the casa grande, and he shot both men in their lower backs, sending them tumbling forward. Again he ducked below the surface to reload and swim to another part of the pool.

Six *matones* were down in under ten seconds; those to the rear of the attack had retreated out of the bright lights from the truck and dived back into the tall grass. But two men, both Jalisco state police, had been advancing up the right side of the pool, near to the truck, as it was turned on remotely. They fired on the vehicle with their M1s, blew out the headlamps but not the floodlights, and then ran past it as their own men began firing in their direction.

The two men made it under the colonnade that ran along the back of the house. It was pitch-black here and free of the wayward gunfire of their own forces. They ran away from the patio doors; after nearly a minute of keeping their right shoulder on the stucco wall, they found themselves turning the corner at the southwestern edge of the building. They continued in the deep dark along the stucco wall enmeshed by thick moneda vines. Far behind them the gunfire had dropped off now to an occasional crack and an answering boom.

They arrived at a window at floor level. It was locked, but one of the men used the butt of his carbine to smash the glass. He reached in and opened the latch, swiveled the window open, and stepped inside. His partner followed behind.

It was not honor or duty or glory that propelled them. It was money. It was the money they would get from this hit and the prestige they would get around their town from having their stock go up with Los Trajes Negros.

They found themselves in a darkened space, could barely make out the large oaken furniture of a master bedroom. On the other side of the window stood a large door, and it was shut. The two cops were both reasonably certain the shattering of the window-pane would have gone undetected by anyone on the other side, especially with sporadic gunfight still going on. The men stood and began crossing the tile floor to the door, were more than halfway there, when a sudden movement on their left caught their attention.

A voice in the dark. 'Guillermo? My son? Is that—'

Both men fired their M1 carbines; in the light from their muzzle blasts they saw an old man, sitting up in his bed. His chest exploded, and he tumbled off the side, rolled head over heels, and settled hunched like a heap in the corner of the room.

Ramses and Martin met up in the *sala*, both responding to the sound of gunfire in the house. The men shouldered up, with Martin in front, and they moved in a well-practiced tactical maneuver that would allow them to attack enemies to the front of them while protecting each other. They arrived at a right angle in the hall, and then, just around the corner, they heard two pops from a pistol and a woman's shout.

The two special operations group officers spun around the corner as if they were attached at the hip: Martin ahead and to the left, Ramses just behind and to the right. They trained their weapon lights on the hall and found Laura Gamboa Corrales on her knees in front of an open door, her back to them, and her pistol pointed into the darkness of the master bedroom.

Just then another loud crack and a flash of light from the bedroom. Ramses Cienfuegos flew back and down to the floor with a grunt as the air in his lungs fired from his mouth.

Martin Orozco opened fire into the bedroom, spraying the doorway just above Laura's head with 9 mm rounds. As he fired, he stepped to the right to cover his fallen partner.

His weapon emptied in three seconds, and he knelt to reload it.

But there was no more shooting from the room ahead.

Martin sprinted past Laura now, and with the light attached to his rifle he saw two dead state policemen by the open window, a wall pocked and broken and chipped from all the gunfire, and then, on the floor on the other side of the bed, the slumped form of Luis Corrales.

Laura had stepped in behind him, and she cried out as she ran past and huddled over her father-in-law.

Martin left her, returned to his partner up the hallway. He was relieved to see Ramses up on his elbows; the gringo was there, too, kneeling over Ramses in the dark. The American was soaking wet. Ramses had taken a round directly into the ceramic ballistic plate on his chest. He'd had the wind knocked out of him, but he was uninjured. The three men looked at one another and breathed a sigh of relief.

The battle was over – for now.

27

Court sat with Martin and Ramses on the southern *mirador*, all eyes were trained on the rear of the property. Court had removed his soaked shirt and replaced it with a denim jacket taken from Luis's closet, but there were no dry pants anywhere in the house that fit him. The acrid smell of gun smoke hung in the air still, soon to be replaced by the smell of the dead bodies on the patio. Court had already decided that he'd tie stone planters to the bodies and roll them all into the pool if it looked like he and the Gamboas would still be here after dawn. The sight and stench of dead adult humans no longer bothered him in the least, but morale would soon suffer amongst the uninitiated civilians here in the casa grande if they had to operate around sun-bloated cadavers crawling with bugs and iguana.

Back in the house he could hear the women crying, then praying aloud, then crying some more. Laura had fallen to pieces when she found Luis's dead body. She was obviously blaming herself for his death. Inez and Luz and Elena had covered the man with a blanket where he died, and as far as Court knew, he was still right there.

Court knew the old man's body would begin to smell by noon.

As soon as the shoot-out was over and the surviving *sicarios* disappeared again into the darkness out towards the southern wall of the hacienda, Court checked on Eddie's truck. His hopes for a quick escape were dashed when he found three of the four tires flat from the barrage of gunfire the vehicle endured after he'd turned on the lights. There were holes in the hood and grille and left front quarter panel, but the engine still ran, for the time being at least.

But that hardly mattered on a truck with only one inflated tire.

Between her sobs and prayers and moments of catatonic staring into space, Inez Corrales had told Court that the barn to the east of the casa grande held an old farm truck. The engine of the truck had not been turned over in years, but as far as she knew, the pickup was operational. Ignacio, while shit-faced drunk, was also an auto mechanic, so Ernesto sent his son out to the barn to check on the potential of the vehicle to help the ten of them escape.

Court positioned young Diego on the north *mirador* to watch the front of the property; he'd outfitted the boy with a carbine retrieved from one of the dead cops, told him to hold it to his shoulder, point it at the target, and just pull the trigger over and over until one of the professionals showed up at his side to take over.

Ramses spoke softly to the American. 'We did good. We lost one out of eleven. They lost eight out of, I don't know, fifteen or twenty maybe. Plus we got rifles and ammo.'

Court didn't see the glass quite so half full. 'Yeah, but the survivors got all the intelligence they need. They know there are just a few of us; they know we can't cover all the points of entry; they know the general layout of the house. These dudes would have been the guys DLR could get here in a couple of hours. This wasn't their A-team by any stretch of the imagination.' He sighed. 'We need to get the hell out of here. We aren't going to make it through another attack.'

'Where do we go?'

'I'm open to suggestions,' admitted Court.

Neither of the *federales* spoke.

Court was tired, frustrated beyond belief, and completely without a plan, and his frustration manifested itself in his next comment. 'So, other than yourselves, you are saying there is not one motherfucking trustworthy Mexican in Mexico?'

The accusation hung in the air for a moment.

Ramses Cienfuegos answered back finally, with the

unmistakable tinge of anger in his voice. 'I know lots of trust-worthy people. Soldiers, cops, civilians, government employees. There are many of my fellow countrymen who can and *do* die fighting against the *narcotraficantes*. But involving them in this will put them at risk. Corruption exists in all levels of every institution in this country, thanks to the sixty billion dollars you gringos spend each year to fuel that corruption.'

Court shrugged. 'Don't blame us for your civil war.'

'Like you Americans would never have a civil war your-selves, right?'

Court ignored the comment, but Ramses was not finished.

'If there was no demand, amigo, de la Rocha and men like him would have to become wheat farmers or some shit. Talk to your fucking drug addicts in the United States; they bear much of the responsibility for all this death and murder. More of my country-men would be trustworthy if only more of your countrymen weren't worthless sons of bitches who break your own laws and, by doing so, destabilize our nation!'

Court nodded in the dark. He got the message, and the message was that he was being a dick. 'Sorry, dude. I'm just pissed off.'

After a moment, Ramses said, 'It's okay. We all are.'

The three men fingered their weapons and looked into the night.

They heard the sounds of Ignacio trying to crank the engine of the truck in the barn, fifty yards off to their left. Eddie's alcoholic brother had the starter spinning up, but so far the machine would not turn over.

Court sighed. If they couldn't get the truck running, they were fucked. Even if they could, he had no idea where they could escape to here in Mexico. He wasn't from around—

Wait. An idea entered his head. 'That's it.'

'What's it?' asked Ramses.

'You said the U.S. needed to take some responsibility. What if we could get Elena and her family into the U.S.? De la Rocha doesn't own the institutions up there.'

'No, he doesn't.'

'It can't be that hard to get into the USA. Your countrymen manage to do it all day long.'

Ramses nodded. 'Last year I was in Mexico City, attached to the AFI, the federal detective force. It's like the FBI in los Estados Unidos. We discovered a gringo who worked in the U.S. Embassy's consular office who was selling papers to get into the States. We had everything we needed to arrest this gringo and stop it, but the operation was shut down. We didn't even tell the Americans what we learned.'

'Why not?'

'Why do you think? Mexico makes a ton of money from people going over the border. There was no reason to stop this guy. I figured we would probably try to help him.'

'Okay. So, you guys are shitty neighbors. How does that help us in our—'

'I know who this guy is. You can buy visas for the Gamboas, get them up into the USA.'

Court thought it over for a moment. 'What if we don't have any money?'

'I have money.' It was Laura. She'd entered the *mirador* from the second-floor hallway, sat down behind them, listening to three men she did not know forty-eight hours earlier now discuss the fate of her family.

Court turned to her. 'You do?'

'There is an army pension for Guillermo, my late husband. I am given a little money every year. I can take it all out at once if I want to, although there is a penalty.'

'How much can you get?'

'Five hundred thousand pesos.'

Court did the math in his head. 'Sixty grand?' He looked to Ramses. 'Is that enough?'

The *federale* shrugged. 'For eight people? No idea. But I'm sure it's enough to get the embassy man's attention.'

Court looked back to Laura. 'You would do this? You would give up all that money for Elena and your parents and—'

'Of course I would.' She seemed offended. 'This is my family. I would do anything for them.'

'And you'd go to the U.S.?'

She shook her head. 'They should go. My mom and dad, Elena and Diego. But not me. My home is Mexico. I do not want to leave.'

'Why not?' Court asked, incredulously.

'I just can't pick up and leave everything behind.'

'Why not?' he repeated himself, then added, 'I do it all the time.'

She looked at him a long time in the night. 'Then you will not understand what it means to belong somewhere.'

Down below them the truck tried to crank again. Gentry could hear the battery weakening, losing more and more of its charge with each failed turn of the key. After a third long and futile attempt to start the truck, those on the *mirador* heard Ignacio cussing loudly.

'¡*Hijo de puta!*' Son of a bitch!

'Well, first things first, we're still a long way from getting out of here,' said Court.

Ramses and Martin moved off to other parts of the casa grande; there was an entire west wing surrounding a courtyard near the chapel that needed an occasional patrol, as no *mirador* covered that side. But Laura sat next to Court on the veranda; they drank strong black coffee and looked out together over the back patio.

'This house is something, isn't it?' Laura said after a time.

Gentry chuckled, looked out on the unkempt estate. 'Yeah, it's a fucking shithole.'

He felt Laura looking at him for a moment, then she turned away. 'I love it. Guillermo and I were going to live here when he finished his tour with the army.'

Dammit, Court. Some time, some day, some *how*, just *try* to say something right. 'I mean ... it's nice ... just needs to be straightened up a little.'

He heard her laugh softly; it even echoed behind them in the bedroom. It was beautiful to hear, though it somehow did not fit her sad, serious, and reverent personality. 'You're right. It would have taken years to fix it up. But Guillermo wanted to take care of his parents, to restart the farm, to have kids here, and to turn it into a happy place.'

'I'm sorry about everything,' Court said.

'Me, too,' she replied.

Two hours later Ignacio was still in the barn working on the truck. Court had relieved Diego at the second-floor window above the front door on the north side of the house. Court lay prone, looking out at the tree line and the windy, rocky drive that snaked down and then disappeared past the dim moonlight's reach on its way to the front gate, a hundred meters or more to the north.

He fingered Luis's old shotgun lying on the tile beside him. He'd given the M1 carbines to the others, had taken some double-aught buckshot shells from one of the shotguns taken from a fallen Tequila *municipale*, but left the man's weapon out on the patio because the barrel had been damaged in the gunfight. Court had found another pump shotgun dropped by a fallen Jalisco state policeman but had been happy with the feel and function of the long, heavy, two-shot relic, so he decided to keep Luis's shotgun as his primary weapon.

He was sleepy, but Luz had just delivered him some more violently strong black coffee, and it would help him along for a few hours more.

He'd need it for the jolt as well as the warmth; it was below fifty degrees, and he wore nothing more than the denim jacket and his damp pants as he lay exposed to the night breeze on the balcony.

Damn, he wanted to get the fuck out of here.

Some progress *had* been made to that end. The battery from Eddie's F-350 had been pulled and brought to the barn by Ernesto and Diego; fresh gas had been siphoned out of the newer vehicle and transferred to the older. It was just a matter of time now before they all piled in like sardines in a can, raced for the front gate with Martin and Ramses leading the way on their motorcycles with their Colt Shorty's blazing, and hoped for a lot of luck to get out of here alive.

Court rubbed his burning eyes, fought sleep for the third time this minute.

He looked down at his watch: 4:06. He knew that if the Black Suits could get another crew assembled in time, then they would come before dawn. There was no way they would not; they had no reason to wait for the light of day.

It was well past the prime time for an attack in normal situations. At first the American was pleased; he hoped that by repelling the first wave his little force had caused the enemy to back off, to leave the hacienda for a while in order to regroup.

But no, that was not it at all. The three a.m. time for normally hitting an enemy position was based on standard guard rotations.

His enemy knew there were not enough here to guard this entire complex in the first place, much less rotate in and out for rest and food.

Yeah, Court realized, his enemies were smarter than he was. He had not even considered the possibility until now. They would hit again before first light. No matter how many or few there were.

Come on, Ignacio, you drunk bastard. Get that truck going!

28

There were only twelve in the second wave, but they had better training, better equipment, better intelligence, and a better plan of attack than that first failed attempt. All twelve were *marinos*, Mexican marines, and they'd driven up to the hacienda from their base in Guadalajara on orders from Spider Cepeda himself.

Though they were regular military men, they moonlighted as *sicarios* for the Black Suits. They were well trained in small-unit assault tactics and armed with HK MP5 submachine guns, flash-bang grenades, body armor, and olive drab uniforms that blended well into the green black predawn landscape of this part of the Sierra Madre Mountains. They'd debriefed the survivors of the first assault over the back wall of the casa grande. The shell-shocked 'fence posts' who'd scrambled back over the wall to safety without shotgun pellets or 9 mm rounds embedded in their bodies had been ordered to stick around to tell the next crew what they were up against. The marines began gearing up alongside their two-ton truck while the cops nervously smoked and told them all they had seen.

The military men had then given their weapons and radios a final check, broken into three four-man squads, excused themselves from the exhausted and overwhelmed amateurs, and began walking towards the walls of the hacienda.

The four men of Team A, 'Antonio' in the Spanish phonetic alphabet or 'alpha' in the English phonetic alphabet, breached the hacienda by climbing over a chained gate on the western wall, deep in the tall grass and wild blue agave. They bound towards the darkened house in teams of two, with one pair covering for the other pair while they moved. They made it to a broken-stone grain silo and approached the chapel that jutted out from the western side of the casa grande.

Team Barcelona scaled the rear wall, near the area where the first wave had gone over three hours earlier. Once inside the hacienda grounds, they pivoted to the right, climbed through the wooden fence of the corral, moved behind an old stable of rotten wood, picking their footfalls carefully to keep from stumbling over the stone and lumber and refuse.

Team Carmen breached the hacienda to the east, landed inside the grounds behind the willow trees near the pond. They moved around to the side and then to the front of the building, directed their attention and their progress towards the old stone and wood barn from where they heard an internal combustion engine desperately trying to internally combust.

Within minutes Barcelona had arrived at the trellis that ran along the eastern side of the patio. They checked in by radio with Antonio and found them in position to the west of the casa grande. This team had sent one of its men towards the freestanding chapel near the house to investigate a light that could be seen through cracks in the old stone.

Seven minutes after breaching the wall, three teams of four men were ready to hit the hacienda's defenders simultaneously from three positions.

Court rubbed his eyes again. Started to look down to his watch.

A shout from the other side of the house. A man – *Martin?*

The crack of a rifle.

Gentry's discipline allowed him to keep his position and to watch the trees and the driveway in front of him.

Only the tips of the pine trees swayed. There was no more movement on this side of the house.

Damn, damn, damn. All his training told him to hold his ground, not to turn, to trust his plan and his fortifications and his fellow defenders to each stay responsible for his or her field of fire.

If Martin's sector was attacked, Ramses and Laura would be on either side, they could see what was going on, and they could respond much better than he, here on the opposite end of the building.

Trust them. Don't leave your post. Just trust your plan.

Another shot. And then a full automatic burst from a submachine gun.

Gentry focused his worry, turned it to a concentrated stare into the dark before him.

Nothing. No movement, no attack. Nothing at all.

Trust your plan, Court.

More gunfire, more shouting behind him.

Trust your plan, Court!

An explosion. A flash-bang grenade detonating inside the house on the second floor.

Shit! Trust your plan, Court!

Then Laura Gamboa's voice. A shout.

A scream.

Fuck the plan.

Court Gentry rose to his knees, leapt to his feet, hefted the heavy shotgun in his right hand, and he turned and ran back into the house as fast as he could, leaving his post behind.

Only by pure dumb luck did he see the first assassin. Court ran into the dark living room along the western wall; the archway to the kitchen was just ahead and on his left, on his right the archway to the formal dining room. He'd planned on shooting past this room to hit the stairs to make his way to the landing and Laura's position down the hall.

But there in the dark, not ten feet ahead in his path, the black tip of a weapon's barrel appeared from the dining room. Gentry reacted in a single bound, let his feet fly out ahead of him, and he dropped to the cold stone tile like a ballplayer sliding into home plate. He slid on past the dining room's archway on his right side, his long shotgun barrel up high towards the threat. As he slid into the archway, he saw the *sicario* in the dark; the man had obviously heard a noise, but he had not yet lowered his weapon towards its source.

Court pressed his shotgun's muzzle into the marine's belt buckle as Court stopped there on the ground, pulled one of the triggers, and pumped nine .33-caliber rounds into and through the man's midsection, nearly ripping him in two and sending him flying backwards through the air behind the echoing boom and short, wide flame. His shredded body landed flat on the dining room table. There it bucked and spasmed as the electrical current from his central nervous system trickled out to his dying muscles.

Gentry rolled up to his knees before the man even came to rest on the table. He had not seen which way the *sicario*'s weapon had flown, and he did not want to waste time searching for it in the darkness, so he got back up and ran on, reloading the smoking barrel of his big gun as he reached the staircase.

He ascended three steps in a bound.

More firing, from two locations now. At the top of the stairs he turned right, heard an incredible blast ahead in a room off the hallway. Through smoke and dust and darkness, he saw Laura Gamboa backing up quickly from the master bedroom. Her pistol was out in front of her, but Court could plainly see it had locked open after firing its last round.

Court shouldered up to her, she stumbled backwards towards him in the hallway, and he caught her before she fell to the ground. At first he worried that she'd been shot, but then he recognized the telltale effects of a concussion grenade. Her pupils were dilated, and she wobbled wildly on her knees. 'How many?' He asked. Her body was small but sinewy and muscular; he helped her regain a standing position.

She recovered a little and looked at him. 'I don't know. *Marinos*. They just appeared in the hallway!'

'They are in the house?'

'*¡Sí!* They are everywhere!'

Court grabbed Laura roughly by the arm, turned, and ran back up the hall, away from the *mirador* and towards the eastern part of the house, running past the landing overlooking the darkened living room.

Gunfire in the near distance did not stop Ignacio Gamboa from making one last adjustment to the carburetor. Neither did the tears fogging his vision and streaming down his face. By the light of a single red candle positioned on the engine, he finished his final turn of the screw. He shut the hood seconds later, staggered around towards the open passenger door, and pulled the half-empty bottle of clear anejo tequila off the rusted roof of the old Dodge truck.

He took a long, gulping swig.

Cracks and snaps and pops of weapons of differing calibers grew in frequency back behind him in the casa grande as the battle intensified.

Ignacio spun, threw the tequila bottle across the barn; it slammed against the stone wall and shattered into wet crystalline shards. He then climbed behind the wheel of the old Dodge and reached for the key. With a single turn the truck fired; the engine coughed and missed here and there, but the engine's power was strong enough and constant enough to trust the vehicle.

Ignacio put his head in his hands and cried.

He had known for the last hour, all along while he worked, that he would get the truck started, he would get behind the wheel, he would put the transmission into drive, and he would drive the fuck out of here and leave everyone behind.

His parents, his sister, his nephew.

His brother's unborn son.

Nothing he could do could possibly save them. And this was the only way to save himself.

He turned on the headlights.

No one survived a death warrant by the Black Suits. Staying

with his family would be suicide, and suicide required a strength Ignacio Gamboa knew well he did not possess. He was not his little brother Eduardo, valiantly fighting his enemies and always providing for his family and friends.

And he was not his little sister, Lorita, giving of herself and relying on her faith.

No, Ignacio Gamboa had neither the gift of valor nor the gift of faith. He was just a man, just a weak man, and he was scared.

He was more like his brother Rodrigo. Weak, scared, looking out for himself and taking what others would give to him.

He'd seen Rodrigo shot through the forehead yesterday morning in the Parque Hidalgo, watched his brains blow apart. Ignacio was like his brother Rodrigo in many respects, but he did not want to be so much like his brother that he ended up dead.

No, Ignacio told himself. He would not die. He would run, and he would live!

Ignacio hadn't mentioned it to the others, but he knew a place to go where Los Trajes Negros would not get them. He had friends who lived up in Durango, in Madrigal country. There were dozens, if not hundreds, of villages there where DLR and his Italian-suit-clad soldier boys would not dare go. Yes, if Ignacio made it up into the Sierra Madres of Durango, he'd have to work for los Vaqueros, he'd have to grow pot or coke or opium, or traffic pot or coke or heroin or meth, or kill others over pot or coke or heroin or meth, but what was the big deal? Better that than ending up like Rodrigo or Eduardo.

He did not tell his family before, because they would not go with him. And he did not tell them now, because they would not go with him.

He'd go alone.

He wiped tears from his eyes with his hairy, sweaty, meaty forearm, and he shoved the vehicle into gear.

He'd planned on just smashing through the closed double doors at the front of the barn, but they creaked open in front of him. Two men appeared in his headlights.

They raised weapons towards him.

'No!' Ignacio Gamboa stomped on the gas.

The two *sicarios* opened fire with MP5s, blasting the windshield and the hood and perforating the heavy man behind the wheel, riddling his spasming, convulsing body with brass-jacketed lead as the truck rolled forwards and past them, veered to the left as his face slammed down on the steering wheel, slowed as his dead foot slid off the gas pedal, and came to rest gently against the stone fountain in the center of the driveway's roundabout.

The *sicarios* reloaded their rifles and fired again into the fat man's twitching body.

Inez Corrales was not where she was supposed to be. Thirty minutes earlier she and Elena and Luz had been in the cellar, as directed by the gringo, lying on bedding, and by the light of a single *veladora*, they had prayed and talked of their lost loved ones. But after an hour there she told the other ladies that she needed to use the bathroom, so she walked down the hallway, past Ernesto Gamboa, who was dozing on the stone steps. At the top of the stairs she passed young Diego, lying on the kitchen floor but awake, and she told him she would be right back. But she entered the living room, crossed it to a long hallway that led to the western wing of the casa grande.

She passed through a small open-air courtyard, walked down a colonnade of cool stone walls, entered a dusty storeroom on the far side, and made her way in the dark towards a doorway leading to the outside.

The night was still save for a gentle cool breeze; she followed a stone footpath overgrown with weeds and moneda vines, took this disused trail to the old chapel. She opened the rotten wooden door slowly; she dared not make a sound that would alert the American or the policemen that she had left the casa, lest they come and take her back to the cellar. When she stepped inside, she closed the door tight so that it would block out any candlelight.

She'd brought a lighter, and she used it to light a *veladora*, which she took to the little altar there on the far wall, and she knelt, slowly so that the knee rest did not creak or even snap from her weight.

She lit a few more *veladoras*, just enough to illuminate the brass crucifix in front of her. Slowly the scent of candle wax and burning wick blended with the mold and dust in the air, and seventy-nine-year-old Inez Corrales Jimenez began to pray.

Gunfire erupted outside soon after. She turned back towards the door, eyes wide in the low light, but she calmed herself.

Turned back to her duty.

She had come alone to the chapel, to pray for her husband, dead now just three hours. She would pray for him here, in the chapel where he had been christened as a boy, where they had come to light candles right after their wedding in 1957, where their own boy, Guillermo, had learned to love Jesus.

The guns outside did not change the beauty and importance of this place in her life, to her family.

She turned back to the crucifix, began praying aloud, a tall glass *veladora* clutched in her hand.

The door flew open behind her; the draft of air whipped the candlelight in the small chapel, sending long shadows across the walls in a back-and-forth jolt.

She stiffened in surprise and fear, but she did not turn back to look. Only lowered her head and quickly made the sign of the cross over her body.

A marine *sicario* shot her once in the base of the skull with a Colt .45 pistol. Her tiny, aged, frail body lurched forward across the altar, came to rest at the foot of the crucifix, the candle in her hand spun through the air and extinguished with the movement.

Diego and his grandfather lay at the top of the staircase into the kitchen, and they fired their carbines at a figure in the living room. The man had shot at them first; Diego knew with certainty neither *tía* Laura, the bearded gringo, nor the two *federales* who'd worked for *tío* Eduardo would do that, so he determined this man in the dark behind the sporadic muzzle flashes to be their enemy.

The sixteen-year-old boy and the seventy-year-old man did not have any training in such things, so they did not space themselves apart properly. Their shoulders literally touched as they fought, affording their attacker the luxury of a single target at which to shoot. Also, they did not know to cover for each other as they reloaded; instead they just fired when they saw fit, stopped when they saw fit, and reloaded when they needed to do so. This created long, dangerous lulls in the fight, during which their enemy could creep closer to find a better angle of fire.

Ernesto rose to a knee to pull a third M1 carbine magazine out of his hip pocket, he leaned to shout something into Diego's ear, and then he spun ninety degrees, dropped the rifle, and clutched high on his right shoulder. He slid halfway down the stairs on his old back, shouted from the shock of the impact, which felt as if he'd been kicked in the shoulder by a mule.

At the bottom of the stairs his wife appeared, a candle in her hand; she began climbing up to him, shrieking and crying; he yelled at her, ordered her back to the cellar, told her that he was fine.

Through the numbness in his arm and a fresh cold chill that now sloshed across his body like a high, cool wave over his little fishing boat, he began climbing the stairs again to fight alongside his grandson, reaching for the wooden rifle on his way.

Ramses Cienfuegos had fought off two men on the second-floor south *mirador*. At first he'd been alongside Colonel Gamboa's sister, Laura, but a flash-bang grenade had been tossed into the upstairs parlor from the *mirador* itself and exploded between them. Laura had stumbled back into the hallway, out of sight, but Ramses had recovered quickly enough to charge forward instead of back. He saw two men on the *mirador*, they were preparing to attack, but Ramses surprised them with his aggressive tactics. The men escaped from him by leaping over the balcony towards the patio below, and when he arrived at the railing and looked down, he saw the marines disappear into the night around the west side of the casa grande. He was certain the assassins would regroup and try to breach from the ground floor, so he sprinted to the staircase, ran down it, and turned into the hallway towards the west wing.

He ran down the hallway, passed several rooms, and then turned sharply and entered a courtyard, made of long open colonnades that formed a box around a garden of weeds with a huge garbage-strewn fountain in the middle. The open sky shone into the space and illuminated it just enough for him to see his way forward down the stone tiles. He ran towards a doorway on the far side.

He cleared the room beyond with his submachine gun, found it to be an old storeroom, and also discovered a wide open door to the outside.

He knew in an instant that the men were already in the house. Somewhere behind him.

Ramses Cienfuegos retraced his steps. He still heard gunfire on the far end of the house, but he also knew that the men he'd seen earlier could not have made it that far in such a short time. He reentered the courtyard, followed the east-west colonnade back to the east, and then turned to the north to go back into the hallway that led to the main portion of the casa grande.

As he jogged, he looked away for an instant, out into the garden, wondering if someone was hiding in the tall grasses and weeds.

When he looked back up, a man was there, thirty feet away and running up the tiled colonnade towards him.

A *marino* in full battle dress, carrying an MP5.

Both Mexicans saw each other at the same time. Both raised their weapons as their eyes widened in surprise and fear.

The *marino* fired his MP5 up the hall, spraying bullets towards the *federale*. Ramses fired his Colt 635 down the hall, spraying bullets back at the *sicario*.

Ramses Cienfuegos went down first, a hot snap into his right biceps, another to his right shoulder, and then his helmet shattered and smashed and leapt straight off his head into the air. He spun away while firing his weapon, supersonic lead arced from the muzzle and nailed the *sicario* in *his* right arm, then across his chest plate, tipping him backwards and knocking him down.

Both fell flat on their backs on the cold tile, only twenty-five feet apart and bleeding in the dark colonnade hallway. Both men's primary weapons were empty, and both men sat up and struggled to reload, encumbered as they were by their wounds and the slick blood coating their weapons and their spare magazines.

'*¡Cabrón!*' Ramses shouted as he rolled onto his right hip, ejected the spent magazine from the well of the rifle, used the same arm to retrieve a loaded spare from his assault vest, and struggled to reload.

'*¡Chingado federale!*' The marine shouted as a reply; his voice echoed in the hallway and across the courtyard. He'd given up on reloading his rifle; instead he pushed the weapon away, reached across his body with his left hand, and with a shout of pain drew his pistol from the drop-leg holster on his right hip. He fought his inertia to roll back to his left to line up a shot.

Ramses gritted his teeth against the scaring burn of the bullet wounds, screamed another obscenity at the assassin, and realized he was beaten. He struggled to pull back the charging handle on the rifle with his one good hand; he looked up to see the black pistol emerge at the end of the *sicario*'s arm, saw the assassin scoot on the tile in his expanding blood pool to get his weapon around for the killing shot.

Ramses knew he could not ready his weapon before his enemy could raise his. He could not pull back the charging handle one-handed without propping the butt of the gun on the tile, and he had no time to do this. He wore no handgun, he'd given it to Major Gamboa's sister, and without a loaded rifle he had no way to engage his foe. So he let the rifle fall to the floor, sat there on the cold tile. His legs splayed out in front of him, and he relaxed, thought of his family, and waited to die.

The marine leaning on his side ahead of him grimaced in pain as his weapon rose. He clearly saw he would get the drop on the *federale*, and his face, contorted in pain, morphed into a smile.

Ramses Cienfuegos drew a long breath and sighed. Watched his killer enjoy the moment.

'¡Come mierda!' Eat shit! Ramses shouted.

And then, as silent and as fast as the predawn breeze that drifted through the hacienda, the American sprinted from around the corner and into the tile colonnade behind the marine. He carried the long, old, side-by-side double-barrel shotgun, and his eyes were down at the open breach of the weapon. He was trying to reload it as he ran, but when he recognized the scene in front of him, the gringo's eyes widened. Ramses watched the gringo discard the two fresh shotgun shells back over his shoulder, and then the wounded Mexican *federale* watched the American toss the big shotgun into the air in front of him while he ran forward as fast as he could.

The marine assassin knew nothing of the danger behind him. He took his time to level his Sig Sauer pistol at the injured man sitting ahead of him on the tile.

The wooden-stocked scattergun spun through the air backwards, the gringo caught it with both hands around the barrel near the muzzle as he neared the unsuspecting marine on the floor in front of him. The American took hold of the weapon by the barrel, reared back as he ran, and swung the shotgun with all his might – like a baseball batter swinging for the fences, like a golfer forcing every ounce of energy behind the head of his driver – and the hickory butt stock of the shotgun connected with the back of the *sicario*'s head, just as the Mexican began to pull the trigger on his pistol.

The impact of hard wood on flesh and bone was sickening, the smack of a melon impacting the street after falling from a truck at speed. It echoed across the courtyard and blood splatter showered the tile and stucco column just ahead of where the assassin sat.

The *sicario* would have died no faster had he been decapitated.

He tumbled forward behind a spray that shone in the moonlight, and he fell on his face. His pistol disappeared under his body.

Ramses blew a long sigh of euphoric relief as the American dropped his shotgun and ran up the hall to check on him.

Just then two more *marinos* appeared behind the gringo; they made the mistake of first looking right instead of left, and Ramses saw the men before they saw their two targets. They recovered in a second though and began turning towards the left, began raising their rifles.

'¡*Atrás!' Behind!* Ramses screamed at the American while sliding his stubby rifle hard down the tiled hallway towards him. '¡*Cárgalo!' Charge it!* he screamed, and the bearded gringo understood immediately, dove headfirst with his arms out, slid forward on his chest to reach the weapon.

The cracks of rounds and the concussion of the withering gunfire of two weapons rocked the narrow hall. Stucco and stone ripped from the walls just above both men, sending sharp shards of two-hundred-year-old building materials through the air like jet-powered hornets. Gentry grabbed the blood-smeared sub gun not ten feet in front of Ramses, he rolled onto his back while racking the bolt back on the little rifle, and began firing before he'd even found his targets.

As the two *sicarios*' bullets stitched lower along the walls on either side of Court and Ramses, Gentry's return fire advanced on the tile floor, creating a fault line–like fissure that chased towards the two men forty feet on. Terra-cotta exploded in sparks and smoke closer and closer to the men, until both marine assassins reeled backwards, spinning and jolting from multiple gunshot wounds as they stumbled and died.

'Fuck!' shouted Court, but he could not hear himself. His ears rang. He kept his eyes and the sights of the nearly empty Colt trained on the two forms slumped in the smoky moonlight ahead. Behind him he heard Ramses crawling forward.

'You okay, amigo?' asked Court without taking his eyes from the gun sites.

Ramses crawled up next to Court, lay on the tile on the American's left side. Ramses spit out a mouthful of stucco and terra-cotta and sweat. He answered back in English that was delivered in some sort of poor impersonation. 'Yeah, dude. That was awesome.'

Court just laughed. He knew the adrenaline running through him would make him edgy for about as long as his ears rang. And after that he would crash hard.

29

Most of the surviving defenders gathered back in the living room fifteen minutes later. A crowing rooster told them the dawn was near, but the sky outside remained coal black.

Gentry stood, his hands on his hips, bloodstains drying on his denim jacket from his chest to the top of his pants. His beard sparkled with perspiration. He'd just returned from the driveway outside, where he'd found Eddie's brother's body lying across the front seats of the old farm truck. Wearily, he announced to the room, 'Ignacio is dead.'

'He died trying to rescue us,' said Luz.

'No doubt,' Court replied, though he had every doubt in the world. A quick glance to Ernesto confirmed Gentry's suspicion that Ignacio's own father didn't believe his son had gone out like a hero, either.

But neither man spoke up.

The five remaining members of the Gamboa family were huddled together on the sofa, sobbing and crying now. Ernesto seemed lost in space at this point; there were tears in his eyes, but he was not as energetic in his misery as were the rest. His wife diligently bandaged her husband's shoulder. Ernesto just kept his chin high and ignored the pain as he gazed off into the darkened corners of the room.

Court continued with the bad news, and Elena translated for those who did not understand. 'Ramses is wounded, shot twice,

but he's a tough little bastard. He'll fight if we get hit again.'
Ramses was in the kitchen just now, pouring clear tequila from
a bottle all over his arm and shoulder. It hurt like a bitch, but it
served as a decent anesthetic. The bandages that Elena had created by tearing bedsheets would help stanch the blood flow.

Court next looked at Laura. 'Inez is dead, too. We found her in
the chapel.' He paused. Tried to think of something 'right' to say.
'She went quick. No pain.'

Laura nodded distantly. Fatigue and shock had blunted the
blow. Court noticed she did not even cry.

Court continued. 'There's more, I'm afraid. The truck is not
going anywhere. It's riddled with bullets and smashed. And ... '

'And?' asked Diego. He held the M1 carbine in his hand like a
security blanket. He'd fired it twenty times at the man who'd been
here in this room twenty minutes prior, and although there was
neither a body nor a blood trail leading away from the room, Diego
felt like he'd protected his family by holding off the attacker.

'And when I was outside, I heard trucks out in the distance, out
past the walls of the hacienda.'

'Trucks?'

'Yes. They sounded like big armor-plated trucks.'

Laura stared through her bloodshot eyes. She understood.
Nodded. *Federales.'*

Court nodded. 'I'm going to assume they are not friendlies. A
half dozen trucks, maybe. I'm guessing there could be fifty men
out there past the wall.'

Court was as shell-shocked as the rest of them. The room just
seemed sucked dry of all life. As if even though de la Rocha's
people had not yet accomplished their mission, they had already
killed much of the defenders' will to survive.

Court searched his brain for a silver lining, no matter how
narrow the strand. Damn, he wished he was a leader, an officer, a
motivator. Fuck, just like he'd been told many times before, at this
moment he felt like he was just a 'door kicker.' A 'breach bitch.'
A 'gun monkey.'

212

Finally, he lightened a bit. 'As for good news . . . there is a little. It's almost dawn, and I do not think they will hit us during the day. They know we have a bunch of new weapons at our disposal, and they can't fight us from inside their armored trucks, so we have until nightfall to find a way out of this mess. We'll come up with something.'

Not exactly the speech Patton would have made at a time like this, Court realized.

Laura shook her head. 'Joe, you have not slept . . . you cannot function like—'

'I'll be okay.' He dismissed her with a wave of his hand. He didn't have time to talk about how he needed a nap. 'I've picked over the dead marines, and in addition to the sub guns, I found radios, a set of binoculars, and a mobile phone. They've apparently already changed their radio codes. I've got to figure the mobile will be tapped or traced, and the tower around here is down, but we can hang on to it. It may come in handy at some point.

They all discussed going to the U.S. for a few minutes, and then it was everyone back to their defensive positions. Court took guard duty on the back *mirador*, still the most likely avenue of any attack. He told Martin and Diego and Ramses and Laura to wander the house, keep an eye out all the windows as best they could, and the wounded and elderly Ernesto was ordered to lie down with Luz and Elena in the cellar. Laura gave her father a pistol to hold, to give him the honor of still taking a nominal role in the protection of his family.

Twenty minutes later Court lay on the second-floor balcony, facing east, and he watched the soft light of a clear dawn roll slowly over the forest. The white of the back wall of the property appeared slowly, as if it were being painted before his eyes on a black canvas.

Although Court did not expect a daylight attack, he recognized a new danger. With the light of day came the potential for snipers in the distant hills; anyone out on these verandas would have to remain on their hands and knees to stay below the level of the railing.

The rooster continued to crow. Damn rooster. Court's veins had been filled and then sapped of adrenaline so many times in the past twenty-four hours, he just needed to sleep now, now that it was time to begin a new day.

He heard a noise in the distance, just on the other side of the wall, and his vision cleared with a fresh rush of adrenaline. A man's shouting. Court fixed his attention on the part of the wall from where it came; he could just see the white band sixty yards from his position. Another shout, and just then something dark flew through the air, over the wall, over the jacaranda vines, and it hit the long grass, bounced high and awkwardly like an oblong ball. It rolled and came to rest in lower grasses, twenty-five yards from the far edge of the murky swimming pool.

Ramses and Martin appeared on the balcony next to Gentry. They had been 'floating' through the house on patrol, and they had seen it, too.

'What is that?' asked Martin.

Court took the binoculars he'd pulled from a dead marine and peered through them; there was not enough light for the small optics, but he could see the roundish shape lying there in the grass. '*No sé,*' he answered. He did not know.

'A bomb?' asked Martin.

'If it's a bomb, we're okay,' said Court; it was still a good distance away from the house.

'A head?' asked Ramses while picking at the bloody bandage on his arm. Everyone knew that *narcos* loved to chop off heads.

Martin chuckled. 'Did you see it bounce? That's not a head.'

Ramses chuckled, too, though he winced from the pain in his wounds as he did so. 'Yeah. It's not a head.'

Court entered into the gallows humor while he scanned the length of the wall. 'Plus, we would know if we were missing any heads. We're not, are we? Should we do a head count?'

Ramses laughed and translated for Martin, who chuckled as well. Court knew they were all near delirious from stress and exhaustion.

Court put down the optics and rubbed his eyes. Sipped the last dregs of coffee that Luz had brought him earlier.

A few minutes later the light improved as the sun rose and morning glowed over the peaks of the Sierra Madres to the east. Court took the binoculars again, squinted, cocked his head, willed the daylight to grow and show him what was there. There was no question the *sicarios* wanted him to see it. They'd called out so that someone would be looking right there when the object came over the wall.

Suddenly, his delirium-induced humor was gone; he had a deep sense of foreboding about this ... thing, out there in the grass.

Whatever it was, he knew only that it could *not* be good.

Wait ... A little more light shone on the left side of the object. It became clearer slowly. 'It's ... it's a soccer ball.' He blew a slow sigh of relief. Held some of the exhalation. Could it just be a soccer ball kicked over the wall at six in the morning?

'Is there a note on it?' asked Martin.

Court kept looking; he just needed a bit more light on the righthand side.

Laura appeared out on the back balcony. Court had no idea if she recognized the threat of distant snipers, but she mimicked the three men, dropping to her hands and knees as she crawled in from the bedroom. Her hands and knees made no sound on the stone tile as she shouldered up to the American and lay down flat. 'What are you looking at?'

Martin explained that someone had kicked a ball over the back wall. He and Ramses and Laura speculated about this, but Court was not involved in the conversation. His eyes were in the binoculars.

'What the hell *is* that?'

A little more light shone in the valley. He forced his eyes open wider to take in more light. Yes, that helped.

215

It was a . . .

No . . . not that.

Oh my God.

Gentry shut his eyes tightly.

Now he knew. He whispered to himself in English. 'What the fuck is wrong with you people?'

'*¿Qué?*' asked Laura.

Court lowered his optics and looked back towards Eddie's sister. 'Laura. I need you to find me a large plastic bag, a towel, a water bottle, and I need your cell phone.'

'The phone doesn't work.'

'Does it have a camera?'

'*Sí.*'

'Bring it to me.'

'*¿Por qué?*'

'Just do it!' he snapped at her. He was tense and angry, but he then caught himself. 'Please.' She turned and crawled off the balcony.

Ramses asked, 'What is it? What did you see?'

'I . . . I'm not sure.'

Martin said, 'It's just a soccer ball, right?'

Court climbed up to his knees, took the double-barreled shotgun in his hand, and began crawling back through the door to the second floor of the house. 'I wish.'

Five minutes later he was out on the patio, crouching low behind a planter full of azaleas. He used the overgrown landscaping and stayed as low to the ground as humanly possible to make his way back to the swimming pool, stopping every few feet to listen for the presence of human noises and the absence of animal noises. He heard chirping birds and even the croaking of frogs at the pool, and this relaxed him a little. He was reasonably certain he was the only person in the back garden of the hacienda, and he used this confidence to propel himself onwards. If the *sicarios* came over the wall, still forty yards away from him, he was well aware he would be fucked. They'd be able to see him lying there in the grass. He only had a weapon that fired two shots without reloading, and reloading from a pocket full of shotgun shells would not be terribly efficient.

He carried the gun as a last resort, but he knew, the last thing he wanted to get involved with right now was a gunfight. Ramses and Martin were up on the *mirador*, covering him with the MP5s taken from fallen marines, but otherwise, he was on his own.

He passed several bodies from de la Rocha's first two waves of killers. Court, Martin, and Ramses had already picked the corpses clean of any useful equipment or intelligence, so he only used them now for concealment as he crawled across the patio, alongside the smelly pool full of mosquitoes and frogs, the pool he'd swam in five hours earlier.

He heard voices again on the other side of the wall. A loud shout, a cackle, like a laugh from an insane person, and he halted his low crawl. It did not take him more than a few seconds to recognize that they would not attack – who would divulge their location only to then come over the wall, exposed to the defenders that they had just alerted? No, Court understood, they were trying to get the attention of the defenders of the hacienda so that they would notice the thing they'd slung over the wall fifteen minutes earlier.

This worried Gentry almost as much as a direct attack.

He started moving again, covered the cold tile a little more quickly now, though he did not actually want to arrive at his destination. He had seen enough through the lenses of the binoculars to understand what he would find. He'd brought along the bag sticking out of the waistband of his pants and the water bottle rolling around inside it as well as the camera in his back pocket for a reason.

He'd brought the binoculars with him as well. Not because he would need them here, crawling along the patio on his belly like a grass snake. No ... he took them because he did not want those back at the casa to see the soccer ball. To see what he was doing. He'd do this alone, make the best of a terrible situation, and then explain the terrible situation to those back at the house as best he could.

Morale was crucial for a population under siege, morale had become terrible in this house of death, and now, Gentry was pretty sure, morale was about to go straight down the goddamned motherfucking toilet.

He entered the tall grass, passed more bodies of corrupt policemen and low-rent civilian killers, and went on towards the object lying in the grass ahead.

Due to literally hundreds of experiences in his life and the things he had seen during those experiences, Court Gentry was a man who, simply put, was almost impossible to gross out. But his face tightened as he reached the ball in the grass, his body recoiled slightly as he noticed the blood smeared on the ground next to it, and his hand did not want to reach out and roll it closer to him. But he did; he extended his arm and put his fingertips on the ball and pulled it to him. His hand felt something cold and soft as he did this, and he almost vomited there in the grass. He steeled himself as he brought the ball in close and looked at it.

The loose and slack face of a human being, a young man, had been sewn with thick black leather thread onto the ball, which was smeared with blood, scuffed with grass stains. There was a tuft of turf lodged into one of the hollow eye sockets. He had no idea who the face was, but he was certain that someone back at the house would know.

This would not be some random local chopped up and made into a grisly toy.

No, this would be someone's loved one.

Someone's family.

This was a message. Give up, come out, or everyone you love will die.

Court put the ball in the bag, rose to his knees, and sprinted low back towards a dilapidated stone garden shed. Inside it was moldy and dark; he left the door open to give him enough light to work with, and he took the ball with the face sewn to it, and washed it with the water from the plastic bottle. He then took the towel and blotted the face as clean and dry as possible. Doing this nearly sickened him, but he saw no other alternative to his plan. When the face was as clean as he could make it, one could not possibly call it 'presentable'; he looked it over a long time. It was only semi-recognizable as being part of a human; the sewing had torn off along the forehead and a flap of skin hung down; Court pressed it back where it belonged. The chin was extended down a little too tightly, pulling the face out of normal proportion like the opposite of a bad facelift.

Gentry groaned, fought a third wave of nausea, and pulled out the camera phone.

Ten minutes later he was back in the huge sitting room of the casa. He'd positioned Martin on the rear *mirador* and Ramses at the front door; each man now was responsible for one hundred eighty degrees of territory, which was far from ideal, but Court knew that he needed to get the Gamboa family together. Court sat on a chair in front of Elena, Laura, Ernesto, Luz, and Diego.

It had occurred to him that he should just keep this information to himself, to not completely kill the spirit of those in the house by giving someone terrible news. But information was important. There was so little of it right now, and he needed to know who had been discovered by the *sicarios* and killed. Was he an informant, someone whose death might shine some sort of light on who the enemies and the friends were in this struggle?

No, Court decided, this was a secret too important to keep.

Court knew there was no chance in hell that he would say the right things right now, that he would break anything to anyone in any sort of way that could be construed as comforting or kind. He told himself that he was not trained to provide comfort and that there was no sense in wasting time on pleasantries when there were matters of life or death to attend to.

But it was not lost on the American assassin that this was just an excuse he used to avoid even trying to communicate with other human beings in a normal, compassionate fashion.

He decided that now, for the good of this operation, he would, at least, give an effort in delivering this news in the best way possible.

'We've been given a message.'

'What kind of message?' Elena asked, and Court worried that she would be the one who knew the dead dude on the soccer ball and that the shock might somehow affect her pregnancy. He couldn't help it, he told himself now. He felt his body tightening, leaving the plan of the gentle delivery behind.

'Look. I'm sorry, but I'm just going to say it. Some hombre has been killed by the *sicarios*; his face has been cut off and sewn onto a soccer ball. The ball was kicked over the back wall, and right now it is in a bag in the garden shed; it's up high, and it's safe from animals. I took a picture of the face in case one of you is able to identify it.' He hesitated. 'I mean ... identify *him*.'

The family just sat there. Stared at him blankly.

'It's going to be someone who means a lot to one of you. Maybe all of you. I'm sorry.'

His audience understood the significance now, and the fresh worry turned faces already contorted by stress into masks of horror and pain. But Ernesto nodded, said softly, 'Show it to me. If I don't know who it is, I will pass it on. There is no use in everyone looking if they do not have to.'

Court nodded, pulled up the image on the camera phone, and handed it to Eddie's dad.

The old man's wrinkles deepened a bit, but he showed no other emotion. He turned the phone to the right and then to the left with his left hand; his right hand was useless to him now because of the wound on his right shoulder. He took a long time trying to discern a face in the stretched strip of flesh affixed to the ball. After a long moment, a moment in which, Gentry saw, the man wanted to save the rest of his family the pain of having to look, he just shrugged.

'*Lo siento,*' *I'm sorry*, he said. 'I do not know this young man.'

Diego reached out and took the phone from his grandfather. He put a hand to his mouth in shock but took it away, did his best to recover; his young machismo was bruised by what he obviously considered a display of weakness.

After ten seconds he said, 'I don't know.'

Luz Gamboa took the camera, looked, and quickly passed it on. The brown bags under her eyes, days of sadness and stress and lack of sleep, seemed to tighten some, but she shook her head. Then it was Laura's turn, and she did not cry, but her face reddened. She crossed herself and mouthed a silent prayer for the dead man. But she did not know who it was.

Elena was last. Everyone wanted to protect her, but she took the camera and looked at the image. She sobbed softly but shook her head.

Shit, thought Court. It *has* to be someone; why go to all the trouble if we don't even know the poor bastard? He asked everyone to make sure, to look again; he found himself pissed off that they couldn't figure out who'd been murdered just to get to them.

But no, no one in the room knew the face.

He wondered if it could have been someone related to the Corraleses. The Black Suits could not know for sure who had been killed in the house, maybe they just—

No. That's not it.

It dawned on him slowly; he wished he'd considered it before forcing the poor people in front of him to look again. But he thought of it now, so he sent Laura up to Ramses's position and Diego to Martin's post. He told Elena and Luz and Ernesto to go to the cellar and try and get some rest.

A minute later the two GOPES officers sat in front of him. Court explained the situation, and both men understood. Ramses took the camera roughly from the American, held it in his good arm, looked at it while Martin stared over his shoulder. Court just watched their faces; he caught himself wanting to see recognition from one of the hardened military men.

And he got his wish. Martin Orozco's face reddened and his eyes shuddered, lowered as his mind left the present and thought back on a memory. Gentry could see it all in his face. It was someone he knew, someone close, someone he'd known for a long time.

A loved one. Just from the expressions on Martin's face Gentry said, softly, 'He's your brother.'

'Pablito.' Martin sobbed the name. Tears ran freely from his eyes as he muttered, in Spanish, 'Oh my God, the sons of whores killed my little brother.' The federal commando's face flickered between rage and horror and utter despair. 'He is just ... he was just a merchant in Cuernavaca. He was not a soldier ... He was nothing to them.'

Ramses Cienfuegos hugged his compadre with his uninjured arm, shook his head in sadness and disgust.

'But you are something to them,' said Court. 'You are here.'

Martin nodded, his face distant.

'They know you are alive.' He turned to Ramses. 'Which means they probably—'

'Know I am alive, too,' Ramses said it gravely. Court could only imagine what was going on in his head. Surely, he was thinking of a wife, brothers, sisters, parents, children.

Times like these Court Gentry appreciated being alone.

'Those *pendejos* are going to pay,' Martin said, still looking at the photo of his young brother's torn face.

Gentry thought over the situation for a moment as he took back the cell phone. He quickly made a determination and put his hand gently on Martin's shoulder. 'Listen carefully, amigo. I need you to leave. I need you to go protect the rest of your family.'

The Mexican shook his head forcefully. 'No. I am here to protect Major Gamboa's—'

'You *know* that you are compromised. If they can get to one member of your family, they can get to them all. I can't have you in here, thinking about what's going on out there. I can't worry they will do something that will make you turn on us—'

'I will never—'

222

'I believe you. I believe *you* believe. But I will not allow you to stay in this operation. You can best help this operation by getting away, taking away the leverage of the enemy. You *know* that, my friend.'

Martin understood. Nodded slowly.

'You need to try and escape immediately,' Court said.

Martin nodded. His eyes remained distant. 'Thank you.'

Court looked to Ramses now. 'You, too, amigo. If they know Martin survived the yacht explosion, then they probably know you did, too. They can't patrol the entire perimeter all the time; if you can make it to the wall without being seen, if you guys go to opposite sides of the hacienda, you can wait for the right moment to climb over and make a run for it through the agave fields.'

Ramses shook his head. 'Joe, you and the Gamboas won't survive one hour after nightfall. No one else has any training or ability to—'

'It doesn't matter. Look. They'll go after your family if they haven't already. They will kill them, torture them; you know how these fucks operate.'

'I will not leave you to die.'

'I need you to make a run for it.'

'What are you going to do?'

Gentry said, 'I have a plan, but I can't tell you in case you get caught by the Black Suits.'

Ramses thought it over, nodded slowly. He took a phone out of a pocket of his chest rig. He winced with the movement, the bullet wounds in his arm clearly painful. He handed his phone to Gentry. 'I want you to keep this with you. If I get out of here, I'll get to a phone. I'll make contact with the guy at the American embassy who can get the Gamboas visas into the United States. If you can get to Mexico City, I will set up a meeting.'

'Perfect.'

'But you will have to get them out of the hacienda, away from all the *sicarios* out there, by yourself. How the hell are you going—'

'I'll get it done.'

Martin had not been part of this conversation. He'd just looked blankly at the tile floor in front of him. His gaze unfixed; his thoughts, Court assumed, were on his young brother Pablo. Court got Martin back into the discussion by going over ideas for the two of them to sneak out of the hacienda in broad daylight. Court thought it unlikely that they would both make it out, but they all agreed, if they went in opposite directions at the same time, one of them would stand a decent chance.

Of course, using their motorcycles would be suicide. There was over two hundred yards of driveway from the casa grande to the front gate, and the enemy would know of the escape attempt in plenty of time to assemble there and kill the biker before he could get away.

So they would have to try and escape on foot, they'd have to do it simultaneously, and all three decided, Martin and Ramses needed to go right now.

30

The two GOPES commandos embraced each other in the front driveway. They'd already said good-bye and good luck to the gringo and the surviving Gamboas. They'd packed water bottles and rolls into the pockets of their pants, taken fully loaded weapons from the dead marines lying around the house; they'd synchronized their watches and discussed the timing for going over the walls – Martin to the east and Ramses to the west. The men walked past their Suzuki crotch rockets and headed off in opposite directions, and Court stepped back inside.

It was only nine in the morning, and Court was dead tired. He had a plan to get out of here, sort of, but it was thin as hell and he knew it. It was so thin he'd decided to wait as long as possible to tell the Gamboas about it, because he was certain they would freak out. But he also knew it was the only possible way they could survive.

Court stopped in the kitchen for some fresh coffee, took it with him to the rear *mirador,* and sat on the tile there and sipped.

He looked to his watch. Ten minutes from now Ramses and Martin both planned to be at the wall, on opposite sides of the hacienda. Court could not see either from his vantage point, so he just sat and waited. Hoped like hell he did not hear any gunfire.

Five minutes now. Laura had come up to see him, had asked him if he thought it was okay for her to take a nap in the cellar.

225

He told her to catch a few hours because she'd need it later, and then she'd lingered a minute longer. She thanked him for all he had done. He'd said no problem; they looked into each other's tired eyes a few seconds longer, and then she'd drifted back down the stairs.

His tired eyes followed her. Damn she was beautiful. Tough and resolute but kind and gentle. He wondered what it would be like to touch her, to feel her touch him, to just be somewhere quiet and safe, and to be together.

Fuck. I'm getting delirious.

Court shook his head, tried to clear his thoughts. Still, he knew now that Eddie had been right about his sister all those years ago. She was something special.

Court looked at his watch. It was time. Right this second both men should be on the top of the wall – one on the east side, one on the west side – looking for a break in the patrols of the corrupt *federales* , hoping to beat the odds and make a run for freedom.

No gunshots. That was good. Not so far any—

A motorcycle's engine revved in the driveway on the opposite side of the casa grande. *What the fuck? Who the hell—*

Court leapt to his feet, ran from the veranda into the bedroom and into the hall, took the stairs three at a time into the sitting room, sprinted past the kitchen. Diego was there, and he ran behind Court as they made it into the entry hall and opened the front door.

Martin Orozco Fernandez shot out of the parking circle on his Suzuki, sending dust and gravel high into the air behind him. He passed the wrecked truck with Ignacio's body, raced down the driveway at high speed, a Heckler Koch MP5 submachine gun in his right hand and held out in front of him. The bike bounced on the stones, but he kept control with one hand as he raced down the drive into the forest and out of sight, heading right for the front gate.

Right into the hands of the enemy, who would certainly be

converging on the noise, positioning themselves there, ready to blast the biker into oblivion.

And this would allow Ramses, on the western wall, time and opportunity to escape.

Gunfire erupted in the distance now at the front gate, sounding over the whine of the motor. Court stood on the front porch, his shotgun in his hand, and he shook his head. Martin was giving his life to buy his compadre a few precious seconds to reach freedom. Somewhere to Gentry's left, a couple hundred yards away, Ramses would hear the bike, the gunfire at the front gate, and he would realize what his friend was doing for him right now.

Court could imagine Ramses Cienfuegos, with two gunshot wounds, rolling over the wall and running across the dirt road there, sprinting into the agave fields with tears in his eyes.

The gunfire in the distance continued.

The motorcycle's engine stopped.

And then the gunfire slowed, and then it trailed off completely.

Court hoped like hell that Martin had earned a measure of his revenge, had killed some of the bastards, had gotten some payback for the torture and murder of his innocent brother Pablo.

Gentry and Diego went back into the house without a word between them.

Ten minutes later, with no more gunfire over on the side where Ramses had made his getaway, Court knew that Martin had succeeded in his last mission.

Ramses had escaped.

Court and Laura were the only two awake in the house at noon. Luz and Elena were asleep in the dark downstairs cellar, Diego was crashed on the couch in the living room, and Ernesto napped in a chair on the *mirador* above the front door of the house, a Mexican Marine's MP5 on his lap. His shoulder wound had begun to sting and burn, but his wife had given him enough aspirin and tequila to deaden the pain slightly, and the old man had insisted on being involved in the property's defenses.

He'd absolutely refused to hide in the cellar with the women any longer.

Court remained at the rear *mirador*; he sat on cool tile in the shade. He'd nodded off a couple of times but had not gotten over sixty seconds of rest. He tried to think up some way out of here for everyone, but the single solution he could come up with seemed like a complete shot in the dark.

A noise on the patio below caught his attention; he leaned forward, knelt between stone columns that had been shot up pretty thoroughly in the first gunfight, when Ramses had used this high ground to fire down on the men on the patio bathed in the light of the Ford truck. Eddie's prized possession now sat like a dead animal in the bushes, listing to one side and showing no possible signs of life. The truck had easily taken one hundred rounds of rifle fire or buckshot pellets.

There, on the patio below him, he saw Laura. She knelt over a dead man in a Tequila municipal police officer's uniform. At first Court wondered if she was scavenging from the body more weapons or cash or anything she could put to use.

Court started to interrupt her from above, to assure her he'd gleaned everything of value from the bullet-ridden body. Just as he began to speak though, Eddie's little sister crossed herself with her rosary in her hand and began to pray.

Praying for the souls of the men who had just killed her brother and had tried to kill everyone here in the casa grande.

Gentry shook his head. He absolutely did not comprehend this level of compassion or forgiveness.

It was not his world at all.

It was not his world, and he had decided he was going to make a run for it.

He found Elena in the kitchen, pouring herself water from a large jug. He asked her to come to the living room. Ernesto remained on watch, Luz remained in the cellar, but Gentry wanted to talk to Elena, Laura, and Diego.

'Listen, even if Ramses makes it to a town, to a phone, or to a car, we can't count on him doing it before nightfall. The *federales* will hit as soon as it's dark; you can bet your life on it.'

'So what are we going to do?' asked Elena.

'I've got to try and break out, to get some help or find a car—'

'Go, Joe. You have done all you can. We would not have made it this far without you. Thank you so much for everything.' It was Laura; she spoke as if she had expected this. He felt defensive.

'You are leaving us,' Elena worded it as a statement. Court saw she had no illusions that she or her baby would survive without him.

'I'm not running out on you; we just can't—'

'It's okay.' She did not believe him; this much was clear.

He turned to Laura. 'If I can make it into town, I can get some sort of truck or something. I'll be back here before you know it.'

'How are you going to get past the *sicarios*?'

Gentry was not ready to be challenged on his plan. He *had* no real plan for what he would do once over the wall. But he trusted, more or less, in his ability to figure something out if he could get out of here and see the lay of the land from another perspective.

'Ramses did it. I'll head over to that side of the property.'

Elena was becoming combative. Court knew she was only thinking of her unborn child. 'Ramses had Martin to sacrifice his life to create a diversion. Would you like one of us—'

'Of course not. I can slip away on my own.' He hesitated, looked into the tired, scared, and shell-shocked eyes. 'I've been doing this for a long time.'

'Slipping away?' Elena asked, angry.

'Yes.' Court admitted. 'But I *will* be back.'

Elena and Diego clearly did not believe him. He looked into Laura's big brown eyes, saw kindness and understanding and compassion, but he had no idea what she was thinking.

Court ripped a camouflaged T-shirt off of one of the dead marines at the back door. The man had been shot in the head, so dried blood had crusted around the crewneck, but Gentry ignored it, took off the denim jacket he'd been wearing, and replaced it with the dead man's shirt.

It was just past two in the afternoon when Court began heading through the house to the west wing. The sun was high over the mountains; the afternoon light was broken by scattered clouds. Elena had returned to the cellar without saying good-bye, but Laura and Diego started to follow him into the hallway.

'You guys stay here. Keep the guard up, but if the *sicarios* hit, don't even try to defend the home. Go into the cellar, and fight them from there. You can do a lot of damage to an attacking force coming up that little hallway.'

Court did not mention the flip side of this truth: an attacking force could do a hell of a lot of damage to a defending force pinned into a little hole with no escape.

'You aren't taking a gun?' asked Diego. He'd noticed Joe was unarmed.

'No.'

'Why not?'

'You need every gun and every bullet. And it won't do me any good. If I start shooting out there on the other side of the wall, there will be fifty guys on top of me in no time.'

Diego shook his head in frustration, 'No. That is not why. I think it is because you feel bad. You are running away, and you feel better by telling yourself: well, I gave them all the guns, what more could I do?'

Court wanted to tell the boy that he needed to learn how to trust people, but he stopped himself. No, actually, Diego did not *need* to learn to trust. Here, he didn't need that kind of advice. Court did not trust, for reasons that were no better than Diego's.

Both of the Mexicans in front of him had been fucked over before, lied to and double-crossed. How could he tell them he was any different?

He couldn't tell them. He'd have to *show* them he was different. He turned and left them there in the hallway.

*

230

Court's low crawl took most of the afternoon. As he pulled his body through the grass, he listened to the cracks of gunfire that emanated from the casa grande every ten minutes or so.

He expected DLR's men to wait until nightfall before attacking, but he knew he could not discount the possibility they would send in individual spotters or sappers during the day to get a better idea of what they were up against. The only way he could think to prevent this, or at least slow down the deployment of these daylight teams, was to instruct Laura and Diego to fire their guns every few minutes throughout the day in different directions. If they did this sporadically and in random patterns, any *federale* infiltrators might think that they had been detected and stay hunkered down, or even retreat back over the hacienda wall.

Court wished that he could move faster, he knew he did not have time to waste, but with the undulating hills and mountains in the distance, he could not just break out into a run across the property. There would be snipers, he would be spotted, and the snipers would shoot him dead.

His low crawl was a worthwhile tradeoff to avoid this eventuality.

It was after five thirty when he arrived at the wall. He scooted under the weeping willows, pulled out a small bottle of water, and drank it down. He was exhausted and sunbaked; his knees and forearms and hands were scratched and bloody, his shoulders and lower back exhausted. The scar tissue in his left scapula, where an arrow had entered seven months earlier, felt knotted and tight; he reached back and rubbed the area while he sat and rested. After just a couple of minutes in the shade he stood and walked along the narrow bank, stepped into mud once or twice as he moved deeper under the foliage of the trees. He saw a water snake floating towards him in the murky pond; he ignored it, moved on a bit further, and then climbed up into a tree whose limbs reached above and over the wall.

Up high enough to look out into the rest of the valley now, he saw the dirt road that ran just on the other side of the hacienda wall. From where he sat he could swing out and drop down onto it, then run to the other side, move low, and dive into the tall, spindly blue agave plants that grew there amidst the high weeds.

He was just about to do that when a red pickup truck drove past from his right. It was loaded full with men with rifles, eight in all, and they passed by just under his position, rumbled and bounced along the track, and disappeared around the wall to his left a hundred yards on.

The men were local *campesinos*, farmworkers in blue jeans and straw cowboy hats, but they weren't tending to their fields. They'd been hired by someone to patrol the perimeter.

Seconds later a *federale* on a motorcycle came up the road from the other direction.

By the time the biker disappeared around the southern edge of the outer wall, Court could already hear the rumbling of a pickup. It appeared; it was black and bore PF markings. A pair of officers stood in the bed and held on to the roll bar with one hand while propping their M4 rifles on the roof of the pickup with the other.

This old dirt farm road surely hadn't seen so much traffic since the hacienda had been a working agave farm and tequila distillery.

Court tucked himself deep into the tree, found a semi-comfortable position, and prepared to wait there until dusk. He hoped there would be some sort of break in the action while the attackers prepped to hit the casa grande, and he hoped to take advantage of that lull.

But waiting till nearly the time of the attack meant that he would have no chance to make it back out onto the main road to commandeer a vehicle or create any other way to help those in the casa grande before the assassins attacked in force. No, waiting until the last moment to escape would force him to rush to save them.

He could still, with little doubt, save himself. He could wait for the raid on the house behind him, and then he could drop down off the wall into the darkness on the outside of the hacienda, and he could walk off into the agave fields and the forests, and he

232

would survive. He could shit-can this lost cause; he could live to fight another day; he could return to Europe and target Gregor Sidorenko, the Russian mobster who had pursued him all the way into the Amazon jungle. He could kill Sid and then get a small measure of his life back. He could find work, and he could forget about Daniel de la Rocha and this horrific civil war here in Mexico, and he could never look back.

All this he would love to do.

But he could not run out on the five people behind him.

They were counting on him. Only because there was no one else, but that did not matter. He would help if he could, and if he could not, then he would die trying.

He would not, could not, leave them behind.

31

At dusk the patrols became much less frequent; Gentry pictured a meeting back at the main gate, imagined the leader of the operation laying out his assault plan to a large group of men kneeling in the dirt with their weapons hanging from their necks.

Court knew he'd have to act fast. Part of any attack would surely include a blocking force outside of the walls on all points of the compass, ready to keep anyone from escaping.

At six p.m. he found the entire east side of the hacienda wall clear, so he slid out of the tree, hung by his arms, and dropped the rest of the way to the one-lane dirt road, rolling to the ground to absorb the jarring shock in his ankles and knees and spine. Quickly, he shot across the hard surface and buried himself into the tall grasses of the overgrown blue agave field. There he knelt for a moment, listened for shouts or gunshots or approaching vehicles. Hearing nothing that worried him, he stood, began moving north through the grass along the road, ready to tuck down into the foliage to duck the next patrol.

The valley had darkened to black by the time he turned at the northeast corner of the hacienda wall. While he made his way through the brush, a half dozen pickup trucks ambled by on the road to his right; they were driven by civilians, and more civilians sat in back with rifles. These were local farmhands, *granjeros*. Deeply tanned men with mustaches and cowboy hats, they were manual labor from the neighborhood, probably offered a week's wages for a day's work. These unskilled laborers would not take part in the attack. No, these men would just patrol the perimeter, perhaps set up a couple of roadblocks, just to make sure that if anyone in the hacienda managed to squirt out during the assault on the building, they would be mopped up before they made it out of the valley.

They weren't evil killers, Court knew. They probably thought they were working for the *federales* and not the Black Suits, though there was no way to be sure. These were not beneficiaries of the drug profits of Mexico in any appreciable sense; they were just laborers who'd lucked into a little work. The Black Suits had access to all the labor they could ever want or need, and Court knew he needed to remember that if he ever got out of this damn valley.

Court knew these were not necessarily bad men. But they were in his way, and he would kill them just the same.

Ahead of him in the distance, at the hacienda's front gate two hundred yards away, Court saw the headlights of several vehicles along the road. Big black SWAT-style armored cars, pickup trucks, a beat-up sedan, even a huge armored Policía Federal mobile command vehicle the size of a bus. He decided to get closer, maybe to grab a weapon or a hostage or a car that he could drive right up to the casa grande and rescue the Gamboas. He moved around an open pasture, dug into a low copse of pine trees, and neared his objective. There were dozens and dozens of men with guns here to prevent him from carrying out this plan, but still he moved towards them in the night. He heard barking dogs but knew the scent of all the other men, and all the other dogs for that matter, would render them worthless as early warning devices.

At fifty yards away he ducked lower. He was close enough to see the *federales* in their SWAT uniforms; they had already broken off into fire teams. Dozens of men rechecked weapons and strapped extra ammo magazines to their bodies. Court heard the fire teams run through their coms checks. Dozens of radios squawked and beeped and crackled through the cool evening.

Then the teams broke apart completely, ten or twelve men to

a unit, some piled into two Policía Federal armored trucks that Gentry recognized as Ford BATTs, or Ballistic Armored Tactical Transporters, and the big black vehicles rumbled to life. Another dozen men boarded the beds of two pickup trucks. Even at this distance Gentry could tell the white trucks were pressed low on their chassis accommodating all the men and their gear.

The two pickups turned right at the road around the hacienda and disappeared into the distance. One of the big BATTs turned left and headed slowly in Court's direction.

The remaining BATT remained at the front gate with its engine running. Court watched *federales* file into it, and the side door was closed and secured. Then another unit stacked up behind it in formation. The Policía Federal armored mobile command vehicle sat behind the rest of the vehicles; men came and left through a side door.

The truck moving to the east passed fifty yards off his left shoulder, everything outside of its bright headlights was black to the driver, and Court knew he could not be seen.

He understood the *federales'* attack plan now, more or less. Three units, each with a dozen men, would assault the hacienda simultaneously from the south, east, and west. A larger force, twenty or twenty-five maybe, would be heading right up the driveway.

The farm hands with the cowboy hats and the scatterguns were outside the walls on the perimeter, ringing the action in clusters on all sides of the hacienda as a sloppy blocking force.

So there it was. Sixty heavily armed, highly trained Mexican Federal Police officers, plus another two-dozen armed locals hanging back in support.

Against a pregnant woman, an elderly woman, an injured old man, a sixteen-year-old boy, and a girl who cries the rosary over assholes who lost their shitty lives trying to earn a paycheck by killing her.

Goddammit, Court thought. Guess it's time to go out in a blaze of glory.

*

Gentry was only twenty-five yards away from the rear of the BATT at the front gate when it drove forward, lumbered into the hacienda proper. The cops on foot jogged behind it in two columns. The driveway to the casa grande was a lumpy, bumpy, winding two hundred yards, and the big heavy armored truck moved slowly up the hill, disappeared into the forest; its headlights and taillights flickered through the trees and made a horror-show dance of ominous shadows all the way back to the gate.

The dogs disappeared up the drive with the foot patrol.

Court got down on his knees, crawled through the brush and grasses and around wild agave plants the size of kitchen tables. He moved slower and more quietly with every inch of progress; he expected there would be sentries back here around the command vehicle, and even though he could not see anyone yet, he knew any sound he made would travel through the night.

Soon he found himself at the road between two parked pick-ups. He was less than fifty feet from the gate; he could hear a group of men talking over the drone of the auxiliary power unit of the big armored command vehicle.

He looked ahead, across the road, and in a shallow run-off ditch on the other side, he saw a dead body, stripped to the waist. Even in the moonlight he could still see the big black bruise on the man's jaw.

It was Sergeant Martin Orozco; a dozen bullet holes perforated his legs, arms, and chest. A final coup de grace wound was centered on his forehead.

'Sorry, amigo,' Court mumbled as he continued forward on his hands and knees.

Looking around the pickup on his left, towards the gate, past the command vehicle, he saw five or six Mexican farmer types with shotguns, their butt stocks resting on hips.

Most of the men stood right up by the gate, as if trying to catch a glimpse of the action two hundred yards away through the forest. Their body postures and tonal inflections showed their

237

excitement. They were spectators; not one of them thought for a second any of them would be in danger or would even be called on to fire their old scatterguns.

Court knew he could hotwire one of these pickup trucks in under a minute. With it he could race up the driveway, get past the armored truck and the men, get the Gamboas in it and then drive through the hacienda, break out at one of the small gates on the west wall, making sure to avoid the *sicarios* who would be attacking from that side.

It would be easy.

Except for the one thousand or so copper-jacketed spikes of lead that would be flying at him and those he tried to protect at three thousand feet per second, each one with the potential to turn a human head into pink mist.

The pickup truck plan was a nonstarter.

If there was still an armored car here at the front gate, and if that armored car happened to be unlocked with the keys in the ignition, well *then* he'd be in business.

But the BATTs were gone, and with them any chance for—

A young PF officer stepped from the side door of the trailer-sized command vehicle, and the door locked back behind him. The officer turned away from the farmers, walked across to the bushes along the far side of the road, and undid his belt. He shook as he tried to force himself to take a quick piss; he rolled his neck to scoot the shotgun that hung in front of him out of the way of the impending stream.

Gentry looked at the locked door of the command vehicle, wondered if the man taking a bathroom break had a set of keys on him. He wished the truck wasn't so fucking big. Still, it *was* armored. It had the plating necessary to stop a rifle round cold; its thick front windshield would hold back dozens of direct hits before failing.

The vehicle would be nearly impossible for Court to drive, but he knew he did not have the luxury of being choosy at the moment.

Dammit.

Across the narrow road the officer pulled up his pants and zipped them, then reached into his pants pocket. Gentry recognized the glint of a key chain.

Court leapt to his feet, and he struck like a cobra.

He ran low and fast across the road as the policeman began to turn back towards the command vehicle. The gaggle of cowboys and farm hands was twenty-five feet off Gentry's left shoulder and still looking up the drive towards the casa grande. Gentry moved like a shadow across the hard surface, drew his knife at the last second, simultaneously slipped it between the turning man's floating ribs on the left side and covered the *federale*'s mouth with his right hand. He pushed the knife to the hilt and kept pushing the man forward into the bushes; Court turned the blade like a key as he followed the man into the thicket and fell with him, on him, onto the hard earth.

Court used his own dead weight on top of the man to stifle his kicks and thrashes. This hombre was probably a soccer player, Gentry thought; he was exceedingly fit, and his body did not play by the rules. Court expected the man to be limp in five seconds; it was nearly twenty before the life left his extremities. Court found himself exhausted, as if he'd been trying to stay atop a bucking bronco while preventing the bronco from making a sound for the entire ordeal. Court reached forward, pulled the keys out of the brush. He felt them for a moment, settled on two possible choices for the door of the vehicle. He held them in his fingers and retrieved the shotgun with his other hand.

Then he stood. Headed towards the armored command vehicle.

Seconds later he was inside. He'd shut the door behind him, turned right, away from the front of the vehicle and towards the back cabin. A man called out from the cab, a question to his partner who was now dead in the brush. Court pulled out his knife, began to turn to deal with the other driver, but he stopped, noticing a metal rack that ran head high along the length of one side of the cab.

All manner of weapons and ammunition rested in the rack or hung from hooks above it.

Gentry's eyes widened, and his face tightened into a cruel smile. 'Oh, *hell* yes.'

He turned away, headed to the front to kill the driver.

The comandante led his men up the driveway towards the front of the house. They had been protected from any threat of fire from the windows or verandas of the hacienda's casa grande by the armored vehicle ahead of them, but his men had widened out as they neared the building and now moved slowly, tentatively in the night. The truck slowed and stopped and shone its bright lights on the front door.

Normally, the comandante would have nothing to do with a frontal assault, straight up the middle towards a defended stone building. But after sending in spotters that morning and seeing the property from the inside, he understood how concealed the driveway was from the hacienda itself. With the thick growth of bushes and trees on both sides, the archways at the front door, even the tall weeds between the cobblestones, twenty-five men heading in two columns straight up the driveway at noon would be more covert than if they jumped over the back wall in the middle of the night.

Even so, he'd waited until nightfall and then one hour more because the defenders might have been expecting an attack as soon as darkness covered the property. Now, at nine in the evening, he could wait no longer. It was time to hit these worthless *cabrones* in the house, kill every last thing that moved – every man, woman, and child, and then the dogs and cats and the chickens and goats.

He wanted to check with the other teams who should just now be approaching from other directions, but one of his damn officers had apparently depressed the transmit button on his radio, and it prevented the comandante from sending commands or hearing from any of his other men. He'd waited thirty seconds for *el chingado cabrón* to realize his error and fix his radio, but still he could not communicate.

In another twenty seconds he would be ready to call for the attack, and if this *hijo de puta* didn't fix his *chingado* radio, the comandante was going to string the *pendejo* up by his *chingado*—

Behind him, lights through the forest. Moving up the driveway towards the house.

He looked to the men around him as he quickly dove behind a low stone wall that rimmed the parking circle in front of the casa grande. He had to get out of the driveway before he was silhouetted by the approaching headlights.

He turned back around, stared at the lights, and he could not believe what he saw.

The mobile command vehicle bounced wildly up cobblestones towards his position.

He'd left the two drivers in the MCV at the front gate, but they had no reason whatsoever to even run the engine much less take part in the attack.

Even though his radio was not functioning, he pressed the button and screamed into it. '*¡Cabrones!* What the fuck are you doing?'

Fifty yards away the vehicle's red brake lights illuminated in the forest.

The MCV stopped in the woods, began turning around in the tight confines of the narrow driveway.

The comandante turned back towards the house. Whatever the hell his drivers were doing, they had eliminated any further surprise. He rose and opened fire on the front of the house with his M16 rifle; this was the only way he had to begin the attack without the use of his worthless radio.

Men on either side of him followed suit; their rounds sparked against the stone facade and tore through the wooden door.

The comandante heard a sound through the gunfire, and he turned back towards the noise. In his utter astonishment he stood up from behind the low wall and lowered his rifle to his waist.

241

The massive armored MCV moved up the rocky driveway in reverse, its speed increasing by the second. The huge blue truck bounced and heaved, its chassis straining under the weight of tons of ballistic steel.

The comandante had driven armored cars enough to know the view out of the rearview mirror was lousy; this *pinche* driver was blindly accelerating up towards the casa grande at a speed that he could not control.

'¡*Alto!*' Stop! The comandante screamed into his radio; the problem with the mike seemed to have been rectified, although every other aspect of this attack was turning to *mierda* in front of his eyes. The MCV shot backwards towards the other armored truck, the BATT that was parked in the parking circle and shining its headlights on the big dark house.

The armored vehicle doing what it was fucking *supposed* to be doing!

The MCV looked like it would flip as it bottomed out at forty miles an hour; it missed sideswiping the other vehicle by no more than a foot, knocking off the driver's side mirrors of both trucks.

Suddenly, the comandante standing at the wall realized three things in rapid-fire succession: One, if his driver had had trouble seeing what was behind him before, now that his mirror was smashed and bouncing up the drive behind him he would not be able to see a thing. Two, that his driver was not *his* driver! And three – that the *federale* MCV moving at forty miles an hour was going to crash up the front steps of the house.

Court let go of the transmit button and tossed the radio onto the floor of the truck and then stomped on the gas. The lumbering vehicle slowly accelerated up the driveway in reverse, bouncing and bumping up the hill. He buckled himself in, and only this allowed him to keep his foot planted firmly on the pedal. The buffeting inside the top-heavy vehicle made him feel like he was a rag doll being shaken by a giant. Still, he did not let up on the gas for an instant.

He'd been aiming, if you could call it that, more or less at the front door to the casa grande, but when he lost his mirror, he gave up on any pretense of precision in his targeting. Instead he just floored it, hung on to the steering wheel for dear life, and pushed his head back hard into the headrest, unsure when the impact would come or even if he would survive it.

He felt a jolting crash that rocked him hard, slammed him tight into his seat, and caused his foot to slip from the gas pedal, but he knew he had not yet hit the house. As the bottom of the vehicle scrapped over stone, he determined it was the angel fountain in the center of the drive. This told him he was heading too far to the left to hit the front doors squarely.

He turned the steering wheel slightly to the right, jammed his foot down on the pedal again as automatic-weapon fire raked across the thick glass plate of the windscreen. He streaked by the broken-down farm truck with Ignacio Gamboa's body in the front seat.

Court's armored bus crashed straight up the steps of the casa grande; it smashed with brute violence into the western side of the archway and turned the two-hundred-year-old oak doors into logs and splinters.

The MCV jolted to a stop. Court slammed the transmission into park, unbuckled himself, and spun into the back. Behind him the confused and tentative smattering of gunfire that had chased the truck up the drive now turned into a heavy fusillade as the Policía Federal quickly came to the realization that this was not a wayward vehicle of theirs but, instead, a breakout attempt by the family under siege.

In the back Gentry fell down twice, stumbling from his dazed headache and lost a moment in the darkness, tripping over weapons that had fallen from their shelves. Seconds later he recovered, found the two items he'd been looking for, and opened the back doors.

Diego knelt in the sitting room behind the couch and fired at movement on the back patio. His grandfather had gone upstairs to shoot from the *mirador*, but he had not heard his *abuelo* fire the M1 carbine in over a minute.

An unreal amount of automatic fire shredded the front of the house. Diego knelt behind the couch as if it would give him some sort of cover; he only lifted his head when he heard an engine's roar. The rear of a huge blue truck crashed into the entry way of the casa grande and continued several feet inside the building. In a panic Diego stood and fired with his pistol, the bullets just making sparks on the rear door. His weapon clicked open and empty.

The sixteen-year-old boy fumbled his reload, dropped a magazine on the tile floor, and chased it to the edge of a wingback chair before retrieving it and seating it in the grip of his gun. Long before his weapon was back in the fight the black doors of the vehicle flew open, and Diego saw a man crouched there in the truck with two massive weapons in his hands.

'Diego! It's me! It's ... ' In the excitement Court had forgotten his pseudonym. 'It's the gringo! Get everyone up here and in the van! *Ándele!*'

It took the young boy five full seconds to comprehend, but when he did, he nodded, spun on his tennis shoes, and ran towards the kitchen. He shouted as he ran. '*Mi abuelo* is upstairs!'

Courted nodded, but he did not go upstairs; instead he turned towards the shattered front doorway. There was little space between the hulking truck and the broken stone and stucco, but Gentry found a firing position, and he raised his right hand. In it he hefted a Hawk MM-1 handheld grenade launcher, loaded with a dozen high-explosive shells. The weapon was heavy and bulky and Court normally would have used both hands to fire it, but the weapon did not require both hands. He pulled the heavy trigger, and with a sound akin to a massive cork popping from an agitated champagne bottle, the first grenade left the barrel.

Boom!

Forty yards away an explosion of fire and smoke and broken earth and spinning *federales*. He fired three more times at the wall lined with attackers before lowering the weapon, lifting an identical device that he held in his left hand, and popping off three missiles loaded with CS agent, a powerful crowd-dispersing tear gas. With the last canister still in the air, he spun in the other direction, fired rounds from both weapons one at a time; they arced through the house, through the broken sliding glass doors to the patio, over the pool, and exploded in the garden behind the casa grande.

Court had lived by luck, but he had no real expectation of hitting one single *sicario* attacking the rear of the house. No, he just wanted to show them the rules had changed; their cowardly attack on women, a kid, and an old man would now subject them to high-explosive rounds being shoved down their motherfucking throats.

He fired one round of CS up the hallway that ran from the main room to the west, hoped like hell he'd have everyone out of here before the gas wafted back inside and made this living room unbearable.

He dropped the CS grenade launcher as he ran up the stairs; it was too heavy to wield along with the high-explosive launcher. He turned to the right, shouted for Ernesto, wished like hell he'd grabbed a shotgun or a pistol or something other than a weapon that he could not use in the short range of a hallway.

He turned towards the rear *mirador*, and he saw the old man there, lying on his back in a pool of blood.

32

Ernesto's eyes blinked, and he drew a shallow breath. He looked up at the American standing over him on the dark veranda.

Gentry reached over the railing of the *mirador* and fired two HE rounds at movement in the moonlight by the corral in the distance. Wood and stone and fire blew twenty feet into the air.

Court knelt back to Ernesto. 'Can you wa—'

He saw it now; the old man's left leg was bloody, twisted to the side. Only held on by bits of meat and the denim in his jeans. Blood covered the tile of the *mirador* in the darkness.

Eddie's father had been hit squarely in the femur with a round from a high-powered rifle.

Court looked back at the man's face, and the eyes had rolled back. A last breath drained from his lungs.

Quickly, Gentry knelt over him, spoke into his ear. 'I'll take care of them. I'll get them someplace safe. All of them.'

Then he stood and spun back into the house as the stucco walls turned to dust around him.

The family coughed and choked on the CS gas as Gentry shepherded them into the back of the truck. He'd retrieved the Hawk that held the tear gas grenades, and he fired the remaining rounds into the driveway and the trees beyond it, hoping like hell he was shooting in the general direction of the bad guys. When the weapon clicked on an empty cylinder, he let it fall to the tile of the entryway. He climbed into the back of the mobile command vehicle behind the family; Luz was right in front of him, and she looked past him, over his shoulder and back into the dark smoky house.

'Ernesto? Ernesto?'

There was no panic at all in her voice, even with everything happening around her. Court just pushed her deeper into the bus, dropped the high-explosive grenade launcher onto the padded bench next to Elena, and shut and locked the door behind him.

'I'm sorry, I have to—'

Court said the word *drive* as he was launched back against the door. Luz fell into his arms as he realized that the MCV was moving forward, its rear tires bouncing down the steps of the casa grande, and that whoever was driving was sure as hell stepping on the gas.

He crawled forward up the aisle, the bouncing and the buffeting of the truck's chassis tossing him about; gunfire raked the walls of armor on both sides, a constant tinging sound like a downpour in hell.

In the front cab he found Laura behind the wheel; she knelt down low, desperately trying to get some sort of a view out of a windshield that was, while still intact, completely white from bullet strikes and cracked from one end to the other.

'I can't see!' she yelled.

Court reached across her body and buckled her into her seat. He shouted into her ear as he did so. 'Don't worry! Just drive! Anywhere is better than here!'

They sideswiped one of the armored cars, ran completely off the driveway and into a pasture, and then Laura jacked the wheel so hard to correct for her mistake that the truck went up on two wheels for an instant before bottoming out and bouncing back onto the rocky drive.

Behind them in the long truck, police gear bounced and slammed around, knocking into Elena, Luz, and Diego.

247

Laura hit a small tree, knocking the MCV hard to the left and sending Gentry flinging into the dashboard.

'You suck worse than me!' Court screamed as he crawled across the front passenger seat, opened the heavy armored door, and leaned outside. They needed some sort of idea of their direction, even if it meant Gentry exposing himself to enemy fire.

'Right! To the right!' he shouted in English, and Laura turned the wheel to the left.

'¡Derecha! ¡A la derecha!' Court shouted.

She fixed her mistake, did not overcorrect this time. 'Sorry! Sorry!'

Court spotted for her, though he heard bullets whizzing past him. They clanged off the rear door and the side panel; Gentry brought his body back inside the truck for an instant then darted his head out again quickly to help Laura find her way through the forest on the long, winding driveway.

They were in the woods twenty seconds later, safe from the *sicarios* at the casa grande, but Court knew good and well that they were not out of the woods, figuratively. The men up at the house had radios, which meant the trucks and the armored vehicle parked near the front gate would now be scrambling into position to block the exit.

Court bobbed his head back into the vehicle. Laura had found a small corner of the windshield that had not been turned smoke white with the impact of bullets. She leaned up and into it, straining against her seat belt, desperately trying to see out of the tiny viewing hole.

Court shouted to the back. 'Diego, give me the grenade launcher!' He said the last part in English; he did not know the words in Spanish.

'The what?' shouted Diego from the dark rear of the vehicle.

Laura shouted back the translation, and within a few seconds young Diego appeared with the big gray cylindrical device. Court snatched it and positioned his entire body outside the MCV now, his feet on a small running board below the passenger door, his

248

right hand holding the open door, his left hand holding the Hawk MM-1 and balancing it on the front door. As the truck bounced and weaved on the bumpy driveway, Gentry found it next to impossible to aim.

They approached the front gate now; Laura concentrated on it. But Court shouted to her from outside the passenger seat.

'I'm going to make us another exit.'

'What?'

Court knew that blasting the cars with high-explosive grenade rounds would damage them, to be sure. But this wasn't Hollywood; the vehicles would not blow sky high and then land conveniently out of his path.

No, he would try to knock a hole in the old wall large enough for them to fit through. The MM-1 had an effective targeting range of one hundred and fifty meters in optimal conditions. The conditions in which Gentry found himself working were absolutely off the other end of the scale from optimum, but he had no choice but to give it a shot.

As he expected, the federal police BATT pulled in front of the open gate, its headlights staring up the drive at him like taunting eyes. Daring him to keep coming.

Gentry aimed his launcher ten yards to the east of the gate.

Pop.

Boom!

Court's first shot hit low, exploded a few yards short of the stucco wall.

'You missed!' shouted Laura. Court wondered how she could suddenly see so much through the windscreen.

He fired again and nailed the hacienda's wall perfectly. Fire, stone, and white dust exploded back and up in the dark. Gentry fired again, hit again, but wide of his last impact. He now saw black openings in the wall, with a five-foot wide 'column' of stone between them. He aimed as carefully as he could at this remaining piece, and he pulled the trigger.

His weapon was empty.

249

Damn. Court climbed back inside, tossed the launcher on the floor in the back between the Gamboas, and quickly buckled up.

'Hit it!' he shouted.

'Hit it?' Laura screamed back her question, disbelief in her voice.

'Right in the middle! As hard as you can!' He then turned back into the back and screamed to the rest of the little clan. 'Hold on to something!'

The gunfire came first. A couple of the *campesinos* at the front gate had gotten in front of the armored cars. Their shotgun pellets tickled the walls and windows of the huge truck looming closer.

Laura Maria Gamboa Corrales slammed the six-ton vehicle through the two-hundred-year-old wall, pulverizing it into stones and dust and whipping moneda vines. Inside the jolt was cataclysmic; the damaged windshield gave in completely, broke apart and away, and slid forward down the stubby hood. The occupants were stunned, but Laura's new wide vision of the road in front of her greatly helped her driving; she pulled the wheel back to the left, crashed through a few low bushes, and nailed the left rear quarter panel on an ancient Datsun pickup. The impact spun the little truck across the road like a toy, forcing shotgunners to dive for cover, their straw hats flying into the air like leaves kicked up by a breeze.

Court Gentry unbuckled his seat belt, rolled onto his knees, and crawled into the back of the van. He grabbed the MM-1 launcher and scrambled to a case of grenades bolted against the wall by the back door. He worked there for a moment; Diego and Luz and Elena just watched him in the dim red light.

'Laura, stop the truck!' he shouted after another ten seconds.

'Are you crazy!'

'Do it!' She slowed the MCV, and Court opened the rear door. He almost fell out; his legs were weak after the concussion of the crash. Back in the dark, one hundred and thirty yards behind, the dozens of *federales sicarios* left behind at the casa grande were now making their way down the driveway towards all the cars positioned there. Gentry hefted the grenade launcher, sighted through its notch and post iron sights, and launched five tear gas grenades at the cars and trucks.

When he finished, even before the last canister impacted back at the gate, he dropped the MM-1 in the road and climbed back in the truck. *'¡Vamanos!'* he called forward to Laura, who put the big tank back into gear. It shuddered and scraped as it moved along now; they'd put the command vehicle through a hell of a lot more abuse than it could be reasonably expected to suffer, but it had kept them alive.

'Where are we going?' Laura asked when Gentry made it back up front.

He climbed into the passenger seat and snapped the seat belt tight around his waist. 'Fuck if I know,' he admitted.

33

If Court hated leaving Eddie's awesome truck behind, dumping the armored car, damaged though it was, just about killed him. It was battered and smoking, the 'run flat' tires were tearing up with each passing mile, and the windshield was gone, but the big MCV still felt sturdy and secure. Still, there was no way they could drive for very long without garnering attention, and refueling would have been impossible without all but drawing a crowd of paying customers to get a close-up look at the shot up *federale* command vehicle.

It was eleven thirty when they pulled behind an auto-salvage yard in the town of La Venta del Astilero, a suburb just west of Guadalajara. They'd stayed off the main roads, more or less, and they'd avoided virtually all of the Tuesday late-night traffic.

With no front windshield, the cool air in the truck was almost unbearable, especially for Laura behind the wheel. Her small-muscled arms were covered in goose bumps visible even in the low light, and by the time they found the salvage yard, she was shivering.

Shivering and crying. Her father's death was just one more heinous punishment to her heart. Court felt terrible for her, wanted to reach out and touch her, to hold her hand while she drove, to tell her it would be okay.

But he did not.

He did not because he did not know how to touch the sad, beautiful girl.

And he did not because he did not really believe everything would be okay.

The four family members stood along the side of the road and waited while Gentry climbed a fence and dropped into the salvage yard. Luz Gamboa rubbed her daughter's arms to warm her, and Elena shifted from one swollen foot to the other, held her full belly to take pressure off her back. Diego stood watch with his hands on his hips. Dogs began barking behind the fence as the family prayed together.

Ten minutes later an engine started and a sheet-metal gate slid open with pushes and grunts. An old pea soup green Volkswagen bus appeared, its headlights off; it pulled into the street, and then Court jumped out, and Diego shut the gate behind it.

Court jogged back to the armored car for a moment, returned with a pair of 9 mm pistols and an extra magazine for each. He passed one weapon to Laura and slid the other in the waistband of his pants.

He looked at Diego. 'It doesn't look like much, but the engine turned right over. I put some plates on it, so you shouldn't have any problems from the highway cops. Head north, just keep going all the way to the border. Sleep in shifts. One sleeps, two awake. When you get to Tijuana, go to a hotel and wait for us. Two days from today, go to the border crossing at ten a.m. Wait thirty minutes. If we aren't there, leave and come back at three p.m. If we still aren't there, do it again the next day. We won't be able to communicate. No phones, no contact. If we get captured, I want it to look like we have no idea where you are or how to get in touch with you.'

The young boy nodded. Court could see that Diego understood that he was now the man of the family, and he shouldered the responsibility in a way Gentry appreciated. The shock and sadness would come later, Court knew, but that was only if they survived until later.

'Laura and I will make contact with Ramses. Assuming he is still alive and he's gotten in touch with the American at the embassy, we will go to Mexico City to pick up the money and the papers.'

Elena asked, 'If you do not show up in Tijuana in two or three days?'

'You'll have to try to make it over the border on your own.'

Everyone just looked at him. He shrugged. 'It's all I've got. I didn't say it was a *good* plan.'

Elena wiped tears from her eyes, stepped forward, and hugged him tightly; he felt the baby, his old friend's baby, kick against him. His eyes widened.

Elena whispered into his ear. 'You have done so much for us, Jose. Eduardo would be proud to know he has a friend such as you.'

Luz hugged him as well, and she said some sort of prayer. He could not understand it, and while she spoke to him, he could not look into her eyes. The tragedy that had befallen this old woman in the past two weeks was unimaginable, even for a man with a history like Court Gentry.

Everyone hugged Laura; of course there were tears, and needless to say there was another prayer. Then the family drew close together. Court watched from ten feet away.

'Perfect. Another goddamned group hug,' he muttered under his breath as they embraced and held one another.

Eventually, the VW bus rattled off. Court hoped like hell it would make the journey, but at this point, it was time to start worrying about his own operation.

By one thirty in the morning they were on the road to Mexico City. Court had stolen a motorcycle out of a shed in a residential area a few blocks from the salvage yard. Laura had wanted to leave an anonymous note saying how terribly sorry she was and promising to send money to this address just as soon as she could, but Court would not allow it. Instead she made a mental note of the little home and told Gentry she would find a way to repay the occupants.

They were 325 miles from Mexico City. It would take a minimum of six hours of hard riding, but with luck they could be there by the time her bank opened at ten. Once they were a few miles clear of the suburbs of Guadalajara, Court pulled over in the darkness and called Ramses with the phone he'd left them. Laura had wrapped herself in a dirty blanket Luz had found in the back of the VW, and she fell asleep in the grass while Court made the call.

Ramses Cienfuegos answered on the first ring. Gentry was relieved to hear the GOPES officer had made it away from the hacienda, but Ramses immediately asked about Martin and the motorcycle engine he'd heard as he dropped over the wall. Court reluctantly confirmed that Orozco had given up his own life so that his friend could escape.

Ramses took it stoically, then said he had made contact with the American embassy man, and told him about someone who needed several sets of documents on the fly. The American consular officer agreed to a meeting at two p.m. in Mexico City, and Ramses gave Gentry the location.

Court and Laura drove on for another two hours then stopped for gas. When Court stepped out of the restroom, he began to veer off a little on his way back to the bike. Laura noticed this and offered to drive for a while. Court's machismo would not allow him to ride on the back of a motorcycle, especially one driven by a five-foot-tall woman. He recognized how silly this was, but he also knew that Laura had likely had as little sleep in the past two days as he had, so they rode a few miles up the highway and then exited, found a thick copse of brush alongside a dirt road through a rolling pasture, and Court stashed the bike.

'Ninety minutes' sleep. No more.' Court said it as he set his watch. They lay down next to each other in the cool grass. Immediately, Eddie's little sister covered Gentry with part of her blanket, and she held him close for warmth.

'I'm sorry. I'm so cold,' she said as she put her head in the crook of his shoulder and rested her sinewy bare arm across his chest.

Court said nothing.

'It's okay?' Laura asked.

'Yeah.' Court stared at the starry sky and tried to control his pounding heart.

Exhausted though he was, it took forty-five minutes for him to drift to sleep.

The Federal District of Mexico City, known simply to Mexicans as 'the D.F.' (*el de-efe*), is one of the largest cities in the world. It is estimated that between fifteen and twenty million people live within its general borders, and many of them live in abject poverty in slumlike suburbs.

Laura and Court hit the outskirts of Mexico City at ten a.m., but with the sprawling expanse of the metropolis, they still had an hour or more ride to their first destination. It was well past eleven when they rolled into the city center. They cleaned up in the bathroom of a fast-food restaurant, and then Court dropped Laura off in front of her bank on the tree-lined Avenida Paseo de la Reforma. He hated letting her out of his sight, but they agreed Court coming in with her might have raised an alarm. He assumed the blurry images of him on TV were recent enough to draw attention to Laura Gamboa, sister of the leader of the team wiped out trying to kill one of the biggest and baddest *carteleros* in the country. So she'd go in alone, wait for her money alone, and then sit in the park outside and wait for Court to return from errands of his own.

He gave her Ramses's phone for emergencies, but they did not have enough cash between them for Court to buy a phone of his own. He really had no idea who she would call if she ran into trouble, but it seemed like the right thing to do. She had the Beretta in her purse, she knew how to use it, and he was comforted by this. Court watched her disappear behind the mirrored-glass doors; he looked down at his watch and then turned away reluctantly.

Gentry had a long to-do list to take care of while Laura picked up her money. He needed to scope out the location of the after-noon meet with the embassy man, to use the last of his money to gas up the bike again, and then to find a decent location to get a hotel room. He'd need Laura and her money to get the room, but Court wanted to drive the streets to get a feel for a secure location.

He did his reconnaissance and his security sweep, gassed the bike, and made it back to the bank ninety minutes after he left. Laura was out in the park along the paseo, sitting on a park bench and drinking coffee. She'd bought one for Court, and he walked up to her, sat down, and reached for it.

She pulled the cup away quickly, regarded him like he was a crazy man, and then her eyes relaxed.

'How can you just appear from nowhere like that? You are like a ghost.'

Court ignored the comment, wasn't going to tell her that dec-ades of training and operational experience had made coming and going discreetly a subconscious action.

'Any trouble in the bank?'

'None at all. They were a little surprised I was taking all the money out, but they did not ask any questions. They were very nice.'

'Where is the cash?'

Laura took a small canvas backpack from a shopping bag and handed it to him.

'Here it is. *You* have it now. I trust you.'

Court slung the bag over his shoulder, smiled as he led her up the street to the lot where he had parked the motorcycle. 'If my intention was to rob you, the past three days would have been a shitty way to do it.'

She laughed a little without really smiling.

The U.S. Embassy was just a five-minute walk up the street on Paseo de la Reforma. In front, huge wrought-iron fencing and cement barriers had been erected in the promenade that ran up the street. All around signs that read 'No Photography' in English and Spanish had been pinned to the fencing. Distrito cops sat in their cruisers or walked up and down the sidewalk; old but hearty Uzi 9 mm submachine guns with folded stocks hung from leather straps on their shoulders.

It didn't seem like the Nation of Mexico gave much of a welcome to the U.S. Embassy, nor did it seem like a terribly inviting building for a Mexican to visit.

But this was the way of the world.

Court and Laura bought two new mobile phones and had lunch in a dark restaurant before their meeting; they sat in the back of the little dining room with their backs to the wall. They were both too tired to talk very much; they drank coffee with lots of sugar and picked at roast pork and rice and beans, waiting for two p.m.

34

The meet was in a mall just a few minutes' stroll up the paseo from the embassy. Court left Laura at the second-floor food court and then went downstairs to the bathroom next to the Starbucks. He knew the route; he'd reconned here just two hours earlier.

Court entered the bathroom five minutes late. His contact was there; Ramses had told him the man's name was Jerry Pfleger. Pfleger was leaning over the sink and looking into the mirror. Gentry got the impression the man had just been squeezing a blackhead on his nose.

He was young, very early thirties, tallish and thin, with short curly light brown hair and a narrow face that looked like it rarely saw natural sunlight. He wore black sans-a-belt slacks and a white shortsleeve button-down shirt. A thin tie that appeared more polyester than cotton.

'Romeo?' asked the young man.

'Juliet,' sighed Gentry in response.

The code had been Pfleger's idea. Court thought it was idiotic.

The embassy man jutted out a hand, and Court shook it. It felt to Gentry as if he were waving a raw fish filet in the air in front of him.

'Okay.' The young American's eyes protruded. 'Okay, first things first. I gotta tell you, this is weird.'

'What's weird?'

'I mean, I do this shit all the time, arrange papers for those who

259

don't want to wait in line. No biggie. But the hombre who called me said I'd be meeting a gringo ... *that's* what's weird.'

'I need papers for a family that needs to get to the States immediately.'

'How do I know this isn't some sort of a sting or whatever?'

'Do I look like I work for the embassy?' Court's long hair was dirty and matted, his beard five months old.

Pfleger shook his head. 'That's all you got? Nothing else to put me at ease here? C'mon, pal.'

'Look, Jerry. I know the guy who called you to set this up. I know the family who wants papers. I'm just the monkey in the middle here. Don't stress. If you can produce what we need quickly, this will be your easiest transaction ever.'

Pfleger nodded slowly, then again more quickly. Court saw evidence of some sort of mood-altering substance in the jerky mannerisms of the young man.

No doubt, Jerry was on something.

Court groaned inwardly. Perfect. This asshole has been snorting coke.

Pfleger continued, his mouth moving fast with the gesticula-tions of his hands. 'I mean, normally, I just work directly with the Mexicans who want to immigrate.' Jerry shrugged. 'I'm usually not doing it under the eyes of a fellow American.' He put his fingers in the air in a double V salute, affected a lousy and paraphrased impersonation of Richard Nixon. '"My fellow American." Ha-ha, Tricky Dick? Right?'

'Right ...' *Fuck.* 'So ... with the papers you will provide, they can just walk right through at the border crossing.'

He nodded. 'Everything they need to get across in Tijuana or Mexicali and avoid the poor-man's routes.'

'What are the poor-man's routes?'

With a jolting wave of his arm he said, 'You know, the desert, the Rio Grande, pole-vaulting the fence or doing the tunnel-rat thing in the sewer. I have colleagues up in Juarez and TJ and Matamoros who do what I do, get the hard-working citizenry of

Méjico over the border to fuel the American economy, but only I can arrange for you to walk through with your head held high. I even throw in worker's visas and green cards. It all looks totally legit because it *is* legit.'

'How much?'

'For the whole enchilada?' Jerry smiled. 'Today I'm running a special. Everything for the low, low price of only fifteen grand a beaner.'

Court's eyes rose at the price *and* the slur. 'There are four in the family.'

'Sixty g's, then.'

'How 'bout a volume discount?'

Jerry laughed, clapped once. Then he cocked his head. After a few seconds he nodded thoughtfully. Court had given him a threatening stare; Court had no idea if it would have any value.

'What the hell? Fifty k.'

Ten grand worth of stare. Not bad. Court wondered if brandishing his pistol would have shaved off another five large. 'We can come up with that. How does this work?'

'I need everybody's photo IDs. I'll take that info and generate everything you need.'

Court reached into the backpack and retrieved the stack of identity cards for the Gamboa family. Court remembered Ernesto's driver's license was still in there. He fished around and pulled it out, stuck it in his pocket with a slight grimace.

He handed the cards to Pfleger. 'How long?'

Pfleger looked them over, and Court watched him carefully. He knew it was likely the American would realize he was dealing with members of one of the families targeted at the rally in Puerto Vallarta. But if he did recognize the Gamboa surname, he showed no evidence of it. 'Overnight. I can have these to you at lunch tomorrow. Mexican lunch, that is. Two p.m. Same time, same place.'

'That'll work.'

'You got a phone? I may need to call you for more info.'

Gentry was reluctant. 'What info?'

'Dude, trust me, there is always something missing on IDs that I don't want to just fudge. These people will be stuck with these identities in the States. They have to have all the t's crossed and the i's dotted.'

Court pulled out his new mobile. Read the number out to Jerry Pfleger.

'Okay,' Jerry said. 'I need a down payment. Fifty percent.'

Court pulled the bag of money from his backpack and pulled out twenty-five thousand dollars. Handed it over to the young American, who counted it out himself. He jammed it into his pocket.

Two boys came into the bathroom, walked immediately up to the urinals without regarding the two Americans.

The men separated with a nod. Court left first, and Jerry went back to the mirror to work on his blackhead.

Court almost panicked when Laura was not in the food court upon his return. His head moved on a swivel, and he scanned the lunchtime crowd and began pushing his way back to the escalator.

He grabbed his phone and began to call her, but he saw a tiny girl with a short bob of black hair in line at the cash register of a men's store. She waved to him and smiled a little. When she came out, she said, 'I got us both some new clothes. I hope you like them.'

He wanted to chastise her, but he realized instantly that she had used her time wisely. They would need new clothes. Little Laura had done well, and he told her so.

She smiled at him, and then together they walked sleepily towards the exit of the mall.

The hotel Gentry picked out was on Donceles Street, just a block north of the National Cathedral in el Centro Histórico, the historic city-center neighborhood. The building was small and recessed from the main street by a guarded gate; there was a tiny hidden parking lot for his stolen motorcycle. The desk clerk took cash and gave them keys to a room on the third floor with two twin beds; Court had asked for a view of the street and was satisfied with his sight line out the window.

As exhausted as she was, Laura was thrilled by the location of the hotel, as it stood directly across the street from la Iglesia de Nuestra Señora del Pilar, a narrow but ornate 250-year-old baroque church and former girls' school. As soon as they were in their room, she told Court she wanted to go across the street and pray. He rolled his eyes and started to follow her, but she suggested he stay in the room and rest. He grabbed the pistol he'd just pulled from his pants, stuck it right back into his waistband, covered it with his shirt, and followed her out the door.

'We stick together, Laura.'

'Good. Will you pray with me?'

Gentry shrugged as they reached the staircase. 'You pray for us both. I'll stand watch.'

They crossed the busy road and entered the church; Court sat in a pew while Laura knelt next to him and bowed her head. Court kept his tired eyes open and darting in all directions, though there were only a few other people in the sanctuary and they were clearly more interested in their salvation than deleting Court or the girl with him.

The altar was high and gilded; the walls on either side of the sanctuary were similarly gilded and adorned by statues. Soft music played through speakers, and the cool air was dim, illuminated by natural light coming through the stained glass and reflecting off the golden walls and ornamentation.

Court began drifting off to sleep. Only when Laura climbed back up to the pew next to him did his eyes relight.

She sat with her hands folded in her lap, her eyes on the crucifix on the altar. She spoke softly. 'You are not a believer, are you?'

'I ... I wasn't raised in the Church. I don't know how it all works.'

She looked up at him and smiled; they sat with their shoulders touching. 'Let me show you.'

'Thanks, but not today. I am really tired.'

'Faith will give you the energy you need.'

'Sleep will give me the energy I need.'

She seemed disappointed. 'Some other time, maybe?'

'Sure.'

Laura then walked forward to an iron stand of votive candles and placed money in the offering box. She began lighting candles, one by one, saying a prayer for each. After the third Court realized they were for the dead of her family.

He stood with her, his back to the wall, watching the front door and the choir loft and the other worshippers. She had a lot of candles to light.

On the way back to the hotel Laura noticed a small bodega, and she and Court agreed they should get some provisions so that they would not have to risk going back out again before the meeting the next day. They bought bread and juice and water and *tortas*, and they made it back to the room just before five.

Laura immediately lay facedown on one of the twin beds and closed her eyes.

Court grabbed the bag of clothes from the men's store and stepped into the bathroom. A long shower washed off days of sweat and grime. Bloodred swirls in the bottom of the bathtub gave him pause: he wondered just which of his many victims' splatter had made it to his skin and just how long the blood had been on him. He shampooed his long hair and more blood ran from it, along with bits of grass and pebbles and broken glass and gunpowder residue. The debris collected in the water around his feet. He watched it swirl or settle, depending on what it was.

To him it was a reminder, a journal of the past few days. The rally in Puerto Vallarta. The hacienda. The armored car. The ride on the motorcycle.

Looking at it all just made him more exhausted than ever.

He turned off the water, stepped out of the shower, toweled off, and looked into the bag.

Pressed brown khakis, a cream-colored linen shirt, a black belt with a square silver buckle, black socks and black tennis shoes, one half size too large, but close enough. He dressed quickly, the fresh clothes felt amazing on his clean body. Though he knew he could sleep for a day, he still felt like a new man.

He stepped back into the bedroom, lay down on his bed, placed the Beretta on his chest, and looked across at Laura. She had rolled over on her back; her eyes were closed, her hands rested on her stomach, and her small breasts rose and fell with her breath.

She was the most beautiful woman he had ever seen in his life.

He forced himself to turn his head, to look away from her. He rolled onto his side, and in minutes he fell asleep.

35

Two white Yukon XL Denalis pulled up in front of the exclusive restaurant in the Zapopan district of Guadalajara just before eight p.m. The drivers remained behind the wheels of the armored vehicles while four men stepped into the road, began looking over the cars on the street, the people passing by. The men wore black Italian-cut business suits, their hands were empty, they were quick and efficient with their movements, but they were not impolite as they moved through the foot traffic to the front door of the restaurant. There they stood, back to the wall, and they all unbuttoned their coats. Their eyes scanned the street in all directions.

Three Guadalajara police squad cars double-parked on the street. Their flashing lights reflected off the glass for a block in each direction. A pair of patrolmen stepped out of each vehicle and began directing traffic to continue on up the street. No one would be allowed to park anywhere near the front of the restaurant.

Four more men climbed out of the gleaming white SUVs and moved directly through the bronze double doors of the restaurant. These men wore black suits as well, carried handheld radios and empty black nylon bags. The manager and the maître d' met the men in the lobby in front of the bar, they spoke a moment, and then the six men broke into two teams.

The maître d' and two Black Suits approached each candlelit table and spoke softly to the diners. Cell phones were confiscated;

266

the men were asked to stand and open their coats, and they were frisked as politely as the brusque act can possibly be accomplished. Some of the customers understood what was going on – most did not. Soon all the phones of all the patrons were in the black nylon bags. An announcement was made to the dining room by the maître d': eat, drink, enjoy yourself, and your meals will all be taken care of by a customer who will be entering shortly. There were gasps, a few claps, a few more stolen glances at wristwatches.

It would be a long night.

Meanwhile, three men checked the prepared banquet room, looked under the table, careful not to disturb the linen or the place settings as they did so. They scanned for listening devices and discussed arrangements with the servers. Then they entered the kitchen; the manager led the way as the staff lined up and underwent a quick frisking, even the women in the back of the house were patted down. Then the pantry was searched, the walk-in cooler, the dry storage areas, and even the freezer.

Everyone in the kitchen knew this routine.

Six more Black Suits arrived in another white Yukon XL Denali; two men headed straight through the dining room, and the patrons wondered if one of them was their benefactor for the evening. But they headed into the kitchen and stepped out the back door. They opened their coats and took up watch in the alley. The remaining four stepped into the dining room from the cool evening, and they moved with military precision into the four corners of the room. Again, coats opened and eyes scanned all in front of them but did not fix on any one thing.

One of the first men in the door spoke into his radio.

Five minutes later three more white SUVs stopped in front of the restaurant. A thick group of men in identical black suits entered; no one would be able to count the number with the speed and tightness of the mass, but there were certainly a dozen individuals. Their clothing and hairstyles, even their trim beards and mustaches, everything was virtually identical. They passed through the dining room; the patrons at their tables strained their necks and gawked; a woman tipped her wineglass as she leaned back to try and pick out the celebrity.

Was he a famous bullfighter? Was he the singer performing at the Auditorio Telmex tonight?

No one knew who it was, because no one could tell one man from the next. In seconds the mass moved into a back banquet room, the door was shut, and two suits stood at the door facing the restaurant.

The main dining room murmured and speculated. Several said, 'Los Trajes Negros,' but none of the men in the black suits standing around nodded or answered back.

Soon the tables began ordering more wine, and the servers poured liberal glassfuls. Champagne corks were popped, and the staid dining room turned into a celebration.

Daniel de la Rocha sat at the end of the long banquet table, sipped his scotch, and gazed at the tea-light candle on the starched white tablecloth. He picked the soft middle out of a slice of crusty French bread and wadded it into a tight ball before popping it into his mouth. The table was set for twelve, but now only five sat with him. The other men paced around the room talking into mobile phones or radios; two were in the corner huddled over a laptop they'd set up on a serving table.

Emilio Lopez Lopez, DLR's personal bodyguard and the leader of his protection forces, stood against the wall not five feet behind his boss.

A waiter in white offered DLR a menu, but he waved it away, asked the server to instruct the chef to prepare him something light. The waiter disappeared, and de la Rocha's attention returned to the candle.

It had not been a good day. Elena Gamboa had survived the attack on the hacienda in the mountains near Tequila and had escaped. Nineteen marines, *federales*, Jalisco state police, and Tequila municipal cops, all under the control of Spider Cepeda, were dead, a couple of *campesinos* as well, and many more were wounded.

Calvo had worked his magic, the news reported that the men died heroically fighting the remaining Madrigal Cartel assassins who had attacked the rally in Puerto Vallarta, but this type of mess did not go away cleanly or quickly or cheaply. There would be blowback from Constantino Madrigal, from the government in Mexico City, from a meddlesome foreign press that Calvo could not so easily influence.

More men sat down now, and de la Rocha lightened a bit. He was with his brothers; they were together, and they would get through this *chingado* mess. The Gamboas would be found, and they would die, and the next wave of 'heroes' working for the GOPES would not be so quick to come after him.

They talked about old times, talked about their days together in the army. Daniel was one of the boys now, and he enjoyed moments like this. He liked getting away from his properties, getting out into someplace different, even if it did require two dozen bodyguards and hours of coordination from the local police.

De la Rocha stood up from his chair. The others seated stood with him, but he motioned for them to sit back down. He stepped over to the corner *nicho*, knelt down at a Santa Muerte placed there just for him, and prayed alone.

When finished, he poured a double scotch for *la virgen* and left it there in the *nicho* beside her, then returned to his table.

Nestor Calvo had been pacing with his phone, but he left the dining room for a moment, returned minutes later, and then sat in his seat on Daniel's right. He leaned into the ear of his *patrón*.

'I've been speaking all afternoon to a man from the American embassy. We use him from time to time, for this and that.'

Daniel's plate came. Filet of sole, not too much butter. A mango salsa. Asparagus. He nodded, lifted his fork, and the waiter went away with a sigh of relief. Daniel did not look up as he responded to Nestor. 'This and that? Time to time? Okay. You aren't telling me much. What about this gringo?'

'He helps Spider get papers for his men to get into the United States if there is someone up there we need to go after.'

Daniel nodded, bit into the hot fish. His face showed no expression.

Calvo continued. 'He ... I am speaking of the *norteamericano*, he called one of my men this afternoon, says he has valuable information, but he will only give it to you directly. I called him back and told him to go to hell. He flew straight in from the Distrito just now to speak to us. Called me from the airport. I finally persuaded him to tell me what he knows, and I had a man pick him up and bring him here.'

'So he didn't go to hell; he came to me.'

Nestor shrugged. 'You are going to want to hear this.'

'Has he been searched?'

'At the airport and again, just now, in the bathroom. Head to toe.'

Now de la Rocha shrugged and nodded, he did not look up from his plate as he ate. 'Bring him in.'

Nestor nodded across the banquet room to a man positioned at the door. He stepped out, and seconds later he returned with Jerry Pfleger.

The American was disheveled, no doubt from the rough feeling up that he'd just endured in the bathroom. Wearing his rumpled white short-sleeved shirt and his thin black tie, he looked completely slovenly in the beautiful dining room amidst the well-coifed men with expensive suits. The guard ushered him to the far end of the table to de la Rocha's left. Daniel stood and shook Jerry's hand.

'Nice to meet you, Your Excellency.' Jerry said it with a wide smile.

Daniel sighed. *Gringos*. 'Don't call me that. Have a seat.' Both men sat back down. De la Rocha looked to the waiter standing against the wall behind him. 'Angelo, bring my *blanco* American friend some *vino blanco*.'

A glass of white wine was poured and Jerry took a long gulp.

270

Daniel had returned to his sole. Between bites he asked, 'What can I do for you?'

'I'm really happy you weren't hurt the other day.'

'Me, too.'

'On the news ... the man who tried to kill you on your yacht. His wife was at the rally in Puerto Vallarta.'

De la Rocha stopped eating. He looked up at Jerry.

Pfleger continued. 'Mister Calvo said you might be interested to know where they are?'

'I might be interested, yes.'

'An American came to me today in Mexico City. He wants me to procure forged U.S. visas for three women and one boy.'

De la Rocha just looked at the gringo, 'And who are these *mojados* ?' *Mojados* was the local translation for 'wetback,' or someone who swims the Rio Grande to get into the United States.

'Luz Rosario Gamboa Fuentes, Elena Maria Gamboa Gonzalez, Laura Maria Gamboa Corrales, and Diego Gamboa Fuentes.'

'Spider!' de la Rocha shouted out, startling Pfleger and making him sit up in his chair. Javier 'Spider' Cepeda had been at the computer in the corner, but he spun around and darted over to his *patrón*. Daniel had Jerry repeat himself to the leader of his *sicarios*.

'They are in Mexico City?' asked Cepeda hopefully.

'I don't know. I just know the gringo is.'

'When will you meet with him again?'

'Two p.m. tomorrow.'

De la Rocha shook his head. 'Seventeen hours. Any way to get to him faster than that?'

'Yes, sir. I got his mobile number. I thought maybe you had a way to triangulate—'

'Esteban.' Now Cepeda was the one interrupting Pfleger and calling across the room. Esteban Calderon was the technical guru of the Black Suits; he'd been the radio operator in their special forces team, and he had degrees in telecommunications and electrical engineering. He hustled over, and the Mexicans discussed the technical hurdles involved in finding someone by their mobile phone signal in a city as congested as the Distrito Federal.

Finally, when it was settled that with enough equipment and men and a little time the location of a mobile phone could be pinpointed, de la Rocha returned to Pfleger. The American had been all but forgotten for the previous five minutes, by everyone except Emilio and the guards along the wall, that is.

Jerry had gulped a full glass of chardonnay and then another half while he waited.

De la Rocha said, 'What do you want, amigo?'

'Your undying appreciation.'

Daniel just stared at him. De la Rocha could see from the man's mannerisms that he was a user of some of the product in which the Black Suits dealt.

When he saw how flat his humor fell, Jerry became serious. 'Honestly, nothing much. I just want the American.'

'The American? You want us to take the family, and you want the gringo to go with you.'

'Yes.'

'And what is your interest in him?'

'Apparently, he is wanted by the U.S. government. The embassy was buzzing this afternoon about some guy on the loose down here. *If* he's the guy they are after, and I *think* he is, then there is a reward. I was thinking I provide you the information, then you could provide ... a group of men to pick them up. You take the Gamboas, and you pass the American over to the embassy. Then you pass me the reward money for my information.'

De la Rocha took a long sip of his wine. 'Why do the *norteamericanos* want the gringo?'

'I don't know. Something classified. There's a guy who showed up this afternoon hanging around the embassy, definitely a CIA spook. Apparently, this spy and the wanted gringo used to work together, and he's hanging around waiting to ID him if he's picked up by the *federales*.

Daniel nodded thoughtfully, and caught Calvo's eye. Both

men stood and removed themselves from the table, found a quiet corner of the banquet room.

Nestor said, 'If la CIA want this gringo so bad, they may be willing to deal for him.'

'I was thinking the same thing. What do they have that we want?'

'It's the Central *Intelligence* Agency. Any hard intelligence they have about Madrigal could be useful.'

DLR stroked his goatee. 'They would know who his government contacts are in Peru, in Ecuador, in Colombia.'

'They certainly might know all that.'

'Would they trade that information for this gringo assassin?'

'I will begin immediately to find out. I will set up a chain of intermediaries to contact the embassy, to get us in touch with la CIA. We will judge how much passion they have for this man.'

'Either way, we need to get Jerry to lead us to Elena.'

Nestor was excited by the prospect of trading the gringo for CIA information. It would be a huge intelligence coup against his organization's archrival.

He was less enthusiastic when his boss returned to the original mission, the killing of the police officer's pregnant wife.

Still, Calvo agreed, and his phone was out of his pocket in seconds. Before dealing with American intelligence he would need to establish a series of cutouts, and this would take time.

Daniel addressed the banquet room full of his men. 'Everyone, we leave immediately for the D.F.!'

Jerry Pfleger rose, held his wineglass up high in toast. The Mexicans in the banquet room ignored him; instead they quickly assembled on de la Rocha, so that they could file out as one unit and limit the chance of an assassination attempt against their *patrón*.

36

At ten o'clock both Court and Laura were awake; they sat across from one another on their twin beds; they nibbled on their tepid dinner and listened to a soft rain blow against the window of the hotel room. Laura had showered, and her wet bangs drooped in her eyes. She had dressed in her new clothes, a black polo-type shirt and blue jeans.

Her rosary hung from her neck.

Court thought it was an efficient outfit, and she looked amazing in it.

They were in for the night; Gentry had unplugged the television and pushed it and the TV stand against the door, along with an oaken chest of drawers. Anyone coming through would not only need a key but also a shoulder and several hard shoves.

There was little conversation until they finished their meal, but once the remnants were in the garbage can, Laura told stories about her family and her youth in San Blas. If she expected Court to talk about his childhood, she was disappointed.

When her stories trailed off and his did not begin, she asked him directly, 'My brother. Was he like you?'

'In what way?'

'In any way? I mean . . . the way you can fight. The way you have protected us. Was Eduardo the same?'

'Eddie was a good guy. A tough guy. But when I knew him? No . . . he was not like me. He was not a killer.'

274

'I don't think you are a killer,' she said.

'Then you haven't been paying attention.'

'No. I understand you have killed people. Of course you have. But only to save us and to save yourself. You have only done what is right. What is necessary. Men around here who are killers do not do it for good reasons. Only for bad.'

Court did not respond. He just sipped water from a bottle.

Laura continued. 'God is working through you. You should know that.'

The sound that came out of Court's mouth was something between a chuckle and a gasp. Water dripped down his chin. 'I don't know about that.'

'I am certain. He sent you to watch over us.'

'You make it sound so simple.'

She considered that comment for a long time, looking into his eyes so intently that he was forced to look away from her. 'No ... maybe it is not that simple. But I believe ... I believe you were sent to us when we needed you.'

'There were about a dozen of you who needed me, and now there are four. What about the others?'

Laura began to cry.

Gentry looked up at the ceiling. Shit. Why the fuck did I say that?

Her sobs softened, and she stood, crossed over to his bed, and sat next to him. Facing him with her legs crossed Indian style. 'Do you believe in good and evil?'

Gentry could feel his heart rate increase with her nearness. He looked across the room. 'I believe in what I have seen with my own eyes.'

'Which means?'

'I believe in evil.'

'You have seen no good in this world?'

Court looked at her again. Felt blood coursing through his body and warming his face and hands. 'I've seen good, sure. Just not enough.'

'Well, I believe what I see with *my* own eyes. And I see much good in you, Joe. You are a good man.'

'I think we should try and sleep. We will be on the road all day tom—'

Laura moved closer. Interrupted Court. 'Do you have someone?'

'Wha – what?'

'A wife. A girlfriend?'

'No.'

'You cannot be alone forever.'

He smiled. Looked away. 'I won't live forever.'

'I mean ... on this earth. God doesn't want man to live alone.'

Court did not reply.

'I have been alone for five years. Since Guillermo died. I know about loneliness, about how difficult it can be to keep everything inside you because there is no one else to share your life. But I have my faith. If I did not ... Joe, I do not know how your heart can survive.'

'My heart is fine,' Court knew this because he could feel it pounding in his chest.

'There is not just darkness in the world, Joe. There is much that is bright.'

'I travel in different social circles than the happy stuff.'

She did not completely understand, but she answered as if she did.

'You are doing God's work.'

'I'm just a guy, Laura. I'm not anything special.'

'No. You *are* special. The devil is fighting for this earth. He does this with evil. You fight against evil here on earth.' She shrugged again. 'You are fighting the devil.' She completed the logic of her thinking. 'You are doing God's work.'

'Thanks,' he said. Sometimes he wondered what the hell he was doing. This girl had her opinion, and it was only that to Court, but it was nice to hear nonetheless.

'We better get some sleep,' he said it again. But she did not get up from his bed.

'May I stay with you? Like last night? May I stay close to you?'

'Sure,' he said it with a phony air of nonchalance, which, he was pretty sure, she had seen right through.

He reached over, flipped off the lights, and laid back, his shoes and pants and shirt still on. His handgun on the table next to him.

She curled up next to him, rested a hand on his chest, and placed her damp head on his shoulder. Even though she was only five feet tall, together their bodies took up the entire twin bed. Soon her leg moved and draped across his lower legs.

The lights were off, but Court's eyes were open. He stared at a ceiling he could not see and tried to keep his breathing slow and shallow.

'Are you afraid,' she asked him, and he thought she was referring to his pounding heart.

'No,' he answered back quickly. 'Not at all.'

'You mean, all the people trying to kill us, and you are not scared? I'm terrified.'

'Oh, that. Yeah. I just ... I am trained, I guess, to use the energy of fear to my advantage. I am scared when I'm engaged in action ... but I was trained to channel it and not freeze up.'

'It sounds like some sort of science.'

'It is.' He liked talking about this. It took his mind off of her leg, which was bent at the knee and resting on his thighs now.

'I am lucky to have you protecting me.'

'I saw how you fight. You've had some training yourself.'

'Yes, when Eduardo was alive, he took me shooting a lot. It was important for him that even though I was only tourist police, I was ready for anything. I trained in kickboxing as well.'

'I noticed you were in good shape.'

'You did?' she said it with a smile in her voice, and Gentry could feel his face warm from embarrassment. Her hand on his chest began moving back and forth slowly.

'I mean, I could tell you exercised. Good for you. You might need those skills again before this is all over. If we run into the Black Suits on the road, we can't expect them to—'

'Joe?'

'Yeah.'

'May I kiss you?'

Yes, he thought. But said, 'I don't think that's a good idea.'

'Why not?'

Court did not know why not. He stammered out something about Eddie, about needing to sleep, about her not knowing who he was or what he was.

'That is crazy, Joe. Eduardo wanted me to find someone else. To find a good man.'

'Laura. I'm not a good man. I am just a man. Just a guy trying to help.'

'Then *help.*'

'Help wha—'

'Help *me.*'

She climbed on top of him, leaned down into his face, and kissed him softly on the lips. His eyes widened, and he did not contribute, but he did not pull away. Again she kissed him, his face and his body went rigid as stone, until the third kiss when his eyes closed slowly.

They opened. 'Wait,' he said.

'No,' she replied, and she pressed her weight against him, wrapped her arms behind his neck, and kissed him more deeply now.

He could see her. When he opened his eyes, they had adjusted to the darkness of the hotel room, and he saw her eyes shut tight, and her wet bangs swaying with the movements of her head as she kissed him: his lips, his cheeks, his eyes, his neck.

Suddenly, she stopped, sat up; her weight pressed against his waist. He noticed his hands had roamed to her hips, and he held her there.

She looked down on him, and he could see her clearly now in the light from the window. 'Your name is not Joe.'

Gentry just shook his head.

'Tell me your real name. I do not want to call you Joe while we are making love.'

Court blinked. *We're making love?* He shook his head again.

She said, 'Tell me what your friends call you, what people used to call you when you were young, something that means *something* to you.'

Court almost said Violator, his code name. It was almost the same in English and Spanish. But he didn't want her calling him that. He thought for a moment more and whispered. 'You can call me Six.'

'*¿Seis?*' she asked, confusion mixing with the lust in her eyes.

'Yes.'

'*Bien. Seis.*' Satisfied, she pulled off her polo shirt, unfastened her bra, and let it fall to the floor between the two beds. She unbuttoned Court's shirt; he put his hands on hers for a moment, tried to pull them away from the buttons, but in truth, he did not want her to stop. He thought about Eddie and Ernesto, men who would do anything to protect this woman, and then he thought about the men who wanted to hurt her. He had been protecting her, but now he did not know if he was hurting her by giving in to her advances. She leaned forward and kissed him. He closed his eyes and opened his mouth, not at all confident that he was getting any better at this.

His mobile phone rang.

He ignored it.

She ignored it.

It kept ringing. Stopped. Started up again.

You have got to be kidding me.

She ignored it.

'It must be the embassy guy.' He barely got the words out; he reached for the phone, but she held his head tight and kept her lips pressed against his.

He almost had to fight her away. 'Hello?'

'Hey there, fellow countryman. Sorry for the late call, I'm burning the midnight oil up here in my office and had a couple of questions.'

'Yeah. No problem.'

Jerry asked Court a few odds and ends about past professions of the four Gamboas. He said it was necessary to have some sort of occupation for their work visas, and although they could make something up, the more accurate the information on the documents, the better they would hold up to scrutiny on the other side of the border.

Court conferred with Laura and answered Pfleger's questions. Half of him hoped that this interruption would quell the heat between himself and Laura; he felt guilty for his actions and intentions with his old friend's kid sister. But the other half of him hoped they could just pick right back up where they left off before the cell phone rang.

Five minutes later Gentry and Lorita *had* picked up where they'd left off. She stayed on top of him, kissing his face like it was some sort of precious treasure, and his strong arms kept her body tight against his while she did so.

When she pulled him up to slip off his shirt, he became nervous. He knew how long it had been since he'd taken a woman to bed. He said softly, and more to himself than to Laura, 'I'm not ... trained.'

'Trained? What do you mean?'

'Never mind.' Shut up, Gentry. Just stop fucking talking.

'Do you think most people go through training for this?'

'No ... I just—'

'Do you think I am an expert of some kind?'

'I didn't mean—'

'You are strange, Six. I really like you. But you are very strange.'

'Yeah.'

Court was self-conscious for a while longer, even distracted when he heard footsteps in the hallway. But the footsteps melted away, and his inhibitions followed them down the hall.

He felt her small fingertips on his belt, then he felt it removed from around his waist. She unbuttoned his khakis, and he did not stop her – he just watched. When his pants were off, she began moving back up his body. She put her right hand on his left thigh, and he winced loudly.

'I'm sorry,' she said, then inspected his leg. Drew a delicate finger tip up and down the length of a deep cut that was, by now, nearly three weeks old.

'What happened?'

'Crocodile,' Gentry said, his mind a million miles from the Amazon tributary right now.

Laura laughed. '*Crocodilo.*' She said it in Spanish and laughed again. 'I don't believe you. So many secrets you keep.' She put her hand on his chest, over his heart. Then she moved it away and began kissing him there. 'You can have your secrets, Six; you can hold them in your heart. But please make a little room in there for me, too. Okay?'

'Okay,' he said, and now he could resist no more. He sat up slowly, kissed her lips, and rolled her gently onto her back.

Her body felt warm and firm, but the tense, hard muscles were shielded by soft, compliant flesh. He felt her racing heartbeat, and it comforted him, made him realize that they were in this together, that she was not just dispassionately watching him like an instructor grading his actions. When he slowed down, she grabbed at him, pulled him forward. When he took a deep breath, she covered his mouth with hers. When he turned his head towards the door or the window, she took his head in her hands and turned it back to her. When he winced with the pain in his thigh, she just pulled him down on top of her and kissed him until the pain went away.

Until, finally, there was no more door and no more window. No more danger and no more pain. There was only the two of them, here, on a little bed and safe from all harm.

They made love for hours.

Gentry woke from a sleep deeper than any he had experienced in years. He felt the sun warm the bed around him.

She was there, wrapped up tightly against his body, her little face in the crook of his arm, her left hand flat on his chest. Her breathing, her body's warmth, the smell of her skin. It was all amazing.

Court had not even known that skin had a smell.

She did not move. He looked down at her face and just saw her full lips and the tip of her nose. Her short, jet-black hair lay tussled; a small rubber band held the longest strands tight behind her ears.

He thought about Eddie, and a panic washed over him. Was this wrong? Emotions of romantic guilt attacked him from nowhere; he'd never felt this way in his life. He thought of standing at his friend's burial plot, just there to say good-bye, and then, three days later, screwing his friend's younger sister, the thing in this world his dead friend had most endeavored to protect while alive.

Her eyes opened, and she looked up at him.

'Are you okay?' he asked tentatively.

She kissed him. He forgot his panic.

'What time is it?' she asked.

'Late. We need to get moving.'

'Where are we going?'

'We need a car. We need it gassed and ready to go. As soon as we meet with Pfleger and get the docs, we are heading up towards the border. We'll sleep in shifts, go straight on through the night. We should make it by three p.m. tomorrow to meet with your family.'

'We are stealing a car?' she sighed. 'You are going to have to help me find a job in the U.S. to pay back all these people for their vehicles.'

Court realized she assumed he'd be crossing the border with her family. He'd told them he didn't have papers, but for all she knew that was something he'd arranged with Jerry.

Shit. He didn't want to mislead her. But he could not tell her that he would be in as much danger in the United States as she was here in Mexico. New guilt hit him from a new angle. Did she only make love to him because she thought they would be together when this was over?

Was there any way he could be with her when it was over?

She squeezed him tight as she yawned and stretched.

'Do we really have to get up now?' she asked with a smile in her voice.

Court heard footsteps in the hallway. He tuned them out to answer her.

'Yes, we do. Grand theft auto in an unfamiliar city is going to require a little time.'

'Can we go across to la Iglesia de Nuestra Señora? Just for a few minutes?'

Court sighed. He should have expected that. Somehow with all the sex he forgot about her penchant for church.

'For fifteen minutes, no more, or we won't be able—'

Court stopped talking.

'¿Qué?'

Silently he turned his attention towards the door across the room.

'¿Qué?'

He sat up quickly, grabbed the Beretta pistol on the side table. Aimed it at the door. It was half hidden behind the television and the chest of drawers. He cocked his head a little but said nothing.

All was silent for several seconds. Laura did not speak again, even her breathing stopped as she looked at the muscular back of the American sitting on the bed. She noticed a nasty scar on his left shoulder blade, but her heart was in her throat. Had he heard something?

Court did not move. Kept his weapon trained on the door, his head cocked for noise. He stood slowly, wearing only his boxers, turned his head to the right to get a look out the window at the street below. He kept his pistol trained at the front door.

He looked down onto Calle Donceles. A few parked cars, no traffic. No passersby. All was quiet. Too quiet for a normal—

Black boots in his face, dropping from above, swinging towards the window. He started to raise the pistol at the threat but he heard the door explode behind him. His gun barrel was swinging still, caught between the two threats.

The glass window crashed in; three feet from his bare chest and face, crystalline shards exploded, and the black boots swung in and hit him squarely.

Gentry flew backwards, the pistol left his right hand and he cartwheeled back. He caught a split-second's glimpse of the *federale* who had rappelled through the window; the man had landed hard on his back but he recovered quickly, sat back up, and lifted an MP5 towards the man on the floor across the room.

To his left Court heard a second explosion, the TV and the chest of drawers flew across the room and crashed against the wall. Behind the wreckage Court saw men file into the room: two, then four, then six. *Federales* in masks and goggles with sub guns and body armor. They appeared more ominous through the haze of smoke from the charges that had blown in the door and the obstructions.

There was the crunching of glass as the rappeller scrambled back to his feet.

Laura was screaming.

Court raised his hands and spoke to her. 'Don't move! Do what they say! They've got us.'

37

It was hot on the floorboard in the back of the sedan. Three pairs of black boots on Court's back, ass, and legs kept him facedown; the electrical tape over his mouth, the cuffs securing his hands behind his back, and the black hood over his head only added to the stifling conditions. A few times the sweat in his eyes burned so badly he cried out, muffled as it was by the tape. Each time he made this noise a boot heel in the back of his head quieted him. He felt the cuts on his chest from the window glass, felt the warm wetness of his blood and perspiration on the rubber floor mats under him. He tried to shift his weight forward to his shoulders to relieve the pain, but this just pressed his face tighter into his hood and made it nearly impossible to breathe.

He felt the tip of the suppressor of an MP5 pressed into the small of his back; it jabbed into his lumbar with every bump in the road.

The car radio played *banda* music at full volume; if there was conversation between the men above him, he could not hear it over the loud accordions and crashing cymbals.

Court assumed Laura must have been tossed into another vehicle; he'd caught a glimpse through the window of several nondescript four-doors pulling in front of the hotel as he was being cuffed and taped up in the hotel room. He'd also stolen a glance at Eddie's sister just before the hood was slipped on and the lights were turned off. Laura's already big eyes were wide with panic; the men had flipped her facedown on the bed and cuffed her there.

She was naked.

Gentry had no idea if these were real cops or, even if they *were* real cops, if they were good guys or bad. He did not know where they were taking him; even a born-and-bred *ciudadano* of Mexico City would not have been able to discern their location after dozens of turns while hooded and facedown.

Finally, the car stopped, and he was dragged out by his shoulders; the perspiration all over his body made the men's gloves slip as they wrestled to take hold. Court was frog-marched forward, and he felt the sunlight leave him and heard the echoes of a large room. He continued on, stepped into what felt and sounded like a freight elevator, and went down what must have been at least three floors.

Once off the elevator, he was pushed forward a few yards and then spun around, his hands were unfastened, and then his body was pressed up against cold metal bars. A fence, perhaps? His arms were simultaneously outstretched and cuffed wide away from his body, two men on each appendage. The insides of his legs were kicked until he spread them, and his ankles were shackled in irons, with his legs spread wide open.

His back and arms and legs and butt pressed up against cold metal.

A pair of long, cold sheers entered his boxer shorts. He tried to recoil from the sharp metal, but he could not get away. His underwear was cut from his body. He was totally naked now, chained spreadeagle against cold metal.

He began to shake in the cold.

Only then was his hood pulled off his head. Steam obstructed his view for a moment as it poured from his hair and beard; thick beads dripped from his eyelashes onto his cheeks and tickled as they trickled down through his facial hair to his chin.

The room was a square, stone basement, twenty by twenty, with a low ceiling and a cement floor. A bare overhead bulb in the center illuminated the middle of the room and the majority of the walls, but left the corners completely black. He smelled the mold in the room, but that was not all.

He also smelled the unmistakable scent of death. This was a kill house, a torture chamber. There was dried blood on the walls, and the cement floor was stained with black rivulets of blood that led towards the drain in the center of the room.

Across from Court was the wooden door of the freight elevator. Next to that was a narrow stairwell with no door.

Four men stood around – two dressed in the uniform of the federal police. They'd removed their masks and goggles and helmets, but their submachine guns hung from their chest rigs.

The other two men wore leather aprons. They were Mexicans; they were not cops; they looked serious and sinister. One of them was short and fat; his head was bald and covered in sweat that shone in the light above him. He was hard at work on some sort of wheeled table not more than six feet ahead and to the left of Gentry. The other was a young man, perhaps twenty, dressed the same as the older.

These would be Gentry's torturers; he was certain of it.

There were no Black Suits in the room, which Court initially took as a good sign, but he had to search hard for that silver lining. A few feet in front of the iron fence or grate onto which his naked body was now chained, a car battery sat on a dolly, and wires wound their way up to a metal contraption on the rolling table. More coiled wires ran from this machine and ended at large roach clips that were fastened to Gentry's grate.

Court had been around. He knew an electroconvulsive torture device when he saw one. And right now, he was bare-assed naked and attached to one.

'Welcome to hell,' the fat man said in Spanish. 'I will be your tour guide as we visit the horrific, agonizing, and slow end to your life.'

Gentry said nothing.

'They call me el Carnicerito.' *The Little Butcher.* The short, fat, bald-headed man said this though he was still distracted by his work; he arranged devices on the rolling table while he talked.

Saws, hand drills, a stainless steel mallet that gleamed in the light of the bare bulb. Knives, forceps, kerrisons rongeurs, and other surgical tools covered the horizontal surfaces of the table. Without looking up from his equipment, he continued, 'I work for Don Daniel. I produce pain, and I extract information from those reluctant to give it. I am extremely good at what I do.'

'Your mother must be proud.' Court affected the macho comment, but he wasn't feeling it. He pulled and kicked against his restraints, and he could tell that he would not be getting himself off of this contraption.

In short, he was fucking toast.

El Carnicerito just smiled. 'This is my protégé.' He waved a fat hand towards the young man in the apron. Then he returned to his work at the table. He turned a dial on the machine slightly, and Court felt electricity tingle his spine. The fat man looked at a dial on the face of the black device. Apparently, it was just a test, because he inflicted no pain. He turned the dial back down and looked up at his victim.

'The electricity is just one measure I have at my disposal. Within the next few hours you will endure indescribable suffering.'

El Carnicerito stepped forward, close to Court's body, and reached up with a rubber glove, began picking glass out of the cuts in the American's chest inflicted by the *federale* coming through the window. Court winced with pain but tried to keep his face as impassive as possible; he did not want to encourage this sadist by showing how much it hurt.

The man smiled; Court could plainly see that an idea had entered the butcher's head. He turned quickly and stepped over to the protégé, and he delivered a quiet command. His subordinate nodded and hurriedly left the room via the stairwell.

As he ran up the stairs and the echoes of his footfalls began to die off, new footsteps clicked down from above. Two men, Gentry could tell, one wearing heavy boots and the other soft shoes.

Within seconds the two new men arrived in the dungeon. One was a Black Suit. Young and well-groomed, he wore the short hair, goatee, and mustache combo common with the leadership of the criminal organization. An HK UMP submachine gun hung from a sling over his right shoulder.

The man's fine suit and clean face contrasted with the sick sights and smells of this basement hellhole.

And the man next to him contrasted with the dungeon as well. He was American. White, thin, curly brown hair. He wore a wrinkled short-sleeved dress shirt and khakis.

Court rolled his eyes.

Jerry Pfleger.

Court scowled at him as he stepped into the light. Dryly, Court said, 'My fellow American.'

The young American embassy staffer looked around the room, clearly taken aback by where he found himself. He was shocked, out of his league, and frightened. He tried to mask it, but Court saw the horror on his face.

'Why is he still alive?' Jerry asked the men in Spanish as he moved into the room.

Pfleger kept looking around the room; clearly, he could smell the death, see the stains on the walls and floor. He knew what this place was. What went on there. He shook it off and looked at Court. 'I'm a businessman, dude. It's the American way. I insisted on coming here to . . . protect my interests in this enterprise.'

Court said, 'They are going to kill the girl; they want to kill her sister-in-law and her unborn baby.'

Jerry nodded. Clearly, he at least suspected this if he did not know it for sure. 'Sucks to be them.'

'You did this for money?'

Jerry nodded then shrugged. 'It's more than money, actually. I am making a statement.'

'What statement?'

'The statement is, dude, I hate it here.'

'You hate Mexico?'

'Of course. Don't you?'

Gentry did not respond.

'Yeah, well, you're banging a hot little beaner, so you'd like it, wouldn't you?'

'You are a trained diplomat? Christ.'

'Have you ever been to Denmark?'

Court lied. 'No.'

'Denmark is the shit. I went to college in Denmark; I speak Danish, know the backstreets of Copenhagen like the back of my hand. I get hired by State, and where do those idiots at Foggy Bottom fucking send me? Denmark? Finland? Norway? Fuck no! Mexico! Are you kidding me? Four years punching visas for beaners. Fuck that! As long as I'm stuck down here, I'm going to make a little dough along the way.'

'And you're making money by handing Laura over to de la Rocha?'

Jerry smiled. 'Oh ... you don't get it, do you.'

'Get what?'

'I'm handing the girl to DLR, yeah. But that's a freebie. I'm making my money handing *you* to the CIA.'

Gentry shook his head. Slowly, he said, 'Jerry, Jerry, Jerry. Think about that for a second. What is Langley going to do when they find out a consular affairs officer is working with the Black Suits? You'll never get that posting to Copenhagen.'

Jerry smiled again, like he was one thousand times smarter than the naked man in chains.

'Los Trajes Negros do the handoff to the CIA, and then they give me the reward. I get the reward, and I'm outta here. Outta Mexico, outta the State Department.'

'You've got it all figured out, don't you?'

'I have a deal with the man himself. DLR.'

'Deals with the devil usually don't pay off in the long run, kid.'

'He's a businessman. I'm a businessman. It's all good.' Then he looked to the Little Butcher, who'd been standing patiently as the men spoke English. In Spanish Jerry said, 'That some sort of electricshock machine?'

El Carnicerito nodded.

'Then juice this *pendejo* once for me, boss.'

The Little Butcher smiled and grabbed an old leather wallet from the table. 'Open your mouth, please. We cannot have you biting your tongue off when we still need you to talk.'

Court did as he was told; he knew what was coming, and he knew the leather in his mouth would help. He moved his tongue away from his teeth, bit down hard, and the Little Butcher turned the dial.

Current ripped through Court's body, from his toes to his anus to his neck. His back arched, his eyes protruded, and a vibrato cry emitted from deep in his throat behind the wallet.

After a few seconds the dial was rotated back down. Fresh sweat shone on the prisoner's face and chest.

The torturer stopped for just a moment. Pulled the wallet from his prisoner's mouth. 'Where is Elena Gamboa?'

'*¿Cómo se dice "fuck you"?*'

The wallet was returned to Gentry's mouth, and he bit down. Electricity pulsed through his body again. His head slammed backwards uncontrollably, slamming his skull into the iron grate behind him.

The torture was stopped. The wallet removed. The question repeated.

'Where is Elena Gamboa?'

'Kiss my—'

The wallet was put back in place. The shocks grew stronger, the pain more intense; the muscle spasms wrenched his body in all directions.

The Black Suit and the two *federales* looked on.

Jerry Pfleger looked away.

Minutes later a technical glitch in the machinery allowed Court a respite from the agony. The Little Butcher worked on his electroconvulsive device, and the protégé returned down the stairs with a bag of groceries.

Gentry's blurred vision followed the young man's movements as he stepped to the table and pulled items from the bag.

An empty plastic pitcher, a large bag of salt, a bottle of rotgut tequila, and a large bag of limes.

Court groaned and let the now shredded leather wallet fall from his mouth to the floor. Immediately, he regretted his show of dread. It would only bolster the fat man. The Little Butcher turned his attention from the machine, and he began slicing the limes in half. The protégé sliced as well; together they looked like a couple of bartenders in a beachside cabana bar. Helped by his assistant, together the two men squeezed the juice into the pitcher and then tossed the peels in behind the juice.

The assistant poured the alcohol on top, and el Carnicerito opened the bag of salt.

Court even managed a quip. 'I'll take mine with no salt.'

The three other Mexicans in the room watched with curiosity. They laughed and joked amongst themselves, but Court wasn't in the mood to concentrate on translating their fun so that he could understand it.

When the pitcher was full of tequila, salt, and lime juice, the torturer hefted it and walked forward to the naked prisoner. He held it up in front of Court's face, slapped him a few times to make sure he had Court's attention, and then the butcher fiddled with a tiny piece of broken glass stuck just below the American's right nipple.

'Can you imagine how this will feel inside your swollen open wounds?' The man smiled as he spoke.

Gentry said nothing.

'I will ask you where Señora Gamboa is hiding. But please ... please, I beg you, do not tell me. I want to do this to you!'

The narcos back by the elevator just laughed. Jerry looked away.

Court nodded, took in a long breath, and then spit in the face of the cruel little Mexican. The Little Butcher's assistant ran forward and punched Court in the nose.

The fat man did not wipe the spit away. Instead he smiled and said, 'You only make my job more enjoyable. In a couple of hours when I saw your head off of your living, breathing, flailing body, I will feel pity. A pity that the day is done.'

And with that he lifted the pitcher, slowly poured the pungent mixture down the American's nude and abraded body, rubbed the liquid with his hands into the open cuts, smeared it in, and cackled almost as loud as the prisoner's screams.

A minute later the elevator was called up to the surface. The two *federale* gunmen in the room put their hands to their ear-pieces, and the Black Suit looked down at his phone and saw that he'd missed a call, unable to hear the ring over the wails of agony in the small chamber.

Before he could identify the call, one of the cops stiffened slightly, looked to el Carnicerito, and said, 'DLR is here.'

Court continued to moan in agony.

Seconds later the elevator started back down; it took thirty seconds for the car to arrive with a thud. The wooden door rose. Three men in black suits emerged, appearing dim in the light.

Court writhed in pain, forgotten by the others in the room. It was several seconds before he could recover from the residual twitching in his muscles enough to recognize Daniel de la Rocha at the center of the three new arrivals.

38

DLR looked the gringo up and down. Jerry, el Carnicerito, his young protégé, Spider's number-two man Carlos, the two police who had brought Court down from the car, stood to the side in the dark cold room. Daniel, Emilio, and Spider stepped up closer to the prisoner.

Daniel stopped three feet from the tip of the American's nose. 'You? *You?*'

The American stared back.

In Spanish the impeccably dressed man said, 'I was expecting ... I don't know. Rambo, maybe?' The room erupted in laughter. And then in English. 'You've caused me some problems, amigo. I'm just curious ... Why?'

The Gray Man did not respond. He wasn't sure if he could speak; he felt his teeth chattering.

De la Rocha shrugged, looked down at the rolling cart with the machine and the surgical instruments, then up at the prisoner.

'What kind of fun have you been having with my friend here, *gordo?*'

'So far just some shocks. I also took advantage of the lesions on his body from the broken glass.' He held up the pitcher, now empty, and de la Rocha sniffed it. His eyebrows furrowed for a moment, and then he smiled.

'A gringo margarita.'

'*Sí*, Don Daniel.'

294

'*Muy bien.*' *Very good.* 'You have not yet used the donkey prod?'

'Not yet. Would you like to watch?'

Daniel rolled his eyes and looked back to his men. 'Would I like to watch?' Back to Gentry. 'Only a *maricón* would like to watch that. I pay him so I *don't* have to watch a cattle prod shoved against your *huevos* and then electrified.'

Court bit his lower lip to stop the quivering.

DLR looked to his torturer. 'Anything about the Gamboa woman?'

'No. He spoke to the other *norteamericano* in English. I did not understand, but he has not said anything of value to me. This one is very strong.'

Daniel regarded Pfleger for just a moment, then looked to Carlos. Carlos spoke English, and he had been in the room during the conversation between the Americans.

'Nothing, *jefe.*'

DLR turned back to look over the man shackled to the fence. 'That is a beautiful scar on your hip there. I see an old bullet wound on your thigh, too.' He stepped forward and looked at it. 'A year old at most.' He then turned Court's head to the left with his fingertips. 'A burn on your neck. Much older. Five years?'

No answer.

'These little cuts on your face and arms? The bruising on your chest?' Daniel shrugged. 'You are no stranger to pain, I see. You may resist our efforts to pry information from you.

'No matter. We have the sister-in-law. I hear you two slept together last night. Did you enjoy your taste of our culture, amigo? Latin women can be very fiery, very passionate, yes? If you don't talk, we will start work on her. The techniques at our disposal will remove that passion within minutes. We will turn her into a zombie in an hour.' DLR smiled at Gentry.

Then asked, 'Where is Elena Gamboa at this moment?'

Court shrugged as best he could with his arms pulled wide.

'Obviously, we know you were attempting to arrange for her to get into the United States.'

Nothing from the tortured man in front of him.

'She will not leave Mexico.' Then the handsome man in the black suit said, 'Why do you care? She is not your family. Do you have family?' No response from Court. DLR continued, 'I believe family is the most important thing in the world. Don't you?'

Gentry took a moment to control himself. Tried his best to sound strong. 'I believe your family is going to miss you when you're dead.'

'Ha, ha. A threat? He finally speaks and he threatens me? Carnicerito?'

'Sí, patrón.'

'It's cold down here. Turn on the heat.'

'Sí, patrón.' The fat man turned the dial without placing the remnants of the wallet in his victim's mouth, and Gentry went wild: his body was out of his control, his mind cleared of all thoughts except a frantic desire to escape pain and find relief, his heart pounded in his chest like when he was underwater with the crocodile above him and he could not find his shotgun and the gnashing teeth were coming closer and close—

The Little Butcher eased back the dial.

Gentry's head dropped forward in exhaustion. Looking down, he saw he was pissing all over the floor. Sweat dripped off his nude body along with his urine and drips of blood. He was thankful he had managed to avoid biting off his tongue.

When he finally pulled his head back up, he saw Laura being shoved into the room from the stairwell, her hands bound in front of her, a single Black Suit pushing her forward from behind. The man handed her off to Spider, then turned around and disappeared back up the stairs.

Even in agony, Court felt the shame and humiliation as his bladder emptied in front of her.

She was dressed in simple blue cotton warm-up pants and a white tank top. Her right eye was black and red. Her lip fat. Even in the dim light where she stood, Court could see her fists were scuffed and bloody.

She'd been fighting back.

Good girl.

Daniel leaned close. 'You almost pissed on my suit. That would have made me very angry.'

De la Rocha turned to the man holding Laura by the shoulders. 'Spider, bring her into the light, put her on her knees in front of her gringo. We will see how deep is their love.'

The man shoved the tiny woman onto the cement, just a few feet in front of Gentry. The leader of DLR's enforcers pulled out a silver .45 automatic pistol and handed it to his *patrón*. Daniel de la Rocha took the weapon and pressed it into Laura's black bob of hair.

'If you do not tell me, right now, where my forces can find Elena Gamboa, I will blow off this pretty head. I will *not* count to three; I will *not* threaten to wound her; I will simply kill her, right here, right now, unless the next words out of your mouth tell me where Major Gamboa's widow is hiding.'

Laura shouted in the small room, 'Don't say—'

De la Rocha pounded the grip of the .45 into her head. Laura went down onto the filthy concrete. Dazed, she struggled back up to her knees.

Court's head rose, and he looked at Daniel de la Rocha.

Slowly, very slowly, he nodded, and softly he spoke. 'Okay. Okay. Listen very carefully.'

De la Rocha pulled the hammer back on the pistol, pressed it tighter against her head. 'Oh, I *am* listening, amigo.'

Court nodded again. Then he shrugged. 'Shoot the bitch. I don't give a fuck.'

De la Rocha just stared, his mouth slightly open. He looked back to the Black Suit behind him. 'He is a cold fucker, no, Spider? Reminds me of you.' Then back to Gentry. 'It is a bluff. A very good bluff, but you are bluffing. You care about what happens to her.' He thought for a long moment; clearly, he had not expected this reaction from the American.

Gentry said, 'I didn't sign up for this shit. The old American guy, Cullen, paid me five grand to watch over his dead buddy's family for a couple of days. Two large in advance, three more after we got back from Puerto Vallarta. He didn't say anything about a goddamned cartel hit on them.'

Now de la Rocha's dark eyebrows furrowed. He took in the English. Weighed the words carefully. 'You are private security? A bodyguard?'

'I was. I just retired.'

DLR conferred with Spider for a moment. Court could not understand what they were saying. Then de la Rocha turned back, shook his head.

'No. No, señor. I do not believe you. It was a nice try, but my associate's men tell him that you escaped the hacienda, and then went back, at great personal danger to yourself, to rescue *la familia* Gamboa. That does not sound like the actions of any hired gunman I have ever heard of.'

Court started to speak, but Daniel continued talking. He was not a man accustomed to being interrupted.

'You know what? Maybe I *won't* kill her now. Maybe I'll have my sickest, most fucked-up *sicarios* rape her *puta culo* until she dies. It will take a little longer, yes, but it will be more rewarding for my men. Maybe I'll have el Carnicerito do it right now in front of you.'

Court looked over at the fat bald man in the leather apron. The torturer licked his lips.

A mobile phone rang. Emilio pulled it from the front pocket of his suit pants and looked down at it. He offered it to his boss. DLR took it, looked at the face, and with a sigh, he flipped it open. 'Nestor, can it wait?' A short pause and then, *'Está bien.'* He took the pistol away from Laura's head and replaced it with his foot. He pushed his Italian loafer hard on the back of her skull, shoving the tiny girl to the concrete floor. When she was down on the urine-soaked concrete, he turned and walked back into the stairwell.

The Little Butcher spoke with the Spider. Court tried to make eye contact with Laura, but she remained on her knees,

her bound hands flat on the concrete in front of her, her head down. He wanted to speak, to tell her the only chance she had to survive was for him to act like he didn't care whether she lived or died. It was a long shot, a hell of a long shot, but he'd seen no alternative.

He had to be cold as ice. He had to play like her life held no leverage with him.

Then she looked up at him from the ground, her eyes full of confusion and, yes, even heartbreak. Court had the impression she did not understand his ploy was for her benefit; she actually bought his bullshit about not caring about her.

Court turned away from her sad eyes and looked up to the *narco* lord across the room. He could hear snippets from DLR's side of his phone conversation, but much of it was either too fast or spoken with too much Mexican slang for Gentry to understand. Still, he picked up some of the exchange.

'No deal. I need time to extract the information. Twenty-four hours – Okay, they can send one man to come look, but they cannot touch – Kill him? That's fine ... Okay, but they only get the body when we have what we need from him. Make that clear.'

DLR hung up the phone and stepped back in the dungeon, conferred softly with Spider for a moment. There was even a brief argument between them, but it settled down quickly. He then spoke to his prisoners. 'Change of plans. Someone is coming to identify this piece of *mierda*.'

Jerry spoke up from the corner. 'Who?'

'Some gringo with la CIA.'

Jerry's next comment squeaked out in a plaintive whine. 'The CIA is coming here? Now?'

De la Rocha nodded. 'They insist on making sure this is the *cabrón* they are looking for. If he is the correct person, then *el hombre de la CIA* will go away, and we can work on this *pinche* gringo here to get the information we need.' He looked up at Gentry now. 'Then they want us to kill him and dump his head near the embassy.'

Pfleger shot out of the dark corner, up to de la Rocha. 'Wait! No! If the spook is on the way, I've got to get out of here! I can't let them see me! I'll go to prison for working with you guys!'

De la Rocha shrugged. Clearly, he didn't give a shit about Jerry Pfleger. Still, he said, 'You are staying here with your prize; that's what you asked for, wasn't it? Somebody give Jerry a mask.' One of the *federales* pulled a balaclava from the side pocket of his cargo pants, tossed it to the American, who pulled it over his head, struggling to orient the holes for the eyes. When he had himself situated, he looked up at Gentry. Clearly, the prisoner could out him still, mask or not. This plan didn't make much sense. Through the nylon mask he said, 'Mister de la Rocha, what if—'

'Enough from you!' Daniel pointed the .45 at Jerry, and Jerry shut his mouth. He stepped back against the wall with his hands up in compliance.

De la Rocha looked to Court now. 'You don't make very many friends, do you? La CIA is desperate for me to kill you.'

Gentry asked, 'And what do you get in return?'

'La CIA will provide us intel from the DEA on the Madrigal Cartel's connections with governments in South America.'

Jerry took a step back towards the light again. 'And money, right? I still get—'

DLR pointed the pistol at Pfleger again. *'Plata o plomo?' Money or lead?*

'Money, *jefe*. Definitely money.' Pfleger backed up again.

De la Rocha continued. 'So I am going to leave you now; my associates insist I not be here when la CIA arrive. But I am going to take your little *puta* with me. The spy will be brought here to identify you and then taken away. The Little Butcher will have the next twenty-four hours to find out what you know about Elena Gamboa, and I will have the rest of my life to find out what little Lorita knows about Elena Gamboa.'

It was quiet in the room.

'The only question is, which one of us will have the most fun with our work?'

Spider took the girl by the hair and pulled her up to her feet. She screamed with the movement. DLR looked at Gentry one last time as he started for the door. 'You have cost me much, and now you will repay me.'

As he entered the stairwell, he called back to the room, 'Carnicerito, help our American friend Jerry here and torture this prisoner so bad he won't be able to speak when the spy comes to identify him.'

The fat man replied, '*Sí, jefe.*' And he turned the dial on the table to its maximum voltage.

39

The Black Suits picked up the CIA man in Chapultepec Park; as prearranged he wore a red tie and stood on the steps of the National Museum of Anthropology. He was a thick man, blond hair that ran just past his collar and a chunky neck from which the tip of his chin barely peeked. He was getting thicker by the minute, too. He'd just finished a dulce de leche ice cream cone, purchased at a stand across from the steps, and had just wiped his thick hands clean of the sticky residue as the Black Suits pulled up.

He'd been one fit and fine son of a bitch a while back, but he'd let himself go.

His current job did not require staying in shape.

A gray van pulled to a stop in front of him on Las Grutas Avenue, the side door slid open, and the thick man from la CIA climbed in.

Four sets of well-practiced hands went to work on him immediately as the van drove off to the south towards Paseo de la Reforma. His briefcase was taken and searched, he was hooded and frisked, his wallet was pulled from his poplin pants, and his white button-down shirt was lifted up to check for a wire.

The hands that felt him up, he knew, would also be the hands that killed him if they were so instructed by their masters.

The van turned left, which the CIA man noted from under his blindfold, but he really did not expect to be able to discern where he was being taken.

He'd been to Mexico City before, yes, but this was not his turf.

He sat quietly between his minders as they drove through traffic; he'd ridden hooded in vans, surrounded by a local gun crew, more times that he cared to remember. In Beirut, in Kosovo, in Thailand, in Somalia, in other shit-splattered dumps around this godforsaken planet.

Usually, he was bundled like laundry into a car or van to be hauled to some secret location to meet with a contact. But this was different. *He* was here, in Mexico, and not some other poor agency sap, for one reason and one reason only.

He had an ability that very few others possessed.

He had the ability to positively identify Courtland Gentry, code name Violator, call sign Sierra Six, nickname the Gray Man, in one second flat.

And why not? They had worked together for five years.

The thick CIA man had spent the last two days in Puerto Vallarta, waiting for word from local case officers that the target had been found. He suspected a wet team from the Special Activities Division had moved into the theater as well, but they wouldn't have any contact with him, nor he with them. Yesterday morning he flew to Mexico City to wait at the embassy for a sighting of the man Langley suspected to be their number one persona non grata ex-employee. The embassy was papered with photos of the guy sliding on the telephone lines above the shoot-out in PV. From just the picture, the thick CIA man in the van honestly had no idea if it was his former colleague or not, but the stunt sure sounded like something Violator would have tried, and like something he could have pulled off.

Hell, the CIA man knew better than to ever bet against Courtland Gentry. When it came to close-quarters battle, when it came to kicking in a door and taking out the bad guys in the room, when it came to sending in a small covert unit against a larger enemy and longer odds, Sierra Six had been the best.

So, the CIA man suspected it was Court; he was here, and he was shooting it out with the *narcos*.

Lord have mercy on the narcos.

A connection had been made between Gentry and the leader of the GOPES team blown up on the boat as well. Eduardo Gamboa had worked in the DEA for years, and Violator and he had shared a Laotian prison cell for a few weeks more than a decade prior.

Tenuous. Tenuous at best, but not too tenuous for Langley to call the thick CIA man, roust him from his bed and shove him on a Company Lear, race him to Mexico and plop him on his fat ass to wait for a chance to positively identify the target.

So now he rocked back and forth, shoulder to shoulder with a vanload of goons from the Daniel de la Rocha organization, the Black Suits, some seriously bad motherfuckers who claimed to be holding Violator, or somebody who looks a lot like him, somewhere in Mexico City. These pricks didn't need money, so it wasn't the reward they were after. It was some quid pro quo worked out high above the CIA man's pay grade. It bothered him that Langley would play ball with these guys, but Denny Carmichael, current head of the National Clandestine Service, had a boner for Violator, so God only knew how Denny would scratch DLR's back if he gave up Court.

The CIA man pondered it all.

Court. Violator. Sierra Six. The Gray Man.

The asshole who ruined my life.

The van stopped for a moment. The American thought this was the end of the road, but no, they moved forward again and made a right turn; he swayed along with the men sandwiching him.

If the Agency's assessment was correct, if this *was*, in fact, Violator, in a few minutes the American would have the chance to let Gentry know how much trouble he'd caused.

And the CIA man had his orders. He had been ordered to identify Violator, yes, but that was not all.

He'd also been ordered, if allowed by Los Trajes Negros, to stick around and watch Court Gentry die.

*

For a time Court realized that he missed the full-body electric shocks provided by the car battery. Twice during a ten-minute zapping by the Little Butcher and his device of misery, Court had blown a breaker switch on the console. The old contraption used fuses that had shorted, and they had been replaced, but the American was able to endure more punishment than anyone that had ever been wired to the fence. So the machine had been put to the side so that a new method could be used on him.

The donkey prod.

At first el Carnicerito had just touched the two sharp prongs to Gentry's bloody chest. The shock was more acute than the all-over electricity he'd been receiving from the shock machine. The prod created a sting and a burn, and it was god-awful but not as bad as the musclewrenching misery of the car battery juice sent through the fence. Then the Little Butcher used the donkey prod in more and more painful locations on Gentry's body, inevitably focusing his attention on his prisoner's genitals. Twice he'd shocked him there. The first time he didn't have the prongs seated correctly, and the gadget just buzzed.

But the second time he rammed the pincers hard against the American's balls, pressed the button, and Court had spewed vomit nearly six feet into the room.

The five Mexicans burst into laughter.

The gringo soon fainted, but smelling salts returned him to his torture session, lest he miss any of the good parts.

Jerry Pfleger stood against the wall to the side; he'd turned away from the cruelty long ago, and he just stared at the moldy bricks in front of him. His body shook; he told himself it was the cold, morguelike air in the basement dungeon, but that wasn't it at all.

He was scared.

He wondered if this was all worth one million dollars.

Jerry looked back over his shoulder when the torturer waddled over to a rubber bucket on the floor against the wall and retrieved a well-soaked iron rod from it. Jerry winced again and turned his head back into the corner. Listened as the dungeon master spoke to his prisoner softly as he prepared the device. 'You have suffered much already, amigo, and the only way to prevent more suffering is to tell me where we can find Señora Gamboa.'

The long device dripped black oil, and the Little Butcher held it up like it was some sort of prize.

Court's head hung low, but still he looked at it. Pfleger watched the muscles of the man's body tighten in revulsion.

He knew where that thing was going.

The elevator again came to life, and the car began to lower slowly.

The rod went back into the bucket, but the torturer said, 'We will get back to our fun in a moment, my friend. You now have some time to think about things.'

The freight door opened, and a large, hooded man in a tropic-weight poplin suit was led in by the two men in *federale* uniforms. The large man's arms were not bound. He was put directly under the light at the center of the room, and then his hood was removed. He recoiled at the bare bulb and then focused on the scene before him.

The nude prisoner, bloody and wet, chained to the metal fence that was bolted into the wall and fixed to iron posts in the cement floor. The wires running to the rolling cart, then on to the battery on the dolly.

The blond man took a few more moments to look around, to size up the six other men in the room with him, and to sniff the air. He took in the odor of decaying human flesh. He looked around impassively for a few seconds more, seemingly unfazed by all in view, as if torture chambers were nothing much to see.

Then he spoke, his words calm and confident like he was a man comfortable with these surroundings. In Spanish he said, 'It looks like you guys started the party without me.'

Court knew an old coworker from the Agency was coming to identify him. He fully expected to be staring face to face with Zack Hightower, his former team leader in the Goon Squad.

But it was not Zack Hightower.

It was Hanley. Matthew Hanley.

Gentry had not seen Matt in more than five years, and even back then they had never spent much time around each other. Hanley was a SAD executive; he had run Gentry's old unit, Task Force Golf Sierra, from Langley, passed instructions primarily through team leader Hightower, who relayed orders on to the rest of the men.

Court had last seen Zack back in the spring, and Zack had told him Hanley was out of SAD and riding a desk somewhere in the Third World, his fall from grace the fault of Gentry himself.

And now here he was, in a secret torture chamber operated by a vicious drug cartel somewhere in or near Mexico City.

No words were spoken between the two at first. Instead Hanley addressed the fat man behind the table. 'You in charge here?'

'You might say this is my office,' came the proud reply.

Hanley just nodded. Then he stepped closer to Gentry.

'I must ask that you do not touch the prisoner,' said the Black Suit from behind. The two *federales* in the room took a step forward but stopped when Hanley nodded again.

The thick American kept his hands to his side, but he moved even closer to the prisoner. He only stopped his slow advance when the two men's faces were inches apart.

Court looked too wounded to speak; his eyes were swollen and vomit coated his bloody lips. As far as Hanley could tell, the younger man was out of it. But Gentry *did* speak, his words soft but strong enough, loud enough, to be understood by anyone in the room who spoke English. 'Do what you gotta do to me, Matt, but the guy in the corner is a State Department dip working for the Black Suits.'

Matt Hanley turned, glanced at the man in the corner. Pfleger's black balaclava mask worn with khakis and a white short-sleeved button-down were an odd combination in a room where the other three masked men were decked out in full SWAT gear and guns. Pfleger did not speak, did not move. Just stared back. Hanley shrugged. 'Not my problem.'

Court spoke again, though the words came out through winces and muscle spasms. 'He's ... he's running a criminal ring ... selling visas to illegals.'

Hanley glared at the bound prisoner. 'Yeah?' He turned back to Pfleger again. 'How's business?'

'I ... I'm not really. I just—'

'Look at me, boy!' Hanley's voice, a low West Virginian drawl, boomed in the concrete dungeon.

'Yes, sir?'

'Take that stupid sock off of your face.'

Pfleger looked to Carlos, the Black Suit in the room, for help, then to the *federales*. Then to the Little Butcher, then to the young protégé with the leather apron. All the Mexicans just stood there, did nothing at all. Slowly, Jerry removed the mask. Stuck it in his pocket.

'Do I look like I'm with the Office of the Inspector General?' Hanley asked, again his voice boomed like artillery.

Jerry shook his head a very little bit. 'No, sir.'

'Okay, then. Relax. I'm not with State, and I'm sure as shit not here for you.' Hanley turned back to Gentry. 'I'm here for the big fish.'

Jerry breathed an audible sigh. Said, 'So this *is* the guy you are looking for?'

Hanley nodded. Confirmed. 'It's him.'

'Awesome. And there is a reward, right?'

'Yep.'

'Awesome,' repeated Pfleger. 'What did he do?'

Hanley looked close into the face of the prisoner once again. Studying it. 'What did he do? What *did* you do, Violator?'

'I did what I was ordered to do. And you gave the orders.'

'Not when you went off the reservation.'

For the first time Court lifted his head, as if his anger gave him strength. 'I *never* went off res. I followed Zack's op orders to the letter. Always! And then you ordered the team to kill me!'

'Ancient history.'

308

'Then why are you here?'

Hanley smiled. Took a step back from Gentry and looked around the room.

Hanley looked over the torturer's gear on the rolling cart. He spoke Spanish. 'Nice. Primitive, but nice.'

'¿*Primitivo?* What do you mean? This is the best—'

'Nah, chubby, we were using shit like this in the late eighties.' That was Spanish, but he turned to Court and switched to his native tongue. 'I lit up a bunch of Noriega's enforcers with one of these bad boys at Howard Air Force Base during "Just Cause."'

Hanley reached for the dial. Switched back to Spanish. 'May I?'

The Little Butcher smiled just a bit. 'Of course, but he is tough. I've blown two fuses on this gringo ... this *norteamericano*, I mean.'

Hanley looked at Court, turned the dial. Sent a strong electric shock into the central nervous system of his ex-subordinate. Gentry's body spasmed and jerked; every muscle flexed taught; the sinews in his jaw looked like guitar strings wound tight under his skin.

After he'd turned the dial back down, Hanley chuckled. 'That never gets old.' He looked at the fat man. 'It's a little weak, isn't it?'

'The battery is drained. This man has taken most of its power.'

'He *is* tough.'

Carlos, Spider's second-in-command, stepped forward and spoke in English. 'Now that you know we have the man you seek, we will take you back to Chapultepec Park. Once we have finished with the prisoner, we will dump his remains near the embassy as agreed.'

Hanley nodded. 'He has some information you are trying to extract, or is all this just for shits and grins?'

Carlos just looked at the blond American. He did not understand. 'Shit ... a ... greens?'

'The prisoner. You need him to tell you something?'

Carlos just nodded.

Hanley looked down to the bucket on the floor. The metal prod jutted out of it. 'Oh ... I see. It's about to get intimate around here.' He continued looking around. At the surgical implements on the table, at a shelf full of containers, restraints, electrical tape, and other odds and ends. He looked back at the men in the room around him.

No one spoke.

Hanley continued. 'I would like to stay for the interrogation.'

Carlos shook his head. 'That will not be possible. We do not know how much time it will take.'

'Too bad,' said Hanley, then he turned back to Gentry. 'Hey, asshole. Wake up. Do you have any idea how much pain you have caused me?'

Court's head hung low again, but he managed a smile. 'You aren't the first to tell me that.'

'I was going places. I was on the way up.'

'Then what happened?'

'Then one day I get word that one of my door kickers fucked up. It was a fuckup that could have been extremely politically damaging for the United States. A deal was done, a deal between us and another nation, and an agreement was made. If we cleaned up our own mess, if we got rid of the offending party, then this foreign nation would let the matter slide.

'So I am told that Gentry goes in the dirt. What the hell am I supposed to do, Court? I send Zack and the guys over to your place. I felt like shit about it, but I had my orders. Next thing I know you slaughtered your entire team.'

'I am familiar with the story.'

'All that shit ran downhill on my head. And now, here I am: fifty-one years old and assistant chief of station in fucking *Haiti*. There's out to pasture, and then there's assigned to the dark side of the moon. I hate the heat; I hate the disease, the bugs, the storms, the drugs; I hate every fucking bit of my life now. And it's all because you could not be a good boy and just fucking die like a soldier!'

Louder and louder, spit flew from his puffy lips.

'You, you worthless piece of shit, ruined my fucking life!'

Carlos, the only Black Suit in the room, stepped forward. 'Enough! The van is ready to return you to the park.'

Hanley looked at the Mexican for a moment as if he had forgotten there were others in the room with him. He put his hands up in apology. 'Fine. *Lo siento, amigo.*' He turned back to Gentry. 'I wish I could stay around and watch you die, you son of a bitch, but I have to go.' He turned away, and the Mexicans around him turned, too. Then he turned back to the prisoner once again. 'A short farewell, a little saying I learned from my ancestors back in the old country.' He looked at Gentry and spoke slowly: '*Tugo zakroi rot I derji ih za sheiu.*'

Court's sweat-soaked brow furrowed.

It was Russian.

Odd.

Matt Hanley's family was Scottish.

Hanley turned towards the elevator, took two steps past the policemen, and just as he arrived flush with the Little Butcher's table full of torture devices, he shot his left arm out and grabbed a long, thin scalpel.

40

Carlos had turned towards the freight elevator; the *federales* had their hands off their weapons so they could replace the hood over Hanley's face.

Surgical steel sparkled in the light of the bare bulb as the spike flashed through the air. Hanley plunged the blade into the neck of the Black Suit in front of him, perforating his carotid artery and causing blood to jet sideways across the room. As the *narco* grabbed at the pain, Hanley spun 180 degrees, towards the *federales*, and grabbed both of the smaller men by their ammo vests, turned them around, and shoved them with all his considerable size and might towards Court and the iron fence. The cops were taken completely by surprise, they stumbled headlong, slammed against the metal grating on either side of Gentry. Court used his outstretched hands, bound at the wrists, to take hold of each man. One by the collar of his uniform, the other by the sling of his rifle.

Hanley knocked the Little Butcher back away from the table; he then spun the dial on the electroconvulsive machine to the max. Gentry just had time to get his hand out and around the back of the neck of one *federale*, and immediately, the two men spasmed under the current of the car battery. The other cop tried to rush away from the fence but was caught by Gentry's hold on his rifle sling, and the *federale* stumbled back on his heels, slammed into the metal, and made a connection with the voltage.

He began writhing as well with the intense current running through his central nervous system.

The torturer's apprentice had taken several spurts of arterial blood from the Black Suit to his face, causing him to spin away from the action and wipe his eyes. Finally, he turned back and pulled a weapon from under his apron. Hanley saw the threat and he stiffarmed the young man, pinned him up against the bloodstained wall, and yanked the small Argentine-made .380 automatic from the apprentice's trembling hand. Matt turned the gun around, pressed it to the protégé's forehead, and shot him dead without hesitation.

Matt then fired twice into the ample gut of el Carnicerito, sending him down to the cold basement floor clutching his abdomen. Hanley turned the electricity dial back down, spun towards the ironwork and the three men there: one nude and shackled to the fence, the other two in SWAT gear and now dropping to the floor stunned and spent.

Matthew Hanley stood over the incapacitated *federales* and fired a round into each man's head, killing them both.

Jerry Pfleger had dropped to the floor in the corner. His back was to the concrete wall next to the dead protégé, blood splatters were painted across his sweaty white short-sleeved dress shirt like a tiedye design. His face was as white as his shirt had been ten seconds ago, and his eyes were open and blinking quickly. He stared at the blond-haired American in the center of the room.

The Mexicans were sprawled out on the floor in various unnaturally contorted positions. The Little Butcher's apron had flipped up over his face. He was alive and bleeding heavily from the stomach.

Matthew Hanley flipped off the overhead light, shrouding the room in near complete darkness. The only faint light now was a dim glow from the stairwell. He then pulled a submachine gun from the neck of one of the dead *federales*, kneeling on the floor below Gentry to do so. He turned low in a crouch, pulled the charging handle back on the weapon, and aimed it at the stairs.

'How many?' he asked. He was all business, intense concentration preparing for the threat to come.

Gentry was barely conscious. That last jolt of electricity, administered by Hanley himself, had almost killed him. Still, he muttered a guess. 'Don't know. A couple of federal cops, maybe more.'

'Okay.'

Several sets of footsteps on the stairs, running down.

Hanley waited.

Court hung from his bindings, a spectator; he felt completely exposed.

Federal police in black appeared in the dim of the stairwell; Matt Hanley fired bursts into their legs to drop them, then more bursts into their faces and necks, hitting them above their body armor. Two men, three men down now. A fourth man took a round to the throat and stumbled on through the doorway before toppling in the middle of the room; his rifle flew from his hands and clanked across the concrete.

It bounced into the lap of Jerry Pfleger. When the embassy clerk recognized what it was, his eyes opened even wider, and he pushed the weapon off of him like it was a live rattlesnake. It landed at his feet, and he kicked it away frantically, his arms raised high.

He didn't want anything to do with that rifle; he made it abundantly clear. He was not going to fight back. He did not want to give Hanley any reason to shoot him.

Hanley grabbed the new weapon and stepped into the stairwell. He neither heard nor saw anyone else.

As he returned to the torture chamber, he flicked the overhead light back on and the Little Butcher grunted. He held his bloody stomach with his fist, looked up at the armed American with eyes of fear and confusion.

'You need him for anything?' Hanley asked Gentry, motioning to the fat torturer with the muzzle of the MP5.

Gentry shook his head. 'Nope.'

Without hesitation Hanley shot the man three more times in the chest, and his groans stopped.

After several seconds of quiet, Court said, 'Thanks, Matt.'

Hanley reloaded the weapon with a fresh magazine taken off the chest of one of the dead *federales*. As he manipulated the magazine release to recharge the weapon he said, 'Fuck you, Violator. I don't like you much more than these assholes.'

'Okay.'

Hanley then began unscrewing the restraints on Gentry's wrists. 'Glad to see you didn't bite your tongue off. I was worried you'd forgotten your Russian.'

'You told me to shut my mouth tight and to grab the men by the throat.'

'Neck, actually, but close enough.'

Hanley got both arm shackles removed then unfastened the ankle bindings. Court staggered forward, went down on one knee, and then sat on the cold concrete floor. His muscles hurt and spasmed uncontrollably. His right leg shook so badly he held it to the floor with his hands to quell the movement.

Matt had already begun stripping the boots and pants off of one of the dead federal police. He stopped what he was doing to reach for the Bersa .380 he'd taken from the Little Butcher's protégé, and he slid the weapon across the floor to Court.

Hanley nodded towards Jerry Pfleger, still sitting in the corner, now shaking with fear.

'I left that dumbass for you. You can kill him if you want. I really don't care.'

'No. I need him.'

Pfleger nodded forcefully; his eyes wide with newfound hope. 'That's right! That's right, buddy! You need me!'

'I don't need you to dance.'

'To dance? What do you—'

Court took the pistol proffered by his ex-boss, shot Jerry

Pfleger in the top of his left foot, a round hole with a tattered edge of sock and leather appeared on his brown loafer.

The young man stared at his bloody shoe for several seconds before screaming.

Hanley winced with the shouting and screaming, and he tossed a pair of black tactical pants to Gentry.

'Did you have to do that?'

Court continued to gasp; he lay back flat on the cold floor for a moment to rest from his torture. Matter-of-factly, he said, 'I don't want him running away. I really don't feel like chasing after him right now.'

Jerry screamed, spit, and snot and vile curses ejected from him like water from a fire hose. 'I'm gonna fucking kill you, you crazy sick mother—'

Gentry crawled on his hands and knees over to the wounded man in the corner; the stainless automatic clicked on the concrete in the process. He sat back down, pressed the muzzle of the weapon onto the top of Pfleger's right hand, pinning the hand to the concrete. 'Don't guess I need you to type, either.'

'No!'

Court hesitated. 'Will you try to mind your manners?'

'No! I mean, yes! Yes!'

'Okay, stop the bleeding. You'll be okay.' Gentry stood slowly on shaky legs, crossed the room to a shelf, and grabbed a towel and a roll of electrical tape, threw them both to the man who, in his writhing on the floor, missed it and had to scramble after it on his elbows, screaming and crying and cussing all along.

Court slid the tactical pants onto his naked body slowly, still dazed and slowed by the electric shocks. Hanley pulled an undershirt off another guard and handed it over.

In another minute they were heading up the stairs.

They made it to the front of the warehouse; it was eight o'clock in the evening, and they encountered no one else on the property other than some dogs fenced in a long kennel. DLR was long gone by now, Court knew, and with him Laura Gamboa. Looking around briefly, he saw barrels of acid lined up against the wall. In the top of the liquid human hair floated. The only remnants of the former guests of this death house.

He and Pfleger staggered out the door together while Hanley hotwired a car in the street. Within minutes they drove out of the neighborhood in a stolen Ford station wagon. Hanley was at the wheel; Court's continued muscle spasms prevented him from driving. Pfleger was in the trunk; Court had used the rest of the electrical tape to bind Pfleger hands behind his back. As they approached a busy intersection, Matt scanned the street signs. He said, 'Okay, I know where we are. Tepito. Bad part of town, but not too far from civilization.'

'Where are we going?'

'We'll find a place to talk in a minute. Then you can take the car. I'll catch a cab to the embassy. DLR's men are going to learn about what happened if they don't already know. You don't want to stick around the capital for long.'

They drove in silence for the most part; Jerry's occasional groans and cusses in the trunk were audible but muffled. Gentry worked on getting control of his muscles; his arms and legs felt weak and rubbery, his abdominal muscles ached, and his back and neck throbbed in pain. There were electrical burns on his back, his butt, his wrists, and his ankles. He wore pants that were too short and a white T-shirt that was too small. There was just a trace of blood on the collar.

Court's feet were bare.

He carried the Bersa Thunder .380 semiautomatic pistol with a fresh magazine he'd retrieved from the pants pocket of the dead apprentice torturer. It wasn't much of a weapon, but it was small and concealable. As Court's mind fought for control of his body, he reserved a portion of his thoughts to work on a plan, and that growing and evolving plan would necessitate a low profile. The MP5s and even the big Berettas the *federales* carried on their hips would just not do.

The Bersa was wimpy, but it was very easy to conceal.

Hanley had retrieved a Beretta for himself just in case they ran into either *narcos* or street thugs while making their escape.

Court was surprised when Hanley pulled up to a bodega on República de Ecuador and hopped out of the car without a word. He returned in less than a minute with a bottle of tequila in his hand. He pulled back into traffic and jabbed the bottle between his legs, unscrewed the cap, and took a long swig.

He offered it to Gentry.

'No, thanks.'

'It will help your muscle cramps. Take it.'

Court accepted the bottle, took a tentative swig, winced, and then took a longer gulp. He fought down the shot, then passed the bottle back to Hanley. 'If you'd picked up a six-pack of Tecate, we could have had a party.'

Matt swigged, laughed, and swigged again. 'Nah, booze is efficient. No time for beer, Violator.'

Finally, Hanley pulled the sedan off the road, down a *callejón* towards the back of a construction site. He found a ramp that led down to a covered parking lot below a hotel that was only half completed. He jumped out to move a pair of orange barrels out of the way, and then he proceeded into the dark lot.

They parked the car, and Gentry popped the trunk so Jerry could get some air. They left a car door open for light and walked around to the back. Pfleger was on his back with his foot propped up. He looked up, terrified, at the two American spies staring down at him in the low light.

'Please don't kill me. I swear I will do whatever you—'

Hanley took another long pull on the tequila bottle. 'Shut up or I'll shut the trunk.'

Jerry stopped talking.

Hanley took Court by the shoulder, walked him over to the corner of the garage, still within the low glow of the Ford's interior lights. Together they stood; Court took the bottle and drank some more tequila, hoping like hell it would mute the shakes in his muscles.

He handed it back to Matt, and the big blond American took a long pull before asking, 'So what the hell are you doing here in Mexico, duking it out with the *narcos*?'

'I just stumbled into this.'

'That wasn't too bright. This drug war is crazy. Worse than Colombia. You ever seen anything as fucked up as this?'

'Yeah ... I have.'

Hanley regarded Gentry then nodded slowly. 'You must have done some work in Bosnia.'

'I must have,' replied Court, in semi-agreement. Hanley let it go. He did not know much about Gentry's pre–Goon Squad work for the CIA, and he did not need to.

'Langley said you knew the GOPES commander, this Major Gamboa.'

'Yeah, long time ago.'

'And now DLR is going after his family.'

Court nodded. 'That's what I've been dealing with.'

'Wish I could give you some support, but officially speaking, my employer doesn't care about Gamboa, and while they do care about you, they only care about making you dead.'

'Why *did* you help me?'

Matt shrugged. 'You *did* fuck up my life, but now that it *is* fucked-up, there's not much more they can do to me.'

Court didn't understand. Hanley saw this and continued. 'Look, you'd have done it for me. In the Goon Squad, you did your job and you did it well. *Of course* you fought back when we turned on you. I can't begrudge you that. I'm not going to just sit and watch the fucking Daniel de la Rocha Cartel torture you to death. You may be persona non grata amongst the top brass at Langley, but I didn't get into this line of work to watch Mexican drug lords murder American patriots.'

Gentry nodded. Leaned back against the cold concrete.

Matt said, 'This isn't the first time I've been sent by Denny to ID you.'

'No?'

319

'Couple of years ago. I was in Paraguay at the time.' He chuckled. 'I didn't know how good I had it in Paraguay. Fucking Haiti, kid. You have no idea.'

'We don't have much time.'

'Anyway, that thing goes down in Kiev. Carmichael has my ass on a company jet from Asunción to Kiev so fast my head's spinning. They were trying to ID you as the operator there, as if one man could have pulled that off, but we both know it wasn't you.'

Gentry nodded. Hanley stared him down, and Court knew the other man was doing his best to read Court's face for any reaction to his statement. Court's face still twitched from the current that had been ripping through his central nervous system; no lie detector–type clues from his limbic system would be reliable in his current state.

Hanley gave up. 'Anyway, got a free trip to Europe out of it, at least.'

Still no response from Gentry.

Matt smiled again, 'You were always the quiet one. The one who did most of the work but never bitched. Hightower was the loudmouth of the group.'

'How is Zack?'

'How *is* he? Is that a serious question? He's dead. They're all dead.'

'All who?'

'All the Goon Squad guys. You killed them all, buddy. You put both barrels of a .44 Derringer into Zack Hightower's chest, sent him cartwheeling out a window. He died at the scene.'

Jesus, thought Court. Matt Hanley really *was* out of the loop. Zack had survived the shoot-out, and Court had run an op seven months earlier in North Africa with him. Zack had been wounded badly in the Sudan, and Court did not know for sure whether or not he'd survived, but clearly, he knew a hell of a lot more than Matt Hanley did about what had been going on at the upper echelons of the Special Activities Division.

The CIA had a shoot-on-sight directive out against the Gray

Man, yet the Gray Man was not as much of an outsider as Matthew Hanley.

'Who put the shoot on sight out on me?'

Hanley looked at the tequila bottle, like he was measuring his consumption. 'Denny Carmichael was the one who contacted me. Told me you had to go.'

'Why?'

'I don't know. I really don't.'

'Bullshit.'

'Carmichael knows. Others at the top. I was told you were the enemy, to execute the shoot on sight. I was shown a presidential finding to that effect; it mentioned something about a foreign nation's involvement, and I asked Denny what that was all about. He told me a deal had been worked out between folks way above my pay grade, and I needed to shut the hell up and execute the finding. I told Denny the only way to be sure to wax you was to drop a JDAM on your head, but he ordered me to use the team to liquidate you. I told Zack, he told the others, and now they are all dead.' Hanley took an exceptionally long pull of the clear liquid. Court saw him wobble a bit from its effects.

He laughed a moment. 'You didn't hear any of that from me.' He laughed some more. 'I am *so* fired.'

Court looked at his former boss incredulously. 'Matt ... for what you did back there in the basement, you aren't just going to get fired.'

'Federal prison? A wet squad at my door? Nah, I'll convince them you got away somehow. I've made a decent living bullshitting my friends and coworkers.' He smiled, but Gentry saw that he *was* nervous. 'It was worth it to waste those *carteleros*.'

'Matt ... Langley will kill you for saving me.'

Hanley shrugged. 'I'll have to sell it. You shot your way out of the basement, took me as a hostage, beat me up, and dumped me by the side of the road as you made your escape with that embassy douche.' He paused. 'We're going to have to make it look good. I'm thinking a pair of black eyes, maybe a cracked rib.'

Court just shook his head slowly.

321

'You have something else in mind?'

'You said it. We're going to have to make it look good.'

Hanley blew out a long sigh, nodded as if he expected this. He drank another three swigs of tequila in rapid-fire succession, then backed up to the wall of the parking garage. He tossed the bottle underhanded, away into the dark. It shattered. Then he pointed to a place high on his shoulder. 'Right there. Do it, Violator!'

Court pulled the Bersa Thunder .380 from his pants pocket. Took a few steps back and raised the weapon. Hanley watched him through eyes squinted in anticipation of the pain and agony that would come. 'Please don't miss, kid.'

Then Court looked away from his weapon's sights and into the man's tight eyes.

'Sorry.'

'Sorry for what?'

The pistol lowered.

'No!'

Court shot Matthew Hanley in the stomach. Hanley brought his hands to the searing pain in his right side. Warm blood oozed through his thick fingers. Softly, he gasped, 'For the love of God, Court.' The heavyset case officer lowered to his knees, fell to the cold cement, rolled onto his stomach writhing in pain.

Court fired again, shot Hanley in the back of the right shoulder.

'Jesus!' screamed Jerry Pfleger. He'd sat up in the trunk and could see the action against the wall. Court turned to him, stormed over to the car with his pistol up, and Jerry ducked back into the trunk. Gentry slammed the trunk lid, then returned to the man rolling around on the bare concrete. Hanley was on his back now; he tried to scoot away from the Gray Man but could not.

As he stood over the big man, Court said, 'Nobody was going to buy a textbook bullet hole in your shoulder. Not from a guy like me.'

'I could have sold it, you fuck! I could have made them believe!'

'C'mon, stop crying. The shoulder is through and through, and the gut shot is lodged in a shitload of fat. Are you the only guy in Haiti putting on weight these days?'

'I'm going to bleed to death!'

'No, you're not. Listen, nobody at Langley is going to question whether or not you were helping me when they find out I shot you three times.'

Hanley was fighting shock. Still his eyes widened.

'Three times?'

Court stood, quickly pointed the pistol again, and shot his former boss in his left thigh.

'Motherfucker!' The thick man screamed, rolled to his side, and grabbed his leg.

'Listen, Matt. I am doing you a favor. Carmichael knows I don't punch people in the jaw who are trying to kill me. I didn't hit any organs, any arteries; you are going to be fine. Better than fine considering what Denny would do to you if he thought you and I were in cahoots. Put some pressure on your gut; don't worry about your leg or shoulder. I didn't hit anything vital.'

'That's fucking easy for you to say! Fuck, Violator! I saved your ass!'

'And I'm saving yours! Okay, Matt, I've got to run.'

'You are leaving? I'm fucking bleeding to death!'

'No, you're not. You're going to be a stud around Langley. You survived a shoot-out with the Gray Man. How cool is that?'

'It's not cool at all, you mother—'

Court knelt, patted him on the head. 'You're going to thank me, I swear.' Another quick pat. 'Gotta go. Thanks again.' Court stood back up and pulled Jerry's phone from his pocket, checked it for a signal. 'Two bars. Call the embassy.' He tossed the phone on Hanley's big gut, climbed behind the wheel of the Ford, and drove out of the parking garage.

Hanley lay in the dark, holding on to his stomach and his shoulder. 'Fucking Violator!' he screamed it at the top of his lungs; it echoed back to him in the empty garage.

Then he took his hand from his shoulder to dial the cell phone with his bloody fingers.

41

Just after nine p.m. Daniel de la Rocha sat on the sofa of his living room in a suburb of Cuernavaca, some forty-five minutes from Mexico City. Next to him, in his lap and up and down the length of the sofa were his children. His wife sat on the floor at his feet. The family watched the huge plasma television, a league match between Chivas de Guadalajara and Cruz Azul, two of Mexico's best soccer teams.

DLR's phone chirped in the front pocket of his black sweatpants, annoying him greatly. He'd instructed his men not to bother him tonight under any circumstances.

The chirping phone caught his wife's attention as well, and she looked angrily at her husband.

'You said no one would—'

He looked at the phone. 'I'm sorry, *mi amor*. It's Nestor; it must be important.'

'I asked for one night of peace with my family.'

DLR's oldest daughter, nine-year-old Gabriella, hushed them as she tried to watch the match.

'Daniel ... the American has escaped. He killed Carlos, el Carnicerito, something like six or seven *federales*; he shot up the CIA man, and he escaped with Pfleger. Apparently, one of them is wounded; there was a blood trail all the way out of the building to the—'

'Wait! Nestor ...' Daniel stood, his nine-month-old son nearly tumbled out of his lap onto the sofa. De la Rocha shot out of the living room, ran in his socks to his study, and shut the door.

'You are telling me that the *chingado* gringo who I saw in the Tepito death house, chained like a piece of meat to the wall, half-dead and surrounded by a dozen armed men, has somehow managed to get *away*.'

'*Sí, patrón*. I am working a lead right now. Pfleger's car is missing; I assume they took it. I have everyone in the D.F. canvassing the—'

'What is going on? He did not do that alone. Someone rescued him.'

'Maybe so.'

'No *maybe*. Madrigal! It must have been los Vaqueros!'

'I'll look into it, *patrón*.'

'I want you to call the CIA right now and tell them that the Vaqueros shot their man!'

'We don't know yet, Daniel.'

'*I* know it! I *know* Constantino Madrigal is behind this!'

Calvo sighed into the phone. 'I will look into all the leads, especially any information that Madrigal's network is involved.'

'Well, we know where they are going, then, don't we? Tijuana!'

'Jerry Pfleger did not create the visas.'

'If he's working with them, maybe he did, and he just didn't tell you.'

'That's true, Don Daniel,' Calvo replied wearily. 'We will have everyone focusing on the border and the highways to get there.'

'Good. You stay on Madrigal, Nestor. You understand me?'

'*Sí, mi patrón*.'

De la Rocha disconnected the call then pressed a button on his desk. 'Emilio. Bring the cars. We are leaving immediately.' He turned back to the living room. His wife stood in the doorway.

'What is it?'

'Work. It is always work, *mi amor*.'

'You are leaving again?'

Daniel nodded. '*Sí*. I am sorry, but I have to go.'

*

325

Court sat in la Iglesia de Nuestra Señora del Pilar, in the same pew as the day before. But Laura Gamboa Corrales was not by his side. He stared at the altar, at the crucifix, at the devotional candles. He smelled the incense and the wax.

And he thought of her.

Jerry Pfleger was bundled in the trunk of his own car now. They'd spent two hours dumping the Ford, taking a taxi back to Pfleger's apartment in la Zona Rosa, getting a few changes of clothes, the twenty-five thousand dollars' worth of pesos Court had given Jerry as a down payment, a mobile phone, and some other odds and ends. They packed all this into Jerry's car. Court strapped a bag of ice onto Jerry's foot to keep the swelling under control, but Jerry limped so badly Court was forced to help the skinny American everywhere he went.

On the way to Highway 85 to head northeast, Gentry took this detour to the church. Operationally, it was unnecessary, no doubt a little dangerous, even though he doubted the Black Suits would still be hanging around Donceles Street.

He could not say for sure why he was here or what he was doing. But he wanted to come here, to sit, to think, just for a few minutes.

He thought about Lorita, wondered what she was being subjected to, what she thought about him right now.

His muscles still hurt, but the twitching was gone. His ankles and wrists were burned and blistered, but he'd survive it. The cuts on his chest burned. They needed some treatment, but they weren't deep enough to worry about blood loss, and the sting would help him focus and stay awake for the next few hours. After that ... after that he'd think about medicine.

He had a plan, sort of. It was paper-thin, but it was action, and at times like these, Gentry preferred action to sitting around and hoping for the best.

He thought of Lorita again, and he wondered if he loved her.

Then he thought of Eddie, of Elena and the baby, and of the life that Eddie had left behind.

Court wondered if he even knew what it meant to love.

He looked around the church. There were only a few faithful here, but he regarded them, wondered about their capacity to love.

No, Court decided. He was not like them. He was not trained to love.

He was conditioned to hate.

And now he was ready to kill.

He stood slowly and left his pew. He had not prayed. He did not cross himself; he did not step up to the altar to kneel before it.

But he did address the crucifix. From the center aisle, before turning for the door, he spoke softly. It wasn't a prayer. It was a demand. Delivered in a threatening tone by someone who, like he had told Laura the day before, did not know how this all worked.

'She trusts you. She is one of your people. You need to help her. To take care of her. I can't do it by myself.'

After the side trip to the church, the Gray Man was all business. He drove to Aeropuerto Internacional Benito Juárez; just a few minutes before arriving, he had Pfleger use the store-bought cell phone to rent a car in his name from the Hertz office in the airport. They parked Jerry's car in long-term parking, picked up the rental, and drove to another part of the airport. Then they took a taxi back into town, into the Reforma district, and here Court and Jerry took a city bus to el Zócalo. Two long blocks south of the main square, with Gentry helping the hobbled Pfleger walk upright, they found a hotel parking lot that was unattended, and here the American assassin hotwired a Ford Mustang.

At two forty-five in the morning, Gentry and Pfleger left Mexico City behind them and headed northeast to Pachuca, a ninety-minute drive. They ditched the stolen car in Pachuca, waited on a park bench across from the main bus terminal until it opened at six a.m., and then took the first bus heading north to Juárez. They would get off before Juárez and take a regional bus to Tijuana.

Twenty-four hours on the road.

As they sat together in the back of the bus, Jerry spoke his first words in hours that were not complaints or curses. 'Why did we do all that?'

'All what?'

'We've been jumping on and off vehicles for a dozen hours. My foot is killing me, dude. I need a doctor.'

'We burned our trail. There is no way the Black Suits are going to find us. They'll look for your car and find it at the airport. They'll think we wanted them to think we got on a plane, but they'll be smart enough to see that you rented a car. They will find the rental there at the airport, and they might think we did, in fact, fly out of Mexico City, but if they are good, they'll check with the taxi company and see that we tried to throw them off. Then if they are good and they are lucky, they might even find out about the Mustang stolen several miles from where the cab dropped us off, but I seriously doubt it.'

Pfleger rubbed his calf with a grimace as the swelling caused the nerves to flare up.

'Even if they managed every bit of that, they'd have to be more dialed in than the FBI to find the Mustang in Pachuca, and even if they did, there was no video security at the terminal there, and we paid in cash, so there is no chance in hell they will track us now.'

'But won't they still guess that we are going to TJ?'

Gentry nodded. 'Oh, yeah,' he said, as if it were obvious. 'They'll be all over Tijuana when we get there, scanning the border, ready to kill us all.'

'That's great,' Pfleger said. 'And then, even if they don't, you are going to kill me when this is all over.'

'Not if you do what I say.'

'Bullshit. I saw what you did to the CIA guy, the guy who saved your ass. You fucking murdered him.'

Court shrugged. Smiled wearily. 'It had to be done.'

'Right. You'll say that about me in a couple of days.'

'Only if you try anything cute.' Gentry pulled a pair of zip ties from his pocket. He'd picked them up at a grocery store back in the capital. He made a two-link chain with them, with his left hand in one of the links and Jerry's right hand in the other. He tightened the bindings. Court found a small sleeping blanket that the bus provided, and he tossed it over his and Jerry's laps. To anyone looking it would appear as if the two men were holding hands. An old woman sitting across the aisle noticed their apparent public display of affection and clucked disapprovingly.

'So we are going to TJ even though we know they will be at the border, waiting for the Gamboas to cross?'

'Let me explain what is going to happen, Jerry. We are going to the border. To Tijuana. When we get there, Elena, Luz, and Diego are going to cross the border. You are going to set up their crossing from this side, and you and I are going to sit in some hotel room together, just sit there and look at each other, until I get a phone call from Elena telling me that they are safely in the United States. If I *don't* get that call, if they *don't* make it across, Jerry, you are going to die a very, very slow and very, very miserable death right there in that hotel room. You have *one* chance to arrange a fucking foolproof crossing for them, so you better start coming up with something quick.'

Jerry began shaking his head before Court finished talking. 'I can't ever be sure someone will make it over! Yeah, if we had the documents, I could just about promise. But with a midnight run there are too many variables. I always tell people I'll get them over within two or three tries.'

'*These* people don't have two or three tries. If they are caught and they go into the system, then de la Rocha can make them disappear. You get one shot at this.'

'I am telling you, I can't promise anything!'

Court shrugged. He closed his eyes and tucked his head against the headrest. He pulled the blanket up high to his shoulders and said, 'Well in *that* case, Jerry, you are going to die.'

329

42

Diego Gamboa Fuentes sat on the park bench, three hundred yards from the border crossing into the United States. His eyes darted to everyone around over the age of ten. He was terrified of being seen by the wrong people, and he was certain the wrong people were crawling all over the place.

This was the third day he had sat here in this spot, and each day he became more and more certain that Jose and *tía* Laura were not going to appear, and more and more certain that the men walking around the park were working for the Black Suits. The air was only seventy degrees, but sweat dripped from Diego's big dark sunglasses and from the scalp of his nearly shaved head.

He'd followed Joe's instructions to alter his appearance, as had *tía* Elena and his *abuela*. They remained at the hotel, a few miles south of here, in hiding, because they just knew the Black Suits were close by.

They'd had a bit of luck the day before. Members of the Tijuana Cartel had spotted some new men in the area, thought them to be a rival cartel up here muscling in on their plaza, and they reacted accordingly, responding in the only way they ever responded to threats to their bottom line – they opened fire. No civilians had been hurt or killed, miraculously, but the daily machine-gun fire in the streets of TJ had picked up considerably since, as more *guerreros* for the Tijuana Cartel had been sent out to find and scare away the new visitors to this lucrative crossing point.

Diego and his family had heard the shooting, but they learned the reasons behind the cartel-on-cartel street battle the evening before on the news. They hoped this meant the TJ *narcos* were, although unwittingly, providing a level of protection for them, giving Los Trajes Negros a little something to worry about while up here in the north.

Diego did not want to come out today, to wait at the park for the three p.m. meeting time. He did not expect to see his aunt or the gringo, and he did not like leaving the hotel. He knew he would have to be the one, eventually, to leave cover and make contact with the local coyote to try and find some transportation over the border, but he was more than willing to wait a few days before attempting this. They had little money, no connections, and a palpable fear of the men of the Black Suits.

Getting over the border on their own was going to be tough.

A man walked past the bench; Diego had not even noticed him approach. His hair was razor short; Diego could tell even though the man wore a ball cap. His goatee and mustache were full but trimmed close to his face; his eyes were hidden behind mirrored lenses. He wore a long-sleeved cotton shirt and baggy jeans, the typical attire of a laborer, not the nicer clothes of a *cartelero*. But when he slowed in front of Diego, the young Mexican stiffened in fear.

'Follow me,' the man said softly in Spanish.

Diego recognized the accent. The voice.

It was Jose. The American.

He had changed his appearance so completely Diego hesitated, even when the man crossed the park, sat down on a small Vespa scooter, and turned back to him. The boy on the bench rose tentatively; he wondered how Joe had pulled up on the scooter and then crossed the park without Diego noticing. It was like he had just materialized out of thin air.

When Diego arrived at the Vespa, Joe started the engine, motioned for Diego to climb on back, and then they drove off down the street without a word between them.

*

Court returned the scooter to the shop where Jerry had rented it that afternoon, then took a taxi with Diego back to the hotel where Luz and Elena were staying. The two women were floored by the American's change of appearance. They both agreed that, with the right clothes, he looked like he could actually be a member of Los Trajes Negros.

Like Diego, the women had made an attempt at a transformation. Luz had dyed her hair red; it did not look natural, but neither did it look out of place for a woman of her age. Elena Gamboa Gonzalez wore a white floral dress that looked new; she'd cut her hair short, into a bob not unlike her sister-in-law Laura's. She wore big sunglasses and high heels.

But Elena was still pregnant. Court appreciated her going to the trouble to try and disguise herself, but he could not imagine the hit men for the Black Suits ignoring a pregnant lady just because her hair was shorter than that of their target.

Diego and Court collected the two women and had a new taxi take them to a supermarket, where they all climbed into yet another cab that drove them south to a local transit bus stop. When the cab drove away, Gentry led the family up the street a hundred yards, then they turned left down a narrow *callejón* and arrived at a horridlooking hourly motel.

Sickly prostitutes stood out front, but Gentry led the Gamboas past them and then up a single flight of stairs in the back. He slipped his key in the lock of a tiny room with no windows.

Inside it was dark. Court had forbade talking on the trip through town, so as soon as he closed the door, Elena said, 'Why are we here?'

As a response Court flipped on the light to the room. A single bed that sagged in the middle, a threadbare comforter, a backpack lying on top. With his eyes Gentry directed the families to look in the bathroom.

Jerry was tied with telephone cord and strapping tape to the plumbing in the tiny and filthy bathroom; his head on the shit-stained porcelain, and his wounded foot positioned high on the rim of the dingy bathtub.

'What took you so long?' he asked as Gentry looked in on him past the three Mexicans in the doorway.

Court addressed the Gamboas. 'We've been compromised.'

'Where is Laura?' Elena asked.

He sighed. 'The Black Suits have her.' He said it in Spanish so Luz and Diego would understand.

Luz cried out, sat down on the bed, and began to wail.

Elena herself cried. 'How?'

'Thank this asshole right here.' He pointed towards the American tied to the toilet.

Elena looked at Pfleger, and Pfleger just turned away from her, gazed at a long centipede crawling across the grimy fake-tile flooring.

'What ... what are we going to do now?' asked Diego.

'We're going to get you all into the United States. And then I'll go and get her back.'

'No! No, I am *not* leaving without Laura,' said Elena.

'Yes, you are. I need you and the family out of the way.'

'How are we going to get my *tía* back?' asked Diego.

Court sat on the bed next to Luz. He said, 'I am going to make de la Rocha give her back. I am going to make de la Rocha's life miserable, and I will not stop making his life miserable until he releases Laura. And then when he does ... I take her, and I leave.'

'You will leave him alive?' asked Diego.

'My only objective is to save Lorita.'

'De la Rocha killed Eduardo,' said Elena.

'I know that, and I would *love* to make him pay. But I don't expect that will be possible, so I am going to concentrate on rescuing Laura.'

Elena Gamboa stared long and hard at Court. He did not understand the look she was giving him at first, but slowly it dawned on him. He had said something, conveyed something, given off some sort of emotion about Laura that Elena recognized.

He turned away, but she came to him, took both of his hands, and squeezed them tightly. He kept his eyes on the

333

wall, then down on Pfleger, who was writhing on the tile next to the toilet.

He heard Eddie's wife sniff back tears. She understood that this was personal now; she had read into Court's words and actions.

Elena must have recognized she was making him uncomfortable, so she turned away without speaking, sat with her mother-in-law, hugged her deeply; tears dripped down both of their faces. Luz looked up at the man she knew as Jose. 'Thank you, Jose. Thank you so much.'

In Spanish he said, 'I haven't even started yet.'

Jerry had spent literally the entire twenty-four-hour bus ride and the next morning in Tijuana working on his plan to get the Gamboas into the United States. He hadn't quite solidified his scheme before the American killer had taken Pfleger to rent a scooter, then returned him to the motel, tied him to the shitter, and left him alone for hours.

Heartless bastard.

The evening before, on the bus north, Jerry had arranged for a criminal contact in Tijuana to vouch for him to a veteran coyote. The *cayote* told him he was arranging for a large group of forty pot smugglers to cross into the U.S. near Tecate late in the evening in two days' time. Jerry was told his group could tag along *if* they would haul packs of marijuana wrapped in hemp cord during the hike, and Jerry readily agreed. He was then given the exact time and place of the crossing.

Next he used an acquaintance in Nogales who owed him a favor. The man put him in touch with a drug ring working the plaza there. He was told of a tunnel that ran from Nogales over the border into Arizona, and the entire morning in Tijuana he worked his new mobile phone to make contact with the right people in the right places. Finally, after the Gamboas were collected and he was cut free from the toilet by the Gray Man, Jerry Pfleger completed the arrangements with more calls to Nogales and Tucson, and promises to everyone he spoke with.

Promises that were mostly lies.

The lies Jerry Pfleger had told in the past twenty-four hours would have a lot of people out to kill him, of this the American embassy officer had no doubt. His plan would fuck over some of the scummiest, most vengeful, and most dangerous men in northern Mexico, a region known for dangerous men. All these men knew his real name, knew his business associates, and knew where he worked. There would be no going back to business as usual when this ordeal was over.

But Jerry Pfleger was more terrified of the Gray Man. If he somehow survived this ordeal, he would deal with whatever came after. For now he had a job to do.

43

Court, Jerry, and the Gamboas drove a stolen Ford Lobo truck east through the morning, arriving at Nogales before noon. There they checked into a motel that was hardly any better than the one they'd left in TJ.

They sat around all afternoon, ate, talked. The Gamboas prayed, and Court and Jerry picked at their raw and red wounds, waiting for nightfall.

Jerry's plan was all about his own preservation. He would tip off the DEA at the last minute to the invasion of pot smugglers near Tecate, he would insinuate heroin was being smuggled along with the pot, and he would exaggerate the number of mules from forty to one hundred.

And he would hope like hell that this took any heat away from the Arizona side of the Nogales tunnel for the time the Gamboas needed to get over the border.

It was the best way to increase the Gamboas' chances because the Gamboas' fate was, to Jerry Pfleger, a matter of life or death.

At eight in the evening Court tied Jerry to the toilet in the bathroom, and he left the motel with the Gamboas. They drove the Lobo up to the border to International Street, made a right, and then drove down a little hill. On their left was the border fence, rusted tin and a few layers of chain link and barbed wire. On their right were some simple homes on the hill. The asphalt road ended, and they continued on gravel and dirt for fifty yards, then parked in front of a wooden shack.

One man stood outside. Even before Court climbed out from behind the wheel, he could tell the man had a gun under his lumberjack shirt.

This was the *cayote*. He'd be crossing with the family, meeting with their ride to Tucsón. He would accompany them all the way there.

The *cayote* eyed the gringo, said nothing at all.

Court didn't like this one damn bit. The lives of these three, four if you counted Eddie's unborn son, all depended on the actions of this drug-running, piece-of-shit scumbag giving him the stink eye.

But neither Court nor the Gamboas had any other options. They had to trust Jerry. Not his honesty or fidelity. No, he wasn't doing this for those reasons. He was doing it for self-preservation, so Court felt his motivation was sufficient.

The *cayote* motioned the Gamboas forward into the shack, and Court stood with them a moment in the darkness on the dirt road. 'I will never be able to thank you,' Elena said to him. She sobbed.

'Just make it over there. Look up some of Eddie's old friends. Navy men, DEA guys. They are good people. They will help you. Have that baby.'

She smiled. 'I will do that.'

She hugged him, tears filled her eyes. 'Please save Laura. You are her only chance. And please be careful yourself,' she said.

She turned and headed for the shack. Court shook Diego's hand next. 'You are in charge; you understand that, don't you?'

'Yes, sir.'

'Your uncle Eddie went to the U.S. as a young man, and he made a success of himself. No matter how his life ended ... he *had* a life.'

Diego nodded, looked into the starry sky. 'I would be proud to live like my *tío* Eduardo.' He turned and disappeared into the shack.

Luz hugged Court a long time. She said a short prayer then crossed herself, turned, and walked away.

Court caught himself trying to understand the words she had said. To take solace in them. To feel empowered by her divine plea. But he did not understand her. And he felt no different.

When the family was gone, Court turned around. He could see over the fence here, more or less. On the other side were a few warehouses; their lights were on but it was still and silent now. A road ran up a hill of scrubland; it was visible in the moon and starlight, a long piece of ribbon candy winding to the north, into the distant night.

That was America. Right there. So close he felt he could reach out and touch it.

Court had not seen his own country in five years. It was no longer home; it was likely the most dangerous country in the world for him.

Except, perhaps, for Mexico.

Still, he looked out over the undulating scrubland longingly, as if the dirt and sand and tumbleweed ahead of him was the land of milk and honey.

It was fucking beautiful.

He was jealous of the three Mexicans he had just sent over the border.

He loved his country, though powerful elements of his country did not love him back. He'd bled for that country. He'd killed for that country.

He would die for that country, if he did not end up dying for something else.

He had a score he'd need to settle someday with Denny Carmichael and others in the upper echelons of the CIA.

But that was for later. Much later.

Court's sad, wistful eyes and the dreamy look of longing on his face hardened, morphed into cold eyes and a gritty expression of determination. He climbed back into the truck and headed to the motel to await a phone call.

*

338

The call came at seven in the morning. It was Elena – they'd made it. The Gamboas had left the coyote behind and were on their own in Tucson, they had bus tickets to San Francisco, and she gave Court the phone number of the mobile phone she'd just purchased in the bus station. Gentry had given them a prearranged code-word. If they were safe, she would tell him they were going to find a hotel. If they were under duress, she would use the word motel. She said 'hotel,' and Court blew out a long sigh of relief. Still, he made her put Diego on the line. Gentry listened hard to him for any sounds of duress, but he, like his aunt, just sounded tired.

He hung up the phone and looked to Jerry. Pfleger sat on the other bed in the small motel room. He'd not slept a wink. His foot throbbed, and his fear over his own impending death had kept him up.

Jerry looked back at the Gray Man. 'You're going to kill me anyway, right?'

Court shook his head. 'No. You did what I asked you to do. I'm not going to kill you.'

Jerry didn't believe him. 'Right. I get up, turn to walk out the door, and you shoot me?'

Again Gentry shook his head. 'No, Jerry ... You can stay here. I've paid up through tomorrow. I'm leaving.'

Pfleger looked confused. Slowly he nodded and said, 'Whatever you say.' He did not believe Court.

'I *do* want you to quit your job. You are done working for the United States. You got that?'

Jerry nodded quickly. Surprised and hopeful now. 'You got it. I can't go back there, anyway. The cartels would fight each other for the chance to kill me now. But ... What should I do?'

Gentry shrugged. 'Whatever. Limp all the way to Copenhagen for all I care. I just don't want to hear about you working for the U.S. in any capacity.'

'You got it, dude. I'm out.'

'And I need another favor from you.'

'Okay.'

339

'Madrigal.'

'What about him?'

'I need to talk to him. Face-to-face.'

Jerry Pfleger just put his head back on the wall behind the bed. 'Man, nobody talks to el Vaquero in person.'

'Bullshit. Make it happen.'

'Look. I know lots of Cowboys. Some of them are pretty high ranking *carteleros*. But I don't know anyone who can get you in front of Madrigal himself. He's a ghost. A phantom.'

'I need to talk to him. Man to man.'

Jerry just shook his head like it was out of the question. But slowly, he stopped. Looked at the man staring him down. 'Let me guess. This is another thing you need me to do, or else you will shoot me again.'

'You are getting the idea, Jerry.'

Pfleger looked off into space, his eyes unfixed, for a long time. Finally, he said, 'Let me make some calls.'

44

Gentry sat on the curb, the bright sunshine and the dust and the exhaust from the passing buses and cars insinuated itself into every pore of his exposed skin.

A boy trotted past on a horse. Looked down at the man on the curb, mystified to see a stranger in his town.

Court glanced down to his hands. They quivered. No, they *shook*. His hands had always been steady, no matter the adrenaline coursing through his body. He'd learned to control his fear, to put it in the back of his mind, to direct his energy towards the problem at hand, to believe in himself. To believe that, no matter whatever perils lay before him, he'd get through it.

But he found himself not believing now.

There was a lump in his throat.

Nerves, Gentry. Just fucking nerves. No problem.

He took a sip of his Coke and a bite of his *torta*. The pork was thick and tangy, but the bright sun of the Sonoran Desert coupled with his worry sapped him of the majority of his appetite.

And the men all around him were seriously pissing him off.

He'd been in town less then five minutes, just off the bus from Hermosillo, when the first intimidator struck. A muscled young man in a straw hat walked up next to him while Court walked towards the center of town.

'Who are you?'

Court kept walking.

'What is your name?'

Court did not even look at the young man.

'What are you doing here?'

Again, no response from the visitor to town. If Court was raising eyebrows amongst the local heavies now, how would they react when they heard his American accent?

The young man stepped on Gentry's foot.

Court stopped. Turned and looked at the guy. Instantly, he thought of the four ways he could kill the man in under two seconds.

But no. He wanted to move to his destination in as low key a manner as possible. Killing folks wouldn't do.

Court walked on. Soon enough a small heard of local men followed him. Many had guns. One yanked Court's ball cap off and threw it like a Frisbee into the dirty street. Another, a teenager, ran up behind Gentry quickly and kicked him hard in the ass with the toe of his cowboy boot. Court stumbled forward but caught himself and kept walking on.

Now he sat on the curb in front of a *tienda* in the center of this little town. The men who had surrounded him had just melted away. No doubt someone got a call or a text, and the order was passed through the locals to hit the road. Court had not heard anyone speak; he imagined a look or a gesture was all it took to get those assholes moving on up the street and out of the way.

His hands shook when he held his drink to his mouth. The burns on his wrists from the electricity weren't bad, mere sunburns, but the entire experience had left him rattled, even four days later. And now he was about to put himself back at the mercy of merciless men, which added to his shakes and his nerves.

A sedan approached slowly. A brown four-door pulled into the gas station across the street, rolled on past the pumps, and stopped. Two men stepped out, *cuernos de chivos* in their hands. They were dressed like cowboys. Pointed boots, white shirts with red piping. They wore thick mustaches but no beards, and their boots were made from gray ostrich hides.

342

They *were* Cowboys. Los Vaqueros. They were henchmen of Constantino Madrigal.

The two riflemen crossed the street, approaching the gringo, who stood slowly, his hands away from his body.

A municipal police car drove by, slowed slightly, but kept going.

It was that kind of town. Dudes with assault rifles crossed a busy street and pointed guns at a man whose arms were raised.

But that was not an affair that interested the police around here.

After all, this was the city of Altar, in the Sonoran Desert, the turf of the Madrigal Cartel.

Los Vaqueros held their weapons at the hip, but the barrels were pointed at Court's chest.

In minutes Court was searched and piled into the sedan; he was driven south, out of town; and the car pulled into a gulley off the side of the road. Here Court was told to get out, and he did so. The car shot off to the south, leaving him there in a cloud of dust.

The dust had not cleared away before a Cadillac Escalade pulled up; it had obviously been trailing them from the city. A back window rolled down; Court thought this might be Madrigal, but no, it was just another Cowboy. This guy was fat and young; he wore Ray-Bans, kept his straw cowboy hat in his lap, and waved a huge Colt Python revolver up by his face so Gentry could see it.

He spoke English. 'I want to see some tan lines, gringo.'

'Excuse me?'

'Take off your clothes. All of them.'

Court shoulders slumped. 'Of course.' He stripped to his underwear, but the fat guy flicked his gun at Court's underwear. He took it off, stood in the hot dirt in his socks, until the fat guy ordered him to remove his socks. He then bounced on one foot and then the other; he had enough burns on his wrists and ankles, he didn't want them on the balls of his feet as well.

Three men climbed out of the SUV, and they went through his clothes like they were checking them for lice. After each garment was examined thoroughly by all three men, it was tossed back to Gentry so he could get dressed. But they searched the clothes out of order, his underwear was the last item to be returned to him, so he just held the lump of dusty clothing in his arms while he waited.

Finally, he dressed; the sun stung his scalp through his short hair as he did so. He climbed into the back of the SUV, next to the fat guy, and the Colt Python was jabbed into his ribs.

Gentry said nothing, just looked ahead, and the SUV rolled off towards the south.

They parked at a tiny airstrip at the edge of a no-name hamlet. It was flat and dry, and the farms around were perfectly square and maintained by donkeys and cheap labor. The airstrip was dirt; the aircraft at the end of it looked forty years old. It was a Cessna 210, a small prop plane that was perfect for running drugs up the length of Mexico. Due to its hardy undercarriage and high wings, it could land at the most rugged of the unregistered runways carved out of the landscape by the *carteleros*.

Court and the fat man boarded the plane. Along with a pilot in a ball cap with a .45 crammed in a leather holster next to his seat, there were two other men in the Cessna. They both held Kalashnikovs in their laps, and Court wondered if they'd ever even considered the difficulties in firing these weapons during flight in the tiny six-seat cabin.

Gentry's brain worked like that. He had no reason to think he was in imminent danger, but as they strapped into their seats and the pilot fired the engine, Court devised a plan to kill, incapacitate, or disarm everyone in the aircraft around him in, he estimated, three seconds. He'd leave the pilot alive and conscious, would relieve him of his firearm, and hope the man would follow Court's instructions to land the plane. If not, he'd just shoot the dude in the head and land the plane himself.

Court was not a great pilot; he'd put a couple of planes down in a manner that made them worthless hunks of twisted metal and smoking oil and, in one case, completely unrecognizable as an aircraft.

So he hoped like hell everyone on board minded their manners for this flight into the mountains of 'Cowboy Country.'

The aircraft bounced on the runway, and then it wobbled as it struggled for the sky. Gentry could tell they were headed south; the Pacific Ocean appeared on his right some time later.

The flight remained uneventful; they landed in the mid-afternoon at another covert airstrip, this one at a small clearing ringed by tinroofed huts in the green mountains of the Sierra Madre Occidentales. Court wasn't sure if they were still in Sonora or if they had made it down as far as Sinaloa, or even into Nayarit, where Court's Mexican nightmare had begun at the grave of Eddie Gamboa.

Wherever they were, he was certain Madrigal's army of Vaqueros would be plentiful.

And he was right.

He climbed out of the aircraft, the fat man followed, and they were met by a large flatbed truck full of AK-wielding men in cowboy hats. Court stepped up into the bed and sat surrounded by the men; they were driven into a village and then up into thick forest. Gentry noticed that the road, while unpaved, was in exceptionally good condition. The bumping and jostling in the back of the truck he was subjected to had less to do with potholes and more to do with machismo and an anti-gringo attitude on display by los Vaqueros.

The road was high quality because it was built and maintained by the Madrigal Cartel. This became obvious when the truck passed a bunker made from felled trees, behind which two men manned a .30-caliber machine gun that covered the road. Below the thick canopy of the Sierra Madre forest, rows of simple buildings appeared, around them men walked and worked. Bare-chested or clad in T-shirts and jeans, they all carried weapons.

This wasn't a drug-processing facility as Court had suspected. No, this looked more like a rebel base. It was a jungle fortress of sorts, though there were no walls or guard towers; the remoteness of the location along with the sheer number of guns and gunners meant nothing less than a battalion-sized element of U.S. Rangers would be needed to take the place.

The truck stopped suddenly; Court pounded shoulders with the man next to him, suffered a few indecipherable angry comments, and then climbed down from the bed.

Court was strip-searched again, right there out in the open; children and women and the elderly around the huts stood and watched the spectacle of the naked gringo. Dogs and chickens milled around him while he waited for his clothing to be tossed back his way.

The men with the cowboy hats and the *cuernos de chivos* watched him dress again, and then they led him up a long narrow pathway, past gun emplacements and armed men on donkeys and horses. Men stared at Court from the woods and rocky dry streambeds that snaked along the route. Wooden steps had been added in a few places, and a razor-wire gate was manned by three men on a path. Court looked at the rocks above him, saw rifles and cowboy hats silhouetted by the sun behind them.

Once Court was through the gate, the path opened into a set of large buildings under a canopy of pines and fir trees. The structures were simple cement blockhouses with tin roofs; a road ran through the middle, and armed men guarded individual doors. Many horses and a few donkeys stood at hitching posts and water troughs. Court was led by them on his way towards a large warehouse-type building halfway up the road.

At the front door the man on Court's right put the tip of his pistol to Court's right temple. The man on the left put the tip of his pistol to Court's left temple. A third man stepped in front of Court and placed his revolver's muzzle on Gentry's forehead, and a fourth gun prodded him in the back of his head.

'*Bueno,*' said the man in charge. He stood in front, spoke Spanish, 'We go into the room slowly. One step at a time.' He began moving backwards, and the entourage moved along in a cluster. Court felt like he was the torso of a spider, arms and legs all around him and moving more or less in unison.

As they passed through the doorway, everyone's weapons pressing and bumping against his face and head, Gentry said, 'You guys are about the most chicken-shit bodyguards I've ever seen.'

The man in front smiled and said, 'If we were chicken shit, we would have shot your white ass back in Altar.' The procession kept moving into the big room; the man in front walked backwards as he said, '*Por favor*, don't make us blow your head all over Señor Madrigal's lunch.'

45

Court looked over the man's shoulder and saw the room was some sort of meeting hall. Against the far wall a row of picnic tables full of food and soft drinks was laid out. A dozen armed men stood around, watching the procession moving towards them across the dirt floor. Seated at the end of the tables, facing Court, was a lone man with a plate of beans; he was sopping them up with corn tortillas. He finished his tortilla then took a long swig of Tecate beer from a can.

A half dozen men stood behind him; they all wore either simple straw hats or baseball caps.

Only after he had placed the can back on the table did he look up at the American surrounded by his men with their guns pressed to his head. The man in front scooted to the side, lowered his pistol somewhat, but he kept it trained on the chest of the Gray Man.

Finally, Court got a good look at the man he'd come to see.

Constantino Madrigal looked more like a *campesino*, a peasant, than a drug lord. He was in his fifties, heavy, more big than fat, with a mustache and bushy hair that was still more black than gray, but just. His denim shirt was open, and his hairy chest gleamed from sweat on either side of a simple wire cross medallion.

He wore a ball cap on his head.

He folded up another tortilla, dipped it in black beans, tore a bite from the soggy bread. Through chews he said, 'Gray Man, they call you. El hombre de gris.' Madrigal lifted his beer and used it as a pointer. Jabbed it out at Gentry. 'Nobody gets a meeting with me. *Nobody*. But everyone is talking about you. Everybody is asking me, "Did you see that gringo on TV in Puerto Vallarta?" You are like a movie star. I had to meet you.'

Madrigal stuck a wet finger into a small pile of white powder on the table next to his lunch, then he jammed the finger into his mouth, sucking off the cocaine.

This act was followed by a swig of Tecate.

Court said, 'Thank you for seeing me.'

'You have killed a lot of the Black Suits' *sicarios*. More than my men have.' He looked around him at the gunmen as he sipped more beer, as if waiting for an explanation from his staff. No one said anything.

Court looked to his left and right, on both sides the muzzles of stainless steel revolvers pressed into his cheekbones. 'Can you ask your men to lower their guns? I'd hate for one of them to sneeze. I came here showing you respect; I only ask you to give me the same courtesy.'

Madrigal smiled as he folded another tortilla. 'I am showing you lots of respect, gringo. You don't think this is respect? You should see how I treat men I do not respect. I know what you can do. You may have a way to kill me still; I don't know.'

'I couldn't kill you if I wanted to.' Court was not above a little ass kissing at the moment.

'Then if that wasn't the plan, what can I do for you?'

'I came to offer my services, free of charge.'

'*¿Tus servicios?*' *Your services?*

'Yes. I would like your help, and your blessing, in going after Los Trajes Negros.'

Madrigal waved his men back; they lowered their weapons and stepped to the side. Still, there were twelve men with firearms within five steps of the American assassin. The *narco* drummed his thick fingers on the picnic table. 'Haven't you been doing that all week without my help?'

'I am talking about a larger-scale operation.'

The drug lord shrugged, motioned for Gentry to sit down. Court took a metal chair on the opposite side of the table. Madrigal spoke while a man with an AK-47 popped open a can of Tecate and placed it in front of Court. 'I am not at war with de la Rocha. I don't *want* war with de la Rocha. There is enough war going on now. DLR has his plaza, and I have mine, and I have enough troubles fighting the army. I'd rather just watch you kill his people without getting involved.' He laughed. 'That's more fun.' The men in the room laughed behind their gun barrels.

Court did not understand everything Madrigal had said; he had a thick Mexican mountain accent peppered with impenetrable colloquialisms, and Court had learned the majority of his Spanish in Spain and South America. A young man was called from across the room; he sat down next to Madrigal.

'My son will translate. We call him Chingarito.'

Court silently translated the boy's nickname then wondered what kind of man would call his son 'Little Fucker.' Court did not ask the question aloud.

The kid was barely sixteen; he wore a ball cap with a gold marijuana leaf emblem stitched on it. He looked somewhat excited to be called to the table for this responsibility. He translated his father's reticence about war with the Black Suits.

Court switched to English. 'Did you know DLR was given intelligence on your contacts in South America by the Central Intelligence Agency?'

The boy translated. Madrigal shook his head. 'No. How do you know this?'

'A man in the CIA told me, and DLR himself told me. He wants access to some of your production.'

'He won't get it.'

'Maybe not. Maybe he will just do what he can to hurt your production. That would strengthen him, wouldn't it?'

350

Constantino Madrigal called another man over. Spoke into the man's ear for a moment. Then he looked back to Gentry. 'Daniel de la Rocha's father was a wise man. A competitor, of course, but a good businessman. Daniel is loco, insane. He has tried to implicate me in the assassination attempt of him by the GOPES on his yacht, and then he tried to implicate me in the assassination of the families of the GOPES officers. But that is his style, not mine. High profile, high body count. Psychological warfare. All that time in the military cooked his brain, made him a mad killer. An unreasonable man. Now they say he worships a street idol from the barrios.' Constantino Madrigal shook his head in disgust. 'The business and intelligence end of his operation is actually run by his consigliere, a gentleman named Calvo. Calvo is my enemy, but I respect him. He is smarter than any ten of these stupid *pendejos* I have working for me.' He waved his arm around the room, and a couple of his men chuckled.

The younger Madrigal relayed all this to Gentry, and then the father continued. 'If Calvo found out who I was working with in South America to fabricate the product and to get it to Mexico, and if de la Rocha decided he wanted to go to war with me, it would cost me much time and money. Money, I have, but that is not how I want to spend my time.'

'I can prevent that,' Court said before the son finished the translation.

'By shooting a few of his men?'

'No. With your help I can harass his operation a lot more than that. I can turn his attention to me, away from you, and you can take steps on your side to protect your interests in South America. He won't even know you are involved.'

When the translation was finished, Madrigal sat quietly for a moment. The man Madrigal conferred with earlier was still standing behind him; the man leaned forward but the *narco* boss stayed him with his hand while he thought.

His son did not say another word.

351

Finally, Madrigal looked at Gentry. 'You are alone. You are not working for the American government. This I know.'

Court nodded.

'Then why are you doing this?'

'DLR has something I want.'

'The Gamboa woman?'

Gentry was pleased that these rough-looking cowboys up here in a remote mountain hideout knew about Laura. It meant los Vaqueros had an intelligence arm with some access to info on the Black Suits.

He nodded. 'I have one mission, and that is to get DLR to release Laura because it is too expensive and dangerous for him to keep her.'

'Young Daniel can be very stubborn.'

Gentry did not blink. 'And so can I.'

'What do you want from me?' asked Constantino.

'Intelligence and material support.'

'Men?'

'No. I work alone.'

'What do you mean, "material support"?'

'Guns and a pickup truck.'

Madrigal smiled widely. Did another finger of wet cocaine, followed by another swig of canned beer. He laughed as he said, 'You sound like a man from Sinaloa.'

Court smiled himself. 'So, we have a deal?'

'I was born in a villa in Sinaloa called Mátalo.' Court translated the town's name silently. The village was called 'Kill Him' in Spanish.

Madrigal continued. 'The Black Suits are army officers, city dwellers, college graduates. Men from Mexico City, primarily. They are cruel. *Sí*, they are very cruel. But de la Rocha and his organization are not *outlaws*. We, los Vaqueros? We *are* the mountains. We *are* outlaws. Our people have been fighting and killing for hundreds of years. We've been cattle rustlers; we've been highway robbers; we've raided Indian camps for their women, army barracks for their guns; we've robbed banks for their money.' The big man sipped beer and smiled. Mentally, Gentry realized, the man was in a happy place.

'Now it is drugs to the USA, so there is more money involved, but I don't care. I am a warlord. I don't give a damn about the money. It is the fight that I love.'

'I'll fight the hell out of DLR for you, Señor Madrigal.'

Another pause from the *narco* boss. He stroked his mustache and sipped beer. 'We ... I mean the leaders of the enterprises here in Mexico, do not touch one another's families.'

'I am not planning on going after his family. I am only asking for information about his drug operations. It will get very, very bloody. But it won't get personal.'

Chingarito translated. Madrigal sipped his Tecate and thought some more. Finally, he motioned over his shoulder. 'This is Hector Serna. My intelligence chief. I will have the two of you work directly together. Less chance for *ratones*.'

'Rats?'

Serna's English was superb. He said, 'Informants. All organizations have them. We are no different.'

'So you have access to rats in the Black Suits? People who can give you information on their whereabouts?'

'We monitor the movements of the leadership of Los Trajes Negros; of course we do. They do the same to us.'

'So you know where they are at all times?'

'At all times? No. But if they communicate their movements to anyone who might also be on our pay, then yes, we hear of it. For example, we know the Black Suits will be in Puerto Vallarta tomorrow; they have contacted their people in the local police and have let them know. If they need to go to a hotel for a meeting, if they need a street blocked off for their security, if they need cars moved out of a parking lot so that they can eat at a restaurant adjacent to it – then we will hear of it from our contacts in the local police.'

'Interesting,' said Gentry. Then he looked at Madrigal. 'Could you arrange for me to get to Puerto Vallarta?'

'Of course,' Madrigal said as he stood and extended a hand.

Court put out his hand. Shook the hand of a murderer of men, women, and children; a torturer of hundreds; a man who epitomized most every reasonable person's personification of evil.

'*Gracias, amigo.*'

46

At eight o'clock the next morning, Court Gentry sat in an old black Mazda pickup truck in a parking lot in the Puerto Vallarta marina. Twenty yards from his dirty windshield, tens of millions of dollars of yachts and other pleasure craft gently rocked in unison on the water. The morning sun warmed a pair of iguanas on the rocks along the promenade. Out his driver-side window, a posh apartment building loomed five stories high. Out his passenger-side window, a long row of *tiendas* and businesses that had not yet opened for the day sat dark and quiet.

Gentry was on the phone with Ramses Cienfuegos Cortillo. Ramses had hooked up with men in Mexico City he trusted. He was still lying low, but Court had called his old phone number, and a recorded message directed him to a new mobile. Court called that, and Ramses called him back minutes later.

Court had contacted the federal officer to give him a warning. Court let him know he was getting intelligence and support from the Madrigal Cartel, but he wanted his friend in the federal police to know he wasn't working for los Vaqueros.

As far as Court Gentry was concerned, he was working for Laura.

'Look, Ramses. This is going to get ugly. I don't know what you have told those around you about me, about you working with me.'

'I have said nothing. I moved my family to a friend's apartment in Miami, and the people I am working with only know that Martin and I survived the attack on the yacht, but Martin was killed in Tequila. These men know better than to ask more questions.'

'You trust these guys?'

Without hesitation Ramses said, 'I trust them. They have all suffered greatly at the hands of Los Trajes Negros.'

'Good.'

'These are honest men. We can help you go after Laura.'

Court paused, looked through the dirty windshield at a middle-aged bald man leaving the apartment building, taking his small poodle for a walk along a grassy strip that rimmed a shopping center just outside of the marina. Then he said, 'If you know honest men, let's keep them honest. What I am about to do ... I don't want to involve them.'

'Just what *are* you going to do, Joe?'

'I am going to scorch the earth. I am going to murder, torture, defile. I am going to go ballistic on the motherfuckers who have Laura Gamboa, and I am going to get her back by killing everything in my path. I am not going to play by the rules.'

'There are no rules here, amigo.'

'I am talking about the rules of humanity, and I am prepared to violate every last one of them.'

'*Dios Santo,*' Ramses muttered. 'I have never met anyone like you who was ... how can I say it? Not on the other side.'

'I am different from other good guys, because I am not afraid to go down to the level of my enemies.

'If you know guys down here, good guys, guys who can still sleep at night ... let's not involve them. I'd rather do what I'm about to do affiliated with Madrigal than with the good guys, does that make sense?'

'*You* are a good man.'

'Thanks, Ramses, but you won't say that when I'm done. You are going to think I am the sickest son of a bitch you've ever met.'

'You have my number. I will help you in any way I can, and not involve anyone else. If you need something, anything, call me.'

'Thanks.'

Court hung up the phone, watched the man with the dog for a moment, and then opened the door to the Mazda truck.

Forty seconds later the poodle was all alone and barking wildly, his leash wrapped around a signpost in front of a *tienda* that had not yet opened for business.

The dank, dark, ten-by-ten storage room smelled of mold. Lizards and spiders crawled the walls and hung from the ceiling, casting frightening shadows when they moved in front of the two-million-candlepower flashlight that Gentry had positioned in the corner, facing the center of the storage room.

There, in the center, sat Captain Xavier Garza Guerro of the Puerto Vallarta police. According to Madrigal's intelligence chief, Garza was a paid *sicario* for the Black Suits, and he oversaw the cartel's security operations here on the west coast of Mexico, from the Guatemalan border in the south to the southern edge of Sinaloa in the north. He had been instrumental in helping de la Rocha's efforts in the region. Protecting his drug shipments, his production facilities, his safe houses, even Daniel's motorcade travel through the city was often aided by squad cars with flashing lights.

Gentry ripped the duct tape off the bald man, tearing mustache hair out by the roots. Captain Garza's left eye was swollen shut, the result of his face's impact with the pavement outside the storage room. His hands were strapped behind his back; his clothes had been cut off with a long, thin fillet knife.

For the first hour Garza had tried to be reasonable with Court, had given him the locations of the meth labs that he knew about up in the mountains to the east. He thought this might buy his freedom; he felt the man must certainly be working for one of the other cartels, and if Garza could only convince him he would play ball, then whoever had sent this man would see that a well-connected police officer, with knowledge of the inner workings of de la Rocha's enterprises, would be much more valuable alive than dead.

But then the gringo stepped in front of the light. He showed himself. The kidnapper made no attempt whatsoever to hide his face from his victim.

And the dirty cop knew what that meant.

Captain Garza was fully aware that now his only chance was to connect himself with Los Trajes Negros, to frighten his kidnapper into letting him go.

He shouted, 'You lay another finger on me, and DLR will send Spider after you!'

The American reached out a hand, pointed his finger, and pushed it hard into the sweaty forehead of Xavier Garza. He finished the motion with a shove.

Then the *norteamericano* looked back over his shoulder at the garage door to the storage room. 'When will he come? I would very much like to see him.'

'You will see him, gringo!' Garza tried to control his anger. 'Look, if you let me go right now, I'll forget this, but if you—'

'Oh, Xavier ... you will *never* forget this. Not for the rest of your life.' Court looked down to his watch. 'You can remember for at least three minutes, can't you?'

'What do you want?' Garza's question came out in a scream.

The American shrugged. 'Nothing from you, asshole.'

'Nothing? Then what is this? What are you doing?'

'I'm just a force of nature, Xavier. You have lived by the sword ...' The gringo turned away, disappeared into a dark corner, returned seconds later with a large metal cleaver. 'You will die by the sword. Or, in this case, by the meat cleaver.'

'You are with los Vaqueros?'

'No.'

'Then who?'

'With the United States of America.'

Garza cocked his sweaty bald head. 'DEA? You are not DEA.'

'No, I'm not.'

Garza thought he understood now. This man was some anti-drug avenger. 'Look, we are just businessmen. All of us down here. We only provide the supply. You gringos provide the demand. We just respond to that demand.'

'So the guy who makes kiddie porn isn't responsible as long as there is someone who wants to buy it?'

Garza looked at the kidnapper. 'You know nothing. You are just a rich American. You don't understand our culture!'

'Actually, I'm getting the hang of it. I'm going to chop off your head and put it in a bag. Does that sound a little like your culture?'

'Go to hell!'

'Most likely. But in the meantime ...' Gentry sat on a brown box in front of his victim. 'Names and numbers.'

'What?'

'Names and numbers. You give me others in your organization, and I'll do it quick and fast.'

'You will kill me quick and fast?'

'That's the best deal I can offer you.'

'And if I don't give you names and numbers?'

Court looked at his watch. Shrugged. 'Buddy ... I got all damn day.'

47

The Puerto Vallarta police cars parked in the street at nine p.m. The officers left their vehicles and began directing traffic, forcing it on, ordering it to continue to the next intersection. One minute later the first in a long series of armored white SUVs pulled up in front of the beautiful seaside restaurant.

The Black Suits working the advance security detail went about their rounds in the restaurant. A stern-looking but polite man went with the maître d' to each table and collected mobile phones while letting the stunned patrons know that their food and drinks would be taken care of. A group of four in the security detail moved through the kitchen with the restaurant manager, checked coolers and freezers, hallways and pantries, bathrooms and loading doors. They frisked the staff from head to toe. A pair of guards armed with .45-caliber Mac-10 sub guns stood in the doorways, two more junior members of the unit patrolled out back with AK-47s.

Daniel de la Rocha sat in an armored SUV with the commander of his bodyguards and his own close protection officer by his side. Emilio Lopez Lopez received the radio call from his advance team unit leader that the restaurant was locked down and secure, so he nodded to his boss, and the driver of the Yukon opened the back door of the vehicle. A team of Emilio's best guards formed around their leader, and they entered the restaurant. Emilio had his right hand on his pistol in his jacket, and his left hand on his *patrón's* lower back. An earpiece connected to his radio gave him updates from his team, and any threat would have Emilio Lopez Lopez shielding his boss, turning him around, and hustling him back to the SUVs in seconds.

Close behind the main scrum of the principle protection force was Nestor Calvo Macias, speaking into his Bluetooth earpiece. Javier 'Spider' Cepeda, the leader of the Black Suit's assassins, was in the crowd, as were a number of local dealers, enforcers, logistics managers, the chief pilot of Daniel's many aircraft, and a few manufacturing and procurement executives.

Fourteen bodyguards on the premises ensured their leader's safety, and nineteen other Black Suits all but filled the private dining area in the center of the building.

The private dining area was open-air, a cool breeze blew in from the Pacific and swirled around the tiled courtyard. Daniel de la Rocha sat at a table in the back of the room, behind a tall gurgling fountain and below a latticework arch of lovingly manicured bougainvillea. Other members of the Black Suits sat at tables of four around the courtyard. This was not a business dinner; it was just a dinner. They were here to eat and then to travel east to the safe house a few miles inland. This was de la Rocha's first visit to PV since the massacre ten days earlier; he had business to attend to in the area and had spent the day working with associates of his commuter airline, and his drug manufacture and transporting enterprise.

The mood among the men was grim because the mood of their leader was grim. He was furious about the apparent escape of the Gamboas and the gringo. He fully assumed they were north of the border, but his hunt was far from over. Right now he had his entire workforce that operated in the United States: in Atlanta, in Chicago, in Dallas, in Los Angeles, in a dozen other cities – he had them all working on finding the Gamboas and the gringo.

361

So far Calvo had failed him, Spider had failed him, his fiftythousand-member-strong criminal organization had failed him.

But that did not really matter. Because all that mattered to Daniel was that Daniel had failed *her*.

Daniel gazed across his table to a corner of the courtyard, just a few feet away. A shrine of la Santa Muerte had been brought in by his advance security team, just a three-foot-tall icon of *la virgen*, dressed in the finest bridal gown handmade by a master dressmaker in Mexico City who worked exclusively on creating high-quality and highprice fashion for icons of la Santa Muerte. She stood on a table festooned with devotional candles that flickered in the sea breeze; the shadows played across the skeleton's face, creating the appearance of movement and life.

DLR stared into her eyes. To him they were not vacant sockets in the plaster; they were windows into an abyss. Viewing portals into the soul of an angry goddess.

A bottle of Gran Patrón Platinum silver tequila was placed at his table by a waiter in a white coat. Next to the bottle a crystal dish of freshly cut limes, a crystal dish of salt, a small shot glass of the same crystal.

De la Rocha ignored the accoutrements and grabbed the bottle by the neck, took a swig of the clear liquor, stared at his idol, and promised her aloud that he would give her the tribute she demanded.

The unborn Gamboa child.

The waiter stood awkwardly with a menu in his hand, waiting for DLR to finish his prayer. While Daniel was still praying, the man cleared his throat.

Emilio Lopez Lopez stood against the wall just behind his *jefe*; Emilio stepped forward to the waiter and grabbed him by the arm of his coat, turned him roughly, and prepared to shove him away for his poor manners. But Daniel raised his bottle of tequila.

'It's okay, Emilio. Thank you.' He looked at the waiter. 'Just have your chef prepare something light. Grilled tilapia would be perfect.'

'*Muy bien*, Don Daniel,' said the waiter, and he shot off to the kitchen, clearly happy to walk away from his error with his life.

Nestor came over to the table, and they talked business for a few minutes, but DLR's heart wasn't in it, and finally he asked his consigliere to leave him to eat his meal alone. The rest of the Black Suits got the message; they ate at other tables and talked in hushed tones, worked their mobile phones or their laptops, tried like hell to be the one who determined just where in the world their targets had managed to disappear to.

A different waiter appeared with a cold watermelon soup, and DLR slurped it while lost in thought and melancholy. He continued to sip the tequila between gulps of bottled water and spoonfuls of soup; he just gazed around in the dark, at his men, at the fountain, at his idol on the table in the corner. Decorative paper lanterns strung across the courtyard on lines above the men's heads swayed in the breeze.

In just minutes another waiter in a starched white coat came to DLR's table; he pushed a tablecloth-covered rolling cart with a covered dish on it. With a subservient bow the man took away the empty plate of soup from the table and then replaced it with the covered dish.

'*Buen provecho*,' said the waiter, *bon appétit*, as he removed the cover and placed it back on the rolling cart.

De la Rocha did not look at the man, did not reply. He just took his fork in his hand, then distractedly glanced down at his plate as he began digging into his dinner.

His hand jerked up and away.

The plate was covered in slimy animal entrails, the reeking head and skeleton of a deboned fish, and other pieces of smelly waste.

'What the hell is this?' Daniel asked.

The waiter answered him in English, '*That*, sir, looks like shit, and *this* ... ' He held his hand out in front of DLR, showed him a device clutched in it. '*This* looks like a dead man's switch.' The device was clearly a detonator, the waiter's thumb was pressed

363

down on a red button, and a wire ran from the device, down the man's palm, and disappeared into his white coat.

De la Rocha looked up at the waiter.

It took a moment with the trim hair and beard, with the darker skin and the black-framed glasses, but he recognized him.

It was the Gray Man.

The American opened his coat and exposed a crude roped vest with two large bricks of yellow material coated in plastic hanging from it. They looked like bags of sand. He said, softly, 'If my thumb leaves this trigger, for even one-tenth of one second, then this ammonium nitrate/fuel oil bomb will detonate, and everyone here will die. Including you.'

Emilio had been standing against the wall; he could only see the back of the waiter's coat. He'd checked to make sure it wasn't the same insolent bastard who had coughed while his *jefe* was praying a few minutes earlier. Satisfied that this was a new, and hopefully more professional, server, he'd not bothered to pay close attention to the presentation of the food. But now Emilio noticed the two men were in conversation with each other. It was not often that his *patrón* spoke to a waiter for so long.

Emilio stepped around the side of the man in the white coat, and when he did, he saw Daniel's wide eyes. Immediately, he reached into his suit coat and rushed the table, recognizing the Gray Man at the same moment. He drew his Venezuelan Zamorano 9 mm pistol and knocked a chair out of the way to press it against the gringo's head.

De la Rocha raised his hands into the air, panicked now that his bodyguard would shoot the American without hesitation. *'¡No! ¡Tranquilo! Tranquilo!' Relax! Relax!*

Guns appeared in the hands of everyone in the courtyard. Handguns, sub guns, a pair of pistol-grip shotguns. Some men approached the table while others stepped back and aimed carefully. No one knew what to do, but they all followed their leader's wishes, and they held their positions.

'Everyone just take a few steps back. Emilio, lower your pistol and step away, but be ready. Spider, keep an eye on this *pinche* gringo and kill him if anything happens to me.'

Spider Cepeda held his Mac-10 with one hand. He stood ten feet away; the muzzle pointed at the face of the American assassin.

'You aren't leaving here with your life, *pendejo*.' He said it slowly and confidently.

48

Court Gentry was fucking freezing. He'd spent three hours in the meat locker, wearing a warm poncho but sitting still in a corner, hiding behind huge sides of beef that hung from the ceiling. He'd slipped into the restaurant at three p.m. with the produce delivery, carrying two backpacks hidden on a hand truck of boxes of fruits and vegetables, then he'd spent a couple of hours in a dry-storage room before finally moving into the walk-in refrigerator as the evening staff went through their afternoon meeting and tasting in the main dining room.

In the walk-in he'd waited until a text came for him from a police officer outside who took money from both Los Trajes Negros and los Vaqueros.

He'd waited thirty minutes more, body shivering and teeth chattering, then he left the refrigerator, dressed in a uniform he'd pulled from a linen rack, and found a rolling cart and some tossed aside fish guts, with which he'd made his entree. Then, still chilled to the bone, he'd headed out into the dining room, looking for Daniel de la Rocha.

Gentry spoke into Daniel's ear. 'Have your men stand down.'

With a flick of his wrist DLR motioned the rest of Los Trajes Negros back a few steps across the courtyard; they all but disappeared in the dark.

But Court raised a hand. He spoke loud enough now for others to hear. 'Not everyone.' He looked back to de la Rocha. 'Which one of these guys is the real brains behind your operation?'

De la Rocha's face flexed like a biceps muscle; Court watched the Mexican's carotid artery flicker. He spoke through a mouth of clenched teeth. '*I* make all the decisions.'

'Sure you do, genius. But you and I need to talk business, and I bet there is a guy in this crowd that you would like to have sit in on our little discussion.' Court motioned with his free hand at the skeleton doll ringed by candles in the corner. 'Unless, of course ... your little Barbie doll can take transcription.' He shook his head and smiled. Displaying a relaxed and 'in charge' demeanor. 'Seriously. What the fuck *is* that?'

Somehow Daniel's fury found a new gear. His face was red, even in the low glow of the paper lanterns hanging from the lines over the courtyard. He hesitated a few seconds, then looked into the dark crowd of men. 'Nestor, *sientate*.' Sit down.

Nestor Calvo sat at the table next to de la Rocha. His salt-andpepper beard sparkled with the sheen of perspiration forming at the skin.

Court looked the older man over for a moment. 'Cool. Adult supervision.'

The Gray Man sat at the table, the rolling food cart to his right. De la Rocha asked him, 'What did you do to the guy from la CIA?'

'I killed the guy from la CIA.' Gentry shrugged like it was no big deal.

'And the gringo from the embassy? Jerry? He helped you escape, didn't he?'

'Forget about Jerry. He is an American asshole. You have enough assholes here without importing. I think you've taken NAFTA just a step too far.'

'I thought you would be far, far away by now. If you had any brains, you would have run. Why are you here?'

'Let me explain what is about to happen to you, Daniel. And Nestor, pay attention, because I'm counting on you to be the reasonable one. Daniel, I am going to destroy your business. I am going to ruin you. Burn your drugs, kill your middlemen, scare off your suppliers, smash your boats and planes and cars and trucks. I will tear all the profit away from your organization, little by little, bit by bit.'

De la Rocha just smiled. 'You do that, and I will kill that little Gamboa bitch.'

'No, you won't, and I will tell you why you won't. Because I am not going to touch your family. That is the one thing you can count on. I want Laura back, and all this blowing shit up that I'm about to do is my audition; it's my proving to you that I can go where I want, do whatever I want, whenever I want. You need to think long and hard about where I might go and what I might do if you do something to Laura. Something to *really* make me mad.'

'You are doing this all for the girl? *¿En serio?*' *Seriously?*

'Yes. If you return her to me, all the bad stuff stops. You can go on being a crystal meth–trafficking piece of shit to your heart's content, and I will no longer be in your way.'

De la Rocha's face was red with anger. After a long time he spoke. 'You are dead, *maricón*. You are dead.'

Gentry shrugged. 'Call ten of your top lieutenants and tell them the same thing, because within seventy-two hours it's a good bet that a lot of them will be.'

'Do you know who we are, Gray Man? We are Los Trajes Negros. We were one of the best-trained units in the Mexican Army. Trained by *your* military, in fact. I am not just some *car-terlero* from the mountains with ostrich boots and a *cuerno de chivo* like that *cabrón* Madrigal. I trained at Fort Benning and Fort Bragg.'

'When you were at Bragg, did you see all those paramilitary forces training there?'

'Yes, and I trained with them. The best commandos in the world.'

'Badasses, one and all. But remember this. Every single one of those special ops organizations has killing me right at the top of their to-do list . . . They've been after me for years, and yet here I sit. You have *never* been up against someone like me, Daniel. You would do well to keep that in the forefront of your consciousness.'

Nestor Calvo had not spoken. Now he shook his head, leaned slightly forward. Said in Spanish. 'But señor, you are just one man.'

Court leaned closer to Nestor. Made long and severe eye contact. 'With nothing to lose.'

DLR looked down at the dead man's switch in the American's hand. 'You think I'm scared of you?'

Gentry smiled, genuinely pleased he had been asked the question. 'I think you are fucking terrified. I see straight through that macho image. You are thinking of your family, and you are thinking of the men you left around Laura, and you hope to God you can call them and tell them to stay away from her before they do something that they cannot undo. Because you know what I have done, and you know what I am capable of.

'Everything just changed in your world. You're no different than thousands of other shitheads around this planet. Your influence, your success, your power – it all comes from fear. If you can't fill people with fear, then you are nothing. You cease to be. Well, guess what, amigo? You aren't the scariest thing around here anymore.'

Nestor drummed his fingers on the table. He leaned forward, towards the American. 'I suppose you have a plan to get away now?'

'I do.' Court reached into the pocket of his waiter's coat, pulled out a small mobile phone.

'Four more pounds of ANFO is stashed under a table in this room. As I walk away from the restaurant, I only have to push one button' – he held up the phone – 'and every one of you dies. As soon as I disappear from view, you might want to think about running out of here, because I have not decided if this is all worth the trouble. Maybe I'll just turn you into dog meat tonight and hope your men let Laura go because there is a new law in town.'

369

De la Rocha looked like he was going to explode from anger. Gentry turned away from him, directed his next words to Calvo, as if the head of Los Trajes Negros was not even there. 'You'll have to keep this guy on a short leash. He's going to want to tear up the country to find me. That's fine; he can waste his time and his energy. But you need to keep letting him know how much my reign of terror on your organization is costing him. All I want is the girl. Handing her over to me will not cost you a dime. You can see how that is in your best interests, even if this dumb fuck cannot.' Court stood. 'Hopefully, he will listen to you' – he motioned to the Santa Muerte statue in the corner – 'and not to that creepy bitch.'

And with that Gentry raised the dead man's switch high in his left hand, and the mobile phone high in his right. 'Tell these assholes to let me walk out of here.'

De la Rocha only nodded slightly; his eyes remained locked on the American. Calvo rose from the table, headed past the fountain and towards the armed men in the courtyard, telling them all to let the gringo leave unmolested.

'I will see you again, Gray Man,' de la Rocha said softly.

'If you do, Daniel, you will end up like your poor friend.'

De la Rocha cocked his head, but Gentry turned away, walked out of the courtyard, past the phalanx of bodyguards. Seconds after that he left the restaurant, both his hands still high in the air.

'What did he say to you while I was gone?' Calvo asked Daniel upon returning to the table. The rest of the inner circle of the Black Suits closed on their leader.

'Something about me ending up like my friend.' De la Rocha and Calvo looked at each other without speaking for a moment. 'What did he mean by that?' Daniel asked his older employee.

Together, slowly, their heads turned towards the rolling cart.

'Emilio. Check that.'

Emilio stepped to the other side of the rolling cart then used the barrel of his pistol to lift a corner of the linen tablecloth. His eyes narrowed as he squinted. 'It's a head, *jefe*.'

'A gringo who decapitates.' Calvo said it with his eyebrows high. 'He is showing us he can play by Mexican rules.'

'Whose head is it?' asked DLR.

Emilio looked again. Knelt down lower. 'I ... I think it is Xavier Garza Guerro.' Garza was the highest-ranking police officer in Puerto Vallarta controlled by the Black Suits and a former army colleague of Daniel's. DLR had known the man for sixteen years. He knew his wife, his kids, his parents.

'Get it out of here.' De la Rocha stood and stormed over to Spider, grabbing him by the lapel of his jacket. 'Listen to me! I want him followed, I want him captured, and I want him tortured like nothing you have ever done to anyone!'

'*Sí, jefe.* I have men in the street ready to follow him until we get you out of here, then we will take him.'

'I swear to you; I want you to have nightmares about what you did to him. I want you to be sick!'

'*Sí, jefe.*'

'Now go! And do not show your face to me until you have the Gray Man. *¿Me entiendes?' Do you understand me?*

'*¡Sí! ¡Sí!*' Spider Cepeda shot out of the room, his phone rising to his ear as he did so.

Then DLR looked around the room, found Emilio right on his shoulder. 'The men on tonight's advance security team?'

Emilio Lopez Lopez raised his chin. 'I have already disarmed them and put them under custody. Tonight I will have this building burnt to the ground, and the manager and maître d' shot.'

'Fine. But this is *your* failure.' His finger jabbed the leader of his security forces hard in the chest.

'I understand, *mi jefe.*' Emilio said it with his head low.

De la Rocha turned around towards Calvo now, who was already speaking on his mobile. 'Call the house. Tell them to keep their hands off the Gamboa bitch.'

Calvo slid the phone back in his jacket, completing a call. 'Done.'

Pent-up rage blew forth from the thirty-nine-year-old de la

Rocha; he screamed and pulled dishes and glasses from his table, crashed them against the stone wall.

Calvo rushed forward. 'Daniel, listen to me! Calm down! Everything the gringo said, everything he did, it was all to get this reaction from you! It was to knock you off balance! Don't play into his plan! Think!'

'I will piss on his beating heart!'

'*¡Tranquilo!*' Calm down!

'I will calm down when someone around me does their fucking duty! I have had enough failure from you *cabrones*!' He threw bottles and knocked over tables. Around him his Black Suits stood watch. No one but Nestor dared speak to him.

And Nestor *did* speak. 'We can end this, Daniel! We can end this right now!'

De la Rocha stopped smashing things; he turned towards his older advisor. Cocked his head. 'You want to give the girl to the gringo. You want to stop hunting for Elena Gamboa.'

Nestor reached out, smoothed the lapel of Daniel de la Rocha's black suit. 'I want to put an end to this madness so that we can get back into the business of making money. Making money for everyone. Building our organization, empowering ourselves against our enemies, protecting ourselves from the government and the—'

'Stop! Stop talking now, Nestor, before I begin to lose trust in you.'

'I am at your service, *patrón*. But as your advisor I feel it necessary to remind you why we are here, why we take the risks that we take. Not for some gringo that la CIA cannot even kill or capture. Not for the life of the unborn child of a cop that we dealt with brilliantly weeks ago.'

DLR shook his head. 'Listen to me, Nestor. You have your orders. The Gray Man must die. The Gamboa woman needs to be found.'

Without a sigh or a change of expression, Nestor Calvo Macias nodded. 'As I said, I am at your service.'

'Good.' De la Rocha turned to another of his men, the leader of his kidnapping operation. 'Roberto, move the Gamboa woman. Double the guard on her.'

'Sí, señor.'

'Emilio!' he shouted. His bodyguard was right behind him still. 'Double the guard on me.'

'Already done, *jefe*.'

'Let's go, before the Gray Man pushes that button on his phone.'

Court did not push the button on the mobile phone, as there was no explosive hidden in the courtyard of the seaside restaurant. The Black Suits lost Gentry in the crowd of the Malecon, the busy beach promenade of Puerto Vallarta. Court ditched his waiter uniform in an alley, went through the entrances and out the exits of a half dozen bars and eateries, then climbed onto a parked pickup truck, leapt to a second-floor balcony of a beachside apartment building. He would spend the night on this balcony, curled into a ball on a soft patio chair, the sea breeze blowing against his face.

Below him the Black Suits ran through the streets, drove convoys of SUVs and pickup trucks through the foot traffic, grabbed shorthaired and goateed Americans and pushed them up against walls, shone tactical flashlights in their faces, and then shoved them back on their way in frustration.

The local cops were out in force as well. They were hunting the Gray Man at the behest of the Black Suits. Gentry imagined word would have gotten to the CIA by now, any American black ops teams in the area tracking him would be racing into downtown Puerto Vallarta.

He wondered if Gregor Sidorenko had operatives in Mexico hunting him, too. If they could find him in the Amazonian jungle, it was a safe bet the Russian mob boss would have a crew here.

But none of these forces had the power to search every apartment in the entire city. He was safe here for a night. And by morning they would have given up, they would have assured themselves that he'd slipped through their net again.

Court scrolled through e-mails on his phone, all from Hector Serna, intelligence chief for the Madrigal Cartel. Each e-mail was a nugget of information. The address of a Mexico City bank; the tail number of a cargo aircraft known to run meth and black tar heroin for the Black Suits; addresses or satellite coordinates of safe houses, warehouses, parking lots of vehicles all purportedly owned by de la Rocha's organization.

Court's target list was an embarrassment of riches.

He sent Serna a text message, requesting some items that he would need the following day. Once Serna replied with details of the drop-off of the goods, Court put the phone in his pocket and looked up at the stars.

He heard another confrontation below, angry men shouting at confused civilians.

To a man, Spider's *sicarios* were scared of Spider. And Spider was surely afraid of Daniel.

Court was a single operator, which freed him of suspicion of others within his organization, simply because he had no organization. He was a lone man with neither friends nor close associates.

He had to be suspicious of everyone, trusting of no one, and he preferred this to working for a group that could turn on him in an instant. This had happened to him in the past. And he preferred this to working for a handler who had double-crossed him. This had happened to him in the past – twice.

Court lay on the softly padded teak chaise lounge, looked at the beautiful night above him, ignored the honking horns and the killers below him, and he knew that this would be his last true rest for many nights to come.

He thought of Laura.

49

Daniel de la Rocha's estate deep in a canyon at the foot of Sierra del Tigre was his largest and most palatial. He'd named it Hacienda Maricela, after his youngest daughter, and he came here to relax as often as his travels would allow. At present his wife and children were at their home in Cuernavaca; it was better suited for kids, thought Daniel, and he was careful to keep la Santa Muerte out of that particular property, if only to placate his devout-Catholic wife.

Hacienda Maricela was a mammoth early twentieth-century home and hunting lodge surrounded by two hundred hectares of private forest. The nearby town of Mazamitla provided its local police force to augment the hundred-man security detail that protected the Black Suits' leadership when they stayed at the residence, and a private airstrip, a heliport, and a paved road dotted with checkpoints that led out of the canyon and up to the highway towards Guadalajara provided safe and easy access for Daniel and his men.

De la Rocha's men had even built a stop on the rail line that passed through the forest so that large goods could be delivered by freight train.

The property was also Daniel's favorite place to train with his men. There were rock walls, obstacle courses, a rappelling tower, an outdoor long-distance firing range, a dojo, and myriad other opportunities for the ex-military men to hone their martial skills.

DLR flew his Eurocopter through the canyons and ravines, horrifying his men with his death-defying flying.

The morning after the dinner in Puerto Vallarta, DLR and Spider were training in the hacienda's massive indoor firing range. A few of Spider's men stood around and watched, and Emilio Lopez Lopez stood just behind his principal, protecting him here even in Daniel's own home.

Javier and Daniel were firing modern FN P90 submachine guns at life-sized rubber human forms attached to hooks that moved on tracks recessed in the ballistic steel ceiling of the firing range. One at a time the targets emerged from behind swinging steel doors in the backstop of the range, forty yards away. Like attacking gunmen the humanoid targets raced forward, darted left and right a bit, even stopped behind the cover of low pine walls laid out on rolling tracks on the floor.

One at a time Cepeda and de la Rocha took turns firing at the moving targets, a dozen times each before they darted off to the side, only to be replaced by the next wave of 'attackers,' coming in from the side or popping up from behind the concrete walls.

It was a state-of-the-art system, costing millions of dollars, and Daniel even had two full-time employees for the range who lived on the property.

Quickly Daniel's weapon emptied while shooting at a target sailing by close from left to right. He dropped the P90 from his hands; it fell and hung taught by the sling around his neck. DLR reached into his black suit, pulled his .45, and snapped four rounds into the humanoid head before it slid from view.

One of the Black Suits behind him shouted. 'That is the Gray Man, *jefe*!' Others cheered.

Daniel smiled, pulled his ear muffs off his head. 'I wish. I get another chance at him, and that is what I will do! Spider failed me last night and let the *chingado* gringo get out of Puerto Vallarta with his life. All of you have failed me!'

Spider's *sicarios* looked down to the floor or up at the ceiling.

'As soon as Calvo's operatives catch wind of where he is, all you fools and your men will be cast out into the street, and your shooting better be as good as mine.'

Nods from the men within the subdued silence.

Spider hefted his P90 from a table, stepped back up to the firing line, but Emilio Lopez Lopez patted his boss on the pack. 'Daniel. Now that you are warmed up, the next targets are for you, as well.'

Spider lowered his P90 and stepped back. De la Rocha shrugged and reloaded his .45 and his sub gun.

Emilio nodded to the range master working in a booth against the side wall. He flipped a switch and the two doors at the rear backstop opened, and the tracked hooks on the ceiling brought targets out into the firing range.

But they were not humanoid.

They were human. Two men, their faces well beaten, their mouths gagged with rough hemp, their hands tied behind their backs, and their bodies hanging from ropes from the hooks, tied tight around their shoulders and causing them to writhe in pain from the strain of gravity.

'*Jefe,*' said Emilio. 'These are two of the men in charge of the advance detail at the dinner last night in PV. After several hours of interrogation last night, we have decided they did not know the Gray Man was in the building. Still, for their failure, I have ordered them to pay with their lives.'

De la Rocha lowered his rifle. Nodded slowly. 'What of the rest of the advance team?'

'Two more died during my interrogation. Two more were junior men who were stationed in the main dining room and were not part of the prescreening of the facility. I do not hold them at fault.'

The hooks conveying the suspended men stopped in the center of the range, the men's feet dangled a foot off the floor. The human targets rocked back and forth, swinging under the hooks.

'You hold the men in charge at fault.'

'Of course, Daniel.'

'Emilio. Those are *your* men. You chose them; you trained them; you sent them to the restaurant. *You* are in charge.'

Lopez stammered.

'You believe in accountability, yes?'

'Of course, Daniel. I hold them account—'

'I hold *you* accountable. You should be out there hanging with them.'

Emilio looked at his *patrón*. He did not move a muscle. Spider had put his P90 rifle down on a table, but he drew his pistol slowly and held it to his side, the leader of the Black Suit's killers daring the leader of the Black Suit's bodyguards to try anything.

Emilio looked at Spider. He recovered from shock. 'That is not necessary. I have my 9 mm inside my coat in a shoulder holster. Shall I remove it or would you like one of your men to take it?'

Spider reached back with an empty hand, waved one of his men forward. The *sicario* stepped behind Emilio, reached around into his coat, and pulled out the gun.

'I ask you to reconsider, *mi jefe*,' Emilio said, his voice calm, but a tremor in his lips belied his emotions.

'You served me well, my friend.'

'It . . . it has been an honor.'

'Too bad some *pinche* gringo had to come and ruin everything.'

'*Mi jefe*, if you give me just one more chance—'

Daniel de la Rocha shot Emilio in the head right where he stood. In a single movement DLR spun, dropped to a crouched shooting position, and sent two rounds from his .45 into the heads of each of his men tied and writhing ten yards downrange. Their struggles stilled, but the impacts of the rounds caused their bodies to swing back and forth.

Emilio Lopez Lopez lay crumpled in a ball at de la Rocha's feet.

DLR stood and said, 'One more chance? A bodyguard does not get another chance. I've been in danger two times in the past week.'

None of the *sicarios* spoke.

Finally, DLR holstered his pistol. 'Spider?'

'*Sí, mi jefe*.'

'You are my personal bodyguard now.'

'Thank you.'

'Don't thank me. You see what happens if you fail twice?'
'I will not fail you again.'

The banker stepped out of the nineteen-passenger Fairchild Metroliner turboprop and onto the tarmac in Manzanillo, two hours south of Puerto Vallarta on the Pacific coast. The sun was high in the sky, and the banker flipped his $4,800 Moss Lipow sunglasses down from the top of his head to protect his eyes.

A limo awaited the banker and his two bodyguards; they were the only passengers on the aircraft, so after taking his time to shake the pilot's and copilot's hands, the banker descended the stairs, his $3,000 Pineider leather briefcase his only luggage.

He approached the limo, and the driver opened the rear door for him. The banker leaned into the limo but then tumbled forward; his chest exploded onto the rich leather interior, splattered on crystal highball glasses, and dripped down smoked windows.

His Moss Lipow sunglasses shot off his head and tumbled across the floorboard. His Pineider briefcase fell free from his grip and bounced against the rear tire of the limo.

His corpulent body slid backwards off of the slimy leather, then slapped facefirst onto the tarmac.

The bodyguards dove atop him as soon as they recognized what had happened, but it was too late.

The bodyguards could do nothing now but guard the body.

Four hundred yards away the Gray Man closed the stock on the collapsible Sako rifle; in seconds he had the weapon stowed in a canvas bag, and the bag tossed into the passenger floorboard of his black Mazda pickup.

He'd killed the banker with one shot. The .338 Lapua round was overkill from only four hundred yards – it could be counted on to drop a man at more than six times the distance – but Gentry found the shack on the hillside not far from the airport's ramp suitable to his needs, and the Sako was the only long-range weapon given to him by Hector Serna.

He wasn't worried about overkill; he was worried about the result. And the result was clear.

With less than an ounce of lead he had eliminated sixteen years of expertise in money laundering.

Yes, Daniel de la Rocha had other bankers, and there was no shortage of qualified men in Mexico ready and willing to replace the corpse that now lay on its back on the tarmac while a frantic bodyguard futilely attempted mouth-to-mouth resuscitation. But the banker's death was a body blow to the finance end of the operation.

Court did not spend one second on remorse or regret. No, he looked at his watch and stepped down harder on the accelerator.

He had two more jobs to do before the day was done.

'Gilberto Moreno was killed by a sniper at noon today.'

It was eleven thirty in the evening, and de la Rocha knelt at the icon of la Santa Muerte. He'd been praying silently in his chapel here at Hacienda Maricela, but Nestor Calvo had entered the room behind him, had exchanged glances with Spider, and then had called out the bad news to his kneeling *patrón*.

'The Gray Man?'

'Undoubtedly. And that was only the opening shot. At five thirty, a small explosion set fire to one of our warehouses in Colima; it destroyed an entire shipment of ephedrine from India. It will push back production of *foco* for a week.'

'Dammit,' DLR said, his eyes not leaving the skeleton bride in front of him. 'He works fast.'

'And then he struck again just minutes ago.'

'Where?'

'Again in Colima. He hijacked a truck containing poppy paste. Killed the driver. The truck was driven off a cliff.'

'How much paste?'

Calvo shrugged. 'Our heroin shipment was not as badly hurt as the *foco* ... maybe two days to make up the production.'

DLR prayed for a moment more, and Calvo stifled a sigh. He

380

kept his face impassive, Spider was looking at him, and he did not need Spider telling their boss that his old advisor was annoyed by Daniel's displays of fealty to the dumb doll in the corner hutch.

De la Rocha looked up at la Santa Muerte. 'She is angry.'

Calvo shook his head. 'No, Daniel. *He* is angry. This is about the Gray Man, remember?'

Daniel stood, walked back across his darkened chapel towards his consigliere. 'One man, in one day, affects my finance operation, my heroin operation, and my methamphetamine operation.'

'*Sí*, Daniel.'

'I trust we have men in Colima looking for him?'

'The entire police force plus other assets in the area. But I assume the Gray Man is gone by now.'

'Gone where?'

Calvo shrugged. 'I do not know. But I wonder if he will go after other aspects of our enterprise. Marijuana, transportation, aircraft, shipping, kidnapping. As long as he is alive, we won't know where he will turn up next.'

'Who is supplying him with the intelligence about our enterprises?'

'Someone with knowledge of the full scope of our operations. I would say either someone in the federal police or perhaps even someone in the Madrigal Cartel.'

'I *know* it is Madrigal.'

'You *don't* know that.'

DLR walked out of the room, Spider close on his heels. Calvo followed.

'It's Madrigal,' repeated DLR to Nestor.

'She told you that, did she?'

Daniel stopped in the hallway. Turned back to Calvo, and Spider took up his position at his boss's side. De la Rocha said, 'Her information has proven better than yours in this matter, consigliere. You would do well to improve your value to me.' DLR and Spider turned away again and disappeared up the corridor.

50

Gentry found refuge in a disused silver mine near La Rosa Blanca, a small mountain town a convenient drive to Guadalajara, with access to the Pacific coast and Mexico City. Both were within a few hours' drive. Hector Serna had equipped Gentry with an old Mazda pickup, and Court used the entrance to a long-dormant horizontal mining shaft in the side of the mountain to store the vehicle during the nights. Court had visited a camping store in Guadalajara and purchased thousands of dollars in gear so he would not be uncomfortable during cool nights on the mountain. His gas stove, his small tent, his dried foods, and his gallon jugs of water kept his needs met. His battery-operated generators kept his mobile phones and his GPS charged, as well as giving him light when he needed it to work on one project or another on the cold ground by his truck.

Court had a lot of projects going in the mine shaft.

And he had a lot of targets to hit around western Mexico. In the past two days he had been busy: he'd killed a territory boss of the Black Suits in Nayarit, he'd destroyed two aircraft at an airport in Tepic owned by de la Rocha, and he'd torched a warehouse northeast of Magdalena.

Now it was the morning of his fourth day of his full-scale war on the Black Suits. He'd been up past three but still managed several hours of fitful sleep in his sleeping bag in the bed of the Mazda. Twice he woke up startled by noises close by; both times he grabbed one of his AK-47s and cut open the darkness around him with the tactical light attached to the fore end of the rifle. Both times hunched furry creatures ran off, deeper down into the black mine shaft.

Even though he was getting a late start, Court had big plans for the day. Hector Serna had passed Court some intel about the Black Suits' locations in the area, and Gentry had noted them on his GPS. He'd set up a series of waypoints that would take him to each target on the way to his most distant destination of the trip. With luck he'd get to five sites before the end of his workday; he did not expect to return to his mine until the middle of the night, though he was not sure he would find things to destroy or Black Suits to kill at each of the stops on his route. Each piece of mayhem he planned had to be weighed against the chance for death or capture, and each location had to be somewhere he felt he could get out of quickly and cleanly.

Before noon he'd pulled into a warehouse district in Guadalajara and watched several train cars off-load crates that Serna promised contained pot grown down south in Chiapas and Guatemala. Court watched from a distance through his binoculars, and he believed Serna's intelligence to be solid, but the loaded trucks idled there within the well-guarded fences of the station for over an hour. He'd tried to pick up the FM radio broadcasts from the walkie-talkies of the men by the trucks, but their handhelds were using some sort of encryption, and Court couldn't read enough of their traffic to find out what the problem was. He'd planned on hitting the trucks on the highway, but they showed no sign of leaving the station, even at two p.m. Reluctantly, he made the decision to call off this mission, anxious to get on to the next waypoint and blow some shit up before the day was done.

His second site was a bust as well. It was a safe house for the Black Suits, but when he entered, kicking in the door and clearing the rooms with his AK, he found no one there and no drugs, guns, or money. He thought about just torching the house, but it was on a city street in the Zapopan district of Guadalajara, and he couldn't be sure he wouldn't end up burning down an entire block. So he climbed back into the Mazda and sped off to the east.

There were three more places on his to-do list; he hoped like hell he could find something worth destroying in at least one of them. He looked at his GPS.

Next stop, another Black Suit safe house, this one in Chapala. Court hoped this wasn't a dry hole as well.

De la Rocha slept on a chaise lounge on the cool balcony just outside of his bedroom. He liked the feel of the outdoors. It reminded him of his time in the army, though in the army he wasn't exactly sleeping on a balcony off an opulent master bedroom in a hacienda on his own 200-hectare property.

Spider was behind him, in the bedroom, sitting on a high-back chair positioned in front of the door. His M4 rifle lay across his lap. Extra magazines jutted from a bag next to him.

With no warning Nestor Calvo Macias barreled through the door. Spider launched to his feet, hefting his weapon as he did so, but the older man ignored him, stormed past, shouted out to his sleeping *patrón* on the balcony.

'The Gray Man hit the safe house in Chapala!'

De la Rocha sat up slowly on the chaise lounge and rubbed his eyes. 'Chapala? *Madre de dios*. Did he steal the money we have cached there?'

'He did not steal it. He burned it.'

DLR cursed, rubbed his face some more. '*¡Qué chingado!* How much?'

'All of it. We had roughly seventeen million U.S. dollars palletized and awaiting transfer to the banks. I'll get the figures from accounting and give you the exact amount.'

'And he just burned it? Set it on fire?'

'*Sí.*'

'What about the men guarding the—'

'One dead. One more missing that we assume—'

'And all the rest? Surely, we had more men guarding seventeen million dollars!'

'We had a dozen men there. The rest are alive; they did not know there was any problem until the fire started. They never saw the Gray Man.'

'Fucking execute every one of those stupid *pendejos*.'

'*Sí.*' Spider said, and he leaned out into the hallway. He barked commands to one of his underlings, sealing the fate of the survivors at the Chapala safe house.

'Daniel,' Calvo said, a soft pleading in his voice. 'In four days he has performed nearly one dozen operations against us. I estimate the value of capital loss and production loss to be, conservatively, somewhere in the neighborhood of fifty million dollars.'

'He is costing me more than twelve million dollars a day?'

'Conservatively.'

'But how long can he continue?'

Spider spoke frankly. '*Mi jefe.* Our organization is set up to effectively fight the military, the federal police, and the rival cartels. We are less equipped to target one man with the mobility and skills of the Gray Man. There is no way to know how long he can operate before we get him.'

Calvo interjected, 'We think it is possible he is getting his intelligence from Madrigal, but we don't know that he is working with the Madrigal organization.'

'Your counterpart in los Vaqueros, remind me of his name.'

'Hector Serna Campos.'

'Right. Reach out to him. Tell them it is war.'

'Daniel, going to war with Madrigal right now would only cost us more money. We cannot—'

De la Rocha screamed as he stormed from the balcony into his bedroom. 'Do not tell me what I cannot do! They are fighting a war with me right now, through this one man!'

'We do not know for sure!'

'I know!' de la Rocha screamed, spit flew from his mouth, and he screamed again, a guttural cry of anger and frustration, pent-up rage without an outlet. 'I *had* this man! I had this man in front of me in chains! I could have pulled the trigger on my pistol and ended this madness a week ago! Why did I not do this? Why did I not kill that *pendejo*? I've lost so many men because I did not pull the trigger.'

Calvo said, 'He'll keep killing your men if you keep chasing him. He's too good!'

De la Rocha regained control of himself. He took a few breaths, rubbed the back of his bare neck, and then waved a dismissive hand. 'Doesn't matter. Men are easy to lose. Pride? Pride is a very difficult thing to lose.'

He turned to Spider. 'My decision is made. As of this moment, it is all-out war on los Vaqueros.'

'*Entendido, señor.*'

'Anywhere we find them, anywhere in the country ...

Spider looked into his leader's eyes. 'They die.'

'*Correcto.*'

Calvo did not throw in the towel just yet. 'Don Daniel. I *beg* you to listen. Spider wants war with Madrigal so that he can show you that his men can fight. They can't kill the Gray Man because of his skill and cunning, but they can shoot a bunch of *pinche* Vaqueros in the streets.'

Javier 'Spider' Cepeda scowled at Nestor, giving him a look countless men had seen shortly before Spider chopped off their heads. '*Mi jefe*, the old man just wants to avoid war with los Vaqueros because he is soft. We have been too easy in our dealings with Madrigal for too long, and look how the Sinaloan Cowboy repays us! We will fight them until they kill the Gray Man or turn him over to us. My men will turn their plaza red with their blood, and within a week the Cowboy will see that the American assassin is only a liability to his operation. Then we can back off, if you order us to do so.'

DLR was nodding before Spider finished. He turned to Calvo. 'Nestor. I want you to communicate with your counterpart in los

Vaqueros. Tell him that we know they are running the Gray Man, and we see this as an all-out declaration of war on our plaza. We will hold them responsible for the loss in property and in lives, and we will respond accordingly as long as the Gray Man is alive.'

Nestor was furious and frustrated, but he did not hesitate. He possessed an astute barometer that could measure the moods of his boss, and he knew this was no time to argue. '*Sí*, Daniel. I will contact Hector Serna immediately and tell him we are at war, and I will then give him the conditions by which we will accept peace.'

The first attack took place a mere thirty-three minutes later. A pair of low-level *sicarios* in Mazatlan who'd been tasked to follow a local underboss in the Madrigal organization got the text message declaring open season on los Vaqueros. Immediately, they got up from their table at an outdoor café, tossed paper plates soaked with tamale juice into the trash, walked into the jewelry store across the street, and shot dead the man they had been tailing, along with his wife and two bodyguards.

Nine minutes after that a truck carrying four Vaqueros was pulled over by a Jalisco state police SUV on the highway from Puerto Vallarta to Guadalajara. The men were lined up and shot, execution style, against their vehicle, their bodies left on the hot mountain freeway like roadkill.

By evening twelve more Vaqueros had been murdered and seven wounded. Four members of Los Trajes Negros had been felled by return fire, and one passerby was wounded by shotgun pellets when a firefight broke out between rival factions of the federal police in Mexico City.

Thirty-two casualties in the first twelve hours of the war was only the beginning.

Two more days passed, and Court worked at a fever pitch through it all. His intelligence from Serna, as good as it was, paled in comparison to the product he was picking up during his raids. In Colima he took the smartphone from a sentry and found an address with the notation 'Foco' by the listing. He knew this was the local slang for crystal, so he drove there and found a fenced storage facility full of shipping containers. There were several guards on duty, but Court managed to slip into the complex and place several ANFO bombs he'd built back at his mine shaft, each equipped with a simple radio transmitter detonator on them. Once clear of the blast radius, he dialed a number on one of his many mobile phones, and six containers of crystal went up in a mushroom cloud of black smoke.

On a hillside nearby he stopped to admire his work, but he saw a single man racing from the scene in a black BMW. Court ran the sport coupe off the road with his pickup, found a member of the Black Suits crawling from the wreckage, and took him hostage. Four hours later the man succumbed to his injuries but only after giving the American a treasure trove of information about de la Rocha's crystal operation in Nayarit and Jalisco.

Court decided to focus on the meth for a few days. According to the dying Black Suit, it was DLR's cash cow; the product was expensive to produce and, therefore, subject to easy disruption by killing or scaring off the skilled labor or destroying the infrastructure of the labs, and to Court this seemed preferable to burning pot plants or poppy fields. He'd still do that, if opportunity arose, but the *foco* seemed like the best bet to make a quick impact.

This led Court to Acoponeta, a small river town on the flatlands along on the road to Mazatlan. He had some addresses gleaned from the dying Black Suit that he wanted to hit before heading up into the mountains to go after a super laboratory.

Before an evening of wreaking havoc, Gentry went into a grocery to resupply with beans, soft drinks, instant coffee, and water, and he stepped into a cantina next door to use the men's room in the back. After using the restroom and washing a small fraction of the grime from his hands, he turned halfway towards the door but stopped suddenly. There, on a wall and staring back at him, was a man's face on a Wanted poster.

Like nothing he had felt in years, unease ripped through his body.

It was him. The fucking picture was of him.

WANTED FOR MURDER
American Assassin of the Madrigal Cartel

A local mobile number was written below.

Gentry realized now that, even if he survived this, even if he got out of Mexico, the U.S. government would label him an assassin for the Mexican mob, and he would never, *ever*, get back into the USA.

Was the girl worth all this?

Court shook his head, hated that the question had entered his brain.

Yes. Of course she was.

He ripped the paper sign from the wall and tossed it in the garbage.

The door on his left squeaked open.

Gentry spun as he drew his weapon, dropping low to his knees in front of the sink.

He centered the weapon on his target's chest, his finger had already taken up the slack of the Glock's trigger safety.

The man's arms flew over his head. He cried out in panic, *'¡Madre de dios!'*

Court looked past the front sight of his Glock 19, felt his finger tight on the unforgiving trigger, and he saw an overweight man in a cowboy hat, just a simple farmer, just a guy in a bar looking to relieve himself after a couple of Coronas.

Court released the slack on the trigger, stood and holstered his weapon, walked past the panicked laborer without giving him a glance.

Dammit, Gentry. Keep it together.

51

It took Gentry an entire day to get into position. For most of that time, while he drove the Mazda into the mountains, while he climbed and crawled, while he hid under a footbridge as armed *guerreros* passed just overhead, while he checked his GPS coordinates against the location given him by the Black Suit who now lay dead back in a ravine near Court's mine-shaft hideout – all the while, he lamented this delay. He wanted to hit the Black Suits every single day, multiple times a day, so he worried that spending twenty-four hours doing nothing but moving unseen through the Sierra Madres, towards a location that might not even exist, would cause his operation to lose momentum crucial to its success.

He did not know, of course, that the day before Daniel de la Rocha had initiated a war against the Madrigal Cartel. This day of travel for Court was still very much a sixth day of bloodshed for the Black Suits, and the fact that Gentry himself was not involved in the fighting had gone completely unnoticed by Los Trajes Negros.

By measure of the number of incidents, by the number of dead and wounded, by the number of convoys hit or safe houses raided, momentum against the Black Suits was only growing.

Court moved through the darkness, the second-generation night-vision goggles provided by Hector Serna were nearly antiques compared to some of the gear that Court had used in his past, but they got the job done. He crossed a valley floor, got close enough to a village full of DLR's men to smell the cooking fires and hear the dogs bark, but he remained invisible to the locals. At one in the morning he found a stream that was right where the dead Black Suit said it would be, and this lifted his spirits. He followed it into a black canyon; in the distance a waterfall roared, but he was not close enough to see it.

He moved on, his night-vision goggles and his GPS leading the way, but his ears, his sense of smell, his knowledge of the wilderness and how to move through it silently, this kept him alive.

By five a.m. he was in position. He shimmied halfway down a rock face that hung over a tiny canyon, and then Court slid below the treetops.

Dawn was still two hours off, but Court smelled tortillas and coffee from his perch in the sheer rock face. A rooster crowed. Dogs barked and goats bleated; there were all the sounds of human habitation. Occasionally, the scent of marijuana wafted up to his hide in the rock wall ten feet above the dirt road. Soon engines fired, large gaspowered generators, and as the natural light trickled into the jungle from above, electric lighting emanated from a clearing fifty yards ahead. A wide building, prefabricated metal painted a mute olive drab, appeared under headlights as a jeep backed up and turned around. A few seconds later it passed under Court's position, full of men and guns.

Still enshrouded in darkness, Court Gentry prepared to attack.

A seven o'clock that morning Nestor Calvo hung up his mobile phone in his office at Hacienda Maricela. He'd been at his desk since five thirty, sitting in his tie and shirtsleeves, his coat draped over a leather chair in the corner. He drank mango juice and sipped coffee while he fired off phone calls and e-mails to his contacts in the United States. While his organization's conflict with Constantino Madrigal grew by the hour, he'd been forced to spend his morning pursuing all leads related to Elena Gamboa. There was evidence that the Gamboas had left Tucson by bus, possibly to the northeast. On that vague nugget of questionable intelligence, Calvo spent ninety minutes contacting members of his network from Chicago to Boston, tasking people with checking all their sources, hunting for a pregnant Mexican woman, aged thirty-five years.

It was a needle in a haystack, Calvo knew, but it was also his job to do the bidding of his master.

His mobile rang again, it was his first incoming call of the day, and he flipped the phone open and answered. '¿Bueno?'

And five minutes later he stormed out of his office, pulling his Kevlar suit coat on as he shut the door behind him.

Daniel de la Rocha worked the gym's heavy bag like an experienced middleweight boxer. He wasn't the only man on the large teak floor – two more Black Suits stood around, already dressed for the business day, and shouted encouragement to him while he sparred with his trainer or worked the speed bag or pounded his gloved fists into the heavy bag. His trainer stood behind the bag in the corner giving instructions.

And Javier 'Spider' Cepeda was there as well; he never left his boss's side now, even though he also spent time giving orders to his underlings who came and went to execute their boss's wishes regarding the war with los Vaqueros.

As was becoming his custom, fifty-seven-year-old Nestor Calvo Macias entered the room quickly, ignored the security detail and the others standing around, and walked purposefully up to his *patrón*.

DLR saw his man in the mirror on the wall. He dropped his arms to rest and turned to face Calvo. 'You bring more bad news, don't you, Nestor?'

'Super lab number six has been destroyed.'

'What do you mean, "destroyed"?'

'Destroyed, Daniel. It *was* there, and now it is not. There is fire. There is wreckage. Twisted metal. Dead bodies. A complete loss of the complex there and all its material.'

DLR just nodded as his trainer wiped his brow with a towel.

Calvo next said, 'The Gray Man destroyed two full batches of product. Plus the capital equipment there. And he killed a few men. Some of the foreigners working there are gone. We don't know if he kidnapped them or if they were killed or if they ran off on their own.'

De la Rocha flexed his chest and arms, then smashed his right fist into the heavy bag.

'Something else,' said Calvo, quietly. 'A laptop was taken from the office of the administrator of the laboratory. The administrator has told my men that everything was locked and encrypted, with one exception. There was one file that was open at the time of the theft. This file had sensitive information on it, which we must assume is now in the hands of the Gray Man.'

De la Rocha punched the bag once again, then turned back to his consigliere. 'What information?'

'Physical addresses of our real estate in Mexico.'

'Shit!' shouted DLR. 'Madrigal now knows the location of all of our properties?'

'If the Gray Man is working for Madrigal ... then yes.'

'*¡Hijo de puta!*' *Son of a bitch!* De la Rocha screamed, punched the heavy bag with all his might. He turned back quickly to his consigliere. 'Cuernavaca? Was the Cuernavaca house on the—'

'*Sí, jefe.*'

'Nestor ... my kids. My wife. That is my fucking home!'

'I know.'

'He said he would not touch my family!'

'With apologies, Daniel, he *has not* touched your family.'

De la Rocha waved away his last comment. 'What do we do?' He stuck his arms out for his trainer to begin removing his gloves. The older man rushed over to comply.

Calvo shrugged. 'Two days ago we complained he has cost us fifty million dollars. But now? To establish new routes and safe houses, to change distribution channels from our current properties into the United States? This could cost us ten times that amount.'

Spider had been silent, but he said, '*Jefe*, we must get you out of here, now!'

'My family,' DLR said softly. 'Move them.' A Black Suit spun away, out of the room, pulling a phone from his belt to contact the Cuernavaca detail and have them move de la Rocha's wife and six children.

But he did not get far. The man ducked his head back into the room. 'I am sorry.' He looked around, did not know whom to address. 'But where do I tell them to go?'

DLR said, 'The property in Portugal. Get them to the airport in Mexico City and have the jet meet them there tonight!'

Calvo shook his head. 'No. The address of the Faro estate was in the file.'

'Motherfucker.' The drug lord said it in English. He'd learned it while serving in the Mexican military, training in the United States. 'He is destroying us.'

'No,' said Calvo. 'Because you will not let that happen. You will give the Gamboa woman back to—'

'No!' DLR grabbed Calvo by his lapels and slammed the older man up against the mirrored wall. 'I will *not*!'

'Daniel, this fiasco is simply costing us too much money, too much time, too much—'

'I don't care! I don't care about any of that. I want Elena Gamboa and this gringo assassin dead! Now they threaten my children?'

Calvo shook his head, undaunted even under the threat of physical violence from his boss. 'No one is threatening your—'

Spider got between them in an instant. '*Jefe*. We have friends who own entire chains of hotels, condominiums, real estate of all kinds. We can send your family anywhere; we can rent out an entire floor, an entire estate! I'll double protection on your family, and you can tell your kids it is a holiday.'

Calvo and de la Rocha stared at each other a moment more, then the younger man let go of the elder's suit coat. Without breaking the staring contest, he spoke to Spider. '*Triple* the guard

394

on them. And notify everyone here. We will leave for Puerto Vallarta within the hour; we have more cops working for us there than anywhere else. I will fly the helicopter. Bring Laura Gamboa with us, we will take over the biggest place we can find there, and we will continue war on Madrigal until the Gray Man is liquidated and Elena Gamboa is found.'

Calvo stormed out of the room without another word. As he walked back towards his office, he decided he would do what he could to end this madness, no matter his master's wishes. The American called him 'adult supervision.' It was an insult to DLR but, Nestor acknowledged, there was some truth to the gringo assassin's words.

52

Court arrived at the predetermined pickup point for supplies from the Madrigal Cartel. He was running low on detonators, ammonium nitrate, and fuel oil; he needed some clean cell phones, a little cash, and more ammo for the Sako.

But when he arrived at the storage unit pickup point, he saw a man standing out front. Still in his truck, one hundred yards from his cache, Court peered through his binoculars.

It was Serna, and he was alone.

He was waiting.

Court pulled up in the truck. Climbed out, looking over the intelligence chief for los Vaqueros. 'Why are you here?'

'The Cowboy wants to talk to you.'

'In person?'

'*Sí*. Immediately.'

This surprised Gentry. 'I don't have time for a face-to-face. Can't I talk to him on the phone?'

'No. We are to take you to him.'

'We?'

'Yes, I did not want to alarm you, so I am keeping them out of sight, but I have twenty men with me. All around us.'

'What does Madrigal want to talk about?'

'I do not know.'

Court looked hard at the *narco* from Sinaloa, but he could not tell if the man was being truthful or not. Court weighed his options. He felt like he could take Serna right now at gunpoint and get the hell out of here, but why? There was no reason for Madrigal to be mad at him. On the contrary, Court had seriously damaged the operations of los Vaqueros's main competitor. By all rights Madrigal should be commissioning *narco corridos*, 'ballads,' about the exploits of the Gray Man and offering him even more help than before.

Court nodded, lifted his arms, and Serna frisked him. Serna removed four weapons, then used a small walkie-talkie to call in his team. Within seconds several massive Dodge pickup trucks appeared at both the front and side entrances of the storage lot. They pulled up the aisle and collected Serna and Gentry, and then headed in a convoy towards the north.

By noon Serna and Gentry were in a small prop plane flying northwest, and by twelve thirty they had landed on a grass airstrip in the mountains. They climbed into big Chrysler sedans and headed through a large town. Court asked Serna where they were, but the intelligence chief only admitted that they were in southern Sinaloa.

After no more than twenty minutes on the road, they entered the gates of a large cemetery. The sky was clear and cool, and Court began seeing armed men in straw hats standing around the ornate mausoleums on the well-manicured grounds. This was nothing like the cemetery where Eddie Gamboa had been laid to rest. No, these crypts were massive, expensive hand-carved cement and marble tile, gilded roofs and life-sized statues in front of the tombs.

Serna answered a question Court had not asked. 'This entire cemetery is for Madrigal's men. He comes here often to visit his old friends. It is a compliment that he invited you to meet with him here.'

Gentry was pretty sure he hadn't exactly been 'invited,' but he let it go. The Chrysler followed the winding road through dozens of crypts, some as large as small homes. Many sported framed photographs on iron shields above the doorways, other accoutrements to the mausoleums such as AK-47s carved from stone, cowboy hats carved from marble, life-sized bronze horses and even actual grilles and front ends of Cadillacs and Dodge pickups jutted from the masonry. In one case, a life-sized stainless steel Piper twin-engine aircraft had been built into the roof of a massive crypt.

And Court imagined half of the red, yellow, and blue blooming flowers in Sinaloa were used here at this cemetery.

The Chrysler pulled to a stop in front of a smaller crypt. This structure looked new, and a dozen armed men stood around it. Madrigal himself was there, with his teenage son Chingarito standing by his side. The Cowboy wore a red shirt and blue jeans, a straw cowboy hat and tennis shoes. A gold belt buckle of a horse's head was the only frill Gentry could find on the man's body other than the simple cross around his neck.

The Cowboy met Court as he climbed out of the car, shook his hand with a smile partially hidden under his mustache.

As he spoke, Chingarito translated. 'Seven days, amigo. One week ago exactly I met you, and you promised to make trouble for Los Trajes Negros. I have to say ... I thought you would kill a few Black Suits, destroy some product, and then die yourself. You have proven to me that you are a warrior.'

'Thank you.'

'Are you positive you were not born in Sinaloa?'

Court did not answer. The 'little fucker' had nothing to translate.

Madrigal continued. 'You have earned my respect. What you have done in seven days, these miserable idiots have not done in seven years.' He waved at the men standing around, and Chingarito laughed while he translated.

Gentry said, 'And I'm just getting started. Another few days and he will be—'

Madrigal interrupted. 'That is why I brought you here.' Chingarito struggled to keep up with the translations.

'Nine of my *sicarios* were butchered last night in Puerto Vallarta. Five Jalisco state police on my pay disappeared in

Guadalajara yesterday. No doubt they will be found dead on a road within the next few days with their dicks in their mouths. The day before yesterday, twelve of my men were murdered, and a shipment of product was hijacked.'

Gentry stared back a moment. 'I don't give a shit if your assassins get killed, and I would only insult your intelligence by pretending like I do.'

Chingarito translated. Madrigal answered back.

'DLR had it done. He suspects you are working with me. He is punishing me for this relationship. I told you this would only work if we could conceal that we were working together.'

'You had to have known there was a chance you would be blamed for my actions. I'm sure you have more hit men and drugs, right?'

'Of course. I could go on like this for years. You are hurting him worse than he is hurting me. But there has been a change in plans. We will not be continuing our war.'

'What are you saying?'

'Your benefit to me has ended. I have made a deal. In return for handing your body over to the Black Suits, I can make this war stop, plus I have been promised some other things in payment. I have agreed to this deal.'

'You made that deal with Nestor Calvo.' Gentry said it confidently. He knew DLR was not the type of man to agree to a compact with Madrigal, his archenemy. He would fight and he would threaten – he would *not* acquiesce.

Madrigal shrugged. Chingarito translated. 'Yes. Nestor Calvo Macias is the center of Los Trajes Negros. He is more powerful than even de la Rocha because of all that he knows. He has offered up one of their remaining *foco* super labs. A gift worth, over time, billions of dollars.' Madrigal smiled. 'You should be proud of your market value.'

'Right.'

The Cowboy shrugged. 'I'm sorry, my friend, but I will have to kill you now. I will honor your service with this beautiful crypt you see here.'

The men around began moving closer. Court looked around frantically for Serna. He found the intelligence chief in the crowd. He did not look happy about this arrangement, but he said nothing.

Gentry looked at Chingarito. 'I can do more for him than Calvo can. Tell him that!'

Chigarito translated.

Madrigal replied. 'You are giving me what I want. I want that super lab.'

From behind, a bag was placed over Gentry's head.

'*Mátalo*,' Madrigal said, and this Chingarito did not translate. Court knew it was the town of Madrigal's birth, but it was also a command.

Kill him.

He heard a pistol cocking close behind his head.

Court shouted one word.

And then Madrigal said, '¡Espere!' Wait. And then, '¿Qué dijiste?' What did you say?

In Spanish Court replied. 'I said Calvo. I can get you Nestor Calvo. Having him in your custody would end Daniel de la Rocha and the Black Suits, and you know it.' Court could not see Hector Serna, but he called out to him. 'Hector, wouldn't you like to pick through Calvo's brain? To find out everything he knows?'

Under the black hood Court perspired; all the muscles in his face and neck were tense, awaiting a shot to the head that he would never feel. He did not think of his own death, but only of Laura. He pictured her now, alone and afraid, and he pictured the men that would come to her when they did not need to keep her in one piece any longer.

He so wanted to help her.

He felt hands on his arms and back, pushing him forward into the mausoleum. There were shouts and orders barked behind him as he walked, and then the door slid shut behind him, and it was cool and dark.

His hood was removed. A man stood on either side of him, each with a pistol jabbed into his temple.

In front of him, from the light of a small, round stained glass window in the back of the crypt, he saw Madrigal, his son, and Serna.

Serna said, 'Calvo is well protected.'

Court stuttered in fear. 'I am well motivated.'

Madrigal spoke now. 'You would say anything now to save your skin. I don't believe you can deliver him.'

'How will you prove to Calvo that I'm dead?' Court asked in English, and Chingarito began a running translation.

Madrigal said, 'I will tell him which crypt you are interred in here. He is planning on sending some men to see your body before the crypt is sealed.'

Court looked to Hector Serna. 'Tell him you want to meet him in person here to show him my body.'

'Why would he do that?'

'He will *have* to do it, because he can't tell DLR that the two of you made a deal. He will honor any reasonable request in order to keep this transaction quiet. And he'll be intrigued, wanting to know what advantage he can obtain out of your meeting.'

Madrigal shook his head. 'He won't agree. It will be too dangerous for him.'

'You can tell him to bring whatever resources he wants. Tell him to bring one hundred gunmen to ensure this is no ambush. Tell him to send his men a day in advance to watch over the location.'

'You can get past one hundred gunmen?'

'Of course not, but he won't bring that many. He is working in secret, without the knowledge of DLR, so he will want to keep these discussions off DLR's radar. He's not an idiot, he *will* bring security, but he won't bring more than his usual close-protection detail. A manageable number so that word of the meeting does not get out around his organization.'

'And you can get through them?'

'I guess I'll have to, won't I?'

Madrigal said, 'But when I get Calvo, how will that help you? I won't trade him away for your little Gamboa *puta*.'

401

Chingarito translated. Gentry's nostrils flared a bit, but he recovered. 'Once I have Calvo, I will give him to you. But I will tell de la Rocha that *I* have him and that *I'll* trade him for Laura. We'll set up a time and a place for the trade. This will give you time to get what you need from Calvo before the Black Suits come looking, and it will give me a chance to get close to Laura, so I can get her back.'

Madrigal looked at Gentry a long time. Then he smiled. 'You think like an outlaw. You scheme as well as anyone I've ever met, amigo.'

'Let's just say this isn't my first rodeo, señor.'

'I am intrigued by your offer, but there is one problem.'

Gentry knew what it was. 'You are worried you have informers in your organization, working for DLR, who will tip Calvo off in advance to our plan.'

Madrigal nodded.

'I have a way to prevent that.'

'How can you pos—'

Before Madrigal's eyes, the Gray Man transformed into a blur of movement. He dropped straight down, out of the line of fire of the two pistols. At the same time he spun on the balls of his feet; his hands came up and shot skyward, knocking the pistols out of the hands of the two men. He then caught one of the weapons as it twirled in the dim, dusty air. He spun back on the balls off his feet, returned to a standing position, and pointed the big revolver at Constantino Madrigal's chest.

All this took place in under one second. The disarmed men around him stepped back; Madrigal, Chingarito and Serna just stood and stared in confusion and shock.

After five seconds of silence, Court let the revolver roll backwards on his finger; it hung upside down from the trigger guard.

He stepped forward and held it out to Constantino Madrigal. 'Here you go. Shoot me with it, or allow me to solve your problems with de la Rocha. If you don't trust anyone here, shoot them, and then the threat of a leak will be gone. I'll stay in here;

402

you can tell everyone they were killed in a fight with me but you finished me off.'

Madrigal's mouth remained open in astonishment. He looked to his son to await the translation, but Chingarito's own mouth hung agape. His father nudged him, and then the boy spoke. While his boy repeated Gentry's words in Spanish, Madrigal looked around at the others in the mausoleum with him, as if to see if they had seen the same incredible act by the American.

The Cowboy took the gun. Slowly, he motioned with it to his guards. 'These two ... I trust.'

He looked back to Serna. 'Hector, as well. And *mi* Chingarito. He is family. Plus he's too smart to cheat me, aren't you, *mi hijo?*'

The Little Fucker confirmed with a nod that he was, in fact, too smart to double-cross his dad.

One of Madrigal's men picked his pistol up from the floor; the other took his weapon back from his boss. They both looked equal parts shocked and embarrassed.

Soon the Cowboy recovered. 'That was good, amigo. Very good. You could have killed me right then and you did not. I will give you your two days. Hector and I will tell no one else what our plan is. But I promise you, if I do not get Nestor Calvo delivered to me, alive, then I will send every one of my men after you.'

Court nodded. 'He will be yours, señor. I promise you.'

For the second time in a week, Court Gentry swallowed all pretense of honor and shook the hand of Constantino Madrigal. It was even tougher this time than the last, chiefly because he knew that what he had just said was a blatant lie.

53

Forty-six hours later, three armored black Chevrolet Suburbans streaked west on a two-lane canyon road in southeastern Sinaloa. The lead vehicle flashed red lights on its dashboard, and the armed driver blew through tiny villas and the occasional inter-section with no regard for any other traffic.

The driver knew the convoy had to keep moving – fast.

In the center seat row of Truck Two, braced on either side by two of the thirteen bodyguards brought along to protect him, Nestor Calvo Macias spoke on his mobile phone to his assistant. Calvo's second-in-command had set up shop at the new property in Puerto Vallarta, and his job for the day was to keep DLR occupied and disinterested in Calvo's whereabouts. Nestor was a professional, he did not like lying to his boss, but Nestor knew adult supervision was called for at the moment. He would not allow some gringo assassin, some ridiculous resin-skeleton bride in a dress, or some distracting quest for a fetus in hiding to ruin all he had built in the past years.

By going against his leader's orders right now and meeting with Hector Serna of los Vaqueros, Calvo would stop a costly gang war, he would present the corpse of his boss's gringo nemesis to him, and he would limit the hemorrhaging of treasure and bodies that had been going on for the past week.

The price would be somewhat heavy to end the Madrigal war, a methamphetamine laboratory in the northwestern tip of Jalisco state. But Calvo had chosen this barter item shrewdly. The lab had been costly and time-consuming to build, but it had underperformed since opening just thirteen months prior. Infrastructure in the area was poor, and access to skilled labor in the region problematic. Further, the army had concentrated on marijuana eradication efforts in the area, and the Black Suits worried constantly about the lab being discovered by some young college-grad army lieutenant who could not be bought off. So Calvo had offered to trade this potential debacle for the life of the man who was costing his organization millions of dollars a day and untold headaches.

An easy enough decision.

Meeting with Serna had been the most worrisome part of the deal for Calvo, but he now decided his concerns had been unfounded. Calvo's security forces had sent an advance team to check out the location of the meeting, and they reported a safe house with only a few of Madrigal's men, including Serna, and no other Vaquero forces in the area.

Nestor had ordered his bodyguards to travel light and undermanned today to decrease the chances of DLR finding out about the meeting. Calvo knew he could never tell de la Rocha about this bit of intrigue. Logic and reason would play no part into his *patrón*'s thinking; he would not agree to a deal with Madrigal in any form or fashion.

As the three-vehicle convoy raced through the narrow canyon on its way to the safe house in the mountains, Calvo continued speaking on his mobile phone to his second-in-command.

'DLR insists la CIA is working with Madrigal. He wants us to send *sicarios* after CIA men in the D.F. He is even talking with Spider about a direct attack on the American embassy. This is absolute madness!'

Two hundred yards ahead of the three Suburbans a large cement truck pulled onto the road from a commercial gravel pit on the left. The big black trucks closed on it quickly as the huge lumbering mixer struggled to gain speed. Its red and white rotating drum revolved as it lumbered up the road.

The driver of Calvo's lead vehicle honked and blinked his lights rapidly as he rushed up from behind.

Calvo was unaware of this, and he continued his conversation. 'The girl was never worth the trouble; the Gamboa family was never worth the trouble.'

The lead vehicle arrived directly behind the cement truck as the canyon narrowed in a turn. There were just a few feet on either side of the narrow blacktop road, which was surrounded by steep, rocky inclines that made passing impossible. The lead driver flashed his lights continuously and honked his horn. The cement mixer was increasing its speed but not fast enough to satisfy Calvo's three expert security drivers. Words were exchanged over the radio between the Suburbans about the slowdown.

Calvo remained unaware.

'I need you to let me know if Daniel comes to you and begins asking too many questions about where I am. I can call him at any time and give him some story. Don't try and fool him yourself. He can smell a lie just like his father could.'

The canyon narrowed further, and the cement truck accelerated to barely forty miles an hour. The lead motorcade driver leaned on his horn now, swerved his truck from left to right behind the mixer, and the front passenger rolled down his window, hefted his M4 rifle, and waved it outside so that it could be seen by the cement truck's driver in his passenger-side rearview.

Calvo glanced up at the persistent honking as he spoke.

'Nothing, just traffic.' He looked down at a notepad on his lap. 'Yes, I will give them the coordinates of the super lab. As soon as we see the *norteamericano*'s body I will contact—'

In the lead vehicle the front passenger had removed his seat belt and positioned half of his body out the window now, angrily waving the rifle in the air. The driver flashed his lights and began cursing loudly as they arrived at the most narrow portion of the mountain canyon. He reached for his radio to warn the other vehicles to be ready for—

Right in front of him, the big cement mixer slammed on its

breaks, skidded to a stop. A two-foot-wide high-pressure stream of wet concrete shot from its five-foot-long chute, and the lead Suburban drove right into the gravelly mixture before braking. It slid hard into the rear of the mixer, airbags deployed, and concrete covered the hood and windscreen. Hundreds of gallons of the gray sludge sprayed the vehicle and splashed onto the narrow road around it.

The bodyguard who had been hanging out the window flew completely from the Suburban; his back snapped, and his weapon slid forward, all the way past the front wheels of the cement mixer.

Just behind this the driver of Calvo's SUV screamed 'Hold on!' Nestor looked up from his phone, out the windshield, and into the morning glare ahead, just as his truck's brakes locked and the SUV slid into Truck One.

Calvo's phone flew out of his hand, and he slammed into the seat back in front of him. The bodyguards on either side of him did the same.

The leader of Calvo's detail sat in the front passenger seat of Truck Two. As he recovered from the impact, his M4 rose from between his knees, and he grabbed his walkie-talkie and shouted to the rear vehicle. 'Truck Three! Back! Back! Back!'

The rear driver jammed his Suburban in reverse, and Calvo's driver did the same.

Nestor climbed back into his seat just as his truck went into reverse, throwing him forward again. The bodyguard on Calvo's right grabbed him and covered him with his body. While doing so, both he and Calvo saw a flash of light on the rocky cliff above and just slightly behind them. The boom of an explosion came a fraction of a second later, and an instant after that, Calvo and his protector watched helplessly as the explosion blasted stone and dirt away from the brown scrub on the cliff. Boulders the size of easy chairs broke from the cliffside and tumbled down towards the convoy, knocking flat shale shingle and trees and dirt free on their way down.

Someone in Calvo's truck screamed, 'Watch out!'

The massive landslide missed Nestor's vehicle. As the driver slammed on his brakes, the intelligence chief of the Black Suits crashed shoulder-first into his leather headrest, the man who had thrown himself over Calvo's body collided into him. Calvo looked out the back window just in time to see the rear vehicle in the convoy catch the brunt of the mass of rock and dirt and dust and greenery; tons of falling rubble slammed into the Suburban, spun the massive armored vehicle 180 degrees on its axis before burying it along with the six men inside.

Wet concrete continued pouring onto the first vehicle in the convoy. The driver recovered from the impact with the cement mixer, pushed the deflated airbag out of his way, and jacked the truck's transmission into reverse. The truck's wheels spun, but it found purchase and began backing up; men in the truck around the driver shouted and screamed, and the SUV backed hard into the grille of Truck Two. Seconds later the cement mixer itself reversed, backed through hundreds of pounds of gray sludge, and crashed into Truck One.

Cement continued to flow from its chute, now directly onto the hood of the truck.

The two bodyguards in the middle seat of Truck Two, one on either side of Nestor Calvo, pointed their weapons at the windows, awaited the order to exit the car. The leader of the detail, the man in the front passenger seat, hesitated. 'Wait!' he shouted. 'We don't know how many there are. Calvo is safe in the truck.'

The men sat silently for a few seconds, then the radio came alive with the voice of an injured man from the rear truck. 'We have wounded. Some are dead, I think. Help us.'

The lead bodyguard switched channels and put a call out for the local police.

Behind him a shaken but highly focused Nestor Calvo had already found his mobile phone on the floor, ended the call he was on, and had begun dialing his own contacts in the area.

The driver of Truck One saw him first. A man in dirty blue jeans, a black leather jacket, and a black motorcycle helmet with

408

a smoked windscreen. Hanging low in his right hand was a black pistol, and in his left hand a black backpack swung at his side.

'¡A la chingada!' Oh fuck! 'El hombre de gris!' The Gray Man! he said, then he grabbed his walkie-talkie to report to the other trucks.

But Truck Two had already seen him. 'It's the gringo!' shouted the guard on Calvo's left, and he threw open his rear door, raised his short-barreled machine gun.

And then flew back inside onto Nestor Calvo's lap. On his forehead and left cheek he wore ragged holes that gushed rich red blood all over Calvo's suit.

The consigliere pushed the man out into the road and dove to pull the door closed, fumbling his phone into the air before his call could be connected.

The leader of the detail attempted to open his door to get out on the far side of the armored truck and engage the Gray Man from over the hood. But yards of thick cement had already pushed back to his side of Truck Two, and he could not get it open.

Instead he turned to the man behind him, on Calvo's right. 'See if you can get out!' He turned back to his own door and began rolling down the window.

The driver of Truck One scrambled across the center console of the front seat, into the passenger side, and he struggled to roll up the heavy bulletproof window left open by the man who'd been ejected during the initial crash with the cement truck. The men in the backseats argued about what to do and screamed into their radios, trying to communicate with the detail commander behind them over the screams and pleas of the survivors of Truck Three.

The man in the motorcycle helmet appeared at the driver-side window of Truck One, pulled a large rectangular object from his open backpack, and slammed it hard against the ballistic glass. When it hit it made a sound like a heavy, wet fish, and it adhered to the clear surface. The armed men inside the vehicle stopped screaming and stared at it for a moment, unsure what they were looking at. It was a black container made of metal, perhaps even iron, and covered in a thick black tarlike material. They saw the Gray Man pick his bag off the ground and move backwards, back up around the side of the huge cement mixer.

'It's a bomb!' shouted the driver.

'Are we safe?' asked a bodyguard in the back.

'Yes,' replied one, certain the bulletproof glass would protect them.

Another man tried once again to call out to the detail commander in the vehicle behind for instructions, and yet another voiced concern that the side window glass was not as strong as the side armor of the SUV.

Finally, after looking at the sticky box on the glass for five seconds, the driver gave the order. 'Bail out!'

Three hands wrapped around three different door handles inside the big black Suburban.

And then the bomb detonated, sent fire, iron shrapnel, and shards of ballistic glass into the SUV's interior behind a shockwave that moved faster than the speed of sound. All the men inside were turned to pulp in eight-one-hundredths of a second, and the heavy vehicle rocked on its fortified steel chassis. The windshield blew out from the inside, shattered against the chute of the cement mixer, and flames engulfed the dead occupants.

The four men still alive in Truck Two, Nestor Calvo included, just watched. When it was clear the armored vehicle in front of them, a truck virtually identical to their own, did not survive the blast, the detail commander gave the order for his men to bail out.

The driver was the first through his door; he drew his .45 pistol as he stumbled out into the road.

In the black smoke billowing from the windows of the Suburban in front of him, the man in the motorcycle helmet appeared, he still carried the pack low on his left, and now his pistol was aimed high on his right.

The driver began to raise his weapon towards the threat, but three rounds to his chest spun him around, caused his .45 to sail from his hands. A fourth shot to the right side of his skull snapped his head to the side and killed him instantly. He fell dead on the blacktop as the two doors on the opposite side of the SUV opened and then closed again.

Inside Truck Two Calvo screamed at the two surviving members of his detail. 'Fight him! Get out and fight him!' The men moved from side to side in their seats, but they were otherwise frozen in terror. They just watched as the man in the motorcycle helmet stood alongside their truck and reached into his bag.

'He has another bomb!' one shouted, but the man instead pulled out a piece of cardboard. He pushed it up to the windshield and the men inside the SUV read the single word written in black upon it.

'Calvo.'

All three men sat silently. The silence was broken by the slapping sound of an iron box covered in tar sticking to the driver-side window of the Suburban. The man in the black helmet stepped away from the vehicle, raised his pistol, and waited.

Twelve seconds later the side door of the truck opened, and Calvo was ejected by the boot heel of one of the two members of his security detail. Immediately, he fell down in thick wet cement that had inched back on the road to his side of the truck. The door shut behind him. He cursed as he tried to stand back up. The man in the motorcycle helmet stepped forward, his pistol still trained on the Suburban, and he grabbed the fifty-seven-year-old by his necktie, pulled him out of the cement and to the side of the road. Court walked backwards up the road, pulling the man with the cement-spackled coal black suit, still covering the SUV with his gun, until he disappeared around the side of the dump truck.

He let go of Calvo and reached into his backpack. He removed a black cell phone and handed it over to the Mexican.

In Spanish the man said, 'Press 4. Then Send.'

Calvo did as he was told. Upon pressing the Send button an explosion rocked the canyon road fifty feet behind him. Shrapnel fired into the cement truck and pelted the hillside.

Thirty seconds later the cement mixer moved forward towards

411

the west, and the only men left alive at the scene were buried under tons of rock and dirt.

A phone call was intercepted by intelligence agents from the Black Suits at three p.m. The call was recorded and then played back for Daniel de la Rocha and Spider Cepeda just twenty minutes later. It was determined that the call was placed from a mobile phone, and the caller was the American known as the Gray Man. The call was received on a landline at a Vaqueros safe house in Mazatlan and then patched through to the mobile phone of Hector Serna, chief of intelligence for los Vaqueros.

The entire conversation was in English.

'Who is this?'

'It's me.'

'Why did you call that number? Where did you get it?'

'The number you gave me is compromised by the Black Suits. Calvo told me himself. I got this number from Jerry Pfleger the other day. I knew whoever answered could get in touch with you eventually.'

'You have Calvo?'

'Yes.'

'Incredible. Still, this line cannot be trusted.'

'It's clean.'

'How do you know?'

'Calvo doesn't know about it.'

'What if he's lying?'

'He is too scared to lie.'

A pause. 'Very well. When will you deliver him to us?'

'Calvo says the Black Suits know about the safe house in Tepic. We need to change the location.'

A long pause. 'All right.'

'I can take him to the safe house where he was going today.'

'No. They obviously know the location of—'

'It's the only other place I know of. They won't be expecting us to hand him over. There is no reason to suspect they will be there.'

'I don't like it.'

'Do you want him back or not?'

'Of course we want him back.' A short delay. 'What time?'

'Midnight.'

'Why not earlier?'

'I think there are others looking for me. CIA. Russians. It will take some time to cover my tracks and get there.'

'We will come to you. Tell me where you—'

'Midnight. The ranch in Concordia. I'll be there. Bring a lot of men and a lot of guns.' The call ended.

54

At five p.m. the leadership of the Black Suits met in the huge main *sala* of the Casa de las Olas, an eleven-thousand-square-foot modernistic mansion overlooking the beach fifteen minutes south of downtown Puerto Vallarta on Federal Highway 200.

The men present in the meeting were protected by two dozen more *sicarios* patrolling the lush ten-acre estate, and they, in turn, were surrounded by Puerto Vallarta municipal police on the payroll of DLR. The cops patrolled the neighborhood in squad cars and sat in a pair of small, armed speedboats out on the water, just past the breakers.

Spider ran the main portion of the meeting while DLR stood next to him.

'Four teams will hit the Concordia ranch at 12:05 a.m., four separate vans will attack from each point on the compass. A fifth team will come in behind the main attack with the objective of receiving Nestor and then taking him out of the area. We will all meet back here by dawn.'

De la Rocha sipped bottled water and looked through the fifteenfoot-high windows off his left towards Bandaras Bay. He was distracted for many reasons, not the least of which was that he would not be going on the rescue mission to recover his consigliere. It was determined to be too dangerous for the organization itself to expose DLR to what was certain to be one hell of a firefight.

414

Spider, the leader of the armed wing, would also be staying behind. Daniel had ordered this, and Spider was not happy about it, but since the execution of Emilio Lopez Lopez, Spider had been in charge of DLR's safety, so it only made since he would stay at the house by DLR's side.

Both men had led forces into battle, and neither man wanted to stay behind at this palace on the beach while their soldiers fought and bled and died and killed one hundred miles north of here. But logic prevailed.

And DLR had a feeling that staying here tonight, with a relatively small contingent of twenty armed men or so, would not be without action of its own.

As the discussions of the coming operation petered out and the men who would soon head off to battle began strapping weapons and gear to their bodies, DLR stepped out of the *sala* and onto a raised dining room open to the great room. As soon as they'd arrived at the rented villa, he'd ordered the long table removed and his largest Santa Muerte idol erected in its place. The skeleton sat on its throne in the center of the room, behind it white curtains hung from the high ceiling down to the wood floor of the dining room, candle sconces ringed the throne and the room itself. Daniel knelt down in front of his patron saint, said a prayer for his family, and said a prayer for the death of the Gray Man.

At the end of his last prayer he looked up slowly into the face of la Santa Muerte, then called out to Spider. Cepeda shot out of the scrum of his men down in the *sala* and up the three steps to the raised dining hall.

'*Sí*, Don Daniel?'

'Do you think the gringo really got the phone number he called today from Jerry Pfleger?'

'No. Calvo gave him that number because he knew his agents were monitoring it. The old bastard is as cunning as they come.'

DLR nodded. 'Yes. He is very cunning.'

Spider stood dutifully over his master.

DLR turned and looked up to him. 'I want everyone staying behind ready for action tonight.'

Spider nodded. Confused. 'Of course.'

Daniel stood and left the dining room through the curtains, heading for his master suite in the back of the mansion.

A cluster of small, uninhabited islands sit in Bandaras Bay, just a few hundred yards off of Mismaloya. Collectively called Los Arcos, they are named for the archlike formations carved out of the rock by centuries of pounding surf. During the day the protected marine reserve around Los Arcos was full of scuba divers, snorkelers, and pleasure boats, but one hour before midnight the only creatures in the waters around the tiny islands were fish, lobster, sleeping blue-footed boobies and other sea birds.

Fifty yards closer to shore a pair of private boats bobbed in the water. In each boat four men sat with M16 rifles in their laps. Two men in each boat had an M203 grenade launcher mounted on their M16s.

Each boat also had a radio and a two-million-candlepower flashlight to scan the calm water in all directions.

They were hardly battleships, but the two converted gunboats would certainly present an obstacle for anyone trying to make it to the back of Casa de las Olas from the water.

Court Gentry knelt waist-deep in water that was surging back and forth in the black recesses of a small grotto in one of the rocks of Los Arcos. His eyes looked past the two small boats and towards the white sand beach beyond them. A pair of men with flashlights strolled back and forth on the sand, rifles hanging on their backs. A wall of white boulders and brown shale ran up to the right of the small beach.

Past the men, past the beach, up the hill, he scanned the palatial estate. It looked a bit like a space station. It was a modern glass-and steel structure, all hard metal edges and glass walls. The focal point of the back of the house was a balcony that ran

416

along a gargantuan window. On the other side of the glass Court could just make out dim lighting, perhaps from candles. Much of the grounds of the property were well lit and, Court assumed, well protected. But from here the building itself seemed buttoned up and quiet.

On the highest point of the southern wing of the huge mansion, a black Eurocopter EC135 sat in complete darkness. Only the few streetlights and glowing buildings higher on distant hills framed its silhouette.

Court took a few minutes to deflate his small rubber boat and to tuck it into a dry nook in the grotto out of sight of the coast. Then he turned to his equipment arrayed on a rocky shelf just above the water line. He donned his scuba gear and his fins, slung a long coiled rope to his tank, connected his Glock to his Buoyancy Control Device, and attached his bag of clothing, extra magazines, and other items to his utility belt.

He pulled a mobile phone out of a protected case, powered it up, and made a phone call. Court said what he had to say and then hung up as the man on the other end screamed and cussed.

The phone went back in the case; the case went back in the bag.

At twenty minutes past eleven p.m. Court sank slowly below the water in the grotto, pushed off with his gloved hands, kicked his legs, and began swimming away from Los Arcos and towards the shore.

He passed the two boats twenty minutes later, traveling sixty feet below them and breathing as slowly and as shallowly as he could to minimize bubbles above. Twenty minutes after that he was below the surf, the ocean floor crept up towards the beach, each wave that surged him forward was followed by an undertow that pulled him back, but he kicked to maximize his progress and, after ten minutes of heavy exercise, he worked his way ashore. He'd let the current push him south of the lights of the building, south of the beach and into the rocks.

He took off his scuba gear, turned off his tank, and stowed it between boulders at the water's edge. He pulled off his fins and his clammy wetsuit. Underneath his neoprene he was dressed head-totoe in black cotton. He slipped into soft-soled shoes, pulled a black ski mask over his face, put his extra magazines in the cargo pockets of his pants and a black Glock into the holster on his belt.

At midnight he began climbing up the rock, careful to stay out of view of the sentries on the beach, the spotlights from the boats, or any guards in the windows of the house.

His progress was slow and arduous, but he made it to the south side of the villa and then proceeded silently to the front, careful to move in shadow and concealment.

Daniel de la Rocha knelt before his throned idol in the candlelit dining room, the huge high-ceilinged main *sala* of the villa was open and empty behind him; both rooms were illuminated by the light of over one hundred white candles as well as a little ambient light that filtered through the *sala*'s window overlooking the bay. On the floor, on tables, on wall sconces, and on tall narrow stands, the burning candles emanated not just light but pungent aromatic wax as well.

DLR was bare chested, his lean and muscular body adorned with tattoos. The large Santa Muerte on his chest in red and black and blue, the names of his six children in ornate script across his back. Guns on his biceps, army unit patches across his midsection, the names of dead Black Suit colleagues wherever a clean space of physique had been found to inscribe them.

He remained kneeling in supplication, all alone in the candlelit room, until slowly his head rose.

He did not turn around as he said, in English, 'She told me you would come.'

No one responded to this comment. DLR then said, 'You knew that we were monitoring that telephone line. You had us send our *sicarios* to Concordia to get them away from here.'

The reply came now, the voice firm and authoritative. 'You

move a fucking muscle, and I'll blow your head all over your girlfriend's dress.'

The Gray Man moved silently closer across the white tile of the large *sala*, his Glock pointed at the back of Daniel de la Rocha's head. As soon as he realized there was a second-story balcony overlooking the *sala*, he spun on the balls of his feet, swung his weapon along the sight line, and scanned quickly for threats above. But it was black and quiet on the balcony, just as it was here in the *sala*, and ahead in what Court could only imagine had been an open dining room before DLR converted it into a throne room for a silly skeleton statue.

'May I stand?'

'Slowly, first thread your fingers behind your head.'

DLR complied, Court closed to within twenty feet or so, but he kept his eyes darting around, confused by the lack of protection for the *narco* boss in front of him.

'May I turn around?' DLR asked. He seemed calm.

Court jacked his head and his weapon back to his six o'clock position, then up again to the balcony on his left and behind him.

Empty. Dark, quiet, and empty.

'Slowly.'

DLR turned, faced the Gray Man below him. 'She told me you would come.'

'You said that. Where is Laura?'

'You did not give Nestor to Madrigal.'

'No, I did not.'

DLR smiled a little. 'The Cowboy is going to be mad at you.'

Court was all business. 'Where is the girl?' He spun around again, kept his weapon's muzzle moving in a blur as he scanned all around.

'You would like to exchange my Nestor for your Laura, correct?'

'That's correct. You can have him back, and then Laura and I will leave together. Everyone wins.'

De la Rocha just shrugged; Court began stepping backwards,

hoping to make his way to a wall so his back would not be exposed to the balcony behind him.

As Gentry backed into a sofa in the middle of the floor, de la Rocha said, 'Nestor told you his men were monitoring the phone line. And that is why you called it.'

Court did not respond.

'Nestor gave you this address as well. He has let me down by conspiring with you. He let me down more by working with Madrigal in the first place. Going behind my back to make a deal for you. I found out all about it this afternoon, and as a result of this knowledge, your bargaining chip has lost all its value.'

'What do you mean?'

'I mean ... if you had brought Calvo with you tonight, I would have killed him myself.'

Court started moving sideways along the long couch.

'So you see, amigo, you come here with nothing to trade for the girl.'

Court's brain worked through the problem. He said, 'There is something.'

'What's that?'

'In exchange for her life, you can have me. She walks out right now, we stand around and look at each other until I know that she's safe, and then I lower my gun. Me for her. Okay?'

'One problem with your offer.'

'What's that?'

'I already have you.'

Court heard the footsteps above and behind him. A dozen men stepped onto the balcony. Six filed over to his left, and six stayed behind. He assumed they'd been watching the conversation on a closed-circuit television.

They all carried M4 rifles.

Fuck.

55

'I did not send all my *sicarios* to Concordia. In fact, this is not all of them. I actually retained the leader of my enforcement arm, just in case I needed his help this evening.' DLR looked to his left. 'Spider?'

The curtain to the left of the throne opened. Behind it, Spider stood in his black suit. His arms were high in the air, and they held a long, shining machete.

Below him, on her knees, handcuffed and gagged, knelt Laura Gamboa. She looked to Court down in the *sala*, and then she strained against her bindings.

Court's weapon turned to Cepeda's forehead.

'You move that blade and I drop you.' His voice quivered and cracked as he spoke.

DLR laughed at him. 'Think about it, amigo! You shoot Spider and then all the men around here fill you with machine-gun bullets. And then, as you lay dead or dying, I step over and chop her head off myself.' Daniel unlaced his fingers and dropped them down to his sides. 'I know what the most difficult thing for you right now is, gringo. It is not saving her, not killing me, not getting away with your life. No, Gray Man, the *most* difficult thing at this moment is trying to not think of the phrase, "Mexican standoff."' He laughed at his joke.

'We can work this out, Daniel. In just a few minutes this—'

'Quiet!' DLR shouted, then turned behind him, opened the

421

curtain, and slid out a small trunk. He opened it and lifted an item out.

It was a black plastic bag, and Court immediately suspected it contained a human head. He was right. Daniel pulled it out and held it high above him. Court focused on the disgusting sight, stared at the face.

Elena?

No. It was a man.

Ramses?

No ... the hair was lighter.

The flickering candlelight from one hundred sources could not bring life to the open, vacant eyes. Court's jaw clenched. He said, aloud, 'Jerry.'

'Spider's *sicarios* caught your American friend yesterday trying to board a cruise ship in Cancun. Under torture we found out the Gamboas crossed the border in Nogales and made it to Tucson. You were smart to not tell him more of their plans. Pfleger was weak. Still, they worked on him all night before they determined he didn't know where you were.

'So, Jerry didn't know where Elena went. He was, ultimately, useless.' DLR tossed the American embassy man's head across the room, towards the huge windows off to Court's right. It rolled into a dark corner and disappeared.

'I need Elena Gamboa. I offered the life of little Laura here to *la virgen*, but she only laughed. I offered her your life, but she told me your death would serve me, not her, and therefore, it is no gift at all.'

Court's eyes scanned the room again while DLR said this. Other than the doorway he'd passed through to enter the *sala* there was one more entrance visible, an archway on his left that, no doubt, led to the front of the house. He suspected there was another archway behind the curtains in the dining room. That would lead towards the south wing of the huge building.

He wasn't sure why any of this mattered, as the dozen dudes who had him in their sights would cut him in half if he made for any of the exits.

DLR said, 'So, I will make you this one offer. You tell me where Elena is hiding; I will send my men there, and as soon as we get her, I will let Laura leave.'

'Keep me. I will tell you.'

DLR shook his head; he seemed almost weary with the discussion. 'No deal.' He turned to Spider. 'Are your arms getting tired?'

Spider kept them high over his head. '*Sí, jefe.*'

'It won't be long now, my friend.' He looked at Court. 'Your decision. Does she live or die?'

Laura's big brown eyes looked up at Court. She was gagged with black cloth, but she chewed at it and tried to stand up. Spider held her down with one hand, kept the machete over her, ready to slice through the back of her sinewy neck.

Outside, in the distance, there was the unmistakable sound of a Kalashnikov rifle firing fully automatic. All bodies in the room stiffened at the noise. Another weapon kicked in a second later. They were a couple hundred yards away, but the volume of fire increased.

Car alarms in the neighborhood began sounding off.

'Who is it?' DLR asked Gentry. 'Madrigal's men?'

Court shrugged. He knew that it was, but the longer he could instill doubt the better. 'Probably CIA. Outside chance it's the Russian mob.'

Court knew it was los Vaqueros because he had contacted Hector Serna himself while in the grotto at Los Arcos. Court told him he could find Calvo at this address. Serna had screamed at him about the change of plans, but Court hung up before listening to much of the man's anger.

DLR started to show concern as the AK fire continued. He barked an order to Spider. 'Keep five here, send everyone else to the perimeter. Have the pilot ready my chopper.' Spider shouted an order to the men on the balcony and then another order into a walkie-talkie on his belt. All but five of the gunmen disappeared, and those who remained all moved to the eastern balcony. They kept their rifles trained on the Gray Man as they did so.

DLR had returned to the trunk from which he pulled Pfleger's head. Now he retrieved a large gun belt. A pair of silver .45 automatic pistols hung from it. He buckled the belt around his waist, tied the holsters around the thighs of his black slacks, and looked back up at the Gray Man.

'You force my hand, fool.'

Court turned his gun away from Spider and back towards DLR. 'You give the order to Spider, and I kill you first.'

Daniel laughed. 'Typical cocky gringo. You are one man with a pistol. If I give the order to Spider, you won't have a chance to shoot any—'

A loud explosion just outside the house sent small snowflakes of stucco from the ceiling. All heads turned towards the noise.

Except one. Court remained focused on his targets, even while his mind raced.

Dammit.

Court didn't like his chances, but he saw no other option.

He had one trick up his sleeve, though, and he'd have to play it for all it was worth.

The gun in his hand looked exactly like a Glock 17, a common semiautomatic pistol. Surely DLR, Spider, and all the gunmen on the balcony had already identified it as such. But it was a Glock 18. The two weapons appear virtually identical, but the 18 is a rare handgun capable of fully automatic fire. Its ported barrel is able to spew 9 mm bullets at a rate of twelve hundred rounds per minute.

Court thought it over in an instant, working on a plan of attack.

Spider and his machete over Laura's neck would have to go first; there were no two ways around that. The men high on Court's left also wore Kevlar suits, just like their boss, and Court's 9 mm rounds would not penetrate Kevlar, so he'd either have to sweep across all five with perfectly executed head shots or, at least, knock them back a bit with a round or two into their soft armor and then finish them off after reloading.

DLR wasn't pointing a weapon at him, as were the *sicarios* on his left, but his two .45s would be in the fight in under two seconds. Court would have to execute an emergency reload of the Glock with perfect speed and precision, all the while avoiding the fire of any of the men with the M4s who'd survived his initial barrage.

Eighteen rounds of ammunition fired in full automatic mode at a rate of twelve hundred rounds per minute. His gun would be empty in a half second.

Oh yeah, there was one more factor Gentry knew he'd need to bring to bear. As soon as he started shooting, reflex alone would send rounds from the enemy rifles right where he was standing. In order to have any chance at survival, he'd have to execute all this precision while diving out of the way, moving his body as quickly as possible from where the five weapons were aiming.

Court felt confident there was no one on this earth with a better chance at executing this. Still, he put his chances at survival at less than 25 percent.

In the gun world, this was referred to as 'spray and pray.'

Gentry was about to do both.

56

'Where is Elena Gamboa?' DLR shouted this time. Another explosion, just outside the mansion. Apparently, los Vaqueros had brought along a few RPGs.

DLR said, 'Spider, if he doesn't answer in five seconds, kill the *puta*!'

Court took a deep breath, blew it out, looked at Laura, and then back at DLR.

He lowered the pistol from Daniel de la Rocha's tattooed chest. DLR immediately began reaching for the silver .45s on his belt.

Time to act. Once the .45s were trained on him, the equation would be unsolvable.

In the dim light of the *sala* Court lifted his pistol in a blur, shifted his aim to the right, remained in place on his feet, and pressed the trigger on the Glock 18. As the pistol lined up on the nose of Spider Cepeda, it popped, and a single round left the barrel behind smoke and fire. With no hesitation or delay to check the results of his shot, Court spun his entire torso hard to the left, his knees went slack, and he dropped straight down towards the tile in front of the sofa. For two thousands of one second his weapon was trained on the bare chest of Daniel de la Rocha, but he did not fire. DLR was at the bottom of his threat matrix, his pistols were not even drawn, so the Glock's muzzle remained silent and the sweep continued to the left.

He heard a rifle crack in the room a fraction of a second before his own weapon went to work; he pressed the trigger as his butt hit the hard floor; his Glock went cyclic as the muzzle began sweeping across the five *sicarios* on the balcony above.

Beyond the gray smoke pouring from the ports in the front of his machine pistol's barrel, he saw black-suited men spin, lurch back, and stumble forward as his supersonic 9 mm rounds sprayed into their bodies from right to left.

Too quickly the weapon locked open, Court had already begun rolling left on the floor to get farther away from return gunfire. As he rolled with his shoulders, passing behind the sofa, he reloaded with his hands, dropped the empty magazine with a thumb press to the release button on the side of the Glock, and pulled a long thirty-two round magazine from the hip of his cotton cargo pants with his left hand. After two full rotations of his body he rolled up to his feet but kept his body in a tight crouch. He ran backwards as he jammed the long black mag in place and dropped the slide forward, chambering a round, all the while trying to survey his handiwork.

He heard another gunshot, which meant not everyone was down. He raised his weapon, while still tracking backwards, and saw Spider on the ground next to Laura, who had fallen to her side next to la Santa Muerte's throne. Scanning to the left he caught a glimpse of de la Rocha's tattooed back as he fled behind the curtains behind the throne where the life-sized skeleton bride sat. A rifle report from the balcony cracked a fraction of a second before Court fired a single round at the curtains. Court then whirled his aim back up towards the five *sicarios*. He held his trigger down and dropped again to his knees, fired the entire thirty-two-round magazine into the Black Suits position above him as he fell forward, prone onto the floor now, desperately trying to keep his body moving out of the weapon sights of his enemies.

The pistol locked open and empty a second time, and Court vaulted back up to his feet while reloading with his last large mag. Again he moved through the candlelit room, this time laterally in front of the floor-to-ceiling windows. He headed towards Laura, his weapon back on target on the balcony. A single man hung over the railing; his rifle's sling was caught in his suit coat, and it caused his coat's tail to hang over his head. Court saw no one else, living or dead, but he fired a pair of short bursts up there anyway to keep any surviving heads down.

As he quickly sidestepped his way across the room, he felt a rush of cool wind behind him, he saw the breeze move across the room as the candles and drapes fluttered. The *sicarios'* rifle fire had blasted the floor-to-ceiling windows looking out over Bandaras Bay. A hearty sea breeze blew into the room, candle sconces teetered and silk draperies whipped around, and in seconds three separate fires had ignited around the *sala*.

He looked down at Laura, his weapon still held high at the mezzanine. The small Mexican woman was still on her side, but she had managed to pick up Spider's machete with her fingertips and was trying to cut through her bound wrists without being able to see what she was doing. Court was impressed with her initiative.

'I've got it,' he said, and finished the job.

The tan-colored wood was wet with blood around them.

Court hoped it was Spider's blood and not hers.

Or his.

Court didn't check for a wound; he had no time. He helped Laura to her bare feet. She hugged him tightly, and his focus slipped away from scanning for threats in the room, the gunfire outside, the burning and whipping draperies. Instead he hugged her back, tightly, looked down into her eyes. They were wide and bloodshot but alive, and he embraced her with his free hand.

She broke away from him after a moment, took off her gag, knelt down, and went through Spider's suit coat. She pulled a micro Uzi free from a holster and stood back up.

Court said, 'Follow me close. I have scuba gear hidden at—'

'We have to kill de la Rocha.'

'No! We don't! I'm here for you! I've got you! Let's go!'

428

Her eyes were wide with emotion, but Court couldn't tell what was going through her head now. The fires had spread to the sofa and chairs, the sea breeze's fuel turning small flames into swirling vortexes of smoking and burning debris. 'I'm *not* leaving him alive.' She turned away from him and disappeared behind the curtain.

'Fuck,' Court shouted, but he followed her.

57

Court caught up with Laura at the top of a staircase. It was dark here and quiet save for a raging battle going on around the villa's grounds. Police sirens wailed along with civilian car sirens, and the nonstop *pop, pop, pop* of rifles punctuated the madness below them. Smoke from the *sala* followed along at the ankles of Gentry and Laura as they headed up a dark hallway. Laura whispered that she'd been kept in the wine cellar since her arrival and admitted she had no idea where they were going.

Fully automatic fire came from inside the house now; it sounded like Madrigal's men had pushed DLR's men into the main *sala*. Laura found another stairwell, and Court noticed a blood trail; he wondered if he'd hit Daniel in the back with his blind shot through the curtains. They moved slowly and carefully at first, but when they heard a helicopter's rotors spooling up above them, they ran upwards through the dark.

As they opened the door to the roof, both Court and Laura raised their weapons and opened fire. A man in a pilot's uniform stood outside the black helicopter with a gun in his hand. Laura missed with her weapon, but Gentry brought the man down with four single shots from his Glock. As his body crumpled to the ground, the Eurocopter's propellers sped up and the craft rose a few inches into the air, spinning on its axis, turning its nose out to the bay.

'It's de la Rocha!' Laura screamed, running for the helicopter.

'He's gone!' Court answered back over the wail of the propellers.

But Laura ignored him and sprinted across the roof, towards the lifting chopper.

Court cussed loudly and then raced after her again.

Daniel de la Rocha had been shot in the upper left shoulder by that *pinche* Gray Man gringo, but he'd be okay, if only he could get away. He was a well-trained helo pilot with over one hundred hours in this model of Eurocopter, and all he needed now was to put some distance between himself and the attack by los Vaqueros. He knew the Gray Man and the girl were chasing after him up the stairs, so he'd kicked the pilot out of his chopper, handed him one of his .45s, and gave him orders to shoot anyone on the roof until DLR could get the fuck out of here.

As he rolled the sleek chopper to the left and began gaining lift, the back door opened up behind him. It was too loud to be heard without screaming at the top of his lungs, but as he lifted off, he did just that. 'I told you to wait on the roof for—'

He felt the hot barrel of a submachine gun press into the back of his head. 'Land!' It was the girl, screaming into his right ear.

He couldn't believe it.

He looked back over his shoulder, saw the girl, and then, behind her, the Gray Man himself climbed up through the open door. DLR increased the throttle and pushed the cyclic stick forward, almost throwing the American back out the door. Finally, the American fell in for good, rolling all the way across the floor and grabbing onto a cargo tie against the wall. Laura had a good hold on DLR's seat, and though the gun wavered from his head for a moment, she jammed it back seconds later. 'Land! Land, or I shoot!'

'You gonna shoot the pilot, you dumb bitch?' he asked, screaming and laughing at the same time. He had no idea if the Gray Man could fly a helicopter; it was a fair bet he could, so de la Rocha increased speed and jacked the chopper violently to the left and right, desperate to keep the aircraft on the verge of falling out of the sky. This way, even if the gringo assassin *could* pilot the bird, he wouldn't be able to take the controls in time to avoid a crash.

He planned on heading into downtown Puerto Vallarta. He owned the cops there, and they would protect him from these two *pendejos locos*.

The chopper shot to the north, zigzagging and shooting just feet above the ocean waves. Though concentrating most of his faculties on flying, DLR did take his left hand off the collective for a moment to pull the .45 pistol on his left hip. He kept it hidden from view of Gamboa and the Gray Man, and placed it under his left thigh where he could access it in an instant.

Laura kept the gun on DLR's head as she looked at Gentry. 'Can you fly this?'

Court was still trying to get his bearings. Climbing into the helicopter while DLR tried to shake him out had kicked his ass. He felt bruised or broken ribs and an incredible pain in his right knee where it made hard contact with the metal floor as he slammed down inside the cabin.

She repeated her question, screaming over the noise. 'Can you fly a helicopter?'

Court crawled over to the door, careful to hold on to a handle behind the copilot's seat so that he couldn't be pitched out, and then he pulled the door shut. It was quiet in the craft suddenly; the three could now speak in near normal voices.

'Six! Tell me, can I kill this *cabrón*? Can you fly the helicopter?' She pressed the barrel of the Uzi hard into the *narco*'s short hair. He screamed and cussed at her while he kept flying north, jacking the collective left and right.

Gentry had been trained on rotary wing craft, yes, but that was a long time ago, and the few craft he'd flown had not been nearly so complicated as this big machine. Now, as he looked around at computer screens and dials and switches and levers and lights, he knew the answer to her question. 'No! Don't shoot him!'

De la Rocha laughed loudly, pulled back on the cyclic stick, and the chopper quickly began gaining altitude. 'You hear that, bitch? If I die, then *you* die!' De la Rocha smiled with open eyes and flared teeth.

Laura held the Micro Uzi against DLR's head. He flew the helicopter higher and higher, feeling safer by the second. He headed north out into the bay and closer to the lights of downtown Puerto Vallarta. 'You can't shoot me, Laura!' he repeated, as if he wanted to be certain she understood the stakes. 'If I die, then you die!'

They were five hundred feet in the air now.

Laura looked to Court with her big brown eyes.

Gentry saw the eyes turn to narrow slits.

Fuck.

She turned back towards Daniel de la Rocha. Shrugged. 'Then I guess I die, *pendejo.*'

'No!' screamed Daniel de la Rocha.

'No!' screamed Court Gentry.

Their shouts were drowned out by a short but loud burping burst of the Uzi. The back of de la Rocha's head exploded and sprayed across the lighted instruments and screens and the large glass windscreen. The remainder of DLR's lifeless body sagged forward in its harness. A .45-caliber pistol dropped out of his left hand.

The helicopter's forward momentum slowed and ceased, and then it twisted slowly to the right until the lights of the Malecon were in full view. It tipped forward, nose down. The bloody windscreen left the bright lights of the resort city and went dark as the black ocean rushed up to meet it.

Laura crossed herself and began to pray.

Like a wild animal Court scrambled and crawled over Laura Gamboa on his way to the copilot's seat. He used his hands and knees and elbows; he felt weightless for a moment, clenched the seat back with his right hand to hold steady just as he grabbed hold of the cyclic control in the center of the console in front of the seat. He pulled this back hard – too hard, in fact – and the craft righted itself quickly, sending Gentry chest first into the radio controls between the seats. The breath was knocked out of him, but he kept crawling forward, twisting his body and diving now to get his hand on the collective on the far side of the seat. He turned it, increased the pitch and the throttle, and he felt the helicopter surge forward again, arresting its downward spiral.

But now he found himself facedown on the seat of the helicopter he was piloting, and the hard turn to the right was keeping him pinned there by centrifugal force. He let go of the cyclic for an instant, just long enough to reach down to push the left antitorque pedal to the floor. This brutal movement caused the high-tech aircraft to stop spinning suddenly, and Gentry rolled forward in the seat, finding himself all but upside down now as his feet were in the air, hanging over the headrest.

'What are you doing?' Laura asked. She had stopped praying enough to watch the American's odd actions.

'Help me!' he screamed frantically. She took his feet and pushed them over to DLR's lap, again the helicopter lost momentum and lift while Court struggled into the seat, but he finally got both hands and both feet where they belonged and brought the Eurocopter to straight and level flight with no more than twenty-five feet between the belly of the helo and the ocean's surface.

They streaked north over Bandaras Bay; one hundred yards off their right side the lights of the Malecon disappeared and the hotel district of Puerto Vallarta came into view.

Court sucked in cool night air, his first deep breath since getting the wind knocked out of him.

He looked to his left. DLR's all but headless body hung to the side. Blood dripped down his bare chest.

Laura was still seated behind him. 'You said you could not fly a helicopter,' she said it with a smile.

'Listen, I think it would be best if we try to land on the water.'

'When is landing in the water better than on the land?'

Court hesitated. 'When the pilot sucks.'

Laura looked at him. 'You are not joking, are you?'

'I'm afraid not.'

'All right,' she said. And she returned to her prayers.

Five minutes later a Eurocopter EC135 came to an awkward hover ten feet above the water in the Marina Vallarta, just north of the city. Those few on the decks of their yachts at this time of the night saw the spectacle of the hesitant aircraft: it hung low to the right for a moment, then low to the left; then it dipped forward, found itself straight and level about five feet above the water; and then, inexplicably, the main engines sounded like they were manually switched off. The craft dropped straight down into the water, the propellers disintegrated on impact, and the chopper began sinking rapidly.

Within seconds of the Eurocopter disappearing under the black water of the marina, a pair of heads emerged. Soon a man and a woman could be seen swimming ashore. The figures disappeared into the black, just as the siren's wail of a harbor police boat filled the air.

58

Nestor Calvo Macias lay hog-tied on his side in the mine shaft. He shook and shivered, both from the cold and from fear. All night long big rats had scurried around and even over him. They were not afraid of him, and why should they be? He could do nothing to fight them off, bound as he was, and with the hemp gag in his mouth he could not even scream out to scare them away.

So he'd spent the night in the dark, in the cold, being walked on, pissed on, and even shit on by *pinches ratones.*

He assumed he would die here. He would starve or die of thirst or succumb to some other ailment in the next day. And if the Gray Man did return, what then? A bullet in the head?

Nestor lay and shook and thought of the rats and the disease, and of starving or dying slowly of dehydration.

He shivered and *hoped* that the Gray Man *would* just come back and put a bullet in his head.

A light up the shaft. The sound of an engine. Soon the Mazda truck appeared in the mine shaft and stopped. The Gray Man stepped out. From the truck's lights Nestor could see that the American looked like hell. His clothes were torn; his face showed pain in each step. He limped over to him, knelt down next to him, and then drew his pistol.

Here it comes, thought Calvo. He cinched his eyes tight.

The cold barrel of the pistol pressed into his temple.

And then the hemp gag was removed from his mouth.

The Gray Man said, 'De la Rocha is dead. Spider is dead. So where does that put you?'

Calvo did not open his eyes. 'I . . . I do not know.'

'I think it ought to put you in charge of the Black Suits. Don't you?'

Now his eyes opened, but they stared ahead, at the far wall. 'I . . . I don't know.'

'I'm willing to make a deal with the leader of the Black Suits.'

'Yes?' Calvo's voice cracked. He looked up to the Gray Man now.

'If you call off the hunt for Elena Gamboa, I will let you go.'

'Of course! Of course I will! I never had any interest in—'

'If anything happens to any of the Gamboas, either here or in the States, then I come back.'

'I . . . I understand.'

The Gray Man cut Calvo free, then he climbed back into his Mazda truck and drove away without saying another word.

Nestor Calvo Macias stood in shock, slowly brushed dirt off of his black suit, smoothed his gray hair back on his head, and began walking slowly forward towards the exit of the mine shaft.

Court sat on a wooden a pew in the sanctuary in the Cathedral of Our Lady of Guadalupe in Puerto Vallarta. His feet shifted nervously while he looked around.

Waiting. Worrying.

Laura appeared through a side door of the sanctuary, scanned the cool bright room, and smiled when she saw him. She approached and they hugged, then she took him by the hand through a narrow archway that led into the small sacristy. Here they sat alone together on a wooden bench.

For a few minutes they talked about the various aches and pains they'd received the week before in Puerto Vallarta. They both looked a lot better now than the last time they'd seen each other: her crying at a roadside bus stop and he pulling away in his Mazda pickup. They'd had time since to clean up and tend to their wounds and figure out where they would go from here.

Court was worried about this conversation. He could not enter into a relationship with this girl, as much as he entertained that fantasy each and every night. He knew his life was in jeopardy, and he knew that, unlike her situation for the past few weeks, his problems would not be solved any time soon. He did not know how to tell her that he would have to leave her behind for her own good. It sounded like bullshit.

But he'd have to do it.

She came to the point quickly, forcing him to prepare himself to let her down as easily as possible. 'Six. I have been thinking and praying about my future.'

'Right.' He said, 'I want you to know—'

'My heart is certain. I know what I want. What I need. I know what will make me happy in my life.'

Holy shit, thought Court. Here we go.

A slight pause. Then she said, 'I will enter the convent. I will become a nun. It is a long process, but my heart knows it is right for me. I feel the calling. I will begin immediately.'

'Holy shit,' said Court aloud.

'I would love for you to come and visit me. I will not be able to see you. I will have to remain cloistered. But it would be nice to hear about you from time to time.'

Court fought to compose himself. He certainly did not envision this course of events. 'Yeah. Sure. I'd like that.'

'And I would also like to pray for you.'

Still reeling, he said, 'Knock yourself out.'

She cocked her head. 'What does that mean?'

'It means, yes, you have permission to pray for me. I would like that very much.'

'The Lord works in mysterious ways. You, Six, are the most mysterious "way" I have ever encountered.'

Court found himself wanting to believe God was working through him and not Satan himself. But he did not know. He did not understand.

But he did not lament the killing he had done, the measures he had taken here. He did not lament for one second one drop of the blood he had shed to save the woman in front of him.

She was beautiful. She was good. She was perfect.

And she was alive.

'Go with God, my friend,' she said, and she hugged him, looked into his eyes, stood, then disappeared back through the sacristy and into the sanctuary.

And she was gone.

Court sat for a few minutes alone, then stood and returned to the sanctuary himself for a moment more. The room felt big and empty, but welcoming somehow. He'd spent time in churches around the world but only for operational reasons, and his mind never drifted beyond the details of his work. Now he looked around, perhaps for the first time in his life, and he wondered about this place. Was there a point to all this?

His eyes turned to the crucifix. He stared at it a long time before whispering, 'Thanks.'

His mobile phone rang. It was the number he'd given Hector Serna.

He walked out of the side entrance to the sanctuary, into a cool sunny afternoon. 'Yeah?'

It was not Serna. It was Madrigal. He spoke in his mountain Spanish, and Court struggled to understand.

'You left Calvo alive?'

'Yes.'

'Why?'

'I think you need some competition.'

A long pause. 'I should have killed you when you gave me that gun!'

'Yes,' Court admitted. 'You should have.'

'I *will* kill you!'

'Take a number, Cowboy.'

'You are a worthless, piece of shit, motherfucking son of a whore!'

'I am an outlaw.'

Another long pause. 'If men ever get to live on other planets, you should be the first man off of this one. Everyone wants you dead.'

'Yep.'

'Someone soon will get you. You must know that.'

'I know that. I find comfort in the fact that so many people will be sad that it wasn't them.' Court hung up the phone, and then tossed it into a municipal garbage can a few blocks away.

EPILOGUE

San Blas felt different to Gentry now. He arrived at eight in the morning, found the weather cooler and an ocean wind off the Pacific swirling garbage in the streets as the locals went on their way to work or school.

By now Court looked positively Latin. He stepped off the bus in his denim jacket and blue jeans, a single cheap backpack over his shoulder; his dark skin and sunglasses and trim hair, beard, and goatee blended nicely with other men his age. He wore earbud headphones in his ears, plugged into his phone, but he was not listening to music.

No, the headphones were just part of the costume, the only rhythms the Gray Man listened to were the footsteps behind him and the soft conversations of those around him. He was on guard here in San Blas, more so now than two weeks earlier on his first visit to the fishing village.

He knew they were after him, and he knew they were close.

He'd given up concentrating on who *they* were ... it didn't really matter anymore.

He walked the road to the hill, past the lobster shacks and the little churches and truckloads of armed marines on patrol, and he took another steep road up a steep hill. He'd taken this same road the last time he was in town, heading up to look for Eddie's grave, and then heading down with Eddie's pregnant wife. So much had changed in that time, but to Court everything felt like it had before. He'd acquired cuts and bruises and scrapes and burns, but his quest now was the same as then.

Mexico was just a bump in the road for him.

He walked up towards the entrance to the cemetery, saw the cheap mausoleums of tin and plastic sheeting and cement block off to his left. An iguana raced by on the road ahead of him. Chickens clucked in the last house up the hill before the beginning of the cemetery and the entrance to an old church and a counting office that dated back to the middle of the nineteenth century.

But he passed the cemetery, kept walking up. It was a normal security sweep for him, more automatic than brought on by any sense of danger or threat. It was second nature to make wide, lazy turns, to stop and retrace steps, to wait in the shadows for someone following, to move through the landscape like a wraith.

He finally turned left well past the cemetery, much higher on the hill, and he entered a grove of low grass surrounded by wild-growing banana trees two stories high. He moved deeper into the woods, turned towards the cemetery. He'd come all this way, a three-hour bus ride, just to see Eddie's resting place one more time. Court thought about leaving something there, under the dirt, as a remembrance for his friend.

But he did not have much with him.

Court was not a sentimental man; perhaps his mind-set was as close to the opposite end of the spectrum as one could come from sentimentality without being diagnosed as a sociopath. But he felt he had to come here, had to take the time and to spend the money and to make the effort to return to the place where this all started for him.

He pushed through some brush.

Coming back was the right thing to do, though he could not articulate why.

He climbed over a whitewashed rock that had once been part of a Spanish fortress.

He would not forget Eddie or Laura or Elena or Daniel de la Rocha, but he needed to put this behind him to move on.

He climbed off the rock and fought through some tight vines, came out just above the cemetery; it began just a few yards down the steep hill.

He'd have to leave his thoughts of Laura, his fantasy of love, and his visions of lust behind him so that he could continue on in his fight against Gregor Sidorenko.

Court stopped dead in his tracks. Lowered slowly to the grass.

Fuck. He did not say it aloud.

When he was certain he was concealed, he crawled backwards on his elbows and his knees, back into the brush and vine and banana, and then he shifted ten yards to his right, still on his belly. It took him nearly ten minutes to do so, but then he sat behind a carved white stone, pulled a tiny set of binoculars from his pack, checked the angle of the sun, and then rolled around the white stone and raised the glasses to his eyes.

Where? Where are you?

He'd sensed movement below him, on the row of crypts south of where Eddie's cross lay. There were iguanas everywhere, but this movement was not natural to the surroundings. It was accompanied by a flash of light, the reflection of glass in the morning sun. That was all he'd been able to discern before his interior warning system had alighted and he had dropped to cover. Now he scanned with his glasses in the area of the movement, looking for whatever had aroused his alarm just a few minutes ago—

There.

Shit.

A figure, a man, prone, eighty yards from Eddie's grave. He wore a fully camouflaged suit, and he looked like the brush around him and in front of him; from under a blanket of twigs and leaves indigenous to the area, a rifle's barrel and the front of a sniper scope protruded.

Behind this man, not far away, was his partner. He was better concealed, he had no barrel to expose or scope that could catch the sunlight, but Court saw him when he turned his head.

Shit. Court scanned the hillside cemetery now. There would not just be two of them. No organization in the world would send just two men on a mission to kill the Gray Man. Court could not find the others, but he knew they were there. Perhaps here with him in the brush above the cemetery. It would be a wise place to hide a follow-on force.

For just a moment he wondered who they were. Sidorenko's men? SAD hunter/killers? Delta Force? Vaqueros? Black Suits?

Did it even matter? He decided it did not.

He turned his optics to Eddie's simple cross.

Court could only see the back side of it down on the hill; he had no idea if more curses had been painted on it. In his pack he'd brought white paint and a brush. He'd planned on doing the work that Elena had been doing when he met her, to restore Eddie's reputation once more before he left this place forever.

But the fuckers below had ruined everything for Court.

Fifty yards away from him sat Eddie's lonely cross, and no one in this town would protect it, no one in this town would visit it. Sooner, not later, Court knew, no one in this town would remember Eduardo Gamboa as anything more than another *cartelero*, another *narco* assassin, another nameless, faceless killer of men.

And Court could not do anything about it at all. He could not even say good-bye.

He lay there in the brush for an hour, watching the sniper, a man as still and as patient as Court himself, and then he backed up through the brush, into the wild banana, out to the road. He went back down the hill, then back past the lobster shacks, and then he caught a bus out of town.

HAVE YOU READ THEM ALL?

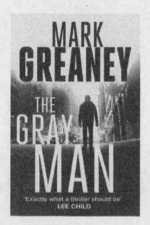

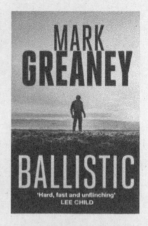

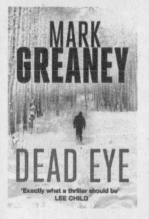

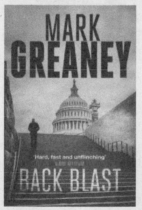

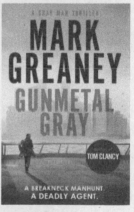

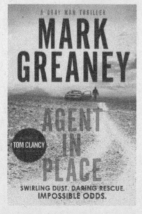

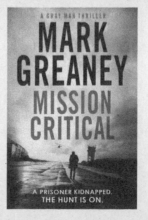